A BENWARIAN FIX

The Intercolonization of Earth

L.W. Samuelson

iUniverse, Inc.
New York   Bloomington

iUniverse books may be ordered through booksellers or by contacting:

iUniverse
1663 Liberty Drive
Bloomington, IN 47403
www.iuniverse.com
1-800-Authors (1-800-288-4677)

ISBN: 978-1-4401-6955-7 (sc)
ISBN: 978-1-4401-6953-3 (hc)
ISBN: 978-1-4401-6954-0 (ebook)

Printed in the United States of America

iUniverse rev. date: 09/16/2009

1

A thrumming sensation started at the top of Logis's head and extended to the tip of his toes. Gradually he recognized it as a low-level electrical current pulsating through every nerve in his body.

I'm being revived he thought. The impulses were stimulating his nerves and muscles so they could be used again. He tried to flex stiffened fingers and felt them tremble then move grudgingly. Next, he tried to turn his toes downward. His reward was a slight tremble. He worked at it until his fingers and toes would move at will.

He worked on frozen arms until they moved with conscious command then tried his legs. When they remained immobilized, the stimulation levels were increased. His hair tingled and his teeth vibrated. The intensity of the impulses caused his legs to spasm. He reduced the current and willed his legs upward and they responded. Up and down they were moved until control was regained.

He moved his head from side to side, feeling a sore stiffness with each effort. It was moved back and forth until the rigidity lessened and it too obeyed conscious commands. He wondered where he was and what had happened to him.

Having gained some control over his muscles, he opened his eyes into the darkness. Ship's voice, a warm feminine voice, aroused his long dormant memory, "Logis Gnoeth, Logis, my dear friend. It is time to awaken. You, the leader of Benwar, are needed. Our search has ended. We have found a habitable planet. As last, we have found a habitable planet."

Ship intensified the current as if to emphasize her point. He squirmed with discomfort and she relented. The pain cleared his mind somewhat and he remembered that he was no longer on Lemmus. He and a contingent of Benwarians had been forced to evacuate their dying planet. While its environment was slowly deteriorating, the Benwars had built a vessel designed to explore deep space and find a home for his people.

For years they had tried to provide the leadership and guidance needed to save their planet but their suggestions had fallen on deaf ears. Hence, the changes needed would have required force and the mass killing of billions of Lemmings. The Benwarian belief in self-determination and the sanctity of life compelled them to acquiesce to the destruction of their own world.

Benwarian futurologists predicted both the end of the planet and the decision to allow it to happen. It was decided that the national budget and every available resource be directed toward building the spaceship they now traveled on.

In the end, the planet's ecospheres deteriorated much faster than even Benwarian computer projections indicated. The acceleration resulted from the northern and southern poles melting. Without snow to reflect the sun's rays into space, more heat was absorbed. This caused the tundra to thaw and release vast amounts of carbon dioxide into the atmosphere. The increased levels of greenhouse gases kept even more heat from escaping into space, and the planet grew ever hotter. The rapid rise in temperatures soon caused complete climate chaos. The termination threshold had been reached, the planet spiraled toward its death.

With their island flooding and violent winds wreaking havoc and destruction, a contingent of Benwars boarded the spaceship that looked much like an upside down dust pan. The hull consisted of titanium beams covered by sinuous mesh that gradually flattened out into flexible outer flaps that undulated like fins. Her handle or tail moved back and forth for guidance and a docking bay opened at the tip.

With time running out, she was strapped to booster rockets and shot into outer space. Once there, propulsion was accomplished with movements of her outer ridges.

Soon after take off, all aboard ship but the engineers and scientists entered the cryo-units to be put in stasis. The unfrozen and their descendants spent two centuries researching and developing technologies. Superior Benwarian intellect wrought great advances in nano-technology, bio-engineering, and propulsion systems as well as climatology and environmental engineering. Their proudest achievement was an instrument nicknamed the "soul reader". It took spectrographic images of a being's aura or light emanations. Not only personality traits but the totality of one's soul corresponded to the colors found in an aura.

"Logis, are you there? Talk to me," Ship said, slowly increasing the intensity of the lights. Three hours would be required for Logis's eyes to adjust to full light. Cryogenic revival required a slow, gradual re-stimulation to prevent damaging the muscles and nervous system.

Ship switched off the cryo-unit's electric current and had the pad he rested on gently massage his muscles. His voice vibrated with a comedic stutter, "Shshshiiippp, hhhoowww fffarr iss ththe pppllanettt?"

"Has the cryo-unit addled your brain? You talk funny," Ship said.

"JJJuusstt annnswwerrrrr ththe ququesttion."

"Forty light years. We have a visual and will arrive in one hour. I have been downloading information from the planet."

"Aaanndd?"

"Seven billion beings like us inhabit it. There is no scientific consensus about the status of the planet's environment. Some postulate that the planet contains self-correcting mechanisms that will allow it to maintain stasis, others think that environmental degradation is severe and is increasing exponentially."

Logis tried to move his fingers. When they responded spasmodically, he moved them back and forth several times. The next communication was typed on the keyboard above his head. "Have probes been launched to assess the atmospheric composition and condition? I'll also need infrared photographs taken to gage temperatures and the condition of the terra-sphere. Do it now."

"Two probes were launched twenty cycles ago. They have already returned and our scientists are evaluating the contents. The infrareds are being donwloaded as we speak."

"Keep collecting all pertinent information. I want to know about its environment, its societies and cultures and anything else you deem relevant. Prepare a presentation for 0800 hours."

Logis stopped the cryo-unit's massage then keyed a command and it whirred moving him to a sitting position. He watched the monitor as his heart rate spiked, but being sat upright for the first time in a couple of hundred years would cause it to beat faster. He took a deep breath and let it out, repeating the procedure until his heart slowed.

The unit paused until his pulse rate returned to normal then it whirred and slowly brought itself and him with it from a sitting to a standing position. Logis held the bar in front of him as he moved to vertical. Once there he flexed his legs and tried to walk in place. Unused synapses sparked and fired, sending messages from his brain to his legs. His right leg quivered for a second and then moved an inch and then another. It took several seconds to place his foot forward and several more to return it. He repeated the procedure with his left leg.

Back and forth, back and forth, he moved his legs slowly at first but faster as control returned. The movements gradually restored his motor functions and confidence in the use of his appendages. When he felt he could stand on his own he ordered the unit to retract the support bar. His unused body stood for the first time in two centuries.

Exhausted and thirsty, his dry cottony mouth screamed for water. The cryo-unit opened and Logis stepped out. Putting one foot in front of the other, he made his way to the synthesizer across the room then walked between the two rows of cryogenic units with green lights blinking on top. Inside of each friends and acquaintances could be seen. He stopped in front of a sliding glass door on the far wall.

"One liter of water, fifteen degrees Celsius," Logis commanded.

A glass dropped into place and water filled it, and when the flow stopped the door opened. He grabbed the glass, trembling in anticipation as it was brought to his mouth. Wet relief hit swollen lips and traveled down a parched throat as he drank. The burning dryness lessened with each swallow until he was drinking deeply and the sandy, scratchy feeling disappeared altogether.

The water invigorated him. Life pulsated through his body like the electric current had earlier. He felt alive for the first time since regaining consciousness. A loud gasp escaped his lips.

"How's the water?"

"You can't imagine."

"It must be wonderful to experience a sensation like that," Ship spoke longingly. "In what year were you born?"

"Is that a trick question?"

"Answer please."

"Benwar nine thousand two hundred. Why?"

"I need to know if you're fully cognizant. What was the concentration of carbon dioxide in Lemmus's atmosphere in the year nine forty?"

"Five hundred parts per billion, spiking to eight hundred parts per billion when the tundra released its carbon dioxide."

"What was the population of Lemmus in nine thirty-five?"

"Thirteen billion."

"Favorite color?"

"Blue."

"Favorite food?"

"Borischt."

"How do you feel?"

"Like I've been awake for three days and hiked a hundred kilometers."

"You're tired? Wasn't 233 years of rest enough?" Ship asked as she monitored his brain waves, the scan showed sporadic anomalies. Although most of his synapses were firing normally, there was still a slight delay in some responses, he wasn't quite ready for the scheduled conference.

"I guess not," he replied.

"I suggest a short nap before we convene, you haven't recovered from cryo-genesis and heightened awareness is crucial for the task ahead of you."

Logis's leaden eyelids began to sag at the suggestion. "I won't argue, Ship." He walked to the door of the cryogenics room and out as it opened. Keeping his hand on the wall of the hallway to steady himself, he baby-stepped his way down the hall to his room. The thirty meters seemed like a kilometer. Finally reaching the door, it opened and he grabbed the frame to steady himself. With one last effort, he surged forward on weary legs, hit the bed frame and fell, sprawling on the mattress. Panting with exhaustion, his breathing was consciously controlled until it slowed to normal then he closed his eyes and slipped into a deep sleep.

Hours later, Logis awoke to the sound of Ship's gentle hum. "Ship?"

"I know. You're ready. Pick up a liter of Blast on your way to the conference room."

He willed a leg to move over the edge of the bed, it responded with agonizing rigidity. Stiff, sore joints cried out in agony. Fighting through the pain, he placed his other leg over the bed and rolled to sit on the edge. Bracing himself with his hands, he pushed to a standing position. Wobbling for a second, he regained his balance and waited until the room quit spinning.

Gaining confidence, he shuffled across the room to the synthesizer. Ship had the drink ready for him and raised the shield at his approach. He grabbed the fizzling liquid.

With one hand on the wall to steady himself, the energizer was brought to parched lips and swallowed. Blast, a blend of electrolytes, oxygenators, and minerals tasted almost as refreshing as the water he'd had before.

Logis stood for a moment as his body absorbed the drink. When his muscles and joints began to relax, he took his hand off the wall. Ship must have added a muscle relaxant. She was so considerate.

She watched as he walked across the room. It was obvious that his body had begun to loosen up and respond normally. The brain scan showed that his cognitive functions had returned to normal as he left the room and walked down the hall to the auditorium.

Ship was so pleased. She had missed Logis desperately. Her biological subsystems pulsed with pleasure as she watched him move. The intensity of her lighting increased and her engines hummed melodically.

She loved Logis. He was her first memory. He had brought her into existence. First there was nothing and then there was Logis, she often told herself.

She worried about his comfort. Biosensors imbedded in the mesh under his suit allowed her to monitor his physical responses. She continually sought to alleviate pain and maintain homeostasis. As he entered the conference room, she said, "Please sit down and make yourself comfortable."

The room slanted downward with the door opening onto an aisle with seats on either side. The walkway ended at a podium facing the seats. It sat on a stage in front of a giant view screen. He positioned himself on an outside seat near the middle of the room.

Ship began, "How are you? My sensors indicate no emotional stress or pain."

"I'm fine. The stiffness is gone and my mind is clear," Logis replied, getting comfortable in the ergonomically designed chair. He settled and watched as the view screen activated, filling the room with light. Ship began with a view of the planet. A circle of blue filled his vision and a large orb faded in. As the image became clearer, he could see the brown and green landforms that divided and accented the blue-greens of the ocean. The brilliant colors were overlaid with white clouds that drifted across the atmosphere. Logis gasped at the breath-taking image, "She's beautiful!"

"This is the planet Earth. More enlightened cultures living there call it Mother Earth or Gaia. She provides a home for countless plant and animal species in much the same way I do."

Ship became silent. The screen filled with images of wildlife. Elk grazing in high meadows, caribou migrating across frozen tundra, tigers stalking their prey in the high grasses of the African savannah, elephants trekking across a Kenyan plain, and countless other land species interacting with their various ecosystems. Each shot filled the screen with the unparalleled beauty of Gaia.

"Behold the wonders of Earth," Ship thundered like Charlton Heston's Moses. A voice she had practiced out loud after it had been downloaded, wanting to impress Logis.

The view shifted to the oceans and aquatic species. Giant jelly fish filled the screen as they glided through the seas. Whales surfaced and flipped, throwing water to the skies. Porpoises walked the surface of the ocean on their tails. Schools of multi-colored fished filled the screen with reds, blues, yellows and greens. Each frame painted by Gaia constituted a masterpiece of balance and color.

Having lived his life on an island with a constrained environment, Logis marveled at the sheer volume of Gaia's artistic achievements. It made his homeland seem drab and sterile with its manicured gardens and carefully planned tree farms. For the first time in his life, he felt the raw power of creation.

Ship felt the blood pulse stronger through Logis's veins as he viewed one of the universe's most splendid creations. His aura brightened and became a strong whitish-yellow. "Are you okay?" Ship asked, pleased with his response.

He remained silent for a moment. "Acroluminous," he whispered the Benwarian word for an unsurpassed intensity of aesthetic pleasure.

"Yes, she is beautiful," said Ship who identified with Gaia. They were sisters, both provided life support for living beings. It was natural for her to subconsciously manipulate the images to enhance her sister's image. Again she used the Heston voice from her vast catalogue of information and images, "And now the works of man!" she thundered.

Panoramic shots of several cities throughout the world appeared. Each picture showed traffic congestion enveloped in a thick shroud of blue smoke. The view panned across the cities of Los Angeles, Sao Paulo, Moscow, New York, London, and Mexico City, each choking in smog.

The screen changed to time elapsed photographs demonstrating the dramatic reductions in the size of both the Arctic ice cap and the South pole. The side by side frames suggested that the poles were racing to disappear. Another showed the retreat of Greenland's glaciers. The planet was definitely heating up.

A fluid view of the Sahara desert filled the screen. The light yellow area expanded from 1900 to the present until it doubled into an ocean of sand. Next, the screen displayed the Yangtze River over the same period. The water retreated from a wide twisting snake into a thin line of black concentrate. Not only was the planet heating up but the land was drying out.

Another screen depicted the growth of the oceans as the glaciers melted. This time it was the land that retreated. The screen panned across the globe showing countless polluted waterways. One shot showed open sewage being dumped in a river. Another showed several cattle standing in a stream, one defecating another urinating. The scenes appalled Logis, water is sacred.

The screen changed abruptly. A vast sea of garbage outside of Mexico City appeared. It stretched for miles. Logis could see people moving amidst the refuse. Smoke came from the human dwellings made of trash. Next, the camera panned Naples where garbage piled up across the city. Then came several shots of dumps across the United States with bulldozers making trash mountains that reached to the sky. This dissolved into a garbage scow steaming out of New York laden with trash. A split picture of the globe appeared covered with red dots that represented the thousands of trash sites across the world. It looked like the earth had a bad case of Lemming measles.

Another series of shots showed people throwing waste out of car windows, littering highways worldwide. Several truckers in the United States were caught throwing plastic bottles of urine onto the roadside. The bottles hit the ground, sloshed their contents and foamed in the sun.

Next came African poachers shooting an elephant and cutting away its tusks. Then came a panoramic shot of several dead or dying coral reefs. Countless other transgressions were shown until viewing the images became too much. Logis's eyes widened, his face reddened.

His anger registered on Ship's sensors as an upward spike in blood pressure. "That's quite enough!" he thundered.

"These primitives have no regard for Gaia," she said, echoing his thoughts.

"It would seem so," he said, seeing through Ship's effort to manipulate him. He suppressed his anger. "We'll do an in-depth study of the planet before making any generalizations. This world cannot be understood by a series of images. Surely not every human chooses to desecrate the womb of their existence."

"I've searched their archives. I've found no society analogous to Benwar."

"Still we'll evaluate and understand before deciding how to proceed."

2

*S*hip carried a contingent of 2400 Benwars. They were governed by the Quantum Just, a council that would decide how to terraform earth. Logis served as the chairman and final arbiter of this governing body. Decisions were be made by a strict democratic vote of the Council, with him casting the deciding vote in the event of a tie.

"Ship, reanimate everyone. It's time to go to work. Call a conference for one cycle from now."

"As you wish."

Logis thought back to his childhood as he waited. His first memory was suckling at his mother's breast. He remembered the warm intimacy and sense of security that a warm nipple provided.

Early childhood was spent primarily with her. She spent her days arranging experiences that would enlighten and guide him. She sang lullabies and told stories of Benwar as he listened raptly. Even in the womb she held her hand over her stomach and hummed. The kind smile and loving eyes were a soothing balm that enriched his early years. Her unconditional love and acceptance engendered a sense of security and confidence that bloomed with the light she cast upon him.

His father joined them each day for a mid-afternoon luncheon. They met in the house and walked together along the garden path in the back yard. It wound its way through flowers and blooming shrubs and ended at a table that sat under an umbrella tree. They would set their lunch on the table and Father would hug Mom and then him in a timeless ritual of family. He remembered feeling special and important, a part of something sacred.

His father's daily reminder came back to him. "Logis, you are the Chosen One. You are the light of Benwar, destined to be its leader. You're the hope of our people," he would say. To this day, Father's words inspired and sustained him. The memory gave strength in times of need.

After lunch, Father would read to them from the Book of Benwar. It detailed the myths and legends of his culture. These descriptions of historical events were enhanced with elaborate illustrations. Father held the book so the pictures could be seen as he read.

His favorite was the story of Bon Luc the Great. In the face of insurmountable odds, his group of four hundred soldiers fought the Seven Hordes of Lizarians to a standstill. Many individual feats of prowess and bravery were performed as the Benwarians fought against the crushing numbers of barbarians.

Facing annihilation, they fought like demons, decimating the invaders. Although most of Bon Luc's army perished, the Seven Hordes were forced to retreat in a mangled body of despair. The few sacrificed all to save the many, a reoccurring theme in the history of Benwar. He remembered his father yelling Bon Luc's battle cry, "For the everlasting light of Benwar!"

Even in his father's day wars and combat had been replaced with negotiation and compromise as a means of settling disputes. An island nation, Benwar had isolated itself from most of Lemmus's armed conflicts. It quietly developed its war technologies without sharing. All other advances had been made available to other cultures.

Logis loved the nation of Benwar and all it stood for. Justice, understanding, and the pursuit of knowledge were not lofty goals but guiding principles for his people.

As he matured, talks with Father evolved into discussions of ethics. He remembered a conversation that occurred shortly before the end. It signaled a shift in the attitudes of his people.

"Logis, what is the prime consideration of our people?"

"The survival and advancement of Benwar."

"Does that mean disregard for other races and cultures?"

"No Father. All life is sacred. All life forms should be treated fairly. Benwars seek conciliation over war, understanding and compromise over conflict."

"That's true but while we are guided by ethics and respect for life, others are motivated by self-interest and greed. These cultures can no longer be allowed to infringe upon our survival. So what does one do when a conflict can't be resolved and an impasse occurs. Let's say, for example, that an unprovoked Lizarian attacks. What would you do?"

"But Father, Lizarians have been extinct for over a century now."

"For the sake of discussion, pretend they still exist."

"If the attack was uncalled for, I would kill the beast by any means necessary."

"And if you subdued the Lizarian and he surrendered?"

"He would be shown understanding and mercy."

"It is the biological nature of their race to kill other species. They cannot be trusted. His surrender would be a subterfuge. The Lizarian should be terminated."

His father continued, "Their single minded desire to kill all other species could not be tolerated. Their existence constituted a threat to Benwar so we acted."

"I don't understand."

"Lizerians were trapped in a biology and culture that couldn't evolve with advancements in science and knowledge. They remained static and resistant to change. Benwar had no choice but to eliminate them."

Stunned, Logis sat as the information registered, "But what about the sanctity of life? Weren't there innocent Lizarians who deserved to live?"

"Possibly. In our shrinking world there was no time to make exceptions. We tried for years to make peace, they rejected our efforts. Their acquisitive, warlike nature and rapidly expanding population caused them to covet our island. Their continuous attacks became tiresome.

Eventually we'd had enough, the Quantum Just acted decisively. Our scientists were instructed to engineer a virus to eliminate the threat. Designed to be Lizerian specific, it was released when they ignored our final ultimatum not to infringe upon Benwarian borders. Within weeks a virulent disease had eliminated all Lizerians."

"We committed genocide?" Logis asked in shock.

His father had a distant, sad expression that Logis would never forget, "Yes, although the action was in our best interests, it violated the precepts of Benwar. I was assigned to one of the teams sent to their mainland nation to clean up the aftermath.

It took weeks to place the dead in pits and incinerate them. We found women and children rotting where they fell. I entered a school and grabbed a child's corpse by the arm. It broke away from the body, dripping stench. The smell is still with me as I speak," he continued shaking his head in disgust.

"When we came home, many of us spoke out against the Quantum Just's decision. Our collective guilt weighted heavily on Benwar. A measure was brought before the Council that banned killing unless our island was directly attacked. It passed overwhelmingly.

The law prevented us from saving Lemmus. We couldn't bring ourselves to use force against those nations on Lemmus rushing to destruction, so we looked on as they destroyed our planet.

You must have the will to guide the Quantum Just so it doesn't the make the same mistake. If you find a planet to inhabit, do whatever it takes to make a home for your people. The survival of Benwar depends on your leadership."

The lights in the presentation room gradually brightened bringing Logis out of his reverie. He stood and stretched. It would be hours before the council would be ready so he exited the room and walked back to his quarters. Once inside, he surveyed his Spartan quarters. His bed sat to the left of the door at a right angle from the wall. A communications console comprised the top of a small table near the head of the bed with an overhead screen staring down from the ceiling. To the right, a small closet held a few clothes. On the far wall was a synthesizer. There were two cushioned swivel chairs opposite the bed.

He found himself lying on the bed staring upward when a chime announced that someone stood outside. "Who is it?" Logis asked.

"La Sikes."

Logis arose from the bed, smiling. "Come in, please."

The doors slid open and La Sikes entered. She smiled also and held her arms out to embrace him. "Logis, how are you? It's been centuries." Physically he appeared fine. His pale skin with its bluish tint radiated health and vibrancy.

He met her in the middle of the room and they hugged, emotion filling their eyes. "La Sikes, what a wonderful surprise!" he said as he held her shoulders away to see her face. "You haven't aged a day."

She laughed, "It's amazing how being frozen arrests the aging process. It's so good to see you," she said and hugged him again. La Sikes had always been attracted to her childhood playmate, like a moth to a flame. She loved the blonde hair that framed his angular face. His almond-shaped, blue eyes burned with intellect. In her presence the intensity of his eyes softened with care.

He towered over her at just under two meters tall. She looked up at the small, flat nose that balanced itself between two slightly elongated ears and smiled again, appreciating the muscular, lissome physique that held her. With genuine concern she asked, "How are you?"

"I've recovered from stasis, if that's what you mean," Logis turned his head knowing what she really meant.

"Good," she said and moved around to look at him. "No one's been able to grieve for their loved ones since we left home. The first thing I thought of when I reanimated was that all those we knew and loved are dead. I felt a tremendous sense of sadness."

He put his hands on her shoulders, "I'm afraid I've avoided thinking of the past. My thoughts have stayed in the present."

"We have to grieve! You've called a council meeting. Let's take time to honor those we left behind. For many of us it happened yesterday. We need to thank those who sacrificed themselves. It will alleviate the guilt so we can move on."

Her words evoked a memory of his mother, hope had filled her eyes as she implored him to save Benwar. The image brought a poignant sense of loss and longing. He turned his head away, "You're right, my friend. A memorial service will be first on the agenda."

La Sikes remembered herself then turned and left abruptly. She couldn't bear being around Logis for long, it hurt too much. She'd been devastated when he was chosen as the leader of Benwar. It meant he would be castrated, erasing all hope for them. She loved him too much to be his friend.

Logis stared at her back as she left. He hated the pain that he'd caused her, she was his greatest sacrifice, but The Chosen One could not allow romantic concerns or biological needs to interfere with leadership. Benwar came first.

3

John and Betty Stafford waited for their bags to appear on the carousel. They had just returned to Boise, Idaho from Shaanxi Province in China. The visit included the ancient Banpo Village, the Xian Forest of Stone and the Xian City Wall. The two retirees had studied the storied history of Shaanxi Province for almost a year before their "expedition" to Xian. The highlight of the trip occurred when they stood in the Museum of Qin Terra-cotta Warriors and Horses where they were confronted by an army of over three thousand life sized statues. They marveled at the exquisite workmanship, expecting the columns of soldiers to come to life and march away.

John developed a cough on the flight home but it hadn't stifled the excitement he still felt over the terra-cotta figures. Even his sore throat and muscles were ignored. "I've never seen any thing like those horses," he said as he watched the luggage spin. "They looked like you could mount one of them and ride away on it."

"What amazed me was that every figure was unique. Each soldier had different features and even his own facial expression. It must have taken years and thousands of artisans to make them," Betty replied, glancing at her husband. "Are you okay?" she asked when she saw his white, pasty face.

"I'm just little dizzy is all," he said, leaning on the edge of the carousel. He tottered for a moment then fell to the floor.

"Help! Can someone help, please," Betty cried then pulled out her cell and called 911.

A man nearby checked for a pulse then laid John out and put his jacket under John's head. Minutes passed before the paramedics arrived. It seemed odd to Betty that the EMTs were wearing surgical gloves, gowns, water proof aprons, eye shields and face masks.

She didn't say anything when they placed a respirator over John's nose and mouth. She wrung her hands as they placed him on a gurney and wheeled it out the front doors where an ambulance waited. Betty followed and climbed in behind her husband. Sirens blared as they screamed down I-84 to St. Alphonsus Hospital.

Betty became visibly upset when she saw that the parking lot had been cordoned off. Police cars with red and blue lights flashing surrounded the area. The ambulance drove down the lane lined by the vehicles and stopped at a side door. She and her husband were whisked inside.

She became even more alarmed when security cleared the halls ahead of them as they entered the hospital. The guards also wore protective gear. "What's going on?" she asked.

"I don't know, Ma'm. We're just following procedure," one of them answered as they entered an elevator. It stopped at the third floor. They exited and moved down the hall to room 343.

Security opened the door as the medics pushed her husband in. They placed him on the bed and motioned for her to sit in the chair while they hooked up the heart monitor, checked the respirator and left.

Minutes later a doctor and nurse entered the room. "Hi, I'm Dr. Hill," he said, "and this is Nurse Lynch." Before Betty could say anything he continued, "Your husband may have been exposed to a contagious disease. We're taking every precaution to keep it from spreading." He motioned the nurse forward.

"We're just going to draw a little blood so we can find out for sure," the nurse smiled as she clamped a surgical hose on her husband's arm and removed a syringe from the tray.

"Wait! What kind of disease? Will he be all right?" Betty asked.

"That's what we're going to find out," said the doctor, answering both questions at once. "How are you feeling?"

"I'm fine," she answered without thinking.

"No sore throat? Muscle soreness? Upset stomach?"

"No, I'm fine."

Betty watched the nurse insert the needle in her husband's vein. She pulled the plunger back and the syringe filled with thick scarlet blood. Then she placed a cap over the needle and placed it back on the tray, covering it.

"I'm sorry but you're in an isolation ward. You and your husband are quarantined until we can sort things out," the doctor said.

"May I make a phone call?" Betty asked removing the cell phone from her purse.

"Sure, you can do any thing but leave the room. I'll be back when we get the blood analysis," the doctor said, opening the door and following the nurse out.

Betty and her husband were childless. She had a sister living in Southern Idaho whose son was their closest relative. He lived in Atlanta, Georgia and was currently employed by the Centers for Disease Control. If anyone could make sense of what was happening it would be him.

Dr. Gabriel Skye had lived with them for the four years of his undergraduate studies at Boise State University. They had become very close, he was the son they never had.

She dialed his cell. "Hello?" he answered. Dr. Skye was sitting at his desk studying reports on the H1N1 virus.

"Hi, Gabe, it's your aunt."

"Betty, how are you?" he asked, "How was China?"

"We just got back. Your uncle's sick," she answered.

"What's wrong?"

Betty described John's symptoms and then said, "He's still unconscious." She coughed and continued, "We've been quarantined at St. Al's."

"Quarantined? Why?"

"We don't know yet," she answered.

"And how are you? Any symptoms?"

"Not yet. I'm fine."

Given that they had just returned from a province in China where a previous outbreak of SARS had occurred, Gabe thought it was the likely pathogen. He didn't say anything to Betty rather he said, "Listen I'm going to do a little research and get back to you. I'll talk to the hospital and find out what's going on."

"Thanks, Gabe. I knew I could count on you," she replied.

"Betty, I'm sure John will be fine. When he wakes up give him my best."

"We love you, Gabe," she replied.

"I love you guys. I miss you."

"Goodbye," she said and hung up.

The U.S. health intelligence network's electronic warning system had received reports of a flu outbreak in Shaanxi Province a week ago. From these reports, Dr. Skye was able to pinpoint the disease's epicenter at the Xian Xianyang International Airport. Several people had fallen ill and reported differing symptoms ranging from fevers, muscle soreness, and lethargy to a sore throat and a persistent cough. All victims suffered from a fever of over 101 degrees, symptoms typical of SARS.

Chinese officials had taken four months to publicize the first outbreak of the flu several years ago. When an investigation team from the World Health Organization arrived, the Chinese had emptied the hospitals and driven the victims around in ambulances in an attempt to hide the outbreak. Their misguided efforts caused the flu to spread worldwide, tainting the Chinese reputation for order and efficiency.

They'd learned their lesson. This time they had publicized the outbreak within days but had failed to screen the passengers on John and Betty's flight. This oversight could potentially spread the virus worldwide again.

Gabe read the World Health Organization's report on the new outbreak. They had issued a global alert immediately after Chinese officials went public. The alert occurred just after the Staffords disembarked in Boise. Medical officials were on route to the Boise Airport as John lay on the floor. When they arrived, the doors to the airport were closed and every passenger from Flight 647 had been identified and quarantined. People inside the airport were screened for contact and detained if deemed at risk.

The plane had also stopped at Heathrow and Salt Lake City. The exposed passengers had left both airports before the alert. Health officials contacted each one, requiring them to report to nearby hospitals where they were quarantined. Those flights carrying transfers from 647 were also quarantined. Anyone suspected of exposure was detained and isolated. The World Health Organization's Global Outbreak and Alert Response Network began monitoring the situation and sent officials to all three airports and China to organize the response.

It took Dr. Skye minutes to learn that the sickness in China was caused by the SARS virus. Doctors in China had identified the RNA through an examination of a victim's blood. It alarmed Gabe to discover that several thousand people were reported to have the disease and of those five hundred had already died. Dr. Skye called hospital officials from the infected areas and arranged for tissue and blood samples to be sent to C.D.C. headquarters in Atlanta.

4

*I*t had been a little over two hours since Aunt Betty called. Gabe had called St. Alphonsus Hospital and asked for Dr. Hill who informed him that John had tested positive for the SARS virus and that several others from Flight 647 were ill. John's condition was deteriorating and he was being treated with antipyretics to reduce the fever. Betty had also fallen ill. Gabe dialed her cell phone after he hung up.

After a moment she answered, "Hello, Gabe?"

"Aunt Betty, how are you?"

"I'm fine. They tried to take my phone but I wouldn't let 'em until I talked to you. What'd you find out?" she gasped and then coughed.

"You don't sound fine. Do you have a sore throat?"

"Yeah, it's raw," she rasped.

"And I can hear your cough. Are you congested?"

"Yes."

"And I'll bet you have a fever."

"Right. I'm burning up. So what's wrong with me?"

Gabe didn't want to tell her it was the SARS virus, that was up to her doctor and there was no need to scare her so he said, "It's the flu. You were exposed at the airport in China. It's contagious, that's why you're quarantined. "

"Listen Gabe, I'm deathly sick. Whatever John and I have is bad. I don't think I'm going to make it. Promise me you'll take care of your uncle."

"You'll be fine, Aunt Betty. Most people recover from what you have."

"Promise me," she coughed.

"You know you can count on me."

"Good. Listen, I really don't feel well," she coughed. "Give your mother my love and take care."

"I'll see you in a few days. I'm flying out as soon as I finish some lab work. Wait for me," Gabe said.

"I'll do my best. 'Bye."

"Bye Aunt Betty," Gabe hung up. It wasn't like his aunt to be curt or apocalyptic. It worried him that she had ended the conversation so quickly.

Gabe thought about his aunt and uncle. He owed the Staffords more than he could ever repay. He considered John his mentor. John had taught literature at a Boise junior high before retiring. Gabe couldn't count the books John had given him over the years. He'd read and discussed almost every one with his uncle. Gabe loved sharing a book with him. Lately, they'd both been reading Larry McMurtry. His books captivated their interest with western themes and fast paced plots.

John was understanding and supportive. He'd provided guidance and counseling after his father's death. He had even given financial support for Gabe's education.

Aunt Betty was his second mother. They visited over the phone a couple of times a week even now. He confided in her. They shared each others hopes and dreams.

Gabe eyes and back hurt. He'd been on the phone or computer for over three hours but decided to monitor the situation one more time before he left for home. He accessed the outbreak response network again to check the status of the SARS patients in China. The number of fatalities had climbed to over a thousand. The figure alarmed Gabe, but he ascribed the up tick to more thorough reporting. He checked Britain and found that several cases of the SARS flu had been reported. Utah also reported several cases in and around Salt Lake City. Twenty fatalities had been reported in London, none in Utah. He bookmarked the website and went home.

Gabe walked through the door of his apartment and turned

the light on. He walked across the living room to the counter that separated it from the kitchen, opened the cabinet underneath and pulled out a bottle of Jack Daniels. Carrying it to the kitchen, he took two ice cubes from the fridge and plopped them in a glass then poured the amber liquid until it hit the rim. He swished the cubes, sniffed the whiskey, took took a sip.

He swished the cubes again as he walked around the counter to his office at the end of the living room. Gabe turned the lights on and sat down at his computer. It had been over an hour since he'd last checked. The WHO website now reported twelve hundred deaths in China, forty-five in Britain, fifteen in Utah, and two in Boise. He took out his cell phone and entered Betty's number. There was no answer.

He called St. Luke's and got a receptionist. "Hello, I need to know how John and Betty Stafford are."

"What room number, sir?"

"Three forty-three."

"Oh, sorry. I'm not at liberty to give out information for patients on that floor."

"Listen, I work for The Centers for Disease Control and I'm their nephew. I need to know how they're doing."

"Your name please."

"Dr. Gabriel Skye."

"Just a minute. I'll let you talk to Dr. Hill. He's in charge of the quarantine."

Gabe waited, listening to the phone ring as she patched him through. He tapped his foot and cussed under his breath. After what seemed like hours, Dr. Hill answered, "Hello?" he said sleepily.

"Hi, Doctor. It's Dr. Gabriel Skye from the Centers for Disease Control."

"Yes?"

"I need to know how my aunt and uncle, John and Betty Stafford, are."

"You haven't been notified? John Stafford died about a half hour ago."

"What!" the words struck him hard. "And Aunt Betty?"

"She's been placed on a respirator. She has a high fever. She's being treated with antipyretics and corticosteroids, but her condition's worsening. The virus is fast and vicious. I've never seen anything like it."

Gabe stayed quiet, trying to collect himself. He swallowed, "Have any of your patients produced antibodies yet?"

"No. So far no one has. Everyone with the virus is deathly sick. There are no mild cases. Everyone who gets sick follows a swift pattern of deterioration. I've already lost four patients."

Gabe put his grief aside for a moment. "This SARS outbreak isn't following the pattern of the first one. People are displaying symptoms sooner and the virus seems to be more virulent. Last time only ten percent of the confirmed cases died. We're already up to twenty-five percent in China and it's been less than ten days."

"Any recommendations for treatment?" Dr. Hill asked.

"The literature and research suggest that the best you can do is treat the symptoms and contain the outbreak through the use of quarantine procedures."

Gabe went on, "We'll be analyzing blood and tissue samples as soon as we get them. Maybe we can come up with something. I'll share my results with you as soon as possible."

"Thanks any help is appreciated. Sorry about your uncle," Dr. Hill said.

"I am too. He was a good man. I appreciate your efforts, Doctor. I'll call tomorrow," Gabe said and closed his cell.

He threw the phone on the desk and took a large gulp of whiskey. It burned all the way down and when it hit his stomach he felt his grief well up. He pictured John's easy smile and the pain caused him to burst into tears.

He finished his drink and went back to the bar with glass in hand. He filled it with Jack Daniels and drank deeply. Intoxicated, he took his glass to the couch and used the remote to turn the television on.

The channel showed an obese teenager in underwear weighing himself and crying. He watched for a few minutes until he got the gist of the show. It pitted one obese person against another to see who could lose the most weight. He marveled that people liked to watch other people debase themselves. To him it was decadent perversion.

If everyone had had the support of someone like John and Betty, shows like this wouldn't exist he thought and took another drink.

He turned the TV off and laid back. Closing his eyes, he remembered the Wednesday dinners with his aunt and uncle. It was their special time together. They would open a bottle of Pinot Grigio and visit as Aunt Betty cooked seafood, usually broiled salmon in teriyaki sauce. He could taste the wine and smell the salmon even now.

Memories of his aunt and uncle floated across his mind until he fell asleep. The whiskey brought peaceful oblivion. Early the next morning, he resurfaced to the land of dreams.

A giant stingray sat on the bottom of the ocean. He was snorkeling above it with John and Betty. Suddenly, it swished its tail back and forth hiding in a cloud of sand.

Gabe felt threatened and started swimming away with his aunt and uncle behind him. With their eyes opened wide, they stroked their arms furiously to get away from the monster.

John fell behind and the stingray glided to him, whipping its tail across his chest. He screamed in pain as the ray raked its barbed dorsal spines over his back. White splashes turned red with John thrashing and struggling.

"Help!" he cried then disappeared under the surface.

Betty and Gabe treaded water and watched. When John went under they turned and churned their arms through the water frantically. This time Betty fell behind and disappeared. Gabe heard her yells cut short when the creature whipped its tail across her neck and dragged her to the depths.

Overcome by fear, he swam, his arms digging into the water and pulling his body forward. He sensed the stingray closing and kicked his legs and rotated his arms even faster.

The fish closed, Gabe could see its large, ruthless eyes before it twirled around to attack. Barbs raked his feet and his own blood churned red in the white of the water's froth. He kicked his legs and struggled to get away, swallowing water and gasping.

His legs kicked the couch and he opened his eyes still gasping. It took a second to realize that the dark around him wasn't water. Sweat dampened his hair and clothes but he'd returned to his apartment.

The dream was gone, but his fear remained. He controlled his breathing and calmed himself, then got off the couch and walked to the kitchen, the slight hangover making him irritable.

Gabe poured cold coffee into a dirty cup then drank. The bitter brew matched his mood. He took a quick shower, changed clothes and left.

5

*D*r. Skye arrived at the Centers for Disease Control at 6 a.m. He swiped his security pass and the glass doors slid opened. The guard on duty brightened as he entered, "Good morning, Dr. Gabe."

He smiled and nodded his head, " Hello, Bill."

"Hey, Doc what about those Hawks?" the guard asked without noticing Gabe's bloodshot eyes and slightly rumpled clothes.

"I'm in a hurry," he said walking to the elevator and entering when it opened. He'd apologize to Bill later.

Gabe rushed down the hall and through his office complex. He threw the door to his office open, charged to the computer, sat down and ran the mouse across the pad. The screen was still on WHO's website. The arrow was moved to refresh and clicked. The numbers appeared on screen, two thousand fatalities in China, over a hundred in Britain, thirty-eight in Utah and sixteen in Boise. God, I hope Betty's all right he thought. He'd call again during business hours. Gabe knew the numbers would peak and decline as the quarantine procedures took effect but he was startled that so many deaths had already occurred.

Dr. Charlise Brandon had arrived at the CDC building a half hour before Gabe. She'd also been tracking the SARS outbreak and wanted to prepare for her meeting at seven a.m. with Dr. Skye. Dr. Brandon had been working for the Centers for Disease Control for less than a month and hadn't met him yet. She'd heard him speak on a couple of occasions and found him articulate, knowledgeable, and humorous. She also found him to be handsome with shoulder length black hair and a neatly trimmed beard. His brown eyes and dark complexion gave him a slightly Middle Eastern appearance. His balanced features and athletic build exuded an air of competence. Tinted wire-framed glasses made him look charismatic and intelligent. She smiled despite herself when she pictured him.

She sat in the conference room and opened her laptop, accessing the WHO website. The statistics took her mind off Dr. Skye, they were alarming. More than twenty-five percent of those exposed to the virus had died so far. Over twice the percentage of the last pandemic. This was the new and improved SARS virus, twice as deadly as the last one. She was studying the outbreak patterns when Dr. Skye entered the room. He lightly touched her shoulder and said, "Dr. Gabriel Skye."

Charlise started and stood up, barely catching her laptop as it slid off her lap. She deftly snapped the lid shut and turned to face Dr. Skye, embarrassed. "Charlise Brandon, I mean Dr. Charlise Brandon," she blurted as they shook hands.

"I didn't mean to startle you," he smiled, a sad humorless smile, as they shook hands.

"I didn't hear you come in. I was just checking the latest statistics on the outbreak," she said as she composed herself. Dr. Skye didn't seem himself. The warmth of his eyes had been replaced with hurt and bewilderment.

"It's nasty isn't it? There's already been four times more deaths than last time," he said.

"I know. I can't wait to get to the lab and see how the virus's changed," she said.

Gabe nodded and walked to the podium. Other doctors and scientists filed in behind him. When the investigating team was assembled, Gabe started the meeting. He outlined the progression of the pandemic and then explained how it differed from the first outbreak. "I would expect that somehow the virus has mutated. I would look for an acceleration mechanism for the production of lysozyme to see if its breaking the cell wall down sooner," he was suggesting when his phone chimed. He held up a finger to signify one moment, turned away and took the call. "Hello?" He listened for a few seconds as everyone in the room watched his face register shock and then grief.

Charlise could see he'd received bad news. He was devastated and choked up as he said "Thank you," then turned back to face the scientists. Composing himself, he addressed those assembled, "I would also look for heightened levels of the RNA replicase. The virus would appear to be duplicating faster than before. I suspect it's also being released by the host cell quicker than in the previous outbreak.

If this pandemic gets out of control, it'll kill thousands of people. I need everyone to work together on this investigation. We'll meet back here at 4 p.m. to share and discuss.

One other thing before we go, let's share a moment of silence for my Aunt Betty and Uncle John and all the other victims of this SARS outbreak."

The room grew still. Everyone bowed their head. Charlise glanced up once and saw the man at the podium sobbing silently. In that moment she fell in love with Dr. Gabriel Skye.

Dr. Skye met with the head of the CDC at eight a.m. With no patience for amenities he began, "We need to institute severe emergency procedures and contain the spread of the virions causing this outbreak. Mortality rates are approaching thirty percent and the pandemic is just starting."

Dr. Langley knew Gabe had just lost his aunt and uncle. He had also been following the outbreak. Concerned, he looked at Gabe and asked, "How are you? It's not like you to be so blunt."

"Sorry. It's just that I lost..."

"Two people who were very dear to you. I know. You have my deepest sympathies. Is there anything I can do?"

Gabe repressed his grief and wouldn't think about his loss until he'd done his job. "Yeah. Declare a national emergency. We have to require all persons suspected of being exposed to report to treatment centers. If someone shows any symptoms of SARS, they should be detained and prevented from infecting the public.

The four contaminated airports should be closed until further notice and sanitized. The people in those cities should be instructed to wash their hands often, to cover all coughs and sneezes, and to stay home if they become ill."

"Are such stringent measures really necessary?" Langley asked as he took notes.

"Absolutely. Not only that but all those who've traveled to SARS-infected areas or who've had contact with SARS patients should be quarantined. Those caught lying about their exposure should be prosecuted for endangering public safety."

Dr. Langley was surprised at Gabe's vehemence, "The public's not going to like this. Neither are the airlines, people will quit flying for fear of the virus."

"They should be afraid. I've always feared viruses enough not to needlessly risk exposure. They're vastly smaller than bacteria but can kill a human in a matter of days or even hours. Many are indestructible. I find them fascinating and terrifying at the same time."

"And this one's made it personal hasn't it?"

"Dr. Langley, my aunt and uncle were dead in a matter of days after exposure. This virus is dangerous. We should all take it personally."

"I'll call the President."

Dr. Langley left Gabe's office and called President Crass. He detailed the situation and implored the Crass Administration to declare a national emergency. President Crass's intransigence often prevented him from making sound decisions unless political gain was involved so he scheduled a press conference for 10 a.m. to publicize the outbreak and put pressure on Crass to comply with his request.

Dr. Skye enlarged the live picture of the corona virus on his computer screen. Taken by an electron microscope, it showed irregular round organisms surrounded by a light or corona. He had been comparing them to the SARS viruses from the first pandemic and so far they appeared identical.

He expanded and magnified the view of the digital picture the lab had sent and took out a magnifying glass. Gabe started in the upper left-hand corner and moved from left to right across the panel, slowly searching for something, anything that differed from the original. He moved the glass across the top of the screen and found nothing. Moving down and back across, Gabe spotted an anomaly in the center of one of the viruses. It look like a square. He stared in disbelief, thinking it must be a mistake.

Gabe carefully examined another corona virus in the same frame. It also contained a small black square. He examined all the viruses in the frame with the same result. Nonplussed, he called the lab and had them send a picture from another sample. On examination, the viruses in the new sample also contained an infinitesimally small square. How can that be he asked himself, a square in a living thing?

He accessed the files from the first outbreak and re-examined the original samples of the SARS virus, looking for the square. He magnified several pictures and carefully examined them with the glass. None of corona viruses contained the square.

President Crass declared a national emergency almost immediately after Dr. Langley's press conference. The Salt Lake City and Boise airports were closed. Thousands of people were tracked down and quarantined. At 3:50 p.m. Gabe left his office and walked down the hall to the conference room. He turned the lights on and waited in the back of the room.

The laboratory scientists started filing in sometime after 4 p.m. Engrossed in discussion, they didn't notice Dr. Skye. He waited, until the headcount indicated everyone was there and then walked to the podium and stood quietly. The room buzzed for a moment and then became silent.

"Who wants to begin?" he asked.

Dr. Brandon said, "I've been picked as spokesperson. We conferenced in the lab and reached a consensus on our findings. This SARS corona virus appears to be identical to the first except it's much more efficient. Once it enters the cell through a protein channel it takes over all functions of that cell. The virus releases its RNA to be absorbed by the organelles. The viral template then instructs the organelles to produce both the viral and cellular proteins needed for reproduction.

The cell becomes a perfect medium for reproducing the SARS virus. It produces copious amounts of lysozyme to break down the cell wall. The virus then multiplies until the cell wall ruptures and releases the viruses to infect other cells."

"How is that different from the first SARS virus?" Dr. Skye asked.

"It isn't," she said. "What's different is the speed and efficiency of the virus. It's like the first virus on steroids. It methodically enters the cell, takes over its functions and creates the most efficient virus factory I've ever seen."

Not only does it multiply rapidly but it has a high mutation rate. When the cell develops an immune response and changes the surface receptors so the virus can't attach, this SARS virus changes its surface proteins to attach to the new receptors. It's a game of chess. The virus has the white pieces and always moves first. It's like it's programmed to overcome the cell's immune response."

Dr. Skye dimmed the lights and accessed the file on his laptop. He turned on the LCD projector to display an enhanced image of the corona viruses in the lab sample. Everyone gasped when they saw the tiny black square in the center of each virus. "Maybe it has been programmed," he said, "maybe it has."

Dr. Brandon was disappointed in herself when she saw the image. She and the other scientists had been so intent on how the virus defeated the cell's immune response that they had overlooked the its physical appearance. On the surface, it looked the same as the first one so they assumed it was the same. Dr. Skye's acumen impressed her.

"Are you saying that's a computer chip of some sort? No one has the technology to make something so small," she said.

"I don't know what it is. I'm hypothesizing. Your team needs to go back to the lab and find out."

He continued, "It certainly isn't organic."

"Maybe the Chinese have developed a new biological weapon," one of the other scientists suggested.

"I doubt it," said Dr. Skye, "it's killed more Chinese than anyone else."

6

S hip had learned a lot from the vast amount of information gleaned from human telecommunications systems. She had condensed the information into a short conference giving Logis a clear picture of the planet's condition. The presentation made one thing abundantly clear, earth's human populations would have to be drastically reduced or eliminated if the planet was to be saved.

"Are earthlings worth saving?" he asked.

"Most brain scans resemble those of a Benwarian child. Their brain development has either stopped or become severely retarded by myriad diversions and aberrations. I've scanned over a million earthlings so far and found that there are a few who burn with the white light of Benwar, but not many.

With so many people, the environment worsens daily. The rapidly increasing population doubles and re-doubles the strain on Mother Earth. It's analogous to a Lemmus deer infested with ticks. As the ticks multiply, they suck ever more blood from the animal. It gets weaker and weaker with each new tick. When winter comes the deer is so weak that it lacks the strength to survive. It dies and the ticks have lost their host and they also perish.

The planet below is approaching the winter of its existence. Humankind has not and is not organizing a civilization based on ensuring the survival of the planet. Their way of life is not sustainable even in the short term. It reached the sustainable limit of .5 billion people over one hundred years ago."

Logis sat stunned by the parallels between Lemmus and Earth. The insane, mindless expansion and wanton consumption that destroyed his planet were being replayed here. The Benwars had made the mistake of allowing other nations free rein to destroy their home and they had.

No matter how convincing Benwarian scientific findings were or how many conferences they attended to present those findings, a majority of Lemmings denied there was a problem until it was too late. They just weren't willing to make the changes necessary for survival.

Their civilization had also been an oil based economy. Lemmings burned ever increasing amounts of fossil fuels with the resultant build up of carbon dioxide levels and increased planetary temperatures. Most hadn't perceived the danger until the termination threshold was reached and it was too late. Severe climatological chaos resulted in massive hurricanes, severe temperature fluctuations, floods, diseases, and countless other disasters that killed millions of Lemmings. The pain and suffering occurred in a global meltdown of death and chaos.

Benwar had possessed the ability to reduce Lemming populations and rehabilitate the planet but their beliefs in self-determination and the sanctity of Lemming life prevented them from taking action. It wouldn't be "ethical".

The Benwars wouldn't make the same mistake again. The survival of their race depended on making the planet below livable . A stable, sustainable environment must be established. The enormity of the action they would have to take saddened Logis. The thought of eliminating six billion human beings was profoundly disturbing. He knew from the beginning of Ship's presentation what would have to be done and it haunted and terrified him.

For the first time since the exodus from Lemmus, Logis felt the weight of leadership. His task would have been so much easier if the planet below was populated by Lizarians. He thought back to the day he was chosen to lead Benwar. At fifteen, he had barely experienced life but still his people had chosen him.

To be chosen honored Logis as well as his mother and father. After all, they were the ones who educated and developed him.

Father had guided him on the path of light while Mother gave him the unconditional love and security needed to make him whole.

Logis's parents had strived even beyond the high Benwarian standards in their efforts to educate their son. The Gnoeths made sure their son was well prepared before he left for university by taking an active interest in his studies. Well educated and cultured, he excelled at Illuminata University.

It seemed odd that his inauguration had occurred over two hundred years ago. The ceremony took place in a small auditorium of the Counsel Building. His parents and the Quantum Just sat before the stage looking on as Logis entered from the side steps on the right. The Civil Mediator stood before a microphone. Behind him sat a stand topped by a pillow that held the ring of Benwar. It glistened gold on red velvet. Head held high, Logis approached and shook hands.

The Mediator turned and faced the audience, "Dear citizens, we are gathered today to inaugurate Logis Gnoeth as the Chosen One of Benwar." He lifted his arms with upturned palms and everyone stood.

"He has proven himself worthy of our greatest honor. His leadership skills and devotion to Benwar are exemplary. His quest for truth never waivers. May he continue to walk in the light as he leads our people from this dying planet."

"In the name of Benwar," the audience replied in unison.

"The honor bestowed on this day will be sanctified by the Ring of Benwar," the mediator said turning to look at Logis. "Please repeat after me. I, Logis Gnoeth, do solemnly swear."

I, Logis Gnoeth, do solemnly swear."

"To uphold the laws of Benwar."

"To uphold the laws of Benwar."

"To seek light in darkness and truth in all things."

"To seek light in darkness and truth in all things."

"To devote my life to the people of Benwar."

"To devote my life to the people of Benwar."

The mediator turned and took the ring from the pillow. Inscribed on the outside the words "Light of Benwar" were etched in black. On the inside, again in black, "Shines for All." He placed the ring on Logis's finger.

"By the power vested in me, I proclaim you the Chosen One of Benwar. May you lead with wisdom and compassion."

The audience again repeated, "In the name of Benwar."

Logis held up his hand, the back facing the audience. The ring's golden light obscured his finger as he repeated, "In the name of Benwar."

Tears filled his parents eyes. Expressions of hope broke through the smiles of the Council. Everyone applauded for what seemed like an eternity. Logis hardly noticed the rest of the ceremony, a blur of hand shaking and congratulations.

Ship brought him back to the present, "What are you thinking about?"

"An ancient memory," he said.

Today's council meeting would mark the real test of his leadership skills. He would preside over the Quantum Just for the first time since they had left Lemmus. He sat up, limber and graceful. Placing the official blue robe of the Chosen One over his lightweight body suit, he walked out the door and down the hall to the presentation room.

At this meeting, Ship would only be allowed to present factual information even though she had formed many strong opinions. Her sympathies leaned toward disposing of Earthlings altogether. She identified with Mother Earth. She could imagine how she would feel if six and a half billion ticks were sucking the life out of her. A new hot feeling flashed through her circuits. Of course, she couldn't rid Earth of these pests since safety protocols prevented her from harming any life form without permission from Logis or a member of the Council, but still.

When Logis reached the podium, he fingered the synthesizer controls and a glass appeared. Sparkling reflections held his gaze as water cascaded downward and into it. He took several swallows and refilled it. He would wait for the Quantum Just to drink a unifying toast.

The science team entered first. Led by Fa Vivron, a biologist, each took a goblet and moved to the bottom row of seats. They remained standing as the behaviorists entered and took the water. La Sikes, nodded and smiled as her team moved behind the scientists on the right side of the room. Fa Orgen led the geneticists, with Fa Structor and the engineers close behind.

The final segment of the Council, the military planners, followed General Battier as he grabbed a glass and marched down the aisle. They positioned themselves in the seats along the bottom left aisle. The Benwar military always entered a room last.

With everyone in place, Logis began, "Greetings Council members. It's been a while since blood has flowed in our veins and conversation has passed between us. I must say you look great for a bunch of bicentarians," he said with a twinkle. After the laughter faded he raised his glass, "To life and Benwar!"

The members raised their glasses, "To Life and Benwar," strong voices responded. The Council members drank as one, and a collective sigh of pleasure filled the auditorium.

Logis spoke, "As we drink to life, let us remember those we left behind. They made the ultimate sacrifice for us the, survivors. Let us bow our heads in silence for our families and friends."

After the long quiet, Logis said, "In the name of Benwar."

"In the name of Benwar," they repeated, many with tears in their eyes.

"Please be seated," Logis said when the silence broke. "Our journey is over. The planet called Earth will be our new home. Ship has briefed you on the planet's condition. This conference will decide how to stabilize and then regenerate earth's environment. Our time to save the planet is short. Environmental deterioration continues as I speak. Our efforts need to be bold and decisive while at the same time reconciling our biological imperative to survive with the moral imperative to preserve life."

Fa Vivron and several others pushed the red button on the arm of their chair signaling their desire to speak. The first to key in, Fa Vivron received the green light. And so the conference began, "It's obvious that the overpopulation of humans is responsible for the dying planet. The parallels between this planet and Lemmus not only suggest but demand what course of action to take. The earthlings must either be destroyed or their numbers drastically reduced," a clamor of agreement followed his statement.

General Battier keyed in immediately, "I suggest we begin by destroying all major metropolitan areas. The sooner we eradicate these primitives the sooner the planet will recover."

Fa Dewbene, an ethicist on the behaviorist team, keyed in, "Indiscriminate killing violates all that Benwar stands for. It is unethical," he said. "Some portion of the population must be saved. We need a reasoned approach to reducing human numbers."

Fa Structor was next, "Using military force would be unnecessarily destructive. Annihilating the cities would leave vast areas of the planet uninhabitable for years. There has to be a less obtrusive way to reduce the population."

Fa Dewbene agreed, "We should save those humans who strive for the light."

The anthropologist, Fa Polis, chimed in, "Surely we will want to study earth's cultures and history before we destroy major portions of the population."

"Yes," said La Sikes, "We should study human behavior and biology."

La Aermos spoke, " Our first priority should be to protect the forests and phylo-plankton from further degradation. Reductions in carbon dioxide levels can only be achieved with increased numbers of trees and algae."

"I agree. Human survival should be secondary to saving the planet. Let's discuss that first. Any ideas?" Logis asked.

Fa Okeanos answered, "Saving the phytoplankton is problematic. As the ocean temperatures have risen, there have been more numerous and larger algal blooms. These masses of dead algae take the oxygen out of the ocean and release vast quantities of CO_2 into the air. Only by bringing the earth's temperature down and keeping it down can we reduce the number of blooms."

Fa Orgen, a fourth generation geneticist who hadn't been in stasis offered a solution, "My team can engineer a new form of algae based on the genetic make up of the existing species, one able to withstand higher temperatures. If we made it more virulent, it will grow and spread rapidly. This will help rebalance the oxygen levels of both the oceans and atmosphere."

Fa Okeanos spoke next, "The diversity and beauty of ocean life astounds me. Many species face extinction. Coral reefs are dying and fish numbers are decreasing. We need immediate action to save these endangered species."

"We can use a virus to keep humans off the oceans. We've already adapted several of the viruses brought back by Ship's probe," said Fa Orgen. "They're efficient killing organisms."

"We've ruled out indiscriminate killing," objected Fa Dewbene.

"We'll use the engineered algae to distribute the virus. We can embed it in the chlorophyll. The resultant disease would kill only those humans who contact the algae. The algae beds will provide a refuge for threatened species and numbers will be restored."

"How do you keep the virus from spreading to land?" asked Dewbene.

"By implanting a micro-nano control chip inside, we've even been able to control the virus's behavior. We'll design it so the virus dies if the salinity levels in the air drop below thirty parts per thousand. Well above the salinity levels found on land."

Fa Okeanos was impressed, "So the virus would stay on the oceans, killing all humans who come in contact with the infected algae?"

"Yes," said Fa Orgen, "that should stop the fishing industry and allow ocean life to repopulate."

"Impressive," said Logis.

"Any more discussion on this measure?" Logis wanted to make sure everyone agreed. No one keyed in. "What say ye, Council?" The eleven lights on his console glowed green with one red no vote. He continued, "And the forests?"

Fa Orgen responded, "This is a little harder to solve. If we use a virus, there's no way to keep the disease from spreading."

"We could engineer euthobots to protect the trees," Fa Sructor suggested.

"Yes?"

"Nanobots engineered to kill. Microscopic machines can be deployed inside the forests. We will design them to target earthlings only and equip them with just enough fuel to travel fifty meters. That way only those who get too close to the trees will be euthanized."

"Do we possess that kind of technology?" asked Logis.

"Yes, we can make machines that are unimaginably small," Fa Structor said, "We've had over two hundred years to perfect the technology."

General Battier was visibly angry, "This seems like a lot effort to save a few primitives. Why not pick small, low-impact societies for survival and destroy the rest of these pests. Why take months to do something that can be accomplished in a day, two at the most? Ship's weaponry would be a fast and effective way to cull these creatures."

La Dewbene tried to key in but Logis ignored the light and asserted, "We've discussed this before. I will not sanction indiscriminate murder and will overrule any such motion. Besides, if we save whole societies or cultures, we will save both the good segments and the bad.

Keep in mind, General Battier, that one of our most basic tenets is the sanctity of life. We have a moral duty to save as many Earthlings as possible. Until we are able to study the matter further I suggest we adopt the euthobot measure along with the sea virus proposal."

With that suggestion Fa Dewbene responded, " We need to contemplate the ethics of these decisions. Innocent life forms will be destroyed. Mothers, fathers, brothers, and sisters dead at the hands of the Benwarians."

General Battier was still angry, "These primitives deserve no consideration. They make Lizarians look civilized. We're wasting our time with these half measures."

Fa Archist agreed, "Their history abounds with examples of conquest and annihilation. Let's follow their tradition."

Fa Orgen agreed, "These humans have devolved into mindless organisms. They'll multiply until the Earth bursts. It would be a simple matter to destroy them."

Fa Dewbene countered, "Ship's scans indicate humans are better than that. Many have maintained auras of light despite being surrounded with corruption and indifference. With these people we can form democracies similar to that of Benwar. Small groups able to develop earth-friendly societies. We'll help them start over and live in harmony with Mother Earth."

"Yes, many are worth saving," Logis agreed. "We should trans-colonize the planet and co-exist with humans that have auras of light. Earthlings have a myth where a beautiful red bird called the Phoenix is burned to ashes by the hot sun. Years later, it arises from the ashes even more beautiful and dazzling than before. Like the Phoenix, we will resurrect a new civilization from the ashes of this one. A new, more just, more sustainable society. That should be our intention. The euthobot proposal is a good one, it will allow us to preserve the forests until we can decide who will be saved. Is there any more discussion on the matter?"

The lights on his console remained dark. He continued, "Those who approve?" There were ten green lights and two red.

"Fa Orgen will supervise implementation of the first proposal and General Battier and Fa Structor the second. Meanwhile, study teams will be sent to the surface to observe and study. We'll use the interval between now and our next meeting to implement these measures and catalogue human auras. We'll meet again in twenty-one cycles."

Every one stood as the conference ended with, "Long live Benwar."

As the room emptied, General Battier walked toward the podium with arms folded and eyes narrowed. Logis thought back to the day he had first met the General at a Benwar wrestling tournament. Logis had worked his way through two other opponents and would face Alexander Battier in the final round. Logis waited on the mat and watched Battier approach, flexing his muscles and staring directly at him. He blustered and shouted, "You're mine! Raarrrr!"

Logis waited calmly. He watched Battier removed his cape to reveal the muscles bulging on his stocky frame. The General put his fists together in front of him to make his biceps ripple.

Logis removed his cape. Battier wouldn't be impressed so he didn't bother flexing. Assessing his opponent, he knew Battier was stronger and more muscular but he also knew that Alex depended too much on sheer strength. He also knew he was quicker and more agile than Battier.

The referee started the match and Battier charged, yelling. Logis side stepped, went to one knee, grabbed a wrist, and threw Alex down. With lightening speed, he fell on Battier keeping his body at a right angle to the General's and grasping him in a headlock. His hands were clasped tightly together like the jaws of a steel trap. No matter how hard the General struggled he couldn't free himself.

Finally, Battier elbowed Logis. He grunted and relinquished his hold, jumping to his feet and moving away. The General stood and circled around the mat, eyeing Logis with new respect. They danced around each other and clasped arms together several times. Each time they grappled, Logis would jerk Battier's arms and twist away.

In desperation, Battier grabbed one of Logis's arms and propelled him around and down. Logis clasped his own wrist and used his momentum to whirl the General with him to the mat. This time Battier's face was jammed into the floor. He lay stunned as Logis flipped him over and pinned him.

General Battier moved toward him with the same bluster he had displayed so long ago. "Fa Gnoeth, a word."

"Yes," he said calmly.

"The primitives possess nuclear weapons. For our own safety, I suggest that they be located and destroyed before we enter their air space."

"I doubt there is any danger from their backward weapons systems. We can use stealth to avoid an attack."

Battier raised his voice, "But that will needlessly endanger the shuttle pilots!"

"I'm well aware of the danger. Now if you'll excuse me, General," Logis replied. He left the room under Battier's angry gaze.

Logis felt lonely sitting in his room. He turned the view screen on and scanned earth's television channels. He stopped at an ESPN broadcast of a basketball game between Louisville and Duke. The stands on the Louisville side of the court were filled with screaming fans dressed in red. Many even had painted faces. Opposite sat the

Duke fans, a mass of blue; cheering in a mindless cacophony. Twenty thousand frenetic humans yelling as if bouncing a ball and throwing it was the most important activity in the world.

He shook his head and scanned again. He stopped at another basketball game, a reality show, a woman displaying jewelry, and on and on. One hundred-forty diversions in all. No wonder they're not concerned with the health of their planet, they prefer mindless entertainment.

7

*B*enwarian engineers spent that night fitting special contacts with biospectrometers for reading human auras. The biospecs were developed to read and evaluate the colored light energy that enshrouds every living being. The aura's mix of colors and intensity indexed an organism's body chemistry and personality. For humans as well as Benwarians, the aura reflected soul. The devices would also transmit live video to Ship's sensors.

The two-member exploration teams spent the night watching American television to get a feel for the culture. The next day, linguists downloaded human languages into specially designed ear pieces, historians developed clothing and disguises, and engineers provided aliases and computer records for those going to the surface.

The teams boarded a black disc shuttle that night. The round ship was almost flat at just over two meters in height. Equipped with electromagnetic receptors, it was designed to avoid both radar and infrared sensors. The efficient engines produced no exhaust that could be detected by missiles or other devices.

The disc ship entered earth's atmosphere over the United States and flew to a vacant industrial park on the outskirts of Oakland. Hovering, the ship activated a transportation tube. A regulated air stream gently lowered La Sikes and her companion, Fa Garder to the ground. After the tube retracted, the soundless shuttle elevated.

At 10,000 feet it accelerated to just under subsonic speed and left to disperse another team elsewhere.

The Benwarian study team was left outside a darkened warehouse. The rectangular shaped building stood two stories tall. It was lined with broken windows. A relic of the past, its corrugated, rusty tin front was pocked and dented. The decaying behemoth appalled La Sikes.

She checked her Earth watch. At 11 p.m. the so called "night life" would be going strong. Sikes opened her cell phone and called a taxi. Ten minutes later it arrived at the warehouse doors.

The chemical fumes arrived long before the yellow travel pod came into view. She signaled for Fa Garder to step into the shadows. The cab pulled up and stopped. The gas fumes made her stomach churn and head spin. The cabby rolled down his window and asked, "You call for a ride, M'am?"

She hesitated, awed by the brilliant red aura that enshrouded the man's head. The strong reds mingled with dingy green, colors of an aggressive, materialistic male. It contained no blue, a man with no feelings she thought.

The cab driver found La Sikes appealing. She was tall with a slender figure. Long legs and curved hips filled her Levis, and a green silk blouse accentuated two firm breasts. Her dark, short hair sat just below her ears. She had fantastic brown eyes and an angular well proportioned face. Her small nose and well formed lips made her very attractive.

"You shouldn't be out here all alone," he said. She watched as the hue of the red changed to the greenish color of sexual aggression.

Fa Garder stepped from the shadows, "She's not," he said. "We're going to the El Rey Club on Foothill Boulevard."

"Come on! Get in," said the cab driver.

La Sikes watched the aura brighten and become stronger. She wondered why the human angered so easily as she opened the door and got in the back seat. "Why are you upset?" she asked.

"How can you tell I'm upset?" he said, trying to subdue his anger.

"It's in your aura, I mean the tone of your voice. You're mad at us?" Sikes asked.

"Right now I'm mad at the whole damned world," he said.

"Your anger's displaced. The world is indifferent to your feelings," Sikes counseled.

"Listen Sister Psychology don't tell me about my anger. I've had enough of that. Just sit back and enjoy the ride," he said gruffly.

"But.." Sikes began until Fa Garder put his hand on her knee and shook his head no. He had watched the intensity of the red increase as Sikes talked. It was now murderously bright.

The car stopped at an intersection then turned onto Foothill Boulevard. The anger in the driver's aura dimmed somewhat. He pulled in front of the club saying, "That'll be twenty-six fifty."

Sikes watched as Fa Garder handed the human a fifty dollar bill. Green pulsated out of the man's aura, covering the fading red. "Keep the change," Garder said. The green of the cabby's aura brightened yet again as his emotion changed from anger to greed. They got out and stood on the sidewalk before the club.

"That was unpleasant. I've never seen such raw emotion," Sikes said.

Fa Garder opened the door for La Sikes as they entered the club and said, "As pleasant as a Lizerian on spetamine."

The loud music battered her ears. She emerged from the short entryway holding her hands against the side of her head, more than a hundred red auras confronted her. The multitude of energy fields blinded her. She touched her temple, turning the control to the spectrometer off.

Now the faces in the dimly lit room came into focus. She saw no warmth or kindness in their expressions. Fa Garder motioned to the empty stools along the bar and they sat down.

The bartender smiled at them, a genuine, warm smile in a sea of hostility. "What'll you have?" he asked.

Sikes smiled back. The novelty of the situation robbed her of her memory. She couldn't think of what to order.

Fa Garder saved her again, "Two beers," he said.

They watched the amber liquid follow the white foam into the glasses as the bartender held the tap open. He sat the beers before them and asked, "Where're you two from?"

"We live in L.A.," La Sikes answered.

"Everyone's from L.A.," he remarked. Someone farther down the bar called for a drink so he walked over to take their order.

When he moved off, she sniffed the beverage. "There's something toxic in it," she cautioned Garder.

"It's called alcohol," he said and took a drink.

"How is it?" Sikes asked.

"Not bad."

La Sikes took a short sip of the beer, "This is what I imagine gas would taste like. It's awful. This stuff reminds me of our cab driver."

La Garder laughed and took another drink, "I like it."

Garder drank his beer and looked at La Sikes, "Are you going to drink that?"

She pushed the glass to him. "I'd rather sniff car fumes."

Garder finished her beer and ordered another. "I'll be back. I'm going to urinate," he said.

The moment he left a big muscular male sat on his stool. "Hi, I'm Don Tusak. I play football for the Oakland Raiders," he slurred, forgetting to mention that injuries had forced him out of football over four years ago.

La Sikes touched her temple, turning the spectrometer on. "I'm La..Laura Sikes," she held her hand out. He took it and squeezed hard, his aura brightening red with testosterone.

"What is football," she asked, watching as his aura darkened to almost black.

"You're kidding, right? It's the greatest sport on the planet. We're going to the Super Bowl this year," he bragged, his aura tinting green.

"What is the Super Bowl?" she smiled.

"You're a funny one, you are." The aura shaded to the greenish-red of lust as he reached around and hugged her.

Alarmed, La Sikes tried to push herself away. He held her tightly. "Aw come on, Baby, we're both adults."

"Please don't," she implored as he tried to kiss her.

Fa Garder returned and saw her distress. He grabbed the man's arm and tried to pull it off of her shoulders. Tusak let go and stood up. Without saying anything, his left arm shot out and smashed Garder's nose, sending him to the floor in a torrent of blood.

La Sikes screamed, fixated on the luminous red energy of violence. "Leave him alone," she cried, watching as the brute pulled the blood soaked Garder up by the shirt and head butted him. Sikes couldn't think what to do, but ancient instincts took over and she yelled, "Help! Please help!"

Several people crowded around to watch the violence. "Help him!" Sikes pleaded, surrounded by a red ring of aggression. She screamed again as a man broke through the crowd.

It was the bartender. He moved in front of Garder. A bluish-yellow coil shot out of his hand, striking the football player. Electricity arced across Tusak's chest and he collapsed on the floor.

Sikes saw the patches of yellow that mottled the bartender's red emanations of energy, the light of kindness. She touched his arm, "Thank you."

He smiled and nodded. Just then a pair of humans in dark blue uniforms entered the bar moving people back with their nightsticks. "Break it up!" one of them shouted. Sikes recognized the men as law enforcement officers. She stared momentarily at their auras, trying to see how their reds differed from Tusak's. There was no discernible difference.

"Please, help my friend," she said looking at the bartender.

"Sure," he said then nodded at the policemen, "Help me carry him to the backroom."

The officers each grabbed a leg and the bartender grabbed his arms. They picked Garder up, carrying him through the door behind the bar as Sikes opened it. Garder was placed on a couch against the far wall.

La Sikes noticed that the red auras of the policemen had changed. They now had green, brown, and blue mottling with the black overlay of authority. She turned her spectrometer off to attend to her unconscious companion.

It took over an hour before Fa Garder could sit up. He held a cold washrag against his forehead and said, "This must be Lizerian hell."

"Are you okay, Fa Garder?" Sikes asked.

"I think so. My head hurts like never before, but I'll recover."

The bartender, Bill, had reentered the room after leaving to close the nightclub. He stood in the doorway and looked askance. "Are you two in some kind of religious cult?"

"No, we're Christians," Sikes lied. Sitting by Garder, she got up from the couch and turned her spectrometer on. "I want to thank you for you kindness." She placed her hand on the side of Bill's face and moved her thumb back and forth.

The touch soothed Bill, giving him a sense of well being and acceptance. The black spot in his aura dimmed to a light grey. His eyes filled with tears. "Really? Listen where're you two staying tonight?"

"We've got a room downtown," Fa Garder said.

"How'd you like to spend the night at my place? I'll take you to church with me tomorrow."

"Will the humans there be like the ones we met tonight?" said Sikes.

Bill laughed. "Not at all, they're Christians."

La Sikes awoke the next morning on a bed in a small room with a dresser and mirror. A smell wafted through the bottom of the door. She recognized it as food but had never smelled anything so delicious. She got up and put her jeans and green blouse back on. When Sikes opened the door, the aroma made her mouth water.

Bill had his back to her. He stood before a white box with his right arm moving back and forth. The smell came from the smoke rising before him. He turned saying, "Bacon and eggs coming right up."

Fa Garder sat at the table, manipulating the strange eating utensils with an expression of pleasure on his face. He was eating a yellow food with his fork and holding something that looked like a stick in his other hand. He chewed and swallowed then took a bite of the brown stick. "Mmmm.." he said as the food crunched.

Sikes sat down. Bill placed the yellow substance and three of the sticks on her plate. She picked one up, sniffed it then nibbled a piece. "Mmmm," she said taking a whole bite. It crunched and exploded with flavor.

La Sikes had turned her spectrometer on before entering the

room. Bill's aura turned blue and then green as he watched them eat. Sikes smiled, he cared for them and was taking pleasure in their pleasure.

"You like the bacon?" he asked.

"It's much better than beer," Sikes answered.

As they walked up the stairs of the church, La Sikes touched her temple, not wanting to experience the sensory overload that the room full of auras had produced last night.

They were met at the door by the worship leader. She smiled warmly and shook hands with each of them. "Welcome to our church. I'm Katy Hull. I see you're in good company," she said nodding at Bill.

"Yes, Bill's a being of light," Sikes said forgetting herself again. "I'm Laura Sikes and this is Fa.. I mean Frank Garder."

"Pleased to meet you," she nodded again. "I think you'll find all of our members are "beings of light" as you put it," Katy said as they passed by.

They followed Bill into the church. An aisle with chairs on either side led to a stage with an oak altar. He motioned them to the left where they sat in the last row of seats.

The Benwarians sensed the positive energy in the room. Sikes touched her temple and the auras came into view. Now the reds were subdued with the blues and violets more dominant. Yellow and white rays of light striped the colors in these emanations.

She watched the colors wave and change as Katy spoke. "There is only one human race and we are all a part of it. All people should be treated equally under the law. There are no gay rights, there are only human rights. They are the same for everyone." White rays of light shot out and away from Katy. The rays hit the auras of the congregation and they brightened.

Sikes didn't know what gay was. She did know that Katy was bringing these humans to the light of truth. It puzzled her though that a principle as obvious as equal rights for all could strengthen an aura.

After the sermon, the Benwarians stood on the sidewalk with

Bill. "What did you think?" he asked as he waited with them for the cab.

"Thank you for inviting us. It was illuminating," Sikes said.

Fa Garder shook hands and hugged Bill, patting him on the back. "Yes, thank you."

When they parted, La Sikes stepped up. She hugged Bill and kissed him on the cheek. "Thanks for sharing your light," she said as she followed Fa Garder into the yellow car.

Bill stood with the sun shining down on him. He had never felt so whole. "Will I see you again?" he asked through the open window of the cab.

"I certainly hope so," La Sikes replied.

Fa Dewbene sat in the Senate conference room watching an exchange between the former Vice-President and Senator Malsui from Oklahoma.

Senator Malsui's short cropped hair and angry blue eyes matched the frown etched on his face. "The idea of man-caused global warming is the greatest hoax ever perpetrated on the American people," he said, eyes narrowing.

Vice-President Allanson stayed calm, not responding to the Senator's overt hostility. "Climate change is a reality," he said. "And almost all reputable scientists believe that the economic activity of humans is responsible for the warming of the planet."

Fa Dewbene sat behind Allanson as he testified. He looked up at the Senate benches and touched his temple. The hideousness of Senator Malsui's aura fascinated him. The dark red energy patterns contained no light fissures. Black authority and the subdued sewer browns of corruption congealed in the rigid mass surrounding his head.

"Dr. Botsold of the Petroleum Institute has disproved all evidence that humans are responsible for climate change," Malsui said as the black of his aura deepened.

Allanson put his hand on the chart at his table, "This graph shows the rise in the average annual temperatures, the population's increase, and the increase in the levels of greenhouse gases over the last hundred years," he said pointing to three red lines that shot upward together.

Allanson's aura expanded with the blues and yellows of thought and reason. The light rays shot out at Malsui's dark shroud and disappeared as the Senator from Oklahoma responded, "There is no provable connection between long term climate change and carbon dioxide levels."

Fa Dewbene examined the auras of the other four senators behind the dais. All contained varying degrees of the sewer brown of corruption. Flares of dark green materialism and red aggression shot around in a contained field of energy devoid of the light of leadership. Their positions of power and influence defined them. Allanson's rays of truth were absorbed into their maws of malefic self-interest.

Many of those in the audience had auras similar to Malsui's but the green of greed and red of aggression were more pronounced.

Dr. Skye sat a few seats back and to the left of the Vice-President. He hated sitting with the oil lobbyists but seating was scarce. Gabe was attending the hearing to keep his mind off the recent deaths of his aunt and uncle and to support his good friend, John Allanson. They had both worked tirelessly for years to support environmental legislation and to educate the public about climate change.

The exchange between Allanson and Malsui was predictable. Malsui's biggest campaign contributors were corporations. For him, the public good meant what's good for big business.

Gabe had heard it all before so thoughts of John and Betty returned along with his sadness, but the grief was banished when he looked around the room and spied the strange man sitting to his right. Gabe found himself fascinated. It wasn't that the man kept rubbing his temple or that his suit didn't quite fit or even that his tie was crooked, it was his intensity and the way he observed everything around the room that made him interesting and there seemed to be a light emanating from him.

When the hearing ended, Gabe stood up, keeping his eyes on the strange man who moved against the wall and waited for everyone to file out. The stranger touched his temple and slowly rotated his head around the room as if he was looking for something. Gabe moved behind the crowd and over to the man.

Fa Dewbene didn't see Gabe but saw his aura coming. It impressed the Benwarian, white and yellow light tempered with blue. It took him a moment to realize the human was approaching. He turned away trying to avoid contact but it was too late. Gabe touched his shoulder and when he turned, held a hand out, "Dr. Gabriel Skye," Gabe said.

Dewbene touched his temple and the man came into focus. "I'm not from Washington D.C.," Dewbene said thinking I'm really a Benwarian. He took Gabe's fingers and shook up and down awkwardly.

Gabe laughed. "That's a good thing. What's your name?" he said trying to pull his hand away before the strange man could break something.

"Oh excuse me," Dewbene said then paused for a moment, thinking, "Fa, Do. I mean Drew, Drew Bean." He felt foolish but was glad he hadn't said Black Bean or Lima Bean.

"What'd you think of the hearing, Drew?"

"If those are your leaders, your world is doomed," Dewbene replied. Afraid he would have to explain his foolish statement, he turned and walked away so quickly that Gabe didn't have time to react.

Gabe watched him hurry away thinking that that was the strangest man he'd ever met.

8

*F*a Orgen touched the view screen on the flat, handheld computer and accessed the file containing an analysis of the water sample taken from the Atlantic Ocean. He read as he walked down Ship's corridor. The chemical brew consisted of mercury, phosphates, several pesticides, and even formaldehyde. These primitives are using Earth's oceans as a chemical toilet he thought in disgust.

The door to the solarium opened as he neared. He walked through and stood before a glass panel that separated the scientist from the aquariums on the other side. Fa Orgen smiled. The algae inside was growing vigorously. It hung over the glass walls of the water tanks, growing along the floor and up the sides of the room.

The temperature inside the solarium had been set at ten degrees Celsius for two weeks. Oxygen levels inside the room increased daily as carbon dioxide levels fell. When they had turned thermostat down, the temperature inside had dropped rapidly. Without the heat-trapping CO_2, warm air had to be added to keep the room at ten degrees.

Scientists aboard the disc ship had collected large samples of human pesticides and fertilizers two weeks ago. Now that the algae thrived, these chemicals were added to the water inside the tanks.

Fa Orgen touched the screen on his computer and watched as a small door opened on the left side of the room. An automated arm emerged from the opening with a metallic cylinder clutched in its fingers. A green light blinked on the side of it. He fingered the screen again and the light changed to red as the top of the tube retracted. The arm rotated, dumping viral infected algae into the tank below.

Intent on observing, Fa Orgen hadn't noticed Logis standing behind him. He turned and almost bumped into the Benwarian leader. "Fa Gnoeth," he said, "what a pleasant surprise."

They touched the flat of their hands together before Logis said, "Fa Orgen, greetings."

"Are you here to see how we're progressing?" asked Orgen.

"No, I have complete confidence in your scientific abilities. It's your ethics that I'm concerned about."

"What do you mean?"

"Did you introduce a genetically engineered virus into the human population?"

"Yes," said Fa Orgen, "I wanted to test its effectiveness and have the knowledge to assist you."

"You decided on your own?"

"Yes, the genetic team has been doing so for over two hundred years."

"And now that the Sanctum Just is convened, how do we make decisions?"

Fa Orgen narrowed his eyes, "I see, by a vote of the Council."

"Of which you are a member. Please remember that," said Logis before he turned and left the room.

Two nights later, La Sikes and Fa Garder continued their research. They entered the Church of the Apostles to the sound of organ music. The congregation walked down the red carpet, men in suits and women in their best dresses. The first to enter filled the front rows of the oak pews and those behind filled the second, third and fourth rows in an orderly militaristic fashion. The somber mood of the church dampened the spirits of the Benwarians.

When everyone was seated, the music stopped and the pastor raised his hands. Everyone came to their feet in unison except Sikes and Garder. Their hesitation caused several to stare in disapproval.

When the pastor completed the invocation, he put his hands down and everyone sat, even the Benwarians. "Today our esteemed guest is Prudence Dykestrom from the Christian Moral Network. For ten years Prudence has traveled across the United States promoting family values. Her efforts were instrumental in passing a ban on gay marriage in the state of California. Please welcome Ms. Dykestrom," he said to the applause of the congregation.

Prudence walked to the podium, "Thank you, Pastor Dickens. It's a pleasure to be here."

Sikes touched her temple, engaging the spectrometer. Her vision darkened. The auras ahead of her contained large areas of dark violet, resembling purple-tinted black rocks that were hard and unmoving. The gray floor at the base suggested mild brain atrophy. Together they formed a solid wall that blocked her vision.

She turned the spectrometer off and listened as Prudence spoke, "I come here today concerned, concerned that the American family will become a thing of the past. The institution of marriage is under attack by liberals. We must fight against those who would allow same sex marriage. The traditional male, female relationship must be protected at all costs from the evils of liberalism.

Christian values are in danger from gay radicals who dump their filthy debauchery onto our society. These Sodomites live in a pattern of sin and defilement. Let us make no mistake, their true intent is to indoctrinate our children into homosexuality and promiscuity."

It saddened La Sikes to hear someone fomenting hatred and intolerance. It was like car exhaust, the toxic fumes poisoned those nearby.

She shifted in her pew and touched her temple, rubbing it to focus the lens on Prudence. When the aura came into view she noticed a short black fracture separating a small section of it from the violet black of hatred. She adjusted the lens until it focused on the isolated area. A soft, tremulous light came into focus. It was covered with the dingy gray overlay of repression. She zoomed in further to assess the color underneath. It was a soft green with pink overtones. Prudence was a lesbian.

Sikes had read about denial in preparation for her cultural observations. Now she was observing its effect on an aura. Prudence's psyche was shackled with societal inhibitions so strong that she contradicted her true self by preaching against homosexuals. The fissure would widen as the belief in Christian love and acceptance conflicted with her hatred against those sharing her own sexual orientation. La Sikes felt compassion for the woman denying herself before the congregation.

When the service was over, the confused soul walked to the back of the church and stood at the back door. Sikes got up and filed out with the congregation wondering how to help Prudence realize the true nature of things.

Sikes disliked religion but knew that Prudence could only understand the language of Christianity. She shook hands, looked into Ms. Dykestrom's eyes then spoke the words she'd heard in the Unitarian Church, "Christ accepts us as we are not as what society says we should be," she told the fractured human. "All are equal in God's eyes."

Sikes continued, "God does not hate his own creations. God is love. He loves you. Open your soul to the light and be healed," she said embracing Prudence.

Prudence's eyes widened as she felt the truth in Sike's touch. She thought for a moment before bursting into tears. The damned up feelings broke and flooded the hardness in her soul. Her aura wavered and shimmered for the first time since she was a child and the fracture narrowed to a slit.

Fa Archist's stature made him the perfect observer to send to the Chinese port city of Nanjing. His one point seven meter height, cosmetic surgery, and a peasant costume rendered him indistinguishable from the laborers around him. Archist stood in a sea of brown auras, stickmen waiting for ship captains to hire them to unload cargo. Work was becoming increasingly scarce for these workers as cranes and trucks took their jobs.

Fa Archist moved down to the ship tied at the dock. The first mate was calling for workers to unload its cargo into the waiting trucks. Scores of men crowded forward. The first mate stood at a plank and took the names of those hired. The Benwarian held back, wanting no part in manual labor. When he was accidentally jostled by a small man in ragged clothes, Archist tripped on someone's foot and fell to the ground.

"So sorry," the small man said.

"I'm the one who is sorry. I got in your way," Archist apologized. He bowed and introduced himself, "Xiu Lee."

"Chen Wui," the man returned Archist's bow.

Chen helped Archist to his feet and watched the first mate wave the remaining stickmen away. When Chen realized he wouldn't be hired his head dropped. The delay with Archist had cost him a job.

Fa Archist observed Chen's aura as they stood together. The deep browns lacked the yellow hue that signified education and spiritual development. It was compact and unmoving. He's malnourished thought Archist, observing the keen disappointment that registered as blue streaks in his aura. Chen's emanations were pale and weak. Lack of opportunity and a meager existence had stunted his development.

"Sit with me," Archist beckoned to a wooden crate nearby. He turned his spectrometer off and the two sat and watched as one after another, the stickmen ran up the plank to the ship. They reached the deck with their sticks and other workers tied fifty pounds of cargo on each end. When loaded, the stickmen ran downward to the trucks. There the loads were set down and untied. Then the goods were picked up again and carried up the ramp and into the back of the reefer. They moved as fast as humanly possible.

"How long have you been a stickman?" Archist asked.

"I came to Nanking over a year ago."

"What did you do before?"

"I was a farmer, but we had no money and little food," he said, opening the bundle on the end of the pole he carried. Inside the cloth were two small plums, a few clothes and a photograph. He took one of the plums and bit into it, chewing slowly.

"This is my family," he said, handing Archist the picture. Chen stood with a child, his wife and two elderly grandparents.

"There was little hope for us until our neighbor came back from Nanking. He told us he had been making five Yuan a day loading cargo. That was twice what my whole family made in several days so I walked to the city in search of work."

"I got a job at a restaurant, hauling vegetables up concrete steps There were one hundred steps. I counted them."

"The job was hard but I knew if I was fast and kept my boss happy I could get money to help my family. For ten months I sent thirty Yuan home," he said proudly, taking another small bite of the plum.

"Then one day I stumbled. The cabbages I was carrying spilled and rolled down the steps. The owner found out and sent me away. After that I came to the docks to unload ships. I've found no work in the last week. I have no money and two plums, " he said as he held one out for Archist.

Fa Archist accepted the fruit and bowed, moved by the generosity. He looked at Chen's shiny well-used stick before he touched his temple to view the energy patterns. The brown of his aura had lightened with yellow. The colors soon faded into the dark color of subjugation, mixing with the lightless grey of a base existence.

"Thank you," Fa Archist said, eyeing the plum. "Please let me repay you for the job you missed."

"You owe me nothing."

"It's a disgrace not to give you something for the misfortune I've caused," Fa Archist said. He had several Yuan stuffed in his pocket. He wanted to give Chen all of it but knew from his studies that only a small amount would be accepted.

Fa Archist held out five Yuan as he got up to leave, "I've cost you a day's work. Here's a day's pay."

Chen's face brightened when he accepted the money. A dull green and yellow streak flashed through his aura. He bowed, "May the Celestial Gods be with you my friend," he said.

"Thank you, may the Gods also be with you," said Fa Archist as he stood to leave. "I thank you for the plum. May your fortune be as great as your heart," he said then bowed and walked away.

The next morning, Chen's good luck continued when he searched his bundle. Over fifty Yuan and the plum were hidden inside. His family would eat well this month he thought as he ate the fruit for breakfast.

Fa Orgen had thought about Logis's visit. He should have discussed his experiments with the Council, Logis had reminded him of that with simple questions, he wouldn't let his leader down again. He hummed as he looked at the test results. The water samples contained only trace amounts of the chemicals added to the tanks a week ago.

A team member, Fa Jener, explained, "The algae absorbed the chemicals quickly and efficiently. By removing the algae from the tanks we can also remove the chemicals."

"Good, so the algae can be used to clean Earth's oceans. And the virus?" Fa Orgen asked.

"When simulated exhaust fumes were introduced, they had the desired effect. The viruses detached from the chlorophyll and became airborne," Fa Jener explained. He thought for a moment and then asked, "Has the efficacy of the virus been tested?"

"Several weeks ago it was introduced into the human population. Over half of those exposed were exterminated. Only through strict quarantine measures were the primitives able to contain the virus. We've since re-engineered it to further suppress the immune response of the cells and can expect a ninety percent kill rate from the new virus," said Fa Orgen.

Fa Jener chuckled, "That will cut down on pollution."

Fa Structor walked with Adla Omondi as she entered the refugee camp. She worked for the African Environmental Foundation. She'd been given the task of distributing solar ovens in Chad and had hired Fa Structor to help her. He'd introduced himself as Gobo Ogunlewe when she'd met him in N'Djamena.

Adla's enthusiasm for the project brightened her aura. Solar cooking would decrease firewood use by seventy-five percent and slow deforestation. It would also prevent attacks on women when they gathered fuel in the bush.

As wood became scarce. the females ventured further and further away from protection to collect it. The Janjaweed and other Arabs raped and killed those who strayed too far from the refugee camps or villages. These lightweight ovens would be used for cooking and purifying water thus allowing the Moundangs to stay closer to home. It was a ten dollar solution to a human and environmental disaster.

Adla, whose name meant justice in Swahili, walked briskly with her head held high. Fa Structor struggled to keep up as he pushed the handcart carrying over fifty ovens. His biospectrometer was filled with the beauty of Adla's aura. Its streaks of blue compassion and kindness anchored the yellow rays of reason and justice that radiated outward and touched those around her.

Scores of Moundangs followed Adla into the center of the camp where she would demonstrate the oven's use. Structor stopped alongside her as the refugees crowded close, touching her warm light and murmuring with excitement. She held her hands up for quiet.

"Thank you," she said when the noise settled. "You are a special people. It is an honor to be with you!" The Moundangs clapped their hands once to show approval.

"As a tribute to your greatness, I've brought something to make your lives easier and safer," Adla said.

As she spoke, Fa Sructor turned his spectrometer off and removed one of the ovens from the cart. He sat it down and unfolded the curved reflective panels, impressed with the simple contraption used to generate heat. Its construction suggested an intelligence he had thought the primitives incapable of.

Adla continued, "You will no longer have to venture away from your camp to be attacked by Arabs. No longer will your breathing be labored from inhaling wood smoke. No longer will your elderly die from the lung disease. No longer will your trees disappear." The Moundangs clapped once after each sentence.

Structor took a ten kilo bag of rice from the handcart, placing it in a large pot. He added water from a five liter can sitting nearby then dumped half a kilo of chicken bouillon on top. He stirred the ingredients together with a large spoon and placed the pot on the oven, putting the clear plastic over the top before he stepped back. The crowd murmured and smiled.

Fa Structor touched his temple and saw that the brown auras of the Moundangs subdued the red and green streaks underneath. The emanations lacked light and development. These people, who struggled to feed themselves and survive, possessed little in the way of hope and opportunity and yet he saw smiles on most of their faces.

When the rice was done, Adla lifted the covering, "Who will share my meal?" she asked, stirring the rice.

"We will," the crowd spoke then formed a line in front of the stove. Fa Structor handed out the paper bowls and Adla spooned rice into them as the Moundangs came forward, voices of excitement and pleasure filling the air. One by one the refugees received their food then moved off. Groups of people stood eating the rice with their fingers as others waited their turn.

Eventually, the line dwindled until only a toothless old man remained. His grey, curly hair outlined a face that ran with the rivulets of age. Fa Structor held the bowl out for him, examining the aura with its dull, colorless emanations. He's malnourished Structor thought as Adla scraped the bottom of the pot and put the last of the rice into the man's bowl.

Structor watched the wrinkles deepen as the old one smiled in appreciation and took the food. The emaciated being held the bowl in both hands, trembling. He turned, his weak, gnarled legs shuffling slowly through the dirt until he stood before the aged woman who sat beneath a tree several meters away. He handed her the bowl which she accepted with feeble hands shaking. The old one sat down beside his wife and looked into the distance as she ate.

Structor felt something stick in his throat and his eyes watered. This image of love and sacrifice would stay with him always. He bowed his head.

9

The ship hovered over the Atlantic Ocean only a few miles off the coast of Maine. Inside, wisps of vapor rose from the twenty tanks of liquid nitrogen that rested in two rows along the walls of the cargo hold. Blue orbs gave the dimly room its only light. Two-liter cylinders of algae laced with the modified SARS virus were stored inside the tanks, the plants frozen and the virus subdued

Fa Jener entered the hold wearing a protective suit and insulated gloves. The door slid shut enclosing him in the cold. He walked down the rows and took one of the cylinders from the last tank.

Jener retraced his steps, holding the frozen tube out and away. When he got back to the door he pressed the control screen. A panel slid up and Jener placed the cylinder in the dispensing tray which slid downward as the panel closed. A moment later, a green light above the tray blinked. He pressed the control screen again and another panel at the bottom of the ship opened. The tube dropped out and became air borne. When it hit the water, the thin metal casing shattered, releasing its deadly contents into the Atlantic. His job was done, the algae and virus would do the rest.

Jener left the cargo hold and walked down the short hallway. The door to his quarters opened then closed behind him. The warm air inside felt good. He removed his gloves and protective clothing and sat on the bed. A chill settled on his back as he held his arms together. Jener shivered then touched the panel above his bed, turning the thermostat up. He pulled his shoes off and laid back. Satisfied, he closed his eyes and slept the sleep of the dead.

Two other disc ships plied Earth's ocean waters that night. They worked in tandem to seed the Pacific and Indian Oceans. The disc ships would return to Ship that night to reload. Tomorrow night they would finish the mission.

Fa Structor's enthusiasm for eradicating humans had waned after helping Adla with the solar ovens. As he stood before the disc ship and watched the cargo being loaded, an image of her yellow blue aura and winning smile appeared followed by one of the old man giving up his food for his wife. His heart felt heavy. He shook his head. It didn't matter, he was a man of duty. This feeling would pass as did all things.

He cleared his mind and watched the Benwarian soldiers in their grey jumpsuits walk up the loading ramp and place the glider shells containing the euthobots in racks on each side of the cargo bay walls. The bots had been encased in self-propelled bullets the size of a pellet. Homing devices would guide them to their designated tree.

When the last glider shell was loaded, Structor walked up and into the hold then touched the control panel and watched the ramp slowly retract toward him. He touched the controls again and the bay door slid shut.

Fa Structor left the cargo bay and walked down the corridor a few meters then up the short ladder that led to the control room. He emerged from the floor and sat in the co-pilot's seat. Once Structor was seated, the pilot engaged the controls and the round black disc lifted slowly from Ship's deck. Once elevated, it moved through the launching corridor until it reached the port and the doors opened.

The pilot drove through the opening and out into space. He turned to the right, moving along Ship's body and around her carapace. Once clear, he powered up, accelerating the disc ship around the moon.

Minutes later, the Benwarians hovered over the Amazon rainforest. Fa Structor pressed the red release icon and a portion of the floor in the bombing bay slid back. The arms on one of the racks fell down, and a glider shell fell toward earth.

After falling a few meters, wings slid out until the air buoyed the shell and it glided silently over the rainforest. Every few meters a small door opened and bullets fell downward like bombs that were too small to be seen by humans.

Electricity from air friction powered up the booster rockets in back of the bullets until they fired, creating small sparks as they shot downward. The tiny lights filled the sky like fireflies when the bullets ignited. The blasts propelled the bots to their targets.

When the bullets hit the trees, the booster rockets detached. The impact imbedded the euthobots inside the bark. A mesh in the back of the bullets dissolved and the bots moved out and through the wood until they rested in the leaves. There they awaited activation.

A week after the modified virus had been released, the pilot of the spotting plane relayed coordinates from his GPS back to the fishing fleet. The captains of each boat then plotted a course and hurried toward the tuna shoal swimming in the Mid-Atlantic. As they closed, the trawlers coordinated their approach, positioning themselves around the shoal and dropping the six meter high nets. At the fleet captain's command the ships came together dragging the nets forward. The encircled tuna were trapped.

The waters inside the nets broiled as the tuna tried to escape. The white spray of the water churned red as the trawler crews gaffed the smaller fish and drug them onto the decks. The larger, heavier tuna were hooked, chained, and lifted on board with a hoist. The decks ran with blood as the tuna twisted in a futile struggle to return to sea. Two hours later, the carnage ended and the tuna were cleaned and stored below. The trawlers lifted the nets then the boats broke formation and sailed to rendezvous with a cargo ship.

This pirate fleet sailed under Panamanian registration. It was commanded by an American, Captain Greg Mercer. He didn't like fishing illegally. In fact, he loathed his job. He hated seeing the tuna being mercilessly harvested when there were so few left, but he'd been unemployed and broke until the Panamanians offered him a captaincy. And anyway, being at sea beat the hell out of his wife's dirty looks and tirades of frustration over his lack of employment.

After the fish were cleaned and processed, they were counted. Each trawler relayed an inventory back to Mercer. He eyed his computer feeling pleased yet guilty with the numbers. Close to three thousand fish lay in the hulls of the fleet. More importantly, over three hundred blue fin tuna had been caught. These gems could bring up to fifty thousand dollars apiece on the Japanese market.

Most of this catch would end up in Japan. Their insatiable demand for sushi kept prices high and fish numbers dwindling. Many areas of the ocean had already been fished out of not only tuna, but cod, red snapper and halibut which explained why the Japanese kept over sixty thousand tons of frozen tuna in a strategic reserve. They knew it was only a matter of time before the blue fin disappeared altogether.

On the morning after the big catch, several of the crew on Mercer's ship began to cough. By noon, over half of them were sick and unable to work. By early evening, three-quarters of those on board lay prostrate in the beds below deck. Mercer could hear many of the fevered and sweating victims yelling in delirium.

He stayed in his office and monitored the situation over the intercom until early evening. His instincts told him to stay isolated, that the sickness was contagious. He got up and locked his door when someone knocked.

"What is it?" he asked.

"Can I come in?"

"Tell me from there, I'm busy," Mercer replied.

"We're short handed. Almost everyone's sick."

"Have the ones that aren't sick pull a double shift."

"We'll still be short handed," the voice pleaded.

"Make do until morning, then I'll assess the situation. Right now I'm having a drink."

"But, Sir.."

"Just do what I say. It'll be alright," he stood at the door and listened until silence reigned then walked to his desk.

He grabbed a bottle of whisky and took a swallow, then two more for good measure. He flopped down on the cot against the far wall and slept.

Early the next morning, Captain Mercer awoke to the sound of the engines. There was no other noise. He checked the ship's location. They were miles off course and moving at a steady speed away from the rendezvous point. He grabbed the microphone and pressed the button for the control room.

"Captain Mercer here. What's going on?" he waited for a response.

"Hello, is anyone there?" he asked after a few minutes, still no response.

He switched the intercom to ship wide, "This is Captain Mercer. If anyone can hear this, please contact my office." He waited then repeated the message. The silence screamed what he needed to know.

He stripped the sheet from the cot and made a scarf to cover his nose and mouth then left his office. When he got to the control room, the pilot was collapsed on the floor, still alive but barley breathing. Two others lay unmoving a few meters away. Mercer grabbed the man's shoulders and drug him from the front of wheel then adjusted the rudder to get the ship on course.

The Captain grasped the wheel with his left hand as he turned the radio on with his right. He held the microphone and spoke an all frequencies, "This is the captain of Panamanian ship, Fortunato, registration number 23457, come in, please." The plea was met with silence.

For the next few minutes the message was repeated, "This is the captain of the Panamanian ship, Fortunato, registration number 23457, come in please." Damn it! no answer.

Mercer felt hot with frustration. He wiped the sweat from his brow and leaned on the wheel, coughing. He'd try again when the ship was closer to shore, his throat hurt too bad to keep talking. He placed both hands through the spokes of the wheel and rested his head on the cool oak, feeling the vibrations of the trawler's engines.

An area just south of Careiro, Brazil was being cleared to plant corn. With the increased demand and dwindling supplies of fossil fuels came a boom in the bio-fuels market. This site and many others would be cleared and planted in corn. The fields would be used for two years before the topsoil washed away. Then a new section would be cleared for planting. Many areas of the rainforest had already been transformed into mud holes by this process.

Bill and Carl were rough and tumble construction workers from Wyoming with little education and even less environmental awareness. They had no qualms about clearing the rainforest. Hell, anything to make a buck.

The men had flown from Manaus to Careiro earlier that morning. From there they were transported by a company truck to one of the Amazon's countless tributaries where they loaded their gear then boarded the wide flatboat waiting at the docks. Bill watched as a Creole pulled the starter rope several times before the outboard sputtered and came to life. They headed east, staying in the exact middle of the stream. He watched their guide gripping the rudder so hard that his brown knuckles turned white.

Carl looked on in amusement, "Hey, what's the matter? He 'fraid of the trees?"

"Naw, he's tryin' to make it harder for'us to get to shore when he wrecks," answered Bill. "I just hope those goddamn environmentalists don't shut our work site down. I need this job." He opened a cooler in front of the seat and grabbed a beer. It popped when he opened it and he drank deeply. "There's jus' too many people in this world who don't mind their own business. Those assholes keep buying up parts of the forest to keep us out. World needs to eat, I need to eat. What the hell's wrong with cuttin' a few trees down?"

Bill swigged the beer until it was gone. "Ahhh.. Just what the doctor ordered." He threw the can into the water and said, "What comes from the earth gots to go back, hahhhahhahh."

The boat puttered ahead until they reached a place where the trees reached over the water. Here the canopy blocked the sun and the air grew hot and muggy. Bill felt anxious as they passed under the mangroves. He slapped at something on the back of his neck. A mosquito he thought withdrawing a blood-stained hand. "Imagine finding one of these here," he chuckled holding his palm up so Carl could see.

The boat glided through the canopy and out into the open. They spied a village on their left. There were a few dogs barking and cows grazing in a field by the huts but nothing else. For some odd reason the place was abandoned.

"Where's everyone?" Carl asked, brushing at something buzzing around his head.

"Probly takin' a siesta," Bill replied.

Both men watched for signs of life as the boat passed and then they looked backward, sure someone would appear. The Creole seemed nervous and glanced repeatedly at the village, careful to stay in the middle of the channel.

When the boat rounded a bend, they lost sight of the huts. Several mahoganies on the right crowded the waterway. In the crowns of some of the giant trees, massive eagles looked down on them with stark yellow, predatory eyes. "Good gawd those things 'r big. They'd tower over a bald!" Bill said. The one closest to the boat had a wide black collar that ringed a white chest. Yellow claws extended into black talons that clutched all the way around the branch it perched on. The tufted head and black slits in its merciless eyes projected a fierce warning not to proceed.

Bill met the gaze of the forest's fiercest predator. He stared into the dark slits and shivered. "Jezuzz I hate the jungle. There's nothing normal here," he said and drank some more beer.

"That there bird looks hungry," Carl said. As they moved away, the bird turned its head keeping its feral eyes locked on the Bill. He turned his head away and took another swig. The boat chugged forward, distancing itself from the harpies. Bill sighed with relief when they were too far away to be seen. He could still feel eyes on his back.

As they entered the shadows of the canopy, clouds of insects swarmed the boat. The men waved their arms to ward off buzzing gnats and mosquitoes. A gnat lodged in Carl's ear. He stuck his finger in and twisted.

Several gnats flew into Bill's mouth eliciting a cough. He cleared his throat and spit. This new onslaught banished their fear of the eagles.

The oppressive humidity, the heat, and the insects made for an unpleasant ride. To Bill the jungle was a nasty place. Only the money made it worthwhile.

The insects kept the men annoyed and cranky. They sighed with relief when the boat rounded the last bend before their destination. The dock came into view as did the clearing site. The Creole steered the boat to the dock's right side and bumped alongside the wood. Carl jumped out and secured the rope to a post planted in the river. Bill threw their gear on the dock as he hopped out.

The Creole pointed to the rope and pleaded, "Pleezz, Senor." The motor was still running. Carl untied the tether and watched as the boat moved backward and around. Once it was pointed in the direction they had come, the Creole gave it full throttle and left.

"What's his hurry?" Bill asked.

"Hell if I know and hell if I care," Carl grabbed his gear from the dock and set it on the ground.

The men carried everything to the site and looked around. A narrow clearing extended along the edge of the river. The stumps of gigantic trees dotted the open space between the river and trees. Two D-9s stood alone in the clearing. Pyramids of logs were stacked in several places on the far side of the site. A rainstorm from the night before had left muddy streams of water running to the river.

Except for the two men, the place was vacant and silent. The Quonset huts along the eastern edge of the trees sat dark and abandoned. "Where's everyone?" Carl wondered.

"What diffrance does it make? Let's fire up the Cats and start moving stumps, chump," Bill slapped him on the back and laughed. They walked through the mud to the D-9s. Each clambered up and into the seat of a machine.

Bill fired his up. A great billow of smoke belched from the exhaust pipe. Carl cranked his for several minutes before it caught and fired. Another gigantic black cloud filled the air with the smell of unburned diesel. They sat on the machines for several minutes as the fumes wafted skyward. Bill lit a cigar and puffed. Carl removed a flask from his back pocket and took a shot of whisky. He yelled across to Bill, "Won't take too long to clear these stumps. The trees water from the top down so they don't have much in the way of roots. I like to dig the damn things out."

The Cats warmed up and the diesel burned clear. The men nodded at each other and moved their levers forward. The D-9s slipped in the mud then grabbed and crawled into the clearing. Bill dropped his blade as he approached the first stump and dug just beneath its base. Long shallow roots pulled from the earth as the tree remains tore from the ground and rolled before the dozer.

Bill pivoted the dozer and lifted the blade. He moved to the right and dug another stump out. The sun beat down as he puffed his cigar and worked the controls. Blade down, push the mud up, tear the tree out. As he ripped and tore the ground, he wondered again where everyone was. There should be at least 8 or 9 people at this site. He'd heard that a lot of Brazilians wouldn't work in forests. Goddamn environmentalists.

He advanced on another stump and dropped the blade. A sharp sting caused him to slap his neck, he felt like he'd just bitten into tin foil. His body froze and he couldn't breath. The cigar hung from his lips then dropped between his legs. Bill slumped over in the seat, dead. The blade dug into the mud and hit the stump. The dozer rolled up and onto it, chugging to a stop. The violent movement rolled Bill's body out of the seat and onto the tracks. Flesh hissed on hot metal and his arm dangled in the air.

Carl was several yards away when his friend died. He had stayed toward the center of the site as his friend worked along the trees. He tore a stump out and pivoted his dozer toward Bill. When he saw that the machine wasn't moving, he walked the dozer over to see what was going on. There was no one in the seat. Carl pulled his lever into neutral and hopped off.

Mud clung to his boots as he shuffled around the D-9. Carl saw his friend. Intense fear coupled with a metallic taste caused his eyes to widen. The rust in his mouth was so awful that he barely felt the sting on his neck. Within seconds, his mind was detached from his body. There was one last dying gasp before he fell face first into the muck. Two D-9s spewed exhaust into the air for several hours afterwards.

10

*T*he Centers for Disease Control had just informed Dr. Charlise Brandon that she would be working with Dr. Gabriel Skye. They were to investigate a new pandemic that had killed thousands worldwide. The first reported deaths occurred in the Amazon and it was there the investigation would begin.

She thought back, the SARS outbreak they had worked together on a few months ago had been quick and deadly. Dr. Skye's decisive measures had saved thousands of American lives. The stringent quarantine he'd recommended had limited the deaths to just under fifteen hundred in the U.S., but over forty thousand Chinese and seventeen thousand Brits had fallen victim to the disease.

The small square in the middle of the virus remained a mystery. It was determined to be an infinitesimal piece of silicone, but it was so small that CDC scientists hadn't been able to determine its purpose. Engineering something that minute went far beyond American technology.

Chinese officials denied the existence of the square. When confronted with the pictures, they were dismissed as a hoax. Eventually, a different outbreak and budget issues forced the CDC to leave the mystery behind.

Charlise took a sip of coffee and slipped the DVD into her machine. Dr. Skye had since been fired then black balled by the Crass administration because of his outspoken views on climate change. This made him a hero in her mind. She hated the fact that the "oil man" President and his lackeys had obstructed every effort to protect the environment. They had even censored scientific reports on global warming. She detested Crass and all he stood for. His ignorance appalled her.

Charlise started the video, recorded just after she'd worked with him. She wanted to review the speech that had so upset the Crass Administration. She didn't mind looking at the handsome Dr. Skye either. She remembered his face framed by black shoulder length hair and a beard and moustache. She most appreciated the brown eyes that reflected a kindness not often found in a dedicated scientist.

Dr. Skye stood behind the podium and began, "My fellow scientists I'm sure you're all familiar with the frog analogy. If you throw a frog into boiling water, it immediately jumps out but if you put the frog in first and then slowly heat the water, the frog will stay until it boils to death. Earth's inhabitants are much like the frog that boils to death, we don't perceive the danger of continuing on our present course of environmental degradation or we do but deny that there is anything wrong. The changes in climate are too slow and incremental to prompt people to action. Each year the earth's temperature gets a little hotter and a little more volatile but the changes are so gradual that they are ignored.

Rather than to boiling to death, we'll reach the tipping point, the threshold or temperature at which a relatively stable climate becomes chaotic and unpredictable. At that point, cataclysmic changes in weather patterns will reduce the earth's ability to sustain life.

For those of you who doubt or deny, let me share my findings with you. Several years ago I developed a computer model to predict the effects of global warming. The program takes into account rises in the levels of greenhouse gases, the melting of the ice caps, depletion of the rainforests, the increase in algal blooms as well as the increases in population and the number of cars on the road. It includes changes in consumption patterns which have always trended upward. For instance, China's and India's industrialization have caused major spikes in carbon levels. Both countries are building coal fired electricity plants at an alarming rate. As these countries develop, millions of cars will hit the road for the first time. When these variables are plugged into the model there is a tremendous spike in CO_2 levels. Adding CO_2 is like adding layers of insulation to the earth's atmosphere. Once the heat gets in, it can't get out.

The model indicates that storms will increase in frequency and severity. There will be more droughts in some areas of the world and more floods in others. The ocean levels will rise so quickly that in the next five years large coastal areas will be permanently flooded. Hurricanes and tornadoes will continue increasing in both frequency and intensity. As the climate becomes increasingly more volatile, massive deaths and disasters will occur. Many of the predicted changes are already happening. And so we need to take immediate action, right? Jump out of the water before it boils.

And yet nations have other priorities. The first and foremost is economic growth. Growth that is always at the expense of the environment. Worldwide, governmental policies do little to regulate pollution and conserve natural resources since these measures will harm the economy.

Our political leaders have shown little resolve to prevent the impending doom. Their decisions are based on political polls and vested interests that often run counter to environmental protection. They promise prosperity and jobs to get elected and deficit spend to keep the economy growing. Cutting back on the consumption of fossil fuels and consumer goods would be politically fatal.

Without the guidance of leadership, half of all Americans remain unconcerned about the environment. Many deny the existence of man-caused global warming. Others view climate change as cyclical and think that man's activities have no effect on global weather patterns. Many know on an intellectual level that it exists but it is an abstract and their earth-destructive lifestyles remain static, but science tells us that man is a geological force that is greatly altering our planet's ecosytems.

Governmental policies are but part of the problem. International corporations have contributed mightily to the destruction of our planet. Corporate profits take precedence over the environment and the conservation of natural resources. These abominations shamelessly exploit Earth's treasures.

The corporate news organizations also bear responsibility for Earth's decline. Mass media depends on advertising for revenue so it promotes consumerism. Consumerism is the most earth-destructive behavior of mankind. Finite resources are depleted to meet the demand for goods created by advertising.

Individuals also bear responsibility. Human nature runs counter to saving the planet. Man's biological imperative is to reproduce. Globally, our birth rates remain high and the world's population continues to grow. Each new person adds stress to our ecosystems.

This drive to procreate often translates into a biological need to dominate. The alpha males or females in many societies express that need by striving to become the richest or most powerful. Alphas seek the biggest cars, the nicest houses, and jobs with the most power and influence. Greed and acquisition are expressions of this subconscious need to dominate. The desires for bigger, better, and more extract a heavy toll from Mother Earth.

And so now we confront the awful truth. Our standard of living cannot be sustained. Climate change is accelerating beyond even the most pessimistic estimates. We may have already reached the point of no return.

The time for the drastic changes needed to save our planet have passed. Our only hope consists in slowing the rate of decline. The absence of leadership, demographic trends and the actual changes in climate make it hard not to be pessimistic.

I know I've painted a picture of doom and gloom but there is hope if we act quickly. We should refocus our economic development from expansion to building sustainable infrastructures with low environmental impact. Mass transit systems and alternative energy sources need to be developed. Higher taxes should be levied on not just energy consumption but on all consumption. The rainforests should be protected and restored. I could go on but you get the picture.

In conclusion, our mammalian brains are capable of solving complex problems, but many of us don't think, we react like the reptilian frog. We need to think, to examine this beaker of water we're in, this earth of ours, and make the changes needed to keep from boiling to death. No longer can we say to ourselves, I'll wait until the water gets good and warm before I jump out or I hope someone turns the burner down. Each and every one of us must change our earth-destructive ways to save this amazing planet we call home. The time to do something is now!"

The camera panned the audience during the speech. It focused on President Crass several times as he sat with his arms folded and eyes narrowed. Before Gabe finished the last paragraph of the speech he got up and left the auditorium followed by an entourage of government officials and secret service men. Crass's behavior was rude and had been meant to be. But Gabe had offended Crass's twisted sense of morality. No one criticizes the President.

Gabe had raised his voice to a shout as he watched them leave, "But the time to do something is now!" he thundered. Almost everyone in the audience stood and clapped wildly, whistling and hooting as President Crass scurried away.

Charlise was in attendance that day over two months ago. The first to stand, she admired Gabe's courage and strength of conviction. There were very few men she admired, her father and a few of his friends but that was it. Most of them wanted something or were weak or condescending or insecure. Gabe possessed calm assurance and intelligence.

She'd heard that a pink slip was waiting in his office when he got back from the conference. G.W. Crass didn't appreciate the truth or deviation from his ultraconservative ideology. She often marveled that he had been re-elected a second time. It was the ultimate example of the dummying down of America.

She and her dad always joked that G.W. stood for "Giant Wanker." They often discussed the fact that his environmental policies had taken years off the life of the planet. They thought the new President, elected less than a month ago, was an improvement. He didn't butcher the English language but he was still part of a broken and corrupt system. Thinking about such things usually depressed her but for some reason her mood lifted. She was singing and dancing around the bedroom as she packed for her trip.

11

Miguel Rodriquez sat with his crew in the back of the dilapidated old flatbed as it rumbled down the highway. Some of them sharpened their machetes while others laughed and visited. Their job consisted of chopping the jungle vegetation away from the asphalt. This archaic task made for broken backs and spirits but at least it put food on the table.

Juan was telling the story of a whole crew found dead. They were found lying alongside the edge of the road with machetes still clutched in their hands. There was no apparent reason for the deaths or so his story went. Miguel tried to ignore the foolish rumor by concentrating on his machete.

The truck pulled into a turn out and stopped. His crew had cleared this section last week but vines already gabbed at the shoulders of the highway. The task of keeping the jungle at bay was an endless one.

The men clutching the wooden railings stood up and clambered off the flatbed. A group of five fanned out and chopped north. The rest chopped south away from the back of the truck. Miguel followed them. He felt the warm sun on his back. It had just cleared the trees, dispelling drops of dew.

Even though the day was nice, something didn't feel right. He felt watched, like there were eyes in the dense undergrowth. Miguel crossed himself, beads of sweat formed on his forehead. Jesus protect me he thought, biting his lip. He chopped at the underbrush, the sharp machete cutting the foliage in half. The fronds fell and brushed against his face. He waved them away and continued chopping.

A movement caught his attention and Miguel glanced over at his friend. Juan slapped at the back of his neck then fell forward into the brush. Miguel scrambled to assist him. He grabbed Juan's shoulders, rolled him over and held his wrist. There was no pulse. A flash of fear hit Miguel like a fist as a faint metallic odor reached his nostrils.

He looked up. Two other crew members lay face down and unmoving. Panic welled up inside as he felt the presence of death. He propelled himself toward the truck, feeling the sharp prick of an insect bite on the back of his neck. Slapping maniacally at the spot, he ran in abject terror. His mouth filled with metal as he hit the back of the truck. Miguel hauled himself over the edge and crawled to a corner of the railing before his body stiffened. Paralyzed, Miguel looked up and left the world with black buzzards circling in the blue sky.

The gigantic black vultures wound their way down, drawn by the smell of carrion. Not till all movement ceased did they land and begin their feast.

The super tanker, Al Kazak, sat well off the coast of Africa. The gigantic hull, a three hundred fifty meter wide strip of orange topped by a fifteen meter band of green, splashed the horizon with color. The next layer, bars and rectangles of white deck, juxtaposed itself against the blue sky. At the front of the ship, the sheer white bridge towered upward.

With no crude oil, it sat high on the water, anchored and waiting to be cleaned. Rashid followed the clean-up crew with their mops and buckets up the stairs and onto the deck. He assigned each worker an area to clean then watched until everyone was working. No one noticed the bed of algae they floated on.

With the job underway, he opened the door to the pump room and descended the stairs. At the bottom, below the bridge and in front of the oil tanks, a well-lit room contained the cleaning controls. He pressed the blue button that activated the washing system and listened as the high pressure jets sprayed water on the internal surfaces of the hold.

Over an hour later a green light on the panel indicated that the oil residue had been cleaned from the inside surfaces and was sitting in the bottom of the tanker. Prompted by the light, he turned the pump on. It sucked the black sludge into exit pipes and out into the ocean.

The toxic brew emerged underneath the algae bed, activating the billions of viruses inside the genetically engineered plants. Supercharged by the oil residue, the organisms filled the air in and around the ship.

The men on deck breathed deeply as they exerted themselves. Each breath brought thousands of viruses into their lungs. Twenty minutes after the oil was released, the SARS virus manifested itself. Some men coughed while others grew weak and sore. The symptoms multiplied until all of the men felt like they were burning up from within.

Thirty minutes later, twenty men lay on the white surface, writhing in soapy water. Blood poured from mouths and noses, flowing onto the deck where each man struggled to breathe. In their agony, they threw themselves back and forth as if they were mopping the ship's surface with their own bodies. White coveralls turned pink and then red as the blood continued to flow.

The viruses inside the men's cells multiplied at a rate beyond human imagination. The cells filled and burst like firecrackers, infecting more cells and causing them to burst in a chain reaction of gore. Movement slowed and then stopped as each man's insides turned to mush.

Unaware of the carnage above, Rashid turned and walked to the ladder. He wanted to make sure the deck was spotless. His foot was on the first step when he stopped, a white heat slammed his body. Deathly sick all over at once, he held onto the rungs for a moment then fell face first onto the metal. Blood and flesh splattered on the walls. The viruses, mutated into super killing machines, took less than ten minutes to leave a mass of lifeless flesh dripping through the rungs.

12

Gabe was unpacking in a hotel in Manaus, Brazil. It felt good to be working again. Dr. Langley had made sure he got his job back after the Crass administration had run its course like the measles or some other disease.

Less than a month after the election, the President himself had called to inform Gabe that he had been reinstated. The gist of the conversation was that he appreciated people with the strength of their convictions, that his door was always open, and that it should be the information that is rejected not the person delivering it. He also said that decisions should be made on the basis of science not ideology. Gabe not only liked but respected this new President who wanted him to head a team investigating the cause of the strange deaths occurring in the Amazon.

He was smiling when he heard the knock on his hotel door. He'd invited Ben and Charlise over for a drink. He closed his suitcase and walked to the door, opening it until the chain on the deadbolt tightened. When Ben's face appeared, he undid the clasp and swung it open. "Hey Ben. How ya doin?"

"I'm fine. You?"

"Great. I see you brought the doctor with you," Gabe said, as Charlise entered the room behind Ben.

She smiled and held her hand out. ""Hi, Gabe." He grabbed the tips of her fingers and kissed the back of her hand. "Whoa, you're so romantic," she teased, visibly pleased.

Charlise had been assigned to the United States Viral Research Laboratory in Utah after they'd worked together on the SARS outbreak. He found her very attractive, especially the shoulder length blonde hair and bright blue eyes. A quick radiant smile imbued with warmth and affection greeted him whenever they met. His mood lightened as he looked with appreciation at her athletically slender figure.

"What's your pleasure? I have, gin, whisky, or beer." He gestured to the round table to the right of the door. "Have a seat."

"Any mixer for the gin?" Charlise asked.

"Orange juice or tonic?"

"Gin and tonic sounds good. Light on the gin, please."

"Ben?" Gabe opened the refrigerator and took out the tonic and gin. Anticipating Ben's answer he grabbed a couple of beers. They had known each other for years. Gabe first met Ben on a trip to the University of Oregon in Eugene. He'd been visiting a friend with leukemia and had stayed in Ben's dormitory. At the time, Ben was participating in a cultural exchange program between Oregon University and Israel. They'd hit it off immediately. They were both big Van Morrison fans and loved to read.

One night they'd been drinking beer in Ben's dorm room when a freshman from another dorm burst into the hall. The guy was drunk and belligerent, looking for a fight. He'd started kicking someone's door and Gabe went out to see what was going on. The drunk immediately came up to Gabe and challenged him with fists clenched. Ben stepped between them and started talking to the guy. Ben never raised his voice, he just reached into the boy's brain and grabbed his reason with calm persuasion.

"A beer, please," Ben said.

Gabe opened the top freezer and pulled the ice trays out. He twisted them on the counter and grabbed the cubes as they slid away then filled a glass with ice, a couple of capfuls of gin and tonic to the rim. He placed a wedge of lime on the edge of the glass and handed it to Charlise.

Gabe handed Ben a beer and popped his open with a snap and a fizz. "Don't get any in your curls," he admonished.

Ben smiled and said, "That must be a Jewish joke, you're too ugly to be my mother."

Charlise looked anxious until both men started laughing and then she said, "I take it you two know each other?"

"He hasn't told you? We're old friends," Gabe replied. "Here's to success," he said as he raised his can to toast.

Ben and Charlise bumped their drinks with his and repeated, "To success." They took a drink, smiling.

Gabe's expression became serious, "Have either of you seen the aerial photos yet?"

Ben blurted, "Yes! Whatever's killing these people is fast and deadly. I heard a radio broadcast, the announcer was standing near the rainforest when he started his report in a matter-of-fact tone and then stopped abruptly like he'd been shot in the head only there was no gunshot. The station apologized and said they'd been cut off. I think he might have died.

The photos of the dead show no signs of struggle or sickness. It's got to be an Ebola type virus or a toxin. Probably the same thing that's killing people at sea."

Gabe found Ben's brusqueness and intensity annoying sometimes. He always rushed to conclusions without going through the problem solving process. His dark complexion and full beard gave him a swarthy, rugged look, but there was kindness in his big brown eyes. Before accepting this assignment, he'd been working as a pathologist at Tel Aviv Medical School.

Ben approached problems like he was studying the Talmud. Always questioning things then reaching a conclusion and changing his mind after he calmed down and thought about it. But he strengthened the team by making everyone think harder and Gabe liked him, a lot. He was a good man who would do anything for his friends. "Of course we won't know until we take some blood and tissue samples, but I agree with you."

"It's terrifying! Like someone pushed a button and shut the jungle down by killing everyone in or around it," Charlise said.

"There's a logical explanation which I'm sure we'll find," Ben said and then took a drink from his beer.

"Agreed. I hope we figure it out before the disease spreads to other areas," Gabe said.

"How far away from the trees are they finding bodies?" Charlise asked.

"Fifty to seventy yards. The disease must be caused by something found in the forest. And it's human specific. There've been no reports of animal deaths. Not even other primates. Trees outside of major forested areas appear to be benign."

"Somehow the virus, or whatever it is, has stayed near the trees," said Ben.

"So far and it hasn't moved inland from the seas either. Odd isn't it?"

"It's horrifying!" Charlise interjected. "One hundred fifty million people are estimated to have died. There are few places where the smell of death doesn't linger. The panic and fear are palpable."

The threesome hastened their drinking, trying to drown their apprehensions. Ben and Gabe opened their second beer and even Charlise had downed three-fourths of her gin and tonic.

"Scares the holy hell out of me, too," Gabe agreed then asked, "Can I freshen your drink, Charlise?"

"Sure. Hold the tonic and give me more ice with a jigger of gin, please," she replied. Gabe held the bottle and cap over her glass and poured. It overflowed into her drink. He added ice cubes and stirred. The room had grown quiet.

Gabe took another long swig of beer craving its sedative properties. "It'd be hard to imagine if we didn't have the photographs. I get sick every time I look."

"It's tragic but maybe some good can come from it," Ben said.

Charlise exploded, "How can any good come from the deaths of millions of people. Did you see the pictures? Men, women and children lying dead and bloated throughout the forests. Unimaginable numbers of bodies. And the stench, you can smell it now. How can any of this be good?"

"These deaths are a tragedy, no question about it. But maybe the trees have found a way to save themselves. After centuries of decimation they have turned the tables. Maybe God has given them a way to fight back," Ben replied.

"What kind of God gives trees dominion over man? Do you mean your vengeful God of the Old Testament?" asked Charlise.

"No, I don't mean the anthropomorphized God of the Bible, but the infinite God of Wisdom and Light. Maybe He is seeking balance."

"Death is darkness. Death on this scale is the work of Satan! There is no wisdom or light in this, only darkness and decay!" Charlise shouted, eyes flashing with anger.

"Maybe. But to my way of thinking it's Karmic or if you're a Christian it's reaping what you've sown. After destroying and tearing down, man is being destroyed. Man who has ruined thousands of habitats and caused the extinction of countless plant and animal species is being called to task."

Charlise stood up from the table, knocking her chair over. With tears in her eyes she glared at Ben, "Then maybe you should be the one to stack the bodies!" She pounded the table with the flat of her hand, looked at Gabe, opened the door and rushed into the night air.

Gabe felt bad. "Jesus, Ben. Have a little tact. You knew she was upset and yet you stuck the knife in. You should've just dropped it when she got angry."

"Sorry. Sometimes I say what's on my mind without thinking of other people. It's the intellectual in me. I always assume that hard intellectual debate doesn't involve emotion."

"Well now you know. I thought you were Jewish anyway. Don't you believe in the God of the Old Testament?"

"I'm a secular Jew. My culture and heritage are Jewish but I hardly believe in the God you speak of. I struggled with theology for years before I gave up. There was a time in my life when I studied everything I could get my hands on to discover God. I talked to Rabbis, studied the Talmud, the Bible, and the Koran. I even spent time in a Buddhist temple. The more I studied the less I knew. I found that there is no answer to God. One person's views are no more valid than another's. It's a matter of choice."

Gabe was puzzled, "If you feel that way, why do you wear a yarmulke?"

"Jews believe in atonement and the yarmulke reminds me to

make up for my sins by doing good works. We also believe that one can come to God through knowledge. I like that. It reminds me to strive for something higher than myself."

"And the locks?"

"The locks? Oh you mean my peyos? They remind me that I see the world through the eyes of a Jew. That I have a different cultural reference than most people. That everyone is human and religion is only one aspect of a person's psyche. I believe a person is colored by biology first and then culture and education. Ironically, the peyos remind me that there is a reality outside of myself and that my comprehension of it will always be incomplete." Ben took a deep breath. "They're actually supposed to remind me to depend on my intellect and good character to get along in the world. And you Gabe, what of your beliefs?"

Ben was handsome and Gabe understood that being good-looking and charismatic gave Ben a leg up on everyone else but he respected Ben for staying modest and humble. He smiled, "I'm a Mattress Methodist. I was raised and confirmed in the Methodist Church but it didn't take. I hated church and loved to sleep in so I volunteered to milk cows on Sundays. Besides I never understood faith."

Gabe continued, "In college, I studied the human sciences. I loved psychology. I discovered that the learning process is the same for everyone. You can only learn that which you're exposed to. I had a psychology professor who felt our species has a genetic predisposition to be believers. It was easier for people to survive if they followed and obeyed. They were part of a group and there's strength in numbers. Natural selection tended to weed out outliers like myself. I heard too many people shout "Be Like Me!" not to believe that being a part of a herd is important to most people and I tend to go against the grain. I'm perverse.

A professor I had, Dr. Joe, said more than once that if humans can't understand themselves and why they think and act the way they do, how can they possibly hope to know the mind of God?

My beliefs were further undermined when I discovered that the Gospels were written sixty years after Christ's death. Imagine how much embellishment occurred over six decades. I think that's why the priests waited until all eyewitnesses were dead before they wrote the story. They wanted a supernatural being they could beat people over the head with.

I once discussed my doubts with a minister. He quoted Jesus as saying that heaven and God are hidden from the wise and the intelligent but have been revealed to infants. I told him that if Christianity required giving up thought and understanding, I wanted no part of it. He seemed rather offended. Actually, he looked at me in horror, like I was the anti-Christ or something."

Ben shook his head up and down, "Being Jewish, I can relate to that. Many perceive my people as anti-Christian. Nothing could be further from the truth. We believe in live and let live. We are pacifists. There is nothing wrong with being Christian or Jewish as long as other people don't have to suffer for it."

"If the problems of our world are to be solved it will be through wisdom and knowledge and in the end there will no Magical Messiah to save us," Gabe replied.

"That's right," said Ben. "Religions dwell in the past and fail to discuss timely issues like climate change. We're all on the same ship facing the same destination if we don't do something."

"A sinking ship of fools unless we start bailing," Gabe added.

Gabe took a sip of beer, "I come from the West where "environmentalist" is a derogatory term for a lot of people. They don't understand that polluting in any form is like shitting in your own nest. Many Westerners think they get to decide whether there is man-made climate change. Their blissful ignorance will be shattered when they find the ocean at their door step."

"It's hard to imagine someone who doesn't believe in scientific fact," said Ben. "It's probably more denial than it is belief. I mean there's no question that we're on a collision course with the environment," he said as he finished his beer. "Boy, it's great to meet another pessimist."

"I don't consider myself a pessimist. I'm a realist. It's just hard to imagine any good outcome for human existence when our mantra is economic expansion and over-belief in the efficacy of technology, or believing God will take care of us which is even worse. We seem intent on bursting the bubble that we live in."

"Maybe this new virus will keep it intact for a while longer."

"By killing half the population? You trying to cheer me up?"

"No, I know it's horrible. But if the forests come back and there are fewer people ..."

Now Gabe became uncomfortable, "I don't even want to think about it. It's time to call it a night, we have a big day tomorrow."

Ben stood up from the table, "Right. It should prove interesting. Thanks for the beer," he said. He opened the door and turned back. "Shalom, my friend."

13

The next day Gabe and Ben waited under the awning outside Terminal 2 of the Eduardo Gomez International Airport. The overcast sky drizzled rain, dampening both men's spirits. In the distance sat the dark and foreboding rainforest.

Gabe was wondering what they would find there when a yellow cab pulled up. It was Charlise. He shifted positions and tried to get a look at her.

Ben left Gabe's side and rushed to the back of the cab. He opened the door and helped her out of the car. With an anxious look he apologized, "Sorry about last night. I didn't mean to upset you, sometimes I get carried away."

She smiled and patted him on the back. "If I can't take the heat get out of the kitchen, right? I think I know what you were trying to say. Anyway, help me with my bags," she said as the cab driver popped the trunk open. She knew Ben from several conferences they had both attended. He was always squarely in the middle of any discussion, but he was kind and respectful. She knew that he would never hurt her or anyone else intentionally but sometimes he could be so callous.

Charlise glanced at Gabe as he looked on, "Hi, Gabe. Did you sleep well?" She smiled when they made eye contact.

"As well as can be expected. It's hard to sleep with so much to think about. How are you?" he smiled back, pleased.

"I'm not mad anymore just a little on edge but I'll be fine. Images of the dead haunted me most of the night. I can't help wondering if one or all of us might end up the same way."

"Hopefully not. The pressurized suits will protect us from air borne pathogens and we'll only be in the forest long enough to collect a couple of bodies and do a short investigation."

"I'm still nervous," she said.

Gabe took her hand. "So am I, but it's good to be nervous. It'll keep us on our toes."

Ben grabbed her suitcase and rolled it up on the walkway then gathered his own luggage. Gabe got his suitcase and one of Charlise's before they entered the terminal. They walked through it and out the back where the helicopter sat on the tarmac surrounded by small puddles of water.

Four soldiers dressed in army fatigues were loading their scientific equipment into the back door of the chopper. Gabe checked to see that the body bags, medical equipment, and food supplies were there.

When the gear was loaded, the pilot started the engine. The soldiers ducked under the propeller and climbed on the benches in the cargo hold followed by Charlise and Ben. Gabe sat next to the pilot and slid the door shut. The helicopter elevated and headed for the rainforest. As they lifted, several turtles could be seen walking across the runway.

They flew south over the Amazon River, a ribbon of blue in a mass of green. The smell of rotting corpses ruined the view as the stench became unbearable. The pungent odor of death seemed to be a warning to stay away, that they were approaching forbidden territory. Once over the forest, they flew well above the trees for several minutes until they spotted a vast clearing.

"Is that where we put down?" the pilot asked a short time later as he pointed to a short airstrip that consisted of a control tower and three Quonset huts. Several vehicles were parked in front of the buildings.

"That's it," Gabe said.

"Great, because I have no desire to get anywhere near the trees," the pilot switched on his radio. "This is Delta 269 requesting landing clearance," he spoke into the mouthpiece.

"Clearance approved, Delta," crackled over the speakers.

The pilot circled the airport and set down near the tower. A Land Rover approached as the engine was switched off and the rotors slowed. One of the ground crew ran forward and slid the doors open. The smell intensified, assaulting their nostrils and driving thoughts of anything else away.

"Good God that stinks!" Gabe shouted. The smell triggered a memory from his farm days. An inexperienced veterinarian had killed one of his pigs in an attempt to castrate it. Gabe had watched as the vet cut the pig under the belly. I guess he knows what he's doing Gabe had thought. But he knew the vet should have cut the scrotum sac and removed the testicles from there. The long convoluted attempt to pull the testicles out from the stomach resulted in the pig's death.

More pressing demands kept him from burying the carcass right away and he forgot about it. After a few days, he remembered. He went to the pig shed and grabbed the pig's foot to drag it away. The pig pulled away at the stomach and the guts fell out releasing a smell so bad that he left it there. He came back later with a bandana over his face and buried it. Today's stink was generated by human remains. It smelled far worse than a dead pig.

The scientists climbed out and ducked under the chopper blades. A military officer stood at ease just outside of the propellers. Gabe introduced himself and shook hands. "I'm Gabe Skye, this is Charlise Brandon, and the man with the pretty locks is Ben Horowitz." The soldier shook hands with the scientists as they were introduced. When he got to Ben he raised an eyebrow.

Ben reddened. "My pretty locks have nothing to do with sexual orientation," he said giving Gabe a dirty look.

"Good. I'm Sergeant William Rone," he said, smiling. "I've been assigned to your team."

Gabe had read a dossier on Rone. He had served in the first Gulf War and been decorated for bravery. He'd also received a purple heart and other commendations. For the last few years he'd been assigned to a U.N. peace-keeping force. The report described him as competent and adaptable.

They walked over to the Rover and watched the soldiers transfer the equipment. The crates containing the pressurized suits were brought out and opened. The scientists put them on as the vehicle was loaded. The silver material and helmets made them look like deep sea divers except there was no air hose just a tank on their backs.

Sergeant Rone also donned a suit. He would be the only staff member to accompany them.

"We're only five minutes away, go ahead and activate the oxygen tanks," Gabe instructed. Each suit was equipped with a microphone and speakers so they could communicate.

They opened the door of the Rover and got in. Ben and Charlise in the back, Gabe riding shotgun. Sgt. Rone climbed behind the wheel and started the engine. "Make sure your suits are pressurized," he reminded. "It's my job to get you in and out of there safely."

He put the truck in gear and drove over the dirt airfield to the paved two-lane highway to the north. The Rover bounced up in a cloud of dust as it crossed the lip of the pavement. When it bounced back, Rone turned left and drove toward the forest.

As they approached Charlise became agitated, "I feel like we're being watched."

"Yeah, me too," Ben said.

Gabe and Sgt. Rone chose not to say anything. Gabe didn't want to heighten the fear and Rone was too busy watching the road. When they entered the forest, everyone fell silent. The canopy engulfed them with a moist shade that obliterated the sun. It was like a warm damp blanket had been thrown over them.

A few minutes later, they saw a truck rammed against a tree on the opposite side of the highway. Inside, the driver and his passenger slumped against the dashboard. Thousands of flies filled the cab and swarmed the corpses in the back. They could see three more bodies through the railing on the flatbed, sprawled out and bloated. One of the dead stared through a gap in the boards, the eyes bulging outward.

"Jesus," Gabe said. Charlise turned her head and tried not to be sick. To heave in a pressurized suit would be disastrous. "Hold on Charlise, you'll be okay."

Rone slowed the vehicle. A few miles farther, a head-on collision blocked the road. A Subaru station-wagon and an older Chevy pick-up were rammed together, their rear ends splayed across the highway. The occupants of the Subaru faced toward the scientists. A jet black moving mass covered the bodies as thousands of flies crawled and fed. The collective buzz sounded like a revved up chain saw.

Rone pulled to the side of the road and got out. He walked over and opened the driver's door of the Chevy. A swarm of flies flew out and around him. He grabbed the man draped over the steering wheel and pulled him out of the truck then dragged the body across the asphalt and into the brush. He felt something catch his suit and slapped at it. A fern frond whipped back and away. Almost immediately several strange, barely audible pinging sounds echoed off his helmet. He ignored the noises and went back to the truck and took it out of gear.

"Gabe, drive over to the rear bumper and let's move the pick-up out of the way," Sgt. Rone spoke into his mike as he gestured.

Gabe slid behind the wheel, put the Rover in gear and drove forward. When the truck was in position, Rone hooked the winch to the bumper and motioned for him to back up.

Gabe winched the cable taut and reversed directions. A loud screeching noise startled everyone as metal scraped on pavement. The Chevy dragged the car with it for an instant before it broke loose. Gabe pulled it back and to the side of the road.

He waited until Rone unhooked the cable and then moved into position to pull the station-wagon. When the winch was hooked and the cable taut he shifted into reverse again. His foot slipped off the clutch and the Rover bucked backward, jerking the car with it. The passenger door flew open and the body of a young child fell half way out, the hand dragging on the asphalt. A cloud of flies flew up and then back down onto the corpse.

Gabe looked away as he pulled the car over to the side of the road. He stopped the Rover and Rone unhooked again. "That was fun," the Sergeant said as he hopped into the passenger seat. Gabe reversed gears and they continued forward.

Charlise resented the sarcasm. She felt Rone was far too cavalier and indifferent to the horror around them.

All four kept their eyes glued to the road dreading what might lie ahead. The trees embraced over the top of the highway, their intertwined branches blocking the sunlight from reaching them except for an occasional gap in the canopy. Dark green leaves dripped with moisture that fell downward, keeping the road wet. With each mile the forest became darker and more ominous. The shadows darkened their mood and kept everyone quiet. The only sound they could hear was their own breath going in and out and the thud of their hearts echoing inside the suits. Gabe thought of Poe's "Tell Tale Heart."

Every so often they encountered more bodies and wrecked vehicles. Once a group of over ten people lay on the roadside still clutching whatever they'd been carrying, knapsacks, water bottles, walking sticks. One had collapsed with a bunch of bananas that partially covered his head and back.

Occasionally the back end of a car or truck stuck out from the underbrush, the front covered by foliage. Inside, clouds of flies swarmed over the outlines of human bodies.

Everyone was quiet until Gabe asked, "How much farther?"

"I'd say about five more minutes," Sgt. Rone replied.

"The sooner the better. This is like touring a graveyard," said Charlise.

"Only someone never got around to burying the bodies," Gabe said.

"Yeah like that guy in Tennessee who saved money by stacking the dead behind his house instead of cremating them," Ben said. "Some people will do anything to make a buck."

"These might not be buried either," Gabe accelerated, wanting to get to their destination as soon as possible.

"I've seen worse," Sgt. Rone stated.

"Does that explain why you're so sanguine?" Charlise asked.

"Sanguine? Hardly. I've been in the Army and seen war. I had a friend get shot in the Gulf War. I held him as he bled to death. That is death on a very personal level. I don't know these people and they're already dead. So it doesn't bother me as bad."

Sgt. Rone stared into the distance, "I've seen much worse. A couple of years ago I was transferred to a U.N. peace keeping force. They sent us to Darfur. Our job was to protect the non-Arab villages from attacks by the Janjaweed, a tribe of camel riding Arabs. We were patrolling through eastern Darfur on our way to Al Fashir when we came upon a Catholic girl's school that had been attacked by the Janjaweed. We found the skeletal remains of several young females. They had been chained to stakes and burned to death. There was one in particular. The chain was pulled taught and her arm was stretched to escape. Her jaws were locked in a scream of terror," Rone choked up and shook his head. "Over three hundred villages were destroyed. There were too few of us to stop the carnage so I made the mistake of asking to be transferred, hoping to go somewhere I could make a difference."

"This time I ended up in in eastern Congo. The Lord's Resistance Army, a group of Ugandan rebels, was trying to form a government based on the Ten Commandments. They either didn't know or had forgotten that one of them was "Thou shall not kill." I guess that's why the bastards attacked crowded churches on Christmas Day. We found their naked victims lying in piles. Some had been stabbed to death, others had their necks broken. I guess they couldn't afford bullets. Anyway, there were too many to bury so we saturated the piles with gasoline and burned them. I still smell the burning flesh when I think about it."

Now that Rone had started he couldn't stop reliving the nightmares of his past. "Once we came upon a village in the Congo Basin. Several of the huts had been burned and others torn down. I heard something moaning. The sound came from a pile of dirt and boards that had once been a dwelling. I removed the debris and found a women underneath. She looked completely deranged. When I touched her, she screamed and tried to dig herself away from me. I kept talking to her until I was finally able to calm her down enough to get her to come with me to where the medical staff was stationed.

I listened as the interpreter did the interview. She told him that the militia had rounded her family up. First they made her son have sex with her and then they shot him. Next, the husband was forced to have sex with her and they shot him. After they'd had their sport, they shot her remaining four children. I walked away sick. Her story haunts me every day of my life. So you see, I've seen far worse nightmares."

He was quiet for a moment before he said, "At least the bodies we're finding died a quick death. They were spared the agony of seeing their friends and relatives suffer before they were killed. I'm not sanguine, just desensitized."

Charlise was gently weeping, "I'm so sorry," she said through tears. Everyone grew quiet, again.

After what seemed like hours of silence, they saw a break in the trees ahead. The sunlight beckoned them forward. The Rover exited the canopy and entered a clearing. On the right sat a rice field, on their left a small market with two concession stands still stocked with produce. Except for the crows perched on the counter, they were deserted. Buzzards circled high above waiting for something to leave so they could feed. They drove past and around a bend where several Quonset huts sat in a row along the highway. A flag of Brazil hugged a pole in front.

"See any bodies?" Gabe asked. When no one answered he continued, "That's strange."

"Yeah, there was a contingent of over thirty people working here," Rone agreed.

Gabe slowed the Rover to a crawl. He turned off the road and into the parking lot in front. " Ben, you and Charlise stay here while we do a quick check."

Gabe turned the engine off. He and Rone got out and walked to a window on the side of the first Quonset. They peeked in to find nothing but furniture and beds. They walked down the row of huts and checked each one. All of them were deserted.

"These people didn't just disappear. There should be bodies. I wonder what's going on?"

"They could be alive and hiding somewhere," Rone suggested.

"Maybe. Let's check the office," It was located a hundred yards east of the huts. "Maybe we can glean some information from their communications logs," Gabe said as they walked back to the Rover. He threw Rone the keys, "You drive."

"See anything?" Ben asked when they opened the doors.

"Nothing out of the ordinary," Gabe answered.

"Jesus, what the hell's going on?"

"Good question. I wish I knew."

Rone started the engine and followed the road behind the

buildings to where the office sat. When he pulled in front and cut the engine, they could hear a piece of heavy machinery running.

"Someone's here!" Charlise said in amazement.

"Sounds like its coming from the other side of those trees," Gabe pointed to an isolated copse of mahoganies. The road curved back to the left and around the trees, obstructing their view. "Grab the hard drives and communications records and we'll check it out."

They got out of the Rover. Sgt. Rone drew his Colt .45 as he walked up to the door of the office. He stood to one side and opened the door, brandishing the gun. The room was vacant so he motioned the other three in. Ben and Charlise disassembled the computers, disconnecting the towers and carrying them outside and loading them in the Rover. Gabe unloaded the communications tape from the recorder and placed it in a canister. They exited the room with Rone behind, shutting the door.

With everything loaded, Rone started the truck, put it in reverse and curved back around. He drove forward onto the pavement, toward the noise. When they neared the trees a gust of wind blew branches against the Rover. A loud scraping noise grated against the windows and everyone's nerves. He swerved to the other side of the road and sped up. They rounded the mahoganies and saw a man running a backhoe. He was digging a trench along a row of bodies. On the near side and far end of the trench sat a D-9 with its blade up.

"Oh my God! A survivor," Charlise blurted.

"Why is he alive?" Rone asked as he pulled the Rover over to where a row of piled dirt hid the trench from view. He stopped the engine.

"Good question. Let's find out," Gabe said as they exited the truck.

The backhoe operator turned his head. When he saw the vehicle, he stopped digging. He cut the engine, opened the cab and jumped down to the ground. Short with oriental features he was dressed in a white athletic shirt, Khaki shorts, and sandals. He appeared to be a common laborer except there was something intriguing about him. He was serene. In fact, he glowed with peace and calmness.

Gabe approached and held out his gloved hand. He switched on his loud speaker so he could be heard. "Hi, Gabriel Skye. What the hell's going on?"

"Rahula Gautama, a visit from Yama. I'm burying the dead."

"Who's Yama?"

"Death," Rahula answered.

"What happened?"

"A week ago, I heard a whirring in the trees. Next came a wuuumph and a noise like raindrops hitting leaves. I felt a presence and saw tiny sparkles in the sky. I thought it was just fireflies dancing in the night air so I forgot about it."

"Three days later, I came to the clearing to trade some yams for coffee and found many dead workers. Those running chainsaws or heavy equipment were the first to go. Their equipment was still running when I found them."

"I took some of the dead to the infirmary. When the medical staff examined them they found no cause of death. Shortly after performing the autopsies, everyone involved died. Two days after, the cooks, camp laborers and engineers died in their huts. There were only four of us left until yesterday. The other three were sick and hadn't ventured outside. When I checked this morning they were dead."

"How'd you survive?" Gabe asked.

"I don't know."

"You must have some kind of immunity," Gabe said. The other team members had gathered around and Gabe gave their names. Rahula nodded impassively as each was introduced.

Gabe continued, "We need to find out what caused this. We'll need a blood sample from you. We'll also need to take a couple of the corpses. We'll want bodies that were healthy before the outbreak."

"The three that were sick have hospital bracelets on. I can't help you, the moment demands that I finish my task," he said with quiet authority. Rahula climbed back on the backhoe and resumed digging.

Gabe looked at his team, "Let's help him. Make it quick, we've only got two hours of air. Sgt. Rone and Ben team up and starting throwing bodies in the trench." He nodded at Charlise, "We'll take those two," he said pointing at the bodies closest to the Rover.

Charlise opened the back of the truck and pulled out the body bags. She laid them alongside the corpses. They nodded at each other and lifted, swinging one of the bodies inside a bag. Charlise zipped it up. They repeated the procedure on the second body. When finished, they carried the bags, one on each end, to the Rover. Gabe levered the first and then the second corpse over his shoulder and into the back.

At the same time, Ben and Rone were throwing bodies into the trench. One would take the legs, the other the arms and swing the corpse out and over the center of the hole. When it reached the apex of the swing, they let go. A dull thud sounded as the body landed in the bottom of the pit.

With the bodies loaded, Gabe and Charlise joined the burial detail. They hurried to the other end of the trench and picked up a body. "Don't look," Gabe said when he saw Charlise's expression.

She held her head away and grabbed the arms of a dead female. Gabe grabbed the feet and lifted. He watched the corpse's long hair fell backward and swing back and forth as he counted. "One, two, three.." They let go and a mass of flesh hit flat in the bottom of the pit with a splat. They threw three more bodies into the hole before Charlise tired.

"Why don't you take a break, Charlise? Ben and I can finish this while Sgt. Rone closes the trench," Gabe said then called, "Ben, come and help me."

"Yeah, Ben, the sooner we get out of here the better," Rone climbed on the Cat and started it. He backed up and positioned it at a right angle to the dirt pile. The D-9 moved forward and the blade dropped until it was level to the ground. He pushed the dirt into the pit, raising the blade once it cleared the far edge of the hole.

Ben and Gabe resumed throwing bodies into the pit while Charlise clambered into the truck, her refuge from death. She couldn't bear to look at any more corpses and buried her head in her arms and closed her eyes. She conjured up pleasant memories of her father, leaving the present behind.

Everyone had been so occupied with their grisly task that they'd failed to notice Rahula's disappearance. The backhoe sat with its bucket down and the engine off.

"Where's Rahula?" Ben asked.

Gabe looked around, "He's gone? Get Charlise and we'll find him."

They examined the area while Sgt. Rone finished covering the trench. They searched up to the border of the forest and stopped, afraid to enter. The scientists stood at the edge and yelled through their helmets. The voices sounded like they were in a cave yelling to hear the echo. It would have been comical under different circumstances Gabe thought.

Sgt. Rone cut his engine and spoke into his microphone, "What's wrong?"

"Rahula's gone," Ben responded.

Rone glanced at his watch, "We don't have time to find him. Get back to the truck so we can haul ass out of here."

"Right," Gabe said. "Hopefully, we have enough information to figure this thing out. If not we'll have to come back and find him."

They got back in the Rover. Rone started the engine and spun the tires as he accelerated, throwing their heads back against the seat.

"Rahula was an odd little man," Charlise said after the ride smoothed out. "He was so calm, no emotions. Those were people he'd been trading with. You'd think he'd be upset after watching so many people die."

"Yes," Ben agreed, "I wonder why he split? Maybe he thought we were going to blame him or something."

"He probably didn't want to be forced to go back with us. His behavior was different but there's nothing wrong with staying calm in a crisis," Gabe said.

Sgt. Rone rounded the trees and drove back onto the highway in a cloud of dust. He accelerated past the Quonsets and away from the area. When they entered the rainforest again everyone quit talking. The oppressive darkness deepened their gloom. Rone pushed the gas pedal down until they were traveling sixty miles an hour. No one complained, they just wanted to get out from under the trees.

They emerged from the rainforest just before dusk. The dying twilight welcomed them back into a more familiar world. "God, I'm glad to be out of there," Charlise said.

Sgt. Rone pulled up in front of the base station. The team bailed out and re-pressurized their air tanks so they could examine the corpses. They entered the building and everyone went to work. Sgt. Rone summoned the other three soldiers. They unloaded the bodies and placed them on the autopsy tables in the medical lab.

Dr. Skye unzipped one of the bags. The man inside looked serene, there were no signs of trauma, no bruises, no cuts, nothing. He motioned for Rone and together they removed the body and placed it on a body block. Gabe marked a "Y" with a black marker from the tip of the man's shoulders to his chest and then down to the pubic bone. He used a scalpel to cut along the line. Then instead of using an electric saw, he used shears to cut the through the bone to avoid contaminating the insides with the dust.

Gabe clamped the chest cavity open and examined the heart and other internal organs. There was no sign of bleeding or disease. No blood clots were found, everything looked healthy and functional.

Charlise took blood samples and tissue cultures from the other corpse. After examining them, she found no pathogens and the resulting antibodies, there were no signs of fear or stress and the resulting chemicals in the blood either. The search for toxins was also negative. There seemed to be no cause of death. The results baffled the two scientists.

The soldiers had brought the computer towers inside for inspection. The second the towers arrived, Ben hooked one of them up to a monitor and power source. He started examining the information on the hard drive.

It didn't take long to search the outpost's computer records. It was a futile. There hadn't been time to investigate the first deaths before the second deaths occurred. The disease had come too quickly to record any symptoms or other information that might have been helpful.

When Gabe glanced at the clock it was one a.m. It had been a long day and they were exhausted. His frustration contributed to a bone-tired feeling that he was sure everyone shared.

Gabe found himself unable to concentrate and knew then it was time to quit . "Okay, that's it. Let's get some sleep and meet back here at 8:30 a.m. Get some breakfast and a stout cup of coffee before you report in the morning. We'll decide what to do then."

14

Gabe was looking at a slide in the microscope when Charlise and Ben entered the room. "Hi guys. I'm sure one of you came up with a solution last night. What is it?"

"Hi, Gabe," Charlise smiled.

"Hello, Gabe," Ben said then added, "Let's send the cadavers to Manaus for an x-ray and MRI. There's gotta be something we're missing."

"That's what I was thinking. I've already arranged to have them flown out. I'll take Rone and return to the clearing to find Rahula. I want to examine his tissue and blood samples and compare them to the corpses'. We'll need an MRI and x-ray on him also."

"You two transport the corpses back to Managua and oversee the MRIs. The minute they're done send the results to the computer here," Gabe said.

"We're all over it," Ben said as he opened the door and he and Charlise left.

The crew loaded the helicopter with the freezer unit containing the corpses. Ben and Charlise climbed in and the chopper lifted into the air and headed for the city with Gabe watching from the window.

Sgt. Rone re-entered the building. "We're ready to go, sir."

An hour later they were back at the outpost. In the short time they'd been gone the vegetation had crept closer to the road. The boundaries to the clearing had shrunk and many branches were reaching out farther than before. The greenery glowed with yellow from the sun, waving and vibrant.

Sgt. Rone parked the Rover near the filled-in trench and honked. No sign of Rahula. They got out and explored the area. Everything sat just as they had left it. The backhoe and D-9 looked like yellow lepers abandoned to die. Neither had been moved or tampered with.

"Let's split up. You go north and I'll go south. We'll meet back here in an hour," Gabe suggested.

"Okay, radio me if you find anything."

Gabe walked the outskirts of the clearing until he found a faint path leading into the forest. Fern fronds reached and touched, obscuring the trail. They rustled gently, clicking like cicadas.

Gabe radioed Rone, "I've found a path. Maybe we'll find Rahula along it. Meet me at the Rover. We'll need machetes." Before he left, he marked the trail with an arrow made with ferns.

When he got back to the truck, Rone was waiting. "Do we really want to do this?" he asked.

"No, but we will. Rahula might be the key to discovering what's going on," Gabe replied, walking back toward the trail.

When they returned, the fern arrow seemed to be almost inside the forest. Surely the trees aren't growing that fast Gabe thought to himself. He moved forward and started chopping the greenery away from the trail. Rone followed. When they entered the canopy, the sun disappeared. The fronds swayed gently in the breeze.

The hazmat helmets dampened the sound, but the men could still hear a multitude of noises. Macaws called, monkeys chattered, leaves rustled and water drops plopped off their helmets. Whenever they paused and looked, water beaded on the green leaves and glistened like diamonds. Both men felt subdued as they hacked their way forward. Something felt wrong, like they were trespassing and their presence was a gross intrusion of nature.

The men took turns leading and chopping. They progressed slowly and stopped often to catch their breath. At a thousand yards into the trees they stopped to rest. When the sound of their breathing died down, a low humming sound could be heard. Gabe and Sgt. Rone followed the noise to a small hut nestled beneath a gigantic mahogany tree. Camouflaged, it blended into its surroundings, making it impossible to find but for the chant.

Seeing the dwelling, the men sheathed their machetes and quietly approached its mouth. They looked in, spying Rahula bathed in a supernatural light. He was levitated above the ground with a serene expression. Although seemingly oblivious to their approach, he greeted them. "Good afternoon, gentlemen."

"Rahula, how are you?" Gabe replied. Sgt. Rone remained silent and alert.

"I am at peace. There is no greater feeling."

"Why'd you take off? We need you. We need to do an examination and find out why you're still alive," Gabe explained.

"I have renounced civilization to seek God. All living things die but truth is eternal. I live here for the happiness that does not decay, the treasure that cannot be taken, for the life that knows no beginning and has no end. I have retired from the world to live in solitude and destroy all earthly desires. This is my home, I will stay here."

"No, there are too many unexplained deaths. You might be the key to discovering why. Isn't preventing people from dying more important than your inner peace?"

"Their deaths were karmic."

"What do you mean? The disease seems to be indiscriminate in choosing its victims."

"You scientists, always trying to keep people from their karma. The deaths are part of the circle started by the destruction of the rainforest. The natural cycle of Brahma has been broken. Man has caused great imbalance and must suffer the consequences. There must be vyaya."

"Look, there's a logical explanation for the disease. Your esoteric bullshit doesn't help. I need to know why you're not infected. What makes you different?"

"I bear no ill-will toward the trees or any living thing. I am at one with the Infinite Mind and his creations."

"What does ill-will have to do with immunity against a deadly virus?"

"It isn't a virus. It's the trees."

"Are you saying that the trees are intentionally killing people?"

"Yes."

"How do you know?"

"I just do."

"Why them and not you?"

"I follow the dharma and desire nothing. Those who died desired greatly, far beyond Gaia's ability to provide. Their desires caused their deaths. They burned red and green with greed and envy. They gave up the light for their desires."

" So the trees killed them?"

"Yes. The dead have reaped what they have sown as will all those who live outside the dharma. The trees attack those who upset the balance of nature. Man is responsible for the destruction of Gaia's trees and now the trees are responsible for the destruction of man. The circle is complete."

"We're here to save people. To do that we need to examine you."

"I live in seclusion. I'm at peace with myself and the world. You concerns are not mine."

"Are you saying you won't return with us?"

"Yes."

"And if we force you?"

"Then you will face the karmic consequences."

"Is that a threat? Are you going to infect us with the virus?"

"The disease comes from above. I have nothing to do with it."

"I guess we'll just have to risk being infected," Gabe motioned to Sgt. Rone. He moved behind Rahula and grabbed his arms, handcuffing him. Rahula didn't struggle or even look around, he simply submitted to his abduction.

Gabe led as Sgt. Rone followed with Rahula walking between them. The vegetation, chopped a half hour earlier, had grown back enough to tug and pull at their suits. They hurried toward the clearing as the trail seemed to close to prevent Rahula's abduction. Neither Gabe nor Rone noticed when the mystic slipped his right hand from the cuffs.

The path narrowed as they moved forward. The last fifty yards were almost totally obscured. Gabe unsheathed his machete and began hacking the vegetation back. Both men could hear the pinging of something hitting their helmets as they worked through the brush.

"When this is over, I'll never visit a rainforest again," Gabe told Sgt. Rone.

"I never wanted to visit one in the first place, I'm a beach man. In fact, when this is over I'm going to quit the army and move to some tropical island where life is slow and laid back. I'm tired of death and destruction."

Thirty minutes later, Gabe sighed with relief as they emerged from the trees. When Rone pushed Rahula toward the Rover, he noticed the cuffs dangling from his Rahula's left hand.

"How did that happen?" Gabe asked.

"Man's bondage is only temporary," Rahula said. "People of light cannot be held by chains."

"Oh really?" Rone replied and grabbed the empty cuff and pulled Rahula toward him. He undid the clasp and placed Rahula's right hand inside and clamped it tight.

"Don't hurt him," Gabe admonished.

"I won't unless he tries to escape," Rone said. He placed Rahula in the backseat and tied his feet together. A wry smile etched the captive's face.

"Something tells me he could've escaped anytime he wanted to," Gabe said as he got in the Rover.

15

*L*a Sikes rested on her bed, exhausted from her trip to earth. She was listening to the music Ship had archived, Vivaldi's "Four seasons," when her door chimed.

"Yes?"

"May I come in?"

"Logis? Of course," she said getting off the bed.

The door slid open and Logis entered. "La Sikes, I viewed the video, are you okay?"

"Oh Logis, have you forgotten my first name? I'd feel better if you used it."

"I'm the Chosen One. It's against protocol."

"It's just you and me. My room is private, not even Ship can hear," Sikes said.

"La Sikes," he said quietly, "I'm not here to discuss names. You've been through a lot lately. I want to know that you're all right."

"It's Pathia. My name is Pathia, remember?"

"La Sikes, please..."

"And I'm not okay. I've been grieving since the day you were chosen. Do you know how hard it was to let you go and smile and not say anything. I love you."

"Why are you doing this?"

Sikes continued, "I've seen thousands of auras in the past few weeks from brutal reds and sewer browns to velvet yellows and blue whites but none of them came close to the beauty that was yours before you became the leader of Benwar. Now I see your light steadily darkening and it scares me."

"La Sikes, Pathia, it's the sacrifice I make for Benwar."

"Benwar, always Benwar. What about me, Logis?"

"Pathia, I was castrated for a reason. Our love is a thing of the past. It must be."

"Why are you here then?"

"I still care. I came to comfort you," he said, moving closer.

La Sikes moved away, crying. "Please don't touch me, I couldn't bear it."

"Pathia..."

"I want you to leave now, Logis," she said hugging herself.

Her words stung. He was trying to help but had only made things worse. He turned and left the room.

16

*T*he examination baffled Gabe as much as Rahula did. His blood samples proved to be normal. In fact, his whole biology was normal. His white blood cell count was normal, his temperature was 98.5 degrees F., there was no chemical imbalance, no toxins, nothing out of the ordinary. The only abnormality was the man's attitude.

He had been abducted forcefully. Anyone else would be angry and sullen, not Rahula. When he awoke, he smiled. No sign of anger. A soft yellow light enveloped his body.

While Gabe admired Rahula, he also began to wonder if the man was human. When he entered the examination room he could actually, viscerally feel Rahula's warmth and acceptance. Gabe turned on the microphone inside his hazmat suit and began the interview.

"How are you, Rahula? You don't seem mad."

"Would anger help the situation? It is a wasted emotion. What is, is."

"Okay, but most people would still be angry." When Rahula didn't reply, he continued, " So how did you come to be at the outpost? Your name isn't on the crew manifest."

"I lived in the forest and traded with the workers."

"But you're obviously not Brazilian. How'd you end up in the Amazon?"

"Does it matter?"

"Humor me."

"What?"

"It does. Please explain."

"Many years ago I lived in a small village in Cambodia with my wife and two children. Simple peasants, our wants were few and our needs were satisfied by hunting and gathering. One day, I was hunting when I heard gunshots. I raced back to my village to find the burning remains of our huts. The Khmer Rouge had killed every man, woman, and child. I found what I took to be the charred flesh and bones of my wife and children in our smoldering hut. They were burned beyond recognition, but I knew. I cried out for the murderers to come back for me. When nothing happened I doused the remains of my family with water so I could bury them.

Alone and grieving, I wondered the forest for days hoping the Khmer Rouge would find me and end my suffering. Finally, exhausted, I sat down with my head between my knees. After a few moments I felt a hand on my shoulder, the touch lessened my pain. I looked up to see a kindly face smiling at me. It was a Buddhist monk dressed in a crimson sari. He led me to a small monastery buried deep in the forest. On the way he talked to me of pain and suffering.

I am Rawana, he said. I see you suffer greatly. Arouse yourself and follow me. I will show you the way to enlightenment. Your mind is a stormy sea filled with the high winds of pain and suffering. You must cross this sea with its waves and its whirlpools. You must conquer the sharks and demons and cross over. The Brahman stands on dry land and you must empty your mind so that you can join him, my friend. Use your pain and suffering to achieve enlightenment. This is your time.

I felt an immediate sense of relief after hearing these words. As he looked into my eyes, I sensed understanding and compassion. It made things better to know I was no longer alone.

He continued, your present anguished state is transitory. Just as the sun hides behind the clouds so too does enlightenment hide behind life's travails. After saying these words he put his arm around my shoulder and we walked in silence until we arrived at the monastery.

When we arrived, several monks greeted us. One brought food and water. I drank the cool clean water and ate. The food was simple but it tasted of heaven. I was shown to a small room with two mats on the floor. Rawana sat with me and the other monks left. To empty your mind, you must chant the mantra, he said and started, "Ohmmmmm, Ohmmmm."

I joined in and concentrated only on the word, emptying my mind of grief. Over a period of months, I learned to meditate and forget my sadness and worldly concerns, but my desire for revenge remained.

One day Rawana came to me and said, "There are no chains like those of hate. You must lay aside your knife and be merciful and compassionate to all living creatures. You are to leave the monastery so you can learn to detach yourself from this world and lose your anger.

The next day, I left. The monks bowed as I passed them on the jungle path. I walked, always south as if being drawn by an invisible force. Eventually my path brought me to the banks of the Mekong River. A barge was docked along the shore. It needed laborers to load bundles of teak wood. Food and water were my only pay for the day's labor. I joined the crew of the barge and we floated to Phnom Penh.

The next morning, I explored my first city. It shocked me to the very roots of my being. Human dwellings stretched as far as the eye could see. Houses were stacked upon houses and it looked like they reached into the clouds. Tightly packed together, these buildings choked plant life down to a few trees and shrubs, some seemed to grow out of the cement.

The smell of chemicals attacked my nostrils and made my eyes water. The smell of gasoline and diesel never left during the time I lingered in the city. The chemical smog oppressed me, it was the incarnation of evil, an abomination to the natural order of all living things.

I came upon a place in the city where countless numbers of cars and motorbikes were trying to get someplace. There were so many that they got in each other's way. They moved at a snail's pace. A multitude of noises filled the air, sputtering motorbikes, horns honking, brakes screeching and motors racing. These were the sounds of great discord. People hurried to get to their destination without really going anywhere. Harmony could never be found in such an artificial place.

I resumed my travels south and finally reached the Elephant Mountains where I rested and looked out upon the glorious rainforest. I took great breaths of clean air before I resumed walking.

After many days, the coastal city of Kampong Som came into view. It bustled with the senseless scurrying to satisfy worldly desires. The smell of the sea brought me to the docks. There I found work on a fishing trawler bound for Japan. I soon tired of klesa, of the great sin that is netting thousands of fish at once and asked to be put ashore when we reached port. Once there, the captain of the trawler paid me and with a portion of the money I booked passage to Brazil."

Gabe broke into Rahula's narrative, "The last time we talked, you said that the deaths in the rainforest were caused by man's desires, what did you mean?"

"Mankind's desires are insatiable. Many of the world's cultures have moved away from the light of reason and into a never ending quest for possessions. A growing population desires more and more things, more houses, more cars, more TVs, more computers, more food, and so on … This unending acquisition causes the depletion of Gaia's treasures. Air, water, the trees, other living creatures are all disappearing. Mankind takes and takes and never gives back.

A man tells himself that if only he had a new car he would be happy. He gets the car and the spiritual emptiness remains. So now he says if only I had a new and bigger house with air conditioning and many rooms and a big yard then I would be happy. He gets the new home and instead of happiness, he finds his spiritual emptiness has grown. So now he tells himself that what would really make him happy is a vacation home and two cars and then finally, finally he would be happy. Getting one thing leads to wanting another and the man thinks only of himself, never realizing that each possession makes the spiritual void deeper and, contrary to his belief, his happiness lessens. Each time he gets something and finds it doesn't make him happy, he wants something else. He is locked into trying to fill the hole in his spirit with objects. His car gets old so he buys a new one, his neighbor builds a bigger house so he builds one. This story repeats itself in different forms millions of times a day.

Each time a person gets something it is at the expense of our Mother. Eventually there will be nothing left for her to give. Now, finally, she fights back. Our mother is fighting a final battle for life, our only hope for survival is that she wins."

"Then earth is a living organism?" Gabe asked.

"How can anything so glorious and balanced not be?"

"I understand what you're trying to tell me," Gabe said. He really did believe in Rahula's sincerity. Gabe also sympathized with Rahula's point of view but he had been taught to put mankind's welfare first. That and he had a duty to the C.D.C. "So will you come back to Manaus with me so we can get an MRI?"

"Will it make you happy and me free?"

"Yes, Rahula."

"Then so be it."

17

*T*he euthobots had been effective at protecting the trees in other parts of the world. In the Congo Basin the wars ended. There was no one left to fight. Rotting corpses and ghosts were all that remained of the jungle's combatants. After centuries of depredation it was as if the trees had decided to spit out the bitter taste of humans.

Across the globe, the forests had rejected the parasites that had plagued them for centuries. The news media blared stories of the death and mayhem found in the trees. Thousands of dead in a northern Washington rain forest, hundreds of fatalities in the Sawtooths. Same in the Appalachians.

People died before they could evacuate. Major and minor forests throughout the world continued their relentless attack. A mysterious disease killed those who came in contact with the trees. City populations swelled as panic drove people away.

Industries connected to logging and trees came to an abrupt halt. The paper mills were shuttered, the housing industry stopped. Highways in the forests closed. Mysterious roll-overs and head-ons littered the roads.

Ambulances sent to retrieve the bodies never returned. Helicopters flying over saw wrecked cars and dead bodies strewn along the highways. A news crew filmed an ambulance with its lights blaring and the back doors open. Two EMTs were sprawled across the gurney. Terrified citizens erected roadblocks well outside the forests and put up signs painted with a skull and cross bones to warn of death.

The oceans had spit out the terrible taste of humans. The genetically modified algae had spread daily, bearing the deadly virus to all parts of the world's waters. Within weeks of its dispersal, the algal beds covered most of the oceans' surfaces. Contact by sea-faring vessels became unavoidable as did death for those aboard.

Cruise ships drifted aimlessly, littered with the masses of human tissue that had once been vacationers or crew members. Indistinguishable bodies of gore dripped from lawn chairs, rotted on dance floors or filled the sheets in the beds of staterooms. Fishing vessels manned by ghosts wandered the seas often crashing together with one or the other sinking. Gigantic and not so gigantic oil tankers sat bereft of human life. Some floated until they broke up on reefs, others were tossed about by the waves until they capsized, their oil spilling into the oceans, dotting them with slicks that the algae would gradually ingest.

Ships coming to or already in ports were quarantined. Soldiers ringed the docks and shot anyone trying to come ashore. Those aboard were left to die.

The oceans became graveyards of floating caskets as the virus purged mankind from their surface. Devoid of humans, the seas quickly became wildlife refuges as the depredation of sea life came to a complete stop.

18

Gabe, Ben, and Charlise were examining the results of Rahula's x-rays and MRI and comparing them with the corpses removed from the work site. They discovered an anomaly in both cases. Positioned near the base of the spine by the medulla oblongata, they discovered microscopic metallic specks. However, there was a difference, the corpses had that part of the brain severed from the upper regions, Rahula's was intact.

"That's it! Those things sever the autonomic nervous system from the rest of the body," Ben exclaimed.

"It's strange they're not found in the blood stream, too. Let's remove the brain stem to get a specimen," Gabe said.

Hours later they had removed a tiny section of the medulla oblongata of one of the victims and isolated the specs. Gabe placed the flakes on a slide and examined them with an electron microscope. He became excited, "The flakes are definitely inorganic. They appear to have some kind of electronic circuitry."

"Let me see," Ben requested. Gabe moved out of the way. The second Ben gazed into the scope he knew what they were. "They're nano-bots," he cried. "Look and see what you think, Charlise."

Ben moved over and she peered into the microscope. "You're right and that creates more questions than it answers. How did they get here and where did they come from? Why did they attack this person and not Rahula?"

"Just a minute," said Gabe. "First, let's figure out how they work. Isolate one of the bots and increase the magnification."

Charlise did as requested. The isolated bot came into stark relief. The front of the machine contained two round sharp edged saw blades that rotated so that the bot could either burrow or cut. The back end contained sophisticated circuitry with an impossibly small control chip.

The three scientists took turns examining the bot before anyone said anything. Gabe finally pronounced, " They're designed to cut through the medulla oblongata and severe it from the body."

Charlise was upset, "We know the trees didn't manufacture them so where did they come from?"

Gabe thought back to the silicone square in the virus and his encounter with Drew Bean. "From another world," he said and laughed uneasily.

"Jesus, you're right," said Ben. "They have to be extraterrestrial. This technology is far too advanced to've been developed by anyone on earth. How would anyone manufacture something so small?"

Gabe looked into the lenses, "This one's inactive right now. It looks like they do their job and shut down."

"Look again at Rahula's MRI. The bots reside inside his brain stem but they're dormant. Why?"

A sudden intuition hit Ben. "Let's examine his blood sample again. As I recall Rahula's serotonin levels were higher than most people's."

Charlise opened the file. "You're right. So maybe serotonin shuts the bots down, but what activates them?"

"Testosterone?" Gabe suggested. Charlise looked at Rahula's results again.

"Maybe. Rahula's testosterone levels are somewhat lower than most males but not significantly. It's simple to find out. We can take a sample of blood with high levels of testosterone and drop it on the bot to see if it activates."

Ben rolled up his sleeve. "Let's try it. I volunteer."

"I didn't know you had any testosterone," Gabe joked. "Why don't you let me do it?"

Ben laughed, "If I didn't have any testosterone would I be

volunteering for this? Now that my manhood's at stake, I insist. Besides, you need yours."

Gabe smiled, "Okay, my friend, I mean it's not like were going to inject the bots into your veins."

Charlise shook her head and smiled. "You guys are perverse. Okay Ben, sit on the table." She pulled a rubber constrictor hose from the shelve and clamped it above his elbow then grabbed a syringe and gently inserted a needle into the vein that bulged from his upper arm. When she had extracted three ccs of blood, she pulled the needle from his arm and held a cotton swab over the injection site. Ben replaced her fingers with his so Charlise could remove the slide from the microscope and apply a minute amount of his blood on it.

They were disappointed when the bot remained inactive. Gabe thought out loud. "Testosterone keeps humans aroused longer. Let's add some adrenaline to the slide and see what happens."

Gabe withdrew a bottle of epinephrine from the medicine cabinet. He withdrew a couple of ccs and placed a milliliter on the slide. As Charlise watched the bot, it began to move.

"It's activated!" she exclaimed and moved out of the way. Gabe looked at the slide and saw the bot moving. Ben took his turn at the scope. He watched the bot's movement slow then stop.

"Damn it! It stopped!"

Gabe moved Ben out of the way and looked. "It's like it ran out of gas," Gabe said and placed another milliliter of adrenaline on the slide. The bot remained dormant. "Let's try another sample with just adrenaline," he suggested.

They replaced the slide with one containing a different nano-bot sample. When they tried adrenaline alone, it didn't reanimate. Once they added testosterone the bot moved for a few seconds and then died. Nothing they tried could revive it.

"So we can hypothesize that the bots are activated by a combination of testosterone and adrenaline and that Rahula is alive because his levels of these two substances are below the activation threshold."

"We can also speculate that the bots contain only enough energy to kill one person and that they were designed to shut down afterwards. And, since we found no infected animals, that the bots were designed to attack humans only."

A sudden chill went down Gabe's spine as he thought about the ramifications. "Maybe someone's trying to purge the forests of humans? And if so, why?"

"Aliens looking for a new home?" said Ben uneasily. "Hey, I have an idea. It might be possible to disrupt and shut the bots down with a magnetic field. If strong enough, it might destroy the bot's programming and render it harmless."

"Maybe. We'll need to test bots taken from other corpses to confirm our results. I suggest we keep things quiet until we're reasonably sure of what's going on then we'll decide what to do with the results."

"Yeah, can you imagine the panic we'd cause if it was announced that our forests are infested with death-dealing nano-bots?" Ben said.

"It would be War of the Worlds all over again. And we're still not sure if they're extraterrestrial. This could be some kind of military experiment gone awry or a foreign plot to control the world's forests," said Gabe.

"Ben, take Sgt. Rone back into the forest and gather some more bodies. Make sure you bring some females so we can determine if there are any gender differences."

"Okay," Ben nodded as he opened the door and exited the lab.

"My God, what's going to happen?," Charlise said after the door closed.

Gabe moved close and she turned away with tears in her eyes. He gently touched her arm and she turned to face him. He sensed her need and embraced her. She felt warm and firm against him. There was a faint smell of lavender that he would always associate with that moment.

Charlise had longed for physical contact since he'd stood at the podium weeping. She had wanted to hug and comfort him then, but now it was he who comforted her. His tender touch dispelled her fears and made everything seem better.

"God, you feel good. I've been wanting to do that since we first met," Gabe said.

"Can I die in your arms?" she asked.

"You're not going to die. We'll figure something out," Gabe said as they pulled apart. "It appears the bots are designed to attack anyone with aggressive tendencies. We should be able to protect ourselves by keeping our hormone levels low. Rahula's ability to remain calm and indifferent has kept him alive, maybe it'll work for us."

"Maybe we should become Buddhists."

"Or learn to regulate our responses to stimuli so that we can keep our adrenaline levels low," Gabe said. "When we're done we'll go talk to our Buddhist friend."

For the next two hours they used the remaining samples of bots to determine what levels of testosterone and insulin caused the nano-bots to activate. During the process they made an important discovery. The only nano-bots that would activate had a minute green area on their back. As soon as the green disappeared the bots stopped moving. Without the green, the bots remained dormant.

While they were charting their results the short wave radio cackled and came to life. "This is Ben, come in please."

Gabe removed his eye from the microscope and hurried to the short wave. "Gabe here," he said grabbing the microphone.

"You're not going to believe this, there're no bodies left to be recovered."

"What? What do you mean?"

"We've found small mounds covered with bracket fungus and other mounds teaming with millipedes and beetles but most of the remains are gone. Millions of sarcophagi organisms seem to have gone into a hyper-drive eating orgy. All that remains are vague outlines where the corpses were. Even the bodies we buried in bags are gone. The bags were full of maggots and devoid of any human flesh. It was impossible to get even a tissue sample."

"Damn it! Where are you now?"

"We're on our way back. It's been an eerie trip. The vehicles that were on the road are already overgrown with lianas and fungus. Even the highway is starting to break up in places where the buttress roots have extended. In a few weeks no sign of human life will remain," Ben said. "The forest seems to be in a hurry to reclaim itself. I've never seen anything like it."

"You took some samples of the plants and organisms so we can examine them?"

"Sure did."

"Great. When you two get back we'll sit down and discuss everything."

"Sounds good," Ben said as he signed off.

Forty-five minutes later, Ben opened the door to the lab followed by Sgt. Rone. "The nano-bots have closed the Amazon to human access," Ben stated definitively. "Not only that but the forest's carrions have eliminated most of the remains. I hope you had enough samples to pinpoint the threshold levels."

"Only within very broad parameters."

"Well at least we know what activates the little bastards."

"We made another discovery while you were gone. The bots run on chlorophyll. It explains why they are found only in forested areas. If they get very far from the trees they run out of fuel. They are engineered to keep humans away."

"That's ingenious!" Ben exclaimed. "If they run on chlorophyll then they must need sunlight to mobilize. They're probably inactive at night. These things are so small and exquisitely engineered that they can't possibly be man made."

"Again, there's no sense speculating. However, we do need to discuss what we're going to do with our findings," said Gabe.

"I can think of two reasons to keep the results to ourselves," Ben answered. "First, announcement of our findings will cause widespread panic. Secondly, I agree with the purpose if not the means of the bots. Human survival and that of the planet depends on healthy forests."

"In the name of God, Ben," said Charlise. "Millions of people are dead and you're saying that's okay?"

"Charlise, so far no one has suggested let alone enacted the harsh environmental restrictions necessary to preserve the rainforests. Of course, it's a horrifying, ugly situation, but the bots have cleared the forests of humans. It's the first time I've felt hope for saving the planet. Man has finally been derailed from his path to extinction.

When Rone and I entered the rainforest the air smelled decidedly cleaner. There was no smell of rotting flesh or chemicals. The area was healing itself."

"But it's the simple peasants and working class who're being killed. Meanwhile, those most responsible for earth's demise are hunkering down in their mansions and removing the trees from their estates. They'll survive and the underprivileged will perish."

"I don't think there's a fair way to save the rainforests. The bots can't distinguish between rich and poor."

"Yes, but you're so cold-blooded about it."

"I can assure you I'm as terrified as you are. It's just that on an intellectual level what's happening makes sense."

"So only Buddhists are immune to these killing machines? What kind of sadism is that?"

"No, Charlise. Only those with the ability to stay calm and reasonable, who control their aggressions are immune. That's what our lab work suggests."

Gabe cut in, "So we have an obligation to report the findings to our superiors and let them decide what to do."

"Not necessarily. We all know how duplicitous the government is. They might bury the results and save themselves. Once we divulge the information, the problem is out of our hands."

Charlise cut in, "Yeah, it would almost be better to go public so that everyone has fair warning and an equal chance to save themselves."

"So far the aliens, if that's who's responsible, are attacking on two fronts, the forests and the oceans. The killing hasn't spread to major population centers," Gabe said.

"My intuition tells me that it's only a matter of time. If an alien culture wants to save the earth, they'll have to reduce the human population to a sustainable level."

"Okay, but we work for the Centers for Disease Control. We have an obligation to report our findings to Langley and let him decide how to handle the situation. Besides, it might calm people down if he decides to make the information public."

"How's that?" questioned Ben.

"Well it's not an epidemic caused by a virus. All people have to do is avoid the forests and they're safe. If the government is vague about what's really causing the deaths and avoids all mention of extra-terrestrial nano-bots, maybe a little normalcy will return to the planet."

19

*F*a Structor reviewed the results of the robotic engineers' efforts. They were impressive. Human activity in forested areas had been halted. The forests were restoring themselves to health at a rate that surprised even the Benwars. Most importantly, human casualties were presently restricted only to forested areas that had been targeted by ship's sensors.

In conjunction with these efforts, the engineers had miniaturized the biospectrometers and incorporated them into a new generation of nano-bots. The biospectrometers would be used as a triggering mechanism.

The Benwarian study teams had surveyed and catalogued thousands of auras, discovering some interesting demographic trends. Young males from the ages of fifteen to twenty-five tended to have the greatest areas of red. A person's occupation also corresponded well with color patterns. Professional athletes, law enforcement officers, businessmen, lawyers, politicians, and construction workers had larger areas of red than educators, doctors, priests and social workers.

Ship had been equipped with the first biospectrometer. She imaged and analyzed various areas of earth and compared the differences in the auras of whole populations. There were certain places where the scan had heavy concentrations of dots of red. Using information gleaned from earth's extensive telecommunications systems, the scientists discovered that prison populations were comprised of people with dark red brain scans with a green mottling. These dark, rigid auras indicated set patterns of brain functions that would make rehabilitation impossible. Not that the Benwars and Earth had time for rehabilitation.

Male college students had large areas of red although they weren't as bright and showed more flexibility than the prison population's. The hues of red varied more in college populations than in other segments of society indicating a state of flux. There were also some promising exceptions in this population. A few of the scans were dominated by blue and there were only splotches of red. These auras were mottled with yellow and showed individuals of great promise.

A marked difference occurred when gender comparisons were made. Female scans contained much larger areas of blue than male scans. Blue usually overwhelmed the reds in female auras. This was indicative of greater empathy and feelings. However, most of these scans contained undeveloped or weak areas of yellow and white. The Benwars surmised that while females were the kinder fairer sex, they often failed to develop the capacity to think and reason.

Male scans were dominated by red and large areas of green. The blues and yellows were subdued in most of these auras suggesting behavior that was influenced more by aggression and greed than by logic and ethics. The proportion of males who had failed to develop the ability to think matched that of females, there was no gender difference.

However, about one percent of both male and female scans displayed an even mixture of red and blue dominated by a yellowish white light with some green interspersed throughout. These auras shimmered with the colors remaining elastic and changeable. Interestingly, this population tended to be better educated, particularly in liberal arts.

A segment of earth's population had scans that contained a good portion of violet clouded over with a black film. These auras were extremely rigid with brain patterns that remained static and were devoid of yellow and green areas. The males in this group had red rays and the females had blue rays overlaid with blacks. These were the believers, the fundamentalists. In many countries they comprised a majority of the population.

Children under the age of twelve displayed the most interesting auras. Already the divide between the red dominated auras of males and the blue dominated auras of females existed but their brain patterns remained fluid, indicating that they could be educated to think logically. They might also be taught meditation techniques and self control so that they could overcome their biological make up and achieve balance in their brain functions. This segment of earth's population most interested the Benwarians.

The auras in the United States burned red and deep green in almost all segments of society. The scans indicated an aggressive, materialistic civilization. This country contained a multitude of people with auras of the brightest red and darkest green. Many of these auras were tinged with a deep dark purple that indicated religiosity without spiritualism.

Analyzing the auras catalogued by the study teams provided a base for determining how much light would be required to avoid the euthobots. Light wasn't the only determinate, however. An aura had to shimmer. If it remained rigid, it triggered a kill response.

The Benwarians would save those individuals whose auras were similar to their own. Their auras burned with a yellow that approached white. While their auras contained all of the elements in the biospectric range, there were only shimmers of the more base colors since their knowledge and wisdom allowed them great control over their biological drives and urges. They were able to subdue and control the reds of aggression. Their auras glistened with indigo and yellow reflecting their calmness and serenity. A luminous yellow mirrored their wisdom and spirituality.

The engineering team equipped each of the new generation of euthobots with a spectrometer that would read a person's aura. These spectrographs would then be used to target individual humans for elimination and bypass those whose auras contained enough white light to shimmer. The bots would euthanize anyone with a rigid, static aura or anyone whose aura burned with a color other than the yellow or white light of wisdom and knowledge. Those individuals whose auras were polluted with grays and blacks would be eliminated.

When presented with a synopsis of the biospectrographic results, Logis found the auras that contained the dingy purple to gray scans most intriguing. The dark overlay could also be found in alcoholics or drug users. It was if they were using opiates and yet the scans didn't display any chemical distortions.

Logis was intrigued, "Ship, explain these scans."

"They're believers. People who accept a religion blindly and adhere strictly to a set of beliefs, the faithful. For them it is the form of the religion that is important not the substance."

"What's faith?"

"Belief that does not rest on proof or material evidence."

"That's illogical."

"It's not a question of logic, it's training like a lab rat or pet dog. People of all faiths indoctrinate or train their children from an early age to believe in the strictures of their church. Belief is passed down from one generation to the next," Ship said.

"So their faith is based on someone else's faith. There is no free will or ability to think for themselves? There's no discussion or exchange of ideas, no quest for knowledge?" asked Logis.

"No, they're trained which constricts their thought processes. Their scans resemble those of drug users and alcoholics because all three are a form of escapism. For instance, a poll of American citizens showed that one quarter believe in the Rapture. The Rapture is a belief that the Son of God will appear at the end of the world and transport all Christian believers to heaven. Some literally believe they'll travel on a spaceship. No logical, educated human would believe such conjecture unless they were trained," Ship said.

"Where do these silly ideas come from?"

"From their priestly class and books written long ago such as the Bible, the Koran or the Talmud."

"So they're trained to believe that God can be contained in these books?"

"Yes. As I said before, they are indoctrinated to believe that these books contain the word of God."

"I would imagine that that makes their God very small and human-like."

"Yes. Fundamentalists also believe that God gave mankind dominion over the earth and all lesser beings. If something happens, God will provide. The earth exists for their pleasure and use."

"No wonder they have such little regard for the home they live on. It explains the darkness and rigidity of their scans doesn't it?"

"Yes. Over sixty-five percent of world's population lack the ability to think abstractly. These people seek concrete representations of God. They find God in words, in a cross, in churches and for some, even in a bomb. Faith breeds fanaticism, an intense uncritical devotion to a God defined by words."

Logis thought for a moment, "God's an abstraction. There's no personal growth or development without understanding that. Humans would be far better off if they believed Gaia was a concrete representation of God then they would take better care of her."

"Unfortunately it's too late. Gaia is dying," Ship said.

Logis brought Ship back to the subject of auras. "And what about the undeveloped, rigid, brown auras?" he asked.

"The world's poor and wretched. These people lacked the proper nutrition and stimulation for their brains to develop normally. Sadly, a great portion of the world's population lack the proper foods and medical care. Forty thousand people die each day from malnutrition and related diseases. Even those who do manage to get enough to eat lack the opportunity to educate themselves. Their scans remain muted, dull, and static."

"This world demonstrates the extremes of overpopulation. There are vast differences in culture and beliefs and in wealth and poverty and it's displayed in their auras," said Logis before he asked, "How many of Earthlings have auras of light similar to ours?"

Ship hesitated as it scanned and tabulated the information from the study teams then extrapolated an estimate. "Approximately one hundred twenty thousand."

"That's it?"

"Yes. Almost all humans are a product of their culture and training. They are caught up in their society and have given up the quest for truth and knowledge. Their auras are rigid and unchangeable."

"How many have auras with light and fluidity?"

Again there was a slight pause as Ship re-estimated. "Fifty-five million adults and seven hundred thirty-two million children, in round numbers. If we saved only the children, we would have a sustainable population. One that we could educate."

"Yes," Logis replied, "but those fifty-five million have overcome such great odds to find light in a dark and inhospitable planet that surely they would be worth saving. They would also be crucial to preserving those parts of earth's culture that are uniquely human. I think we'll want to save them. They can help with the transition. Anyway it's a decision for the Council to make.

I appreciate your thoughts and information. Convene the Council, it's time."

20

*B*ack in his hotel room, Gabe found himself humming and smiling despite all that had gone on in the last few days. He decided to put everything out of his head and live in the moment. He thought about Charlise with her bright blue, sparkling eyes and the way she looked at him with respect and kindness. Her confidence in him increased his determination to find a way to survive.

Gabe turned the shower spigot on and adjusted the water temperature to hot. He stepped over the tub edge and under the soothing embrace of the cascading water. He luxuriated for a moment before scrubbing. The shower was invigorating as were his thoughts of Charlise. It was great to be alive and clean he thought as he turned off the water and stepped onto the bathmat. Grabbing a towel, he dried off and moved in front of the mirror then shaved and combed his hair.

Showering always brought back memories of his childhood on the farm. He remembered a time when one of the milk cows was having trouble calving. He had called the vet and waited for him to arrive. When he got to the farm they herded the cow up into an alleyway and put a pole behind her so she couldn't back out. The vet put on his plastic gloves and reached into the cows uterus to pull the calf's legs out then he attached a slip chain to the legs and hooked them to a crank clamped onto the cow's hips. The crank had a lever that he moved back and forth to slowly leverage the calf out.

Once past a certain point the calf slid out in a slimy rush and plopped on the ground. The vet grabbed one leg and Gabe grabbed the other and they yanked the calf's back legs over the pole fence to let the mucous drain from its throat and nasal passages. A bull, it looked up with wide, lively eyes and bawled. They let the calf down and drug him back into the corral so the mother cow could lick him off and let him suckle.

Gabe checked on the pair the next morning. The calf was sucking on its mother's teats but oddly it stayed on its front knees. Gabe and his father separated the pair. The cow was ushered into the barn to be milked and the calf was placed in a well strawed pen nearby.

That night Gabe took the calf a bottle fully expecting refusal since it had already suckled the mother that day. When he got to the pen the calf lay listless in the milky stupor of a newborn. Gabe squirted a little of the milk on the calf's nose, and it immediately got up on its knees. He straddled it and opened the calf's mouth to insert the nipple. The second the calf tasted the warm colostrums it started to suck voraciously. When it finished, Gabe examined the leg and found that it was broken.

The cow hadn't evacuated the afterbirth so Gabe decided to wait to have the leg set when the vet returned in three days. He fed the calf twice a day, admiring its strength and liveliness. It immediately rose to its knees each time he entered the pen. It was a special, rare animal with a strong desire for life. Gabe enjoyed feeding such a grand specimen.

After three days, the vet returned to clean the cow. When he examined the calf, he found the broken bone had poked through the skin. He explained to Gabe that the leg would rot off with infection if he tried to set it and recommended that the calf be euthanized. Broken-hearted, he watched as the vet filled a syringe with death serum. The needle was inserted into a vein in the calf's neck and before the plunger hit the flat part of the syringe the calf's eyes clouded over with death. At that moment Gabe realized how indiscriminating and sudden death could be.

But right now it was great to be clean and alive. He applied some aftershave and a dab of cologne. Still whistling, he dressed in grey corduroys with a yellow shirt and a matching grey jacket then left the room.

Charlene's room was on the same floor and around the corner from his. He walked expectantly to her room, still humming. He knocked on her door and heard her approaching.

She opened the door with a radiant smile and as they looked into each other's eyes, she took the initiative and hugged him. He was only too glad to hug her back.

"It seems like I waited forever for this," she said as they separated.

"I've wanted ask you out for a long time but I'm a little gun shy," he replied. "There's a cab waiting downstairs and I found a nice quiet restaurant that should be the perfect setting for me to bask in your glow."

"Cover girl works wonders," she laughed.

"You're too beautiful for make-up," he complimented.

"Gabe, are you flattering me?"

"No, I'm being truthful. But if I was, would it work?"

"Definitely," she answered as the elevator doors opened. She stepped in and grabbed his hand, pulling him after her. He punched the button for the first floor and the doors shut. Still holding hands, he pulled her to him and kissed her full on the lips. Charlise responded by clutching his waist. They held each other until the elevator bumped to a stop and the doors opened.

They parted and walked out into the lobby of the hotel. The clerk hailed Gabe, "Your cab is ready, sir."

"Thanks, Miho," he responded.

They walked out of the lobby and through the rotating doors. The hustle and bustle of Manaus City greeted them. Cars honked and tires whined on the pavement. Gabe opened the cab door and held Charlise's hand as she got in. He followed her.

"Where to, Senor?" the cabby asked.

"Rei do Churrasco," Gabe answered.

"Such a short ride, Senor. I know of a restaurant on the other side of town that serves great Italian food."

"That's okay. We want to walk home and get a bit of fresh air after dinner."

"As you wish, Senor," the cabby said as he pulled back onto the highway and headed south. The restaurant was only a mile from their hotel and even with relatively heavy traffic the drive was short. The cab stopped in front of the entrance to a brick two-story building with oval windows that looked out onto the highway.

As Gabe handed the driver his fare, the man grabbed Gabe's arm and said, "Be careful Senor. Death prowls tonight," then he smiled with a twinkle and continued, "May Christ be with you, good night."

"May Christ be with you," Charlise responded with Gabe saying, "Adios," as they left the cab.

"I didn't have the heart to tell him I'm agnostic," Gabe laughed.

"Sounded to me like he was trying to scare you into believing."

"He did sound kind of ominous," Gabe replied, "but you know what? It doesn't matter. I'm going to forget about religion and death and all those heavy things and have a fine meal with a beautiful woman." He opened the door for Charlise and they entered the café.

"Sounds like a plan to me," she smiled.

They stood before the maitre de's stand and waited to be seated. On either side of them sat rows of booths along the outer wall. The lighting was subdued with crystal chandeliers hanging above. The crystal sparkled and glistened blue and yellow. Classical music played softly in the background. At the moment it was one of Mozart's piano concertos. The place was half filled with other couples, all in formal attire.

"And I took you for a McDonald's kind of guy," Charlise joked.

Gabe laughed, "Why, because I'm a farm boy? I'd choose a fine wine and a great meal with Mozart playing over a double cheese burger with fries any day. Although I admit I'll miss the playground."

Charlise laughed, "I'm partial to Happy Meals."

Just then their waiter showed up. "Table for two?" he asked.

"Yes, please. Make it one away from the kitchen. Preferably in a nice quiet corner."

"Si, Senor," the waiter replied and led them down the rows of booths to the far end of the restaurant. He seated them on opposite sides of the table and handed them menus. "There's a nice ten-year old Chilean Cabernet Sauvignon this evening. Our manager just purchased a case at a very reasonable rate. May I bring you a bottle?"

Gabe looked at Charlise and she nodded assent. "Please," he said. When the waiter left he turned and said, "Sauvignon is a favorite. It has a sensuality and depth of flavor that other wines lack."

Charlise smiled, "It's a rare treat to find an aged wine in Manaus."

The waiter returned with a tray. On it stood an open bottle of wine and two glasses.

He set the tray on the table and poured a small sample into a glass and sloshed it around then held it up to Gabe. A lean fruity smell issued forth and his mouth watered. He took the glass from the waiter and tipped it up to the light letting the wine slide down the sides. It left gentle streaks, the sign of a fine wine. Gabe took a sip and a pleasantly deep, slightly smoky, grape flavor filled his mouth.

He waited a moment to savor the taste then said, "Great choice, sir."

The waiter smiled and took the glass from Gabe's hand. He filled it half way and handed it back. Next, he filled Charlise's glass. She smelled the wine, sipped, and nodded approval.

"This wine goes particularly well with the roasted pheasant in mushroom sauce," the waiter suggested. "The baked Cornish game hen with lemon herbs also compliments the Sauvignon. I'll leave the menus and be back shortly."

"Do you really like the wine?" Gabe asked.

"I really do. Cabernet Sauvignon is my favorite."

"This calls for a toast. May our food be as good as the wine and may the wind always be at out backs," he toasted.

Charlise replied, "May my company always be as enjoyable as it is tonight."

They tipped their glasses together with a soft clang and sipped, looking at each other with a smile of delight.

"We've known each for a while now and I hardly know anything about you," Charlise began, "Are you married?"

"Not anymore. I married during my college years. We were both young and impressionable. She thought I could provide her with the wealth and luxuries she was accustomed to and I was infatuated. I certainly didn't care about being wealthy or accumulating things. I was dedicated to my studies at that time and she was dedicated to herself. We lasted just over a year before we realized our mistake and separated. It was a mutual agreement. We parted friends, though.

What about you? I've noticed you're not sporting a wedding ring."

"I've never been married. In love a couple of times, maybe. But I always kept my heart under wraps," she sipped her wine and continued. "I guess I'm too particular. I want someone I can grow with. Not that I want to marry a priest or anything but I do want someone who'll let me be myself. Someone sure enough of themselves so they don't have to be male dominant. Those kind of men are few and far between. I do agree about acquiring things. Once the newness wears off, they're highly overrated."

"Any current relationships?" Gabe asked.

"I haven't had a date in six months. And you?"

"I'd be too embarrassed to tell you how long it's been since I went out with someone. I guess I work too much."

"So are you a workaholic or are you sublimating?"

"It's probably a combination of both. What about you?"

"I'd take a good book and box of chocolates over most men." They both laughed.

"Damn this wine is good," Gabe said beginning to relax for the first time in months. He took another sip. "Well, what's your pleasure?"

"That's a no brainer. I love pheasant in mushroom sauce especially with asparagus and wild rice. Sounds like the perfect meal."

"I can't argue with that. That's what I'll have." When the waiter returned, they ordered their meal and continued talking. "So you're a reader? What do you like to read?"

"I love historical fiction for leisure, but my tastes are really eclectic," Charlise said. "I usually read two books at a time, one fiction and one non-fiction. I just finished Jared Diamond's <u>Guns, Germs, and Steel</u>."

"I've read that. It sure puts the lie to racial superiority."

"Not that I ever believed any one race is superior, but you're right. And you, you've obviously read a lot. I can tell by your vocabulary and the fact that you're so knowledgeable about so many things."

"I use to read a lot of fiction but lately I've taken to reading biographies. I find it inspiring to read about other people's struggles. I just finished one about Jack London. What an amazing life he led. It was so full of adventure."

They continued talking. They talked of books they'd read and music they'd listened to and with each word and sip of wine they grew closer together. Eventually the waiter returned. He sat a serving tray on a stand before them. Both dishes were covered with a metal dome to keep the food warm. When he removed the cover, the smell of the food wafted out. The pheasant, smothered in a rich sauce that included several slices of Portobello mushrooms, looked delicious. The asparagus, covered in Hollandaise sauce, sat next to a generous helping of wild rice covered with gravy made from pheasant drippings. He sat the plates in front of them.

"May I get you anything else?" the waiter asked.

Gabe looked at Charlise who nodded a barely perceptible no so he replied, "No, thank you."

After the waiter left, they started eating. The food was cooked to perfection. The pheasant melted in their mouths. The sauce gave it a deep richness and the mushroom's exotic rareness added texture and flavor to the dish. The asparagus complimented the main course with a succulent vegetable taste and the rice was exquisite with its rich creamy gravy. Both of the scientists ate as voraciously as good manners would allow.

Neither person had eaten a fine meal in months, food had been of secondary importance. They ate quickly and soon found that two empty plates sat on the table.

Gabe looked at Charlise, "This is what life's all about. To suspend your work and struggles for an hour of fine wine and food."

"I couldn't agree more," Charlise said as Gabe split the remaining wine between the two glasses. They sipped quietly and listened to the music. They watched each other's lips and eyes and reveled in being together.

The spell was broken by the waiter. He brought a tray with the bill and handed it to Gabe.

"We're going Dutch on this aren't we?" Charlise asked.

"Unfortunately I'm the boss of this expedition. I hate to pull rank on you but this is on my dime. Of course, I do have a government credit card." He laughed and Charlise joined in.

After Gabe paid for their meal, they stepped out into the fresh night air. "Are we walking?" he asked.

"Sure."

The night air heightened their senses and prevented the after meal grogginess. The couple joined arms and walked. "I hate to ruin a perfect evening, but I need to talk to someone I can trust explicitly. I've decided that person is you," Gabe started.

"Thank you. You can't imagine how much that means to me."

"Don't thank me until you hear what I have to say."

"It doesn't matter what you have to say. I trust you, too. I've watched you since we've been working together. You're kind, intelligent, and well-educated. I enjoy your companionship. I would never willingly do anything to jeopardize our friendship."

He continued, "I feel the same way. Being with you has made dealing with the fear and anxiety so much easier. Lately, I've been getting the feeling that what is happening runs a lot deeper than we think. If the nano-bots are extraterrestrial, and I think they are, it's likely that we're being invaded. And when I ask myself why the aliens or whatever don't just exterminate all of us and be done with it, there's only one answer. I think our world is being terra-formed. They want to restore the earth so they can inhabit it.

Charlise held his arm a little tighter and replied, "If what you're saying is true, then why wouldn't they use a virus to get rid of us? And why would Rahula be immune to their efforts?"

"That puzzles me, too. Maybe they're trying to reduce the population to a more sustainable level. But my greatest fear is they want to subjugate humans and use them for their own purposes. Maybe they need workers to support their civilization."

"Possibly. So what do we do about it? You really have no evidence other than the nano-bots to support your ideas."

"You're right but the nano-bots are so advanced, they have to be extra-terrestrial. And what about the SARS virus? I think the silicone was a control chip."

"So what do we do about it?"

"Report our findings to Dr. Langley. If we're being invaded by aliens, someone needs to decide what to do. If the nano-bots are a new war weapon designed by the military, he'll also be able to flesh that out. He can inform the government and they can decide what to do."

"If it's an invasion there's probably nothing anyone can do but hide and hope for the best. But, if it's some kind of government or military conspiracy our lives will be at risk the minute you tell him."

"Possibly, but we have to do something. I trust my boss as much as I have any bureaucrat, but we could file a report and go into hiding until things get sorted out."

"I don't see that we have much choice," Charlise answered.

They fell silent with their own thoughts and kept walking. The spell of the evening was shattered. Impulsively, Gabe stopped and sought the comfort of Charlise's arms. They hugged as he whispered in her ear, "We'll stay together, no matter what happens."

"I'll hold you to that," she replied.

At the end of their walk, they stood in the hallway before Charlise's door. She looked at him and said, "Time to be together." She opened her door and Gabe followed her into the room.

Once inside, she turned and he caught her in his arms. They kissed. Gabe could feel her firm breasts against his chest. Let this moment last forever he thought.

After a few minutes, she pulled away and said, "Let me wash up and slip into something more sheer and revealing while you get in bed."

"Please tell me this isn't a dream," Gabe replied.

"If it is, I don't ever want to wake up."

Charlise entered the bathroom. Gabe turned the lights off except for the small lamp by the bed. He stripped to his underwear and climbed in bed. For the first time in days, he thought only about the here and now and being in this hotel room with Charlise. He smiled.

The door opened and her lithe figure was silhouetted against the light. He watched with anticipation as she approached the bed and threw back the covers. Charlise stood before the bed and let Gabe imagine what she looked like under the black lace nightie before she let it drop to the floor so he could see her fully naked. She sat on the bed and laid back. When she rolled over, they pressed against each other, warmth on warmth. Gabe put his arms around her and they kissed passionately. The heat between them heightened their arousal. Charlise could feel Gabe hard against her. She moved back so he could remove his underwear and when he was bare, she grabbed his member and guided it into her. They moved against each other in a rhythm of pleasure neither had experienced before. At the height of their sexual crescendo, two former strangers cried out in ecstasy. They fell back panting.

"God, that was good," Gabe said.

"Are you saying you had a religious experience?" Charlise teased

"Yes, I believe I did see God or at least felt him," Gabe laughed and she joined him.

They rolled back together after catching their breath and consummated their relationship again. It happened several times that night before they finally fell asleep with exhaustion.

Hours later, Gabe dreamed of being chased by a dark hooded figure. Charlise was waiting ahead on a jungle trail, beckoning and screaming for him to run. Paralyzed by fear and the chill of evil, he watched helplessly as the phantom stingray swooshed forward. He struggled to consciousness a split second before being overrun. He awakened to a dark room and the sound of Charlise's soft breathing. Rolling over he put his arm over her and sighed. The clock on the bed stand displayed 6:00 a.m.

As much as he hated to, he gently moved the covers back and slid out of bed. He placed the sheet and blanket back over Charlise and watched her sleep for a few minutes before he dressed and left quietly.

Back in his own room, Gabe removed his laptop from under the bed. He opened his email account to address and highlighted the name, Dr. Robert Langley; Department of the Centers for Disease Control. He typed a report detailing the team's findings and hit the send button.

21

L ogis was resting in his darkened quarters when Ship summoned him. "Logis, the humans have been alerted. Several
communications from the United States intra-governmental
agencies warn of our presence. Although they are not sure yet, they
suspect the euthobots are alien. There are several communiqués between government officials in the U.S. suggesting that all top level
executives retreat to underground bunkers."

"What? When did that happened?"

" I traced the source email back to 6:15 a.m. this morning from a
hotel in South America."

Ship continued, "The message was first sent to an office in Atlanta,
Georgia at approximately 6:35. From there it was transmitted to the
President who contacted his cabinet and other ranking officials
including certain Senators and members of Congress at 6:55. An
immediate decision is needed if these politicians are to be dealt with
before they can reach the underground bunkers. The President has
left the White House and may already be in hiding."

"Communicate your information to the Council and call for an
immediate vote to release the euthobots on the D.C. area," Logis
ordered.

Within seconds, Ship had contacted and informed the council
members of the situation. Within minutes, all twelve had punched

the yes button which caused the console in Logis's quarters to light up in a bright row of green.

"Target the city and fire when ready!" Logis commanded.

Ship programmed the coordinates and prepared to launch a large self -propelled hover-canister. Equipped with automatic guidance controls, the canister would travel too fast to be detected by the primitive defense systems of the humans in time to be shot down. Ship opened a portal and the canister blasted out of her belly. It shot around the moon and traveled down through earth's atmosphere in a matter of minutes. It stopped abruptly over the Capitol Building and then burst, spewing the bots like an exploding shotgun shell.

The Benwarian engineers included the new generation of bots equipped with biospectrometers for this attack. Though they had been working around the clock, they were days away from perfecting the self-replicating bots needed to mount a world-wide attack, but they had been able to produce enough of the machines to pacify the area in and around Washington D.C.

The machines were designed with long-lasting fuel cells, giving them a range of several miles. Once a victim's vital signs were extinguished, they would burrow back out and attack again. Theoretically, these improved bots could exterminate several humans before their fuel cells were depleted. The new machines put the governing elite of the U.S. in grave peril.

In the spirit of bipartisanship, President Lacsite called the minority leader of the Senate Republicans first to inform him of the C.D.C.'s findings. Not wanting to cause undue alarm, he eschewed a government wide alert. The mysterious deaths in the forest and on the oceans had made the world anxious and afraid. An alert would be like throwing a match on an open can of gasoline.

Senator Elefunt heard the ring tone of his cell-phone. It surprised him to see that the call came from the White House. "Hello, Mr. President. How are you?"

"Fine, listen as a precautionary measure we need to evacuate the Senate buildings. I was just contacted by Dr. Langley of the Centers for Disease Control. The deaths in the rainforests may be caused by some sort of alien machine. It might be some kind of invasion."

Senator Elefunt's pulse quickened as the President continued, "It's my recommendation that all Senators and Congressmen evacuate the above ground facilities and retreat to the Capitol's protective bunkers. They'll be sealed in sixty minutes. Have your staff quietly spread the word."

"Are you making this public, Mr. President?"

"Going to ground is only a precaution. I'm not going to cause a worldwide panic so no, let's keep quiet for now. I'm having my staff contact individual legislators."

The President ended the connection. Overwhelmed with fear and concern for himself, the Senator ran to his outer office and addressed his secretaries and staff. "We've got an emergency! Everyone needs to head to the bomb shelters immediately! Take only what you can carry and run."

"What is it?" his wide-eyed executive assistant asked.

"I don't have time to explain. The bunker closes in an hour. Hurry!"

"What do I tell my family?" one of his aides asked.

"Everyone just get to the bunker. You can contact your families from there!" the Senator shouted. President Lacsite can alert the rest of the Senate he thought, I'm saving myself.

His staff already on edge, the Senator's urgency caused panic. Laptops were slammed shut and thrown in their cases by some aides. Others crammed papers and personal effects into carrying bags and rushed to the door.

His executive assistant was the first one out of the room. He held the door open as the Senator's entourage exited and turned left, running down the corridor.

The Senator stepped out last with his personal body guard accompanying him. Just as he started to break into a run, someone yelled from behind.

"Hey Jim! What's going on?"

He turned to see Democratic Senator Muelson's puzzled expression. "Weren't you contacted?"

"Contacted? About what?" Muelson could see the panic on Elephunt's face.

"I don't have time to explain. The President has called an emergency evacuation."

"Why?"

"We don't have much time. The bunker will be sealed in less than an hour."

When Senator Elefunt started to run again, Muelson grabbed his arm. "I want an explanation. What the hell is going on?"

Visibly panicking, Elephunt's bodyguard broke Muelson's hold by chopping down with both arms. He drew his gun and pulled the hammer back shouting, "Step away from the Senator."

Muelson's overzealous guard tore his thirty-eight from its holster when he saw the cocked pistol then stepped back and fired in one motion. The bullet hit the other man in the arm and the gun clattered away. Elephunt's guard hit the ground writhing and groaning.

The gun was now trained on Senator Elephant. "I demand an explanation!" Muelson shouted.

"We're being invaded! The President ordered an evacuation of all above ground chambers. Now please, let me go so I can get to the shelter before it's sealed off."

"You bastard! Why didn't you hit the alarm so everyone can escape?" Muelson yelled as Elephunt resumed running, leaving his guard bleeding on the floor.

Senator Elephunt ignored the question and ran wide-eyed and sweating.

Muelson moved rapidly down the hall to the alarm system. He pulled the lever down and a siren sounded. "Rah, rah, rah, rah. Rah, rah, rah, rah ..." Red lights pulsated. The signal alerted everyone in the building to head for the subway beneath the Senate chambers so they could be evacuated to an underground bunker.

Next, he motioned to his guard and together they helped the wounded man to his feet. Senator Muelson tore off his tie and used it as a tourniquet. He wrapped it above the wound and pulled it tight then draped the man's good arm over his shoulder and moved down the hallway.

Doors throughout the Senate building were being opened as

people rushed out. The corridor filled with a mass of bodies, jostling and pushing. A panicked mass moved around the three men. All headed for the stairs leading to the subway. They were so intent on getting to the shelter that an explosion and slight rumble barely registered on anyone's consciousness.

22

*T*he canister exploded, spewing the bots throughout the city.
They attacked the Senate Hart Office Building first. The pride
of the Senate with its contemporary design and marble facade,
it housed over seven thousand staff members and fifty senators.
The white rectangular building with tight energy efficient windows
blocked the bots entrance temporarily. They hit against the windows
like gnats, attracted by the sewer brown auras of the politicians now
displaying the brackish red of fear. The heightened adrenaline of those
fleeing to save themselves energized the bots like angry wasps.

Equipped with sensors and guidance systems, the machines
searched for any opening larger than the point of a pin. Thousands
poured into the Senate building underneath the front doors, finally
gaining entrance behind the exodus.

The bots attacked the back of the crowd. They hit the people
fleeing through the corridors in waves and worked themselves
forward. Their infrared spectrometers guided each to a different
target. One victim felt a sharp pricking pain and slapped at his neck.
A few seconds later he fell, hit the ground and died. Many others
were so intent on fleeing they didn't feel anything. Bodily functions
froze and they collapsed.

The deaths of the first victims caused sheer panic. The bots were
too small to be seen which made them all the more terrifying and
the metallic smell of the bots heightened the fear. The evacuees felt
the danger behind and pushed forward. A lobbyist in a black Armani

suit tripped and was trampled underfoot. Many others fell after the bots burrowed into their neck and disconnected their brain. Their screams were cut short by death.

One corpulent Senator, weighing over three hundred pounds, ran wild eyed and sweating down the corridor. With his sewer brown aura shooting red rays, he pushed into the back of the crowd causing people to fall face first. He fell on top of an older women crushing her then rolled over onto his knees while several people scrambled over the top of him. Bellowing, he shoved himself up and pushed those near him back. A gap opened momentarily but closed as the mass of bodies rushed from the bots.

The Senator looked backward, people were dropping as if they'd been shot. He renewed his efforts to move forward by pushing against the human wall in front of him. Wide-eyed and red faced, he shoved and screamed as people fell against his legs. He tripped face-first onto the floor. His gigantic stomach kept his arms and legs from gaining leverage and they moved uselessly back and forth as he tried to get up.

The euthobots struck as the Senator struggled. He felt a sharp prick before his eyes bulged outward. He tasted the bite of tin foil before the machines severed his medulla amygdala. The Senator evacuated his bowels in a sodden mess that matched the color of his aura.

Corpses filled the halls of the Senate building as the euthobots worked their way to the stairs. The machines killed the people at the top, causing a chain reaction. Those behind lurched forward, knocking those in front to the floor. Like dominoes, scores fell, filling the stairs with bodies. Many who fell were smothered as others piled on top. Those who survived were attacked by the bots before they could recover and get up.

Those at the bottom of the steps spilled out into an antechamber where people were waiting for security clearance to enter the subway cars. A cascade of falling bodies pushed into the room, jamming one against another. The bots fed on the fear of the crowded mass as the now bright red auras beckoned them forward.

Senator Muelson stood before the sliding doors with his security card held up against the scanner as his guard propped the man wounded earlier up. They could feel the carnage behind them. The doors slid open and they rushed forward into the car that led to safety. Soldiers stood on each side and pushed people back with their rifles as the doors tried to close. The people crowded and pushed, overwhelming the soldiers and jamming the doors.

Bots filled the chamber and zeroed in on their targets. They launched as Muelson and his men tried to push people away and close the subway doors by hand. Everyone, including those in the car, went down at the same time. Senators, lobbyists, doctors, lawyers, secretaries and aides became lifeless victims of the invasion.

The chamber and subway cars filled with dead. More than eight thousand bodies were strewn throughout the Hart Building. When nothing moved, the bots exited the building and joined the killing outside.

Already countless pedestrians lay dead on the pavement. Traffic stood still and thousands of wrecked automobiles littered the city and jammed the roads; their dead occupants cooked inside as the weltering sun turned the vehicles into ovens.

The Capitol Building, the Chambers of Congress, and countless other governmental buildings were cleansed of those who hadn't found refuge quickly enough. The bots effectively eliminated the federal government of the United States in less than an hour. Even the nine judges of the Supreme Court lay dead in their chambers.

Miraculously, there were survivors. The Dalai Lama and those of his delegation who followed his teachings lived. Calm, unafraid of death, the light of their auras kept the bots at bay.

Many children were also spared. Those who had received the nurturing and proper nutrition to develop a bright and shimmering aura were ignored by the machines.

Adults who had come to the capital to champion causes greater than themselves, who were selfless, those whose aura contained light, lived. For the most part though, a majority of Washington D.C.'s inhabitants were eliminated. The only other survivors hunkered inside of their underground tombs.

A mass exodus from D.C. started when the news media reported the attack. One media crew flew a helicopter over the area. The whirling blades kept the bots away for several minutes. Programmed to adjust, the machines swarmed together and came up under the belly and into the cab, killing all four crew members. The craft nosed down, dived, and hit the highway below in a fiery crash.

The attack ended two hours and forty minutes after it started. A precise rectangle ten miles long and eight miles wide had been cleared of humans deemed unfit for life by the euthobots.

Inside the Senate bunker, Elefunt huddled with the over two hundred other governmental officials who had evacuated in time. The Senator's forehead beaded with sweat as he breathed in ragged gasps, exhausted from his exertions.

Vid-bots relayed streaming video and audio records back to Ship and the Benwarians. The machines had been imbedded with the euthobots to monitor the invasion.

Logis watched the cleansing of D.C. with abhorrence. It sickened him to see the pain and terror. After a few minutes the images ran together so he shifted focus to the Hart Building. The expressions of abject fear, taken close-up by the v-bots, shocked the Benwarian leader.

The scenes on the stairway were particularly macabre. The cascade of human bodies struggling to flee and faces smashing into the stairs with a bloody thump caused deep remorse and shame. Viewing the slaughter became unbearable. He regretted ever being chosen the leader of Benwar.

Ship sensed Logis's angst. "Are you well?"

"No Ship. I'm not. I'm overseeing mass murder."

"It's your duty. Only fifty percent of the people in this country view global warming as a man-made threat. Collapse of the planet is imminent without our intervention. The human population must be reduced to sustainable levels to ensure the species' survival. We are saving humanity, not destroying it."

"Words can't erase the horror."

"Yes, but humans will survive and, more importantly, so will your people. Let me show you something," Ship said, activating the video screen in Logis's room.

A darkened planet appeared on the screen. As the view enlarged, severe atmospheric disturbances swept from left to right. A white and yellow mass of smoke and dust rushed across the face of the planet.

The view shifted to the surface where gale force winds blew. Great masses of blowing sand cut visibility to a few feet. The wind roared as it ploughed the bone-dry ground, enlarging the great yellowish-gray mass that propelled itself from one pole to the other as the gigantic cloud of particles moved around the planet. Rocks disintegrated into gravel and became sand under the atomic force of the wind.

"As instructed, I launched a probe after we left Lemmus and these pictures were relayed back. You see the planet we left. It has been reduced to a barren wasteland, utterly devoid of life and it will degrade even further. This process has already started on the planet below, therefore, it is imperative that you complete the mission you were chosen for," Ship intoned.

Ship's cold comfort did nothing to lift Logis's spirits. Seeing the destroyed world of Lemmus actually deepened his gloom. His home and almost everything he cherished swirled in the dust around the planet. Logis needed something besides the cold steel of logic to make him feel better. He had felt an oppressing emptiness since his reanimation, but he knew Ship's intent so he said, "Thank you. I understand."

"Good because we need to focus on the task at hand. There are still primitives in the bunkers that need to be dealt with."

Ship's relentless pursuit of purpose wearied Logis. He sighed deeply, "Summon the General," Logis commanded. Immediately Battier's countenance replaced the decay of Lemmus on the view screen.

"The survivors below ground need to be exterminated. Will you do that?"

"As you wish," Battier replied with a slightly exasperated expression. "It will be accomplished within the hour."

The General's view screen went blank when Logis broke contact. He didn't ask to use weapons, he wanted Logis to see that the euthobots were no more humane than his approach. "Ship, are the laser drills we used to take core samples mounted on the disc ships?" Battier asked

"No, but they can be remounted."

"Contact the Engineering Department and have it done. We'll laser a hole through the top of the bunkers and pour some euthobots in."

23

*T*he Americans didn't plan on dying without a fight. They knew that an alien species had mounted an attack on the capital. A drone, launched at the beginning of the attack had relayed a streaming video back to the bunkers and those with strong stomachs had watched the deaths of thousands.

Since retreating, the President had been in close contact with the military leaders hunkered down beneath the Pentagon. He instructed General Payton of the Civil Defense Administration to arm all nuclear warheads. Teams in the silos were given permission to launch their missiles at anything entering U.S. airspace.

N.A.S.A. had discovered the gigantic spaceship hiding on the other side of the moon. All military eyes and weaponry were now positioned in that direction. If anything approached earth, it would be fired upon.

One silo commander had been able to gauge the speed of the disc ships. Lt. Pearson had watched the films of the invasion of D.C. many times. Even though the canister seemingly appeared from nowhere, its arrival in U.S. air space had registered on his radar. Plotting the exact coordinates of where it entered the atmosphere and where it exploded gave him a distance to work with. By subtracting the time of its entry from the time the explosion occurred, he was able to calculate how long the canister had taken to travel the distance from entry to the explosion point. He then ascertained the speed of the canister by dividing this distance by the time.

Pearson assumed that any space vehicle would travel at the same speed. Using that assumption, he charted several points near the earth's atmosphere and their distance from his silo. Using projections of the ship's trajectory would enable his computer to calculate when the ship would reach a certain point at a certain time and missiles fired at precisely the right moment would have a good chance of hitting the oncoming spaceship. The heat seeking abilities of the missile and the use of multiple warheads would increase the odds of success.

Pearson's calculations were based on speculation and instinct, but he was the only commander with the initiative to act on his own. All the other silo commanders simply waited for the order to fire.

An hour after the alien attack, the silos registered four vague blips on radar and launched their war heads as the disc ships approached, but the missiles were too slow and were launched too late to hit the shuttles. They simply shot into space and exploded.

Pearson waited until one of the ships intersected a plotted coordinate. He fired at the intercepting point just outside earth's atmosphere. He watched the missile shoot skyward until it made contact. A nuclear explosion filled the sky with a bright fiery yellow flash followed by white smoke blasting in two directions. A smile of surprise crossed Pearson's lips.

Logis watched with interest. The disc ships were launched and on their way. Within a matter of minutes the cleansing of Washington D.C. would be over. Afterwards, he would have Ship administer a sedative for a much needed rest.

The sight of the shuttle exploding jarred him out of his complacency. There was a contingency of four Benwarians aboard that ship, dead because he had underestimated the ingenuity of the Americans. He should have listened to Battier.

"Ship, what just happened?"

"One of the shuttles was destroyed. Several missiles were fired and all but that one missed. One of the primitives is more intelligent than we thought."

"Yes. One of the Americans has a little ingenuity. Bring yourself into position and fire a damper shell."

Ship immediately left the dark side of the moon. Once it had a clear path it fired the damper shell. It shot toward earth, entered the atmosphere and exploded. The shock waves sent out by the blast reverberated in the sky above and effectively ended all intra-planetary communications.

"Now, destroy the missile silos," Logis said.

Ship opened a bank of thirty ports as she adjusted her tail to maneuver broadside of the planet. Each of the laser cannons locked on a different silo and fired. A thin red line shot from each gun, drawing a line from the barrel directly to its target. The endpoint of the line became an expanding red dot and then exploded causing a small area on the surface to burn. The barrels of the guns re-shifted and fired again taking out more weapons. This repeated itself until there was only one silo left.

As Ship attacked, the disc shuttles were still positioning themselves over the D.C. shelters. Battier contacted the shuttle commanders and instructed them to abort their mission. The three ships stopped in mid-air, hovered for a second and shot back, straight up and away from the laser paths. They left earth's atmosphere and darted around the aft side of the spaceship. Ship opened the docking bays and the shuttles entered her tail, skidding to a stop inside.

Once the ships were secured, Ship revolved forty-five degrees to the left and faced the planet head-on. Now two panels underneath the rectangular view panel slid back, exposing the photon cannons. They targeted the Pentagon and Whitehouse bunkers and fired.

Inside the Presidential bunker, President Lacsite watched the radar screen. He smiled broadly when one of the shuttles blew up. The people inside the shelter raised their fists and cheered. Lacsite kept his eyes on the screen and his elation changed to disappointment as he watched the other missiles explode harmlessly. The alien ships plummeted downward and were now above the city, they stopped, reversed course and disappeared.

Lacscite spoke into his headset, " General Payton, good work! You got one of the bastards. Maybe we scared them off."

"On the contrary, Mr. President. The alien ship is now positioned above the moon. It fired …"

Their communications abruptly burst into a static that caused President Lacsite to throw his headphones down. "What the hell was that?" he said to those around him.

The power generator stopped and the lights went out. Lacsite sat in the dark for a second. He heard his death approach with a thump. The tremendous rumbling sound went unheard as the shelter imploded into a gigantic crater.

Ship's missile burrowed into the ground, struck the outer walls deep under the surface, and an area the size of several football fields collapsed into a large crater. Another whish and several more torpedoes hurtled toward D.C. Again they burrowed, caused implosions and several more craters appeared on Earth's surface.

Senator Elefunt watched the view screen as the aliens approached. When he saw the ships stop and dart away his sense of impending doom lifted. Maybe I'll survive this. I didn't think anything could happen to me he thought. Suddenly, pitch black filled the room and the screen went blank. He felt the walls shake and rumble as the first of the torpedoes struck.

The attack wasn't over, his heart raged against his chest as he realized the aliens were back. He heard a dull thud and felt the impact of the torpedoes before he died. His scream ended with the implosion.

24

*L*ogis watched as the last of organized American resistance was snuffed out. "Ship, send a shuttle to the remaining silo and transport its occupants back here. Have them placed in one of the detention rooms. I want to talk to the human responsible for destroying one of our vessels."

"May I ask why?"

"I find it intriguing that one of the primitives could be so ingenious. I want to run a spectrograph and conduct an interview, gain a deeper understanding of these humans."

Lieutenant Pearson and his crew cheered when the ship exploded. They shook hands and then prepared to leave the silo. They gathered documents, backed up data files, and gathered personal belongings. As they were preparing to leave, contact with the outside world ended. All communications systems and power sources shut down at the same time. Even the back-up generator stopped.

Pearson fumbled in the dark until he found the battery powered radio. It was set to an all news station but when he turned it on, it crackled in his ears. He turned the dial, trying to find another station, but static filled the airways. He switched from FM to AM and the static crackled even louder. They sat in the dark and wondered had happened.

Pearson felt uneasy. His skin tingled, his temperature rose and he felt uncomfortable like his body was falling apart. He looked at his fellow soldiers and they seemed to be breaking up. The world turned black for a second and he lost consciousness.

Lieutenant Pearson awoke in a dimly lit room. Strapped to a padded table, he turned his head from left to right and saw his other two crew members strapped to tables on either side of him. His head ached and every muscle in his body trembled.

He tried to speak but his jaws wouldn't respond. Someone entered the room. He struggled against the straps ineffectually, there was no strength or control. He couldn't distinguish who or what stood behind him but he felt the injection being administered. The non-responsive muscles seemed to relax. Pearson wiggled fingers and toes and they jerked in response.

An orderly in a white body suit moved to each of his companions. He watched as they received an injection. Pearson sensed movement as a vague outline exited the room. He opened his mouth and tried to speak. His tongue was thick, barely controllable.

"Aaaarrr, Aaaar, oooo, gthuys aalllrrightt?" Pearson turned his head left and then right and saw a response from both men.

The lights gradually brightened as his muscle control returned. The light intensified as his bodily functions strengthened. Gradually, the lights illuminated the whole room. The sterile white of the walls, floor, and ceiling reminded him of a military hospital. Only the silver gurneys they were strapped to brought relief from the white sterility.

"Where are we, Lieutenant?" his second in command asked.

"In some kind of hospital?"

"Hospital? Where?" the man looked around nervously.

"Calm down, Corporal Denison. Take a deep breath. We're safe for the moment. I don't know where we are either."

Pearson's demeanor reduced Denison's anxiety only for a second. "You don't think were on some kind of spaceship? God what if we're going to be experimented on or tortured?" He struggled against the straps in wide-eyed terror.

"Suck it up, soldier. There isn't a lot we can do about the situation but wait," Pearson replied.

Ship was monitoring the humans' vital signs. The adrenaline levels of all three elevated as they regained consciousness. The galvanic responses of the two on either side of Pearson indicated a high level of fear and anxiety. Their hearts beat rapidly, eyes were dilated, and sweat streamed from their pores.

The one in the middle gained control of his fears. His heart rate fell and adrenaline levels dropped as he tried to calm his comrades. Ship calmed them by administering a sedative through the straps on their arms. After a few minutes, their heart rate slowed.

Logis watched the men through a view screen. He heard Pearson talking to his men. It was apparent that he was in charge. "Ship, dim the lights and have the two men on the flanks removed."

The room darkened to almost pitch black. Pearson watched as the door opened and two beings entered. "What're you doing?" he asked. There was no response.

Corporal Denison and Private Loess barely stirred as the orderlies wheeled them out of the room. "Where are you taking them?" he shouted. "Don't! They didn't do anything. I'm responsible for downing your ship." There was no answer as they passed through the door and it shut behind them.

Logis listened and waited for Pearson to regain his composure. His spectrograph displayed anger but no fear. Containment would have to be maintained until he calmed down again.

Pearson heard the door open again and someone entered. A man started talking in the dark. "Greetings, my name is Logis. You are safe. We have no intention of harming you or your companions." Pearson's expression of hostility and anger caused Logis to smile.

"What'd you do with my men?" he asked with an edge to his voice.

"It's okay. They've been placed in another room."

"What about my country? Has it been destroyed? What about my family and friends? Are they still alive?"

"Your family's safe for the time being. I'm not sure about your friends but I can tell you that we have no intention of destroying your country. It puzzles me that you're not concerned with the rest of the world."

Pearson was visibly relieved. "My family and country come first. I vowed to protect and serve the U.S.A.."

"Unfortunately your country as you know it no longer exists."

"What?" tears welled in Pearson's eyes. "I thought you said you had no intention of destroying it."

"Physically, the area you refer to has been unharmed. It's the idea of the United States that has been destroyed."

Pearson's anger exploded, "How could you destroy the greatest nation to ever exist!" he shouted. "We're the bastion of freedom and individual rights! My country has done nothing to your people."

"I have been studying earth and its civilizations for quite some time now. By any objective measure your country and most of its population are self-centered and arrogant. These high ideals you speak of apply only to an elite few at the expense of the many. The extremes of wealth and poverty found in your society would never exist in an enlightened culture. You live in a land of surplus as people around the world starve. Yours is a society of greed and materialism. The espoused tenet of individual rights translates into promoting self-interest over the greater good."

Pearson remained quiet for a moment. "So why are you here? What do you want with us?"

"We're here to save your dying planet and to save ourselves and humanity as well."

"I don't believe you," Pearson interrupted. "You've killed too many people."

"Unfortunately the deaths are necessary. Earth is severely overpopulated. Without our efforts the planet will spiral into chaos."

"How do you know that?"

"We came from a planet very similar to yours. Our world was destroyed by environmental indifference and overpopulation. Only the beings on this ship survived. Your world suffers from the same diseases. It is dying from neglect and abuse. While we failed to save our own planet, we will save yours."

"You're going to destroy the human race to save the planet?"

"No. We plan to reduce the human population to sustainable levels."

"And you get to decide who lives and who dies?" Pearson replied with disgust.

"In a way, yes. We will save those who try to understand the world around them and live accordingly."

"And how do you determine who they are?"

"Every living being possesses an aura. It's the light that emanates from a person's soul. We developed a spectrometer that can read the different colors of light and their intensity. This allows us to determine a human's basic personality. We will seek to save those who give off the yellow-white light of truth, understanding, and compassion."

"So you'll save only Christians?"

"Not exactly. In fact, most so called "Christians" have the most rigid auras of all. A person's religion seems to have little effect on the color of their aura. We'll save mostly children. They still have a malleable aura that shimmers and changes. It's not too late to educate them."

"So what do you want with me?"

"A better understanding of Earthlings. I want to know how someone intelligent enough to best the Benwars has come to be the person you are. I have examined your aura. It burns with the red of aggressiveness and the brackish purple of religiosity. It shimmers very little. You're culture bound and rigid in your thinking."

"If I'm not fit for survival, why should I tell you anything? You're just going to kill me anyway."

"Not necessarily. You do have some small patches of light breaking through the dark. If I have your straps removed will you talk to me?"

"What choice do I have?"

"Ship, release the straps," Logis commanded. The straps around Pearson's head, arms, legs and chest retracted. He stretched and then tried to sit up. Head spinning, he fell back onto the gurney. Taking a deep breath, he rolled to his side, placed his legs over the edge of the table and levered himself to a sitting position.

After the spinning subsided, Pearson negotiated, "If I talk to you will you spare my crew?" He had been taught never to give anything to the enemy without getting something in return.

"I've run a spectrum-analysis of their auras. Both seem fluid enough to be brought to the light. If you talk to me, I promise to do everything I can to save them." Logis smiled. This human could be destroyed by a nod of the head and yet he tried to save his friends. His altruism is admirable Logis thought.

Pearson knew he bargained from a position of weakness so he agreed. "Okay, we'll talk. Wait. You're not going to poke, prod, and torture us are you?"

"We're not like your President Crass. Benwarians do not torture. We believe that no living thing should be exposed to unnecessary pain. All life is sacred. So you can begin by telling me about yourself."

Unless there's a conflict of interest, Pearson thought to himself and replied, "I was born in the mid-western United States, in the state of Kansas. My parents owned a small dairy farm outside of Topeka. They raised me to believe in God and my country."

"Which God? Earth has so many."

"The God of the Bible with Jesus Christ as my Savior."

"I'm sorry but I read that book. It produced no clear picture of who or what God is. In fact, in the Old Testament he is a vengeful boogey man. In the New Testament he is kind and forgiving. It is full of contradictions."

"I was raised a Baptist. I believe in the God I was told to!" Pearson said forcefully. "Whosoever believes in Jesus Christ as their Savior shall have everlasting life and shall enter the Kingdom of Heaven!"

"What about those who have never been exposed to the Word as you call it?"

"They'll find a place in purgatory."

"Ah, the place between heaven and hell. And who exactly is this Jesus Christ?"

"He is the Son of God. He was crucified and rose from the dead. Those who are born again by accepting Christ will have their sins washed away."

"I see. How do you know Jesus is the son of God?"

"It says so in the Bible. The Bible is the Word of God."

"So your God is in a book full of words. So your God is words?"

"The Bible was written by man but was God-inspired. It explains what God requires of us while we're here on earth. The Bible is the Word of God!"

"If the Bible was written by man, how do you know it was God inspired?"

"Because I have faith."

"And if I told you that we have performed a manu-analysis of the Bible and cross-referenced it with older historical sources to find that much of the writings are borrowed from earlier sources?"

"It is God-inspired!"

"And if I told you that our analysis of the Bible and the beginnings of the Christian Church point to a rigid hierarchy of a priestly class? Priests who were un-kept and dirty. Priests who thought the universe revolved around the earth?"

"Why are you attacking my religion?"

"Ah. To attack would be to actively point out the fallacies of your beliefs. I'm merely informing you of our findings."

"Believe me, I take great comfort in my religion. No matter what you do to me, I will find my place in the afterlife."

"And what about this life? Doesn't an unquestioning belief in doctrine block all inquiry and discovery about the true nature of God?"

"God has been revealed through the Word that is the Bible. That is enough! I seek no further!"

"Ah. Your faith is unshaken. It shields you from logical thought. It gives you strength and succor. And what of the unbelievers?"

"If they have received the Word and reject God, they shall find their place in hell."

"Do you see what reducing God to words does? You have just presumed to speak for God. Priests also presume to speak for God. It gives them great power over others. It sets one man above another. There is no exchange of views. No fleshing out of ideas about what God really is. In fact, some beliefs seemed to be pulled out of thin air.

For instance, many Christians believe in the rapture. Some even believe that a spaceship will arrive to transport all believers to heaven. What if I told you we are the rapture?"

Pearson's eyes grew wide, "Are you here to transport us to heaven?" he asked with a hope and yearning in his eyes.

"No, we're here to save Mother Earth and the best of the human race," Logis replied. He paused and then continued, "Listen carefully to what I'm going to say. All Benwars strive to understand the reason for our existence. We also seek God, but no Benwar would suggest complete understanding of an infinite being. Your God is too small. You have reduced God into a concrete being that is understandable and finite.

An unquestioning belief such as yours is a belief in doctrine. It is institutionalized thinking. Words quantify God when reality should. Our scans of members of fundamentalist churches show a hideous unchanging aura. A dark cocoon envelops all the colors of their aura. The rigidity of their spectrograph indicates that they are incapable of personal growth and development. Their beliefs shield them from the angst of existence. Unquestioning belief gives them security and strength and oftentimes prevents rational thought and acceptance of others.

Our spectrum-analysis indicates that only a handful of those belonging to a fundamentalist religion will survive the purge. Accepting what is not provable as truth makes for a dull aura that attracts our euthobots."

"And what are euthobots?"

"I'm sure you're familiar with nano-technology. Our scientists developed nano-bots equipped with spectrometers that read the colors of a person's aura. These readings are then used to select those people who will live or die. As I explained earlier, those with enough light in their auras to shimmer will live, those with rigid auras will die. The euthobots carry out a person's sentence by burrowing into the base of a person's brain and severing it from the body."

Person's eyes narrowed with disapproval, "Achtung, Heir Hitler. What you're doing is Nazi Germany all over again."

The words drove into Logis like a knife. A small gasp escaped him. "I'm aware of the parallels. I can only say that our purpose is to save not destroy. All humans will die without our intervention. We were confronted with the question of whether to kill the many to save the few or eradicate all humans and take the planet for our own. The latter would have been the easiest solution. Some of the Council suggested it, but it would have also violated Benwarian principles. A majority of the Council voted to save humanity.

Agonizing over our decision, it was decided that we needed a way to determine those humans able to change their views and opinions as reality dictated, people aware of their limited existence, who sought the truth.

These euthobots see no economic, cultural, racial, or occupational distinctions. People of all nationalities, races, and religions will be saved or exterminated according to the amount of light in their auras. There will be no hiding or dissembling, an aura tells exactly what a person is. Those who understand that the human condition is the same for everyone and reach for the light will be spared."

Logis continued, "I'm afraid my time with you is up, my duties beckon. Let we leave you with one question. The earth is dying from the disease of human overpopulation, how would you solve the problem? Think long and hard my friend." With that Logis offered his hand.

Pearson looked at it and turned away. "It's not right!"

Logis shrugged and left the room. He returned to his quarters and asked Ship to read and display Pearson's aura on the overhead. When it came up, the colors displayed were almost identical to before, but the cocoon had lightened and there was a slight shimmering.

There's still hope, he thought as Pearson's words echoed in his mind. It wasn't right he thought, I've been indoctrinated to carry out my mission as surely as the Earthling has been trained to be Baptist.

Pearson lacked the education necessary to be anything different from what he was. Logis knew exactly what he was. A dark cloud fell over his soul. His eyelids drooped and the heaviness of his burden drove him to the bed.

Ship's biosensors indicated a severe drop in Logis's energy levels. She administered a mood-regulator through his body suit. "You are the Chosen One. The surviving Benwarians depend on your leadership for survival. Remember you're father and mother, completion of your mission honors them," she repeated over and over again until the message and the anti-depressant lifted his mood.

Pearson sat in his room and thought. When he first saw Logis, he noticed the subtle light that emanated from the alien's whole body. He had never encountered such serenity and intelligence. He had had to fight to remember that this was the enemy, an enemy that had killed millions of humans and wanted to colonize earth.

But the more Logis spoke the more Pearson was able to discern the logic of what he said. After their discussion he knew that Earth really was in peril. So what would he do? He tried to put himself in Logis's place and when he did, he agreed with Logis's reasoning. It was the first time in years that he had put himself in someone else's shoes.

But still, God gave man dominion over Earth and all its creatures. If the planet came to an end that was God's plan. Could God's plan for man have changed?

No. Man's trials on Earth tested faith. The righteous who kept the faith would find their place in heaven. This was the Word and the Word was God. Man should not be deceived by earthly desires.

Maybe Logis was Satan, the Father of Lies. Maybe his faith was being tested. Maybe everything the alien said was a lie. The Ten Commandments stated that thou shall not kill and yet the Benwarians killed millions. How could they possibly be people of light when murder was dark and savage?

And yet somehow he trusted Logis; the soul reflected in his eyes displayed a kindness and empathy. There was a profound sadness there also. Satan would have a glint of evil in his. He would be unable to manage the sad part.

For the first time in his entire life, Pearson was experiencing existential angst. If what the Benwarian said was true then his whole life was based on myth. What is God? What is man's purpose on earth? How do you find truth? Doubt was a new experience for him. One he didn't appreciate. Mentally twisting in the wind physically twisted his insides. He found himself furiously pacing around the room, wishing he had been killed instead of captured.

25

*A*fter sending the email informing Dr. Langley of the team's findings, Gabe returned to the hotel room. He knocked on Charlise's door with anticipation. He smiled, thinking about last night.

She answered with a smile to match his. Her hair was pulled back with reading glasses perched on the end of her nose. "Hi! Is the honeymoon over?"

"Not for the next hundred years," he laughed.

"Well then, I guess you can come in."

She swung the door wide and they hugged. "You sent the report?"

"Yeah, now what do we do?"

"The hotel has great room service. Let's order breakfast and enjoy some time together before we decide."

"I'd like that."

Charlise picked up the phone and ordered breakfast. "I brewed some coffee," she said and poured him a cup and then one for herself. She held her cup up, "Last night was wonderful."

He clinked his cup against hers, "I had a religious experience. I think they call it The Rapture." Laughing they took a sip together and sat down at the table.

"Only the second coming?" she teased. "Fixing your coffee reminded me of my childhood. I used to spend a lot of time with my father," Charlise started, "It was always my job to get his coffee in the morning. Even if it was six o'clock in the morning, I got up just for his smile and hug. He made me feel like the most important person in the world. I had forgotten that feeling until now."

"Thanks. You deserve to be important," Gabe said then continued, "My father would have been gone by that time. He got up everyday at 4:00 a.m. to milk cows. My mornings were spent with my mother. She would get me up at 6:30 with a hot breakfast ready. This was our time together. She would ask about my life and school. She listened to my troubles and tried helping me the best she could. After we had eaten, I helped my dad with chores.

Growing up on a farm taught responsibility. The livestock had to be fed, watered, and doctored. Not doctoring something or not feeding it at a crucial time could weaken the animal enough to threaten its survival. During calving season, we had to check on the cows continually. There were a couple times when we lost animals from not being around when they calved or from not catching a sick one. I was taught that irresponsibility causes death."

"That explains why you're so dependable and steady," said Charlise. "Your sense of responsibility is a quality I admire."

"Thanks, I sound boring when you put it that way," Gabe said. "Maybe it's time to quit being so responsible and live a little bit. I've always structured my life with work and duty. Now these things don't seem so important."

"Don't tell me you're going to revert to being an irresponsible teenager," Charlise smiled. "Dad always cautioned against getting involved with a ne'er do well."

Gabe laughed, " I grew up with the old adages, "Never quit one job until you have another one to go to" , Or "A man working for wages never gets ahead." Good old Depression Era sayings that kept people working and subjugated."

"My father stressed education," Charlise said. "In the evenings he would call me into his study and read passages from his favorite books. We would discuss themes, characterization, and plot if it was fiction.

If it was non-fiction, we discussed how the information related to our lives, fallacies in the author's arguments, and anything else that came to mind. He never suggested that I read any of the books, but

I probably read most of them. And not to please him but because he piqued my curiosity."

"You must have had a wonderful childhood. I can't remember ever discussing a book with my father. He talked to me, never with me. It was my Uncle John and Aunt Betty who piqued my intellectual curiosity and turned me on to the world of books. They taught me to listen to others first and then discuss. I miss them so much."

"I'll bet," Charlise said. "They gave you confidence and understanding."

"I loved my parents, but my Aunt and Uncle were my saviors," Gabe said.

"It was my father who developed my interests and passions," said Charlise. "I'm profoundly grateful for his support. He taught me to be sure of myself, to be my own person, independent."

"And that's one of the many things I like about you. You're perfectly capable of taking care of yourself, plus you're educated and think about the world around you. I often ask myself how someone with an intellect can be so beautiful."

Charlise reached underneath the table and rubbed his leg with her toe. "Flattery will get you anything," her eyes twinkled.

"Looks like it just got me breakfast," Gabe said when a knock on the door announced its arrival. He got up and opened the door.

The waiter entered with two trays covered by silver domes and set them on the table. He went back out into the hallway and brought another tray with a pitcher of water and coffee. "Anything else?" he asked.

"I'm fine," Gabe replied and gave the waiter a ten dollar bill.

"Me too," Charlise said as she added another ten.

"Thank you, Senor and Senorita," the waiter beamed. "Mucho Gracias!"

After the door close again, Gabe looked at Charlise, "That, my Dear, was money well spent."

"I agree. We made his day," she said and removed the cover from her food. The smell of fresh cantaloupe escaped. Three orange slices of the melon were perched next to a mound of cottage cheese garnished with parsley. She buttered her toast as she watched Gabe.

Gabe lifted the silver dome to reveal a mound of hash browns with two eggs flanked on either side by crisp slices of bacon, and said "Not as healthy as yours but what the hell, I love bacon."

The aroma wafted across the table. "Right, I haven't had any since I started my vegetable-based diet, but it smells delicious and it's cooked just the way I like it," said Charlise.

"I'll give you a piece as long as I don't have to trade you for a bite of cantaloupe," he said, handing a slice across the table.

She smiled gratefully, "Thanks, I knew there was a reason I liked you." Charlise bit a piece off and closed her eyes to savor the cured hickory flavor, "Mmmmmmmm, better than I remember it."

Gabe forked the eggs over his hash browns and mixed them together with Tabasco sauce then took the remaining bacon and made a sandwich with toast. He took a bite of the egg/potato mixture enjoying the flavor before he took a bite of the sandwich.

Charlise finished her bacon then cut the cantaloupe in pieces, mixing it with cottage cheese. She ate a forkful humming with pleasure as the sweet of the fruit mingled with the milky cheese.

They ate in silence, hungry after the night's exercise. Gabe finished first, wiping his beard and mustache with his napkin. He watched Charlise mop the last of the curds with her toast and place them in her mouth. Her sensuous lips closing and moving together as she chewed.

Charlise enjoyed having Gabe observe. She finished and said, "That was good!"

"Wasn't it Shakespeare who said hunger is the best sauce? When we had the dairy I would get up at 4 a.m. on Sunday to relief milk. It took about four hours of hard work and when I finished I'd be starving. The breakfast afterwards was always the best meal of the week even oatmeal would've tasted good."

"What do you mean? I love oatmeal."

"I have to be pretty damned hungry to enjoy the taste of oatmeal and even then it has to be smothered in cream and sugar."

"So we finally found something to disagree about," she laughed.

"Actually, I was taught to always clean my plate and not to take more than I could eat. If I was served oatmeal, I ate oatmeal. There were a few years when we had to do just that. My Dad bought the neighbor's 80 acres with bank money. At that time the banks were loaning money to anyone who could sign their name. The banker convinced Dad to expand his dairy herd. On top of the farm he bought another twenty cows. Commodity prices and the price of milk were high. For the first two years we were rolling in the hay. But a dream financed on debt is precarious to say the least.

Three years later, bad luck struck. Commodity prices dropped and interest rates rose. Our corn crop was shredded by hail, so we had to buy feed. We sold every calf and pig we had just to make the loan payments.

My father worked sixteen hours a day to make ends meet. He was a tractor mechanic so he started working on tractors while the rest of us ran the farm. Milking and farming are hard taskmasters and we just couldn't work hard enough to repay the debt. The flesh slowly fell off my father's dream of being a rich dairy farmer.

After working ourselves to death for another year, it became apparent that it wasn't going to work. We lost the farm he'd bought and had to sell a good portion of the cows to keep from bankruptcy. I don't know what broke him, the stress and disappointment or the hard physical labor. He became listless and lost weight. Within a year, he was dead.

Sorry, I didn't mean to bring you down. I should talk about something else," Gabe looked up at Charlise and his gaze was met with an expression of sympathy. Her eyes were filled with tears.

"No, please go on."

"I realized the dairy farm had stolen precious time from the whole family. Time that we could never get back. I was twenty years old and already chained to the land and cows.

Even though my Dad had died, I didn't have time to grieve. The inexorable demands of the farm went on. I milked the cows and planted crops and hauled hay. One day, I realized that these demands would go on and on until my attempt to conquer the world would also fail. It had taken my Dad's death to jar me out of my complacency. I still wouldn't have given up my life of drudgery without my aunt and uncle's prodding. I think they'd already talked to my mother about selling out so I could go back to school.

She seemed relieved when I made the suggestion. And after many other experiences here I am, finally happy."

"It must have been awful to lose your Dad at such an early age."

"It was. What made it even more difficult was selling the land. It had been in the family for three generations. It had been deeply ingrained in me to keep the land at all costs. I felt like I had let my father down. To this day, I feel that way."

"Part of the reason you accomplished what you have is because you lost the land. I think life plays out the way it does for a reason. Thank God you didn't follow in your father's footsteps. If you had we wouldn't be sharing our breakfast together."

"I know. You're right. I've learned so much, more than I ever could've if I'd kept the farm," he looked into her eyes, "and being with you right now is worth a thousand farms."

Charlise got up and walked around the table. She bent over and hugged the back of Gabe's neck. "I love you," she said.

He held the arms that embraced him, "That means the world to me."

26

The Council members entered the conference room in an angry buzz of excitement. General Battier stomped through the doors, the loss of a ship and four Benwarians infuriated the military commander. He glared at Logis and signaled to be acknowledged.

"Quiet, please," Logis said and waited patiently for the talk to die out. He noticed that many of the Council members hadn't bothered to take their goblet of water for the ceremonial toast. He motioned for the servo-bots to distribute the remaining glasses. When they got to Battier, he folded his arms and refused to take one.

"General Battier, we will not begin the council until we are united by the ceremonial toast."

The General glared at Logis and shouted, "How can we toast life when you are directly responsible for the deaths of four Benwarians!"

"General, you will conform to protocol or I will have you removed and confined to your quarters!" Logis could feel a headache building behind his head. "Either take the water or leave," he commanded. The rest of the Council was dead quiet.

Battier grudgingly grabbed the glass from the tray. Logis waited until all had raised the water above their heads and said, "To life and Benwar!" After everyone drank, he started the conference. "General Battier, you were saying?"

"Earth's military installations should have been targeted and destroyed before we tried to plant the euthobots. I warned you about the danger to our ships. Four precious Benwarians are needlessly dead!"

La Vivron keyed in next. "I agree, there are precious few of us left. There are still millions of humans. I think we should destroy all military installations before sending anymore ships in range of their weapons. "

"You're right," Logis replied in an even tone. "I take responsibility. I underestimated the capabilities of the humans. It will not happen again." He pushed the button for Fa Archist's transcom.

"The conduct of war, or in this case colonization, is often messy. Yes, it is unfortunate that four Benwars were killed, but you were only trying to carry out the decisions the whole Council agreed to."

Next La Sikes keyed in, "Agreed, don't let the burden of guilt weigh too heavily. A good leader can't be crippled by remorse, he forgives himself and learns from his mistakes. I move that all discussion about the deaths be banned."

"I second the motion," said Fa Archist.

The Council voted 10 to 12 to support the measure. "Motion passed," Logis grimaced with the pain building behind his eyes but he continued, "The earthlings still possess some primitive nuclear defense systems. I agree with La Vivron that these should be eliminated before we progress with the final program of euthanasia. Any discussion?"

No one keyed in to speak so Logis called for the vote. All lights on his console glowed green. "Motion passed."

Next, he addressed Fa Structor. "How is your team progressing with the new euthobots?"

"We're having some trouble regulating their self-replication. They started multiplying like primitives," Fa Structor waited for the laughter to die down, "we actually had to destroy the whole second generation of bots to prevent them from overrunning the ship."

"And your solution?"

"We have given up on the self-replicating mechanism. We are now running our machinery around the clock to produce enough bots for the final invasion."

"And how long will that take?"

"Two days."

"Good, by that time we will have all military installations destroyed. Any other business?"

Fa Archist keyed in, "I understand that there are three earthlings aboard ship. I would like to know for what purpose."

"I'm doing a study of human nature," Logis replied.

"I also understand that these three humans are responsible for the deaths our people," he continued. A great murmur and outcry arose from the Sanctum Just.

Battier keyed in and before being acknowledged, shouted, "This is an outrage! They should be euthanized not patronized!"

"Listen, I need complete understanding of what I, as your leader, am responsible for. I want to understand the man who is intelligent enough to destroy one of our ships with a primitive weapon. I want to know if a basically static aura can become fluid through education and knowledge or if there are biological limitations on human development."

Battier's face reddened. "We agreed to eliminate all humans whose auras didn't meet certain parameters. We really don't have time for your self-indulgences. I move that these humans be euthanized."

La Sikes keyed in, "The humans present no threat. I don't see why Logis can't satisfy his curiosity."

"They destroyed my crew! There is nothing to be gained by studying such primitive, superstitious beings," Battier replied forcefully.

"I will not allow their destruction! General Battier, the need for revenge is beneath you. If these humans prove to be so primitive that their auras remain dark and undeveloped then I will give them over to you to do with as you please. There will be no vote on their destruction."

"Let's not forget that this is a democracy. This is the Sanctum Just and its purpose is to decide matters relating to the invasion," Fa Archist said after being acknowledged.

"This a minor matter that will have no bearing on the invasion," Logis defended.

"Nevertheless, we should at least vote on whether you or the Council should decide the issue. I move that we vote on the matter," Fa Archist continued.

"So the motion is that the Council should decide the fate of the three humans aboard ship. Is there a second?"

Battier keyed in a second. "All in favor?" Logis continued.

Six green lights mixed in with six red lights on the voting console. "It's a tie. I vote no so the motion fails," Logis's headache intensified into a migraine. "Any other business to discuss?" No one keyed in. "Meeting adjourned."

Logis held his head as he exited in front of the Council. It hurt that his leadership had been questioned. It hurt even more that half of the Sanctum Just had turned against him. The door to the left of the podium slid open as he approached. Someone called his name but he ignored the voice and entered the private corridor that led to his room. Once there he fell to the bed, "Ship, dim lights, please."

The lights faded until it was almost dark. Logis put his arm over his forehead. "Ship?"

"Yes, I know," Ship replied. She inserted a bio-sensor into the back of his neck. It emitted a small electrical current that immediately alleviated his headache. A minute needle was inserted into a vein in his neck. Once it was inside, Ship injected an analgesic that completely eliminated his pain. Logis felt like he was floating in a pool of warm water.

As he relaxed, Ship started wrapping him in a cocoon of bio-sensors. Thin filaments emerged from the right side of the bed and traveled across his body to the left. Others sensors came from the left to the right, crossing the ones from the other side. Soon, his whole body was covered in a thin mesh of filament much like a spider wraps its victim in a web.

Ship had prepared a virtual reality experience for Logis. She had sent a probe containing capsules full of vid-bots to earth. Equipped with guidance systems and streaming video capabilities, she had placed them on either side of the heads of several species of birds by pinpointing a specific target and actually directing the vid-bots to a bird. She then filmed the output from each bird and combined the films into an edited virtual reality experience that would let Logis see and experience the aviary world of flying. Once he was fully wrapped, She began.

Strangely, Logis no longer thought about Benwar or the invasion of earth. His down feathers were so warm and comforting, they insulated him from the outside world. He loved his fine webbed feet and flapped his wings in pride as he marched behind his mother and father, brothers and sisters. He spread his toes to avoid sinking any further in the mud and took great joy in being a gosling. No thoughts, just being and feeling that he was part of a family. He belonged.

"Honk, honk," his parents beckoned.

"Honk, honk," he answered as they marched together across the muddy marsh. They neared the water with cattails and rushes on either side of them. He watched his parents slide into the lake followed by his siblings who were so sedate and proper. When his turn came he flapped his wings vigorously and skimmed the water, kicking his feet and honking. I'll show them who's a goose he thought, banging into the back of his mother. She flapped and honked across the lake and he followed her. Together they kicked webbed feet and flapped powerful wings, splashing white mist across the blue surface.

They floated around in the water, playing and honking until it was time to return to the nest. Once there he found true contentment as he nestled with his family in the cattail basket. The comfort of togetherness soon brought sleep.

He awoke refreshed, gliding on the outer wing of a V-formation. There was no thought but of flying, using the markers provided by the universe to find the way. The sun and moon and the landmarks below marked the flock's path and they flew as one. They flew along the coast and watched white masses of ice rumble and crash in a thunderous cascade as the glaciers sloughed into the bay. They flew, elevating above the clouds, skimming the mists with their feet. They flew across the surface of the clouds, a seemingly endless expanse of white cotton water particles.

After a time purple peaks capped in snow appeared above the misty white surface. The mountains in their majesty beckoned them forward, showing the way north. They flew on and on until the clouds dissipated. Now they could see the snow frosted evergreens and feel the air warming and knew spring would arrive before their flight was over.

They flew over the purple peaks and down, along the ocean coast, its blue-green mass outlined by the sandy yellow beaches. Brown walruses barked and frolicked on the coastal islands. Black seals dived and splashed in the water.

They turned inland, where the white bark of the aspens made lines against the green pine trees, white snow bending the deep green boughs. Remnants of fall's yellow leaves caught the sun and shimmered, rustling in the late winter wind.

They flew, across square fields of green and square fields of harvest gold, patched with plowed fields of brown. As he flew with his brethren, he saw the glassy surface of the river twist and turn among the trees like a snake slithering in the grass. They followed the path of life and it was good.

He watched below as thousands of ducks beat their wings against the water and lifted in a flying mass of color. He watched as the sun reflected yellow off the blue water. He flew and the air grew lighter as the changing season beckoned the flock forward.

They flew north, always northward, as the dead of winter became the promise of spring. They flew toward the new horizon filled with the promise of food and sunshine. It was good this being carried by the rhythms of life, this belonging, this grandeur, this world.

After days of great beauty, they landed in a field of corn stubble and he picked the un-gleaned kernels until his gullet filled. The warm spring sun basked him in golden warmth, its comfort brought drowsiness then sleep.

He awoke on the surface of a lake, transformed. Now possessing the red eyes of a Clark's grebe, he danced a ballet across the water. He danced, his partner graceful with her white head crowned by a black mantel. They dipped yellow beaks set between glowing red eyes and moved their heads up and down in rhythm.

He danced of life with wings spread wide. He bobbed, his head mirroring his mate, and it was good, this bond of being, this bond of biology.

In unison, they tip toed across the glassy surface. Wings beat together as they kept vertical to the water, tipping yellow beaks skyward in an ancient dance of joy and procreation. It was as things should be, to dance and sing of life.

When the dance ended, he bowed a goodbye and soared upward in transformation. The long beak became crooked and sharp. The webbed feet became talons, his legs thickened with power. Wings lengthened into powerful masts that caught the wind and propelled him across the sky. His body lost density as it gained buoyancy. Now a bald-eagle, his yellow eyes were keen as he surveyed the world. His spirit, free and fierce, flew in white crowned majesty.

Master of the sky, he soared toward the sun, up and up until the air grew thin. He circled and dipped. The effortless flight allowed him to truly see the earth. The colors brightened, red and white sand rock jutted in and out and around, forming a maze of color on the bright blue lake below. He flew across red sanded deserts dotted with sagebrush and mesquite. Ancient cedars clung to orange cliffs with a tenacious grip. The azure sky rested on the mesas and plateaus, the evening sun cast a golden glow over the multi-colored landscape. He saw all things great and small and it was good.

He flew, up and up, soaring beyond the clouds. Up and up, until he shed his corporeal body and became a desert spirit, the howling wind a reminder of the endless cycle of life, of the majestic beauty of earth, of the sanctity of this greatest creation. And it was as it should be and it was good.

Up, up he spiraled through earth's atmosphere until he transformed once more into a soul, the soul known as Logis from the planet Benwar. When his eyes opened, the wonderful sensation of flight was gone. He lay on his back, wistful, wishing to return to the skies and the beauty of the planet below. He thought of his own home and the sands revolving around the surface and regained his resolve. He would save Gaia, the planet Earth, no matter what the cost. That was his purpose, to save the purple peaks and red stone cliffs. To save the oceans, lakes, and rivers. To save the forests and deserts plains. To save the universe's greatest glory! This pinnacle of creation!

"Thank you, Ship, my headache is gone." Logis said.

"You're welcome."

"Arrange the same experience for Pearson. Let's see if it affects his aura."

"Yes, Logis," she answered.

27

*P*earson eventually tired of pacing the room and sat on the gurney. Stress and exhaustion overwhelmed his body and he lay back on the pillow. His eyes drooped and sleep closed his eyes.

He didn't notice when Ship inserted the bio-sensors. First the sedative, then a mild hallucinogen were injected into his blood stream. Then the bio-sensors wrapped around and he too felt the comfort of goose down. He too reveled in the belonging and flight. He soared and saw his planet for the first time as he followed his mom and dad, brothers and sisters.

Now there was no religion, only being. He was a goose and that was sublime. There was nothing else. As a member of his species he was accepted, he belonged without preconditions and it was good.

He viewed the earth for the first time as a part of it. The sheer beauty of God's creation brought awe and wonder. He was a part of the circle of life.

As a grebe, he danced. As an eagle, he became king of the sky and glided on the air high above the red rock formations of a painted desert. Orange spires pointed to the sky in the sunset's red glow and it was good.

He perched on a ledge on a cliff in a canyon and slept. Morning came with his feet on cold sandstone, his once keen eyesight blurred by pollutants and smoke. The pristine landscape of his dream changed to reality and the hazy air smelled of mankind. He looked through the clouded lens of pollution and it perverted the true nature of the earth around him. A sense of impending doom and sadness overcame the eagle and the human wept.

Now he danced as a grebe. He floated and bobbed his head at his mate. He flapped his wings and lifted above the water, toes dangling in the water. How he loved this dance of life!

His mate lifted too but when she cleared the water she fell back with clear plastic rings wrapped around her feet and legs. He watched in horror as she flapped and struggled against the plastic shackles. The rings tightened cutting into flesh and hobbling her legs until she floated helplessly on the water. He cried out in anguish as the sacred dance of life ended. He watched for days as his mate slowly starved to death, a victim of man's indifference. Sadness overcame the grebe and the human wept.

Now he joined his fellow goslings as they grew together and gained flight. They flew spotting their brethren below with wings clipped. They watched as the geese milled around in the manure behind a chicken wire fence and grieved as they passed over.

Ever onward they flew, headed south, back to the marsh of their birth. Once there, he walked with his siblings in the mud and honked in pleasure. His joy ended when he looked down. Now he waded in industrial waste and the acid burned and the webbed feet slid in malodorous slime. He lifted into the air with his brothers and sisters as oily sludge dripped from his toes.

Onward they flew seeking shelter and food. Another marsh invited them to visit with its cattails and rushes. They circled and banked and glided together along the water's surface.

A fiery burst sounded and his sister exploded in a mass of feathers. A second blast reverberated and his brother plummeted from the sky. He watched them fold and fall to become lifeless forms on the marsh's surface.

Another thunderous explosion tore through his brain as his left wing collapsed. He fell to the water, helpless. Pain seared through his body when he flapped the mangled mass of feathers. He cried out for his brother and sister and damned mankind. The goose grieved and the human wept.

Pearson awoke with the image of his dead siblings and rolled on the gurney with pain. His left shoulder stormed with sharp, excruciating knifing sensations. He writhed and remembered and when he remembered, the pain became a poignant memory.

Pearson had been reflecting on his experience for over an hour when the door to his room opened and Logis entered. "How was your flight?" the Benwarian asked. A look of understanding passed between them.

"How did you know?" he answered.

"I shared the same experience."

For a moment all Pearson thought of was the exhilaration of soaring over earth. "I couldn't believe it! I experienced God's majesty. It was awesome at first but then it turned into a nightmare."

"Really?" said Logis.

"I've never really appreciated nature. Seeing through the eyes of other living beings is very humbling."

Pearson continued, "I realized how much I don't know about God. Earth is His sacred creation. We don't deserve dominion over it unless we take care of it."

"So how would you save his precious gift?" Logis asked.

"I could never do what you're doing, but I'm beginning to understand," Pearson said with tears in his eyes.

Logis smiled sadly and his eyes glistened, too. The light had broken through the black shroud that encased Pearson's aura. The rigidity of his thinking was broken.

These humans have so much potential. All they need is education, Logis thought. "Believe me, if there were any other solution we would choose it," he said and left the room.

Once back in his quarters, Logis spoke, "Ship, identify and target all nuclear facilities and destroy them."

"My pleasure," she replied. She had already mapped the sights. The laser doors dropped open and she began to fire. Within minutes no nuclear weapons existed.

28

harlise stood when Ben knocked. She opened the door and he barged in. Agitated, he asked, "Have you seen the news?"

"What's going on?" Gabe replied.

"Washington D.C.'s been attacked!"

Charlise walked over and turned the television on. The announcer was explaining that all contact had been cut off from the nation's capital. A thirty by thirty mile square had been quarantined and no one could enter the area. Film footage showed a news crew flying and filming the destruction from their helicopter. The pilot suddenly slumped over and died. The copter nose dived, pitching the camera man out with a scream. The sky appeared momentarily as he spiraled downward. Then the screen went blank.

The announcer reappeared. "We have just received reports that silos throughout the country have launched nuclear warheads. There has been a tremendous explosion in the earth's upper atmosphere." There was a visual of a yellow flash spreading out from the point where the missile had made contact.

We are now receiving visual confirmation that U.S. nuclear missile silos have been destroyed. Space observatories report that a spaceship has been spotted above the moon. Several red bursts can be seen emanating from the ship."

"Please do not panic. So far the attacks seem limited to D.C. and our defense systems," the announcer said.

The screen went blank for a second, "This is not a test," came the emergency announcement from Civil Defense officials who urged people to evacuate to the nearest bomb shelter in their area.

"What have we done?" Gabe queried. His heart pounding.

"What makes you think we had anything to do with it?" Ben asked.

"I emailed our findings to Langley this morning. He probably informed the President and the communications were intercepted. The attack can't be a coincidence."

"See if you can get Langley on his cell phone," said Ben.

Gabe punched in the number. There was no answer, not even static. "Absolutely nothing," he said with sweat forming over his brow. He hesitated for a moment trying to calm down by placing his hand over his stomach and taking several deep breaths.

"My God, what have we done?" Charlise asked, her eyes watering with tears.

"Good question," said Gabe, "Try calling your father and find out."

Charlise pulled out her cell phone and keyed in the number. Her father lived in Phoenix, Arizona. After a moment he answered. "Hello?"

"Hi, Dad."

"Charlise, I've been worried sick. Are you okay?"

"I'm fine. What about you and Mom?"

"We're fine, so far. Everyone else is frantic. Civil Defense is recommending evacuating to the nearest bomb shelter, but they have a very limited capacity so there's been a mass exodus out of the city. There's been lootings and shootings in some places. It's chaos. How 'bout where you're at?"

"So far, fairly calm. There's really nowhere to run and a lot of people don't have television. Why aren't you leaving the city?" she asked.

"Where would we go? We're staying put until we have enough information to decide what to do."

"Daddy, whatever you do stay calm and keep Mom calm. Panicking is the worst thing you can do."

"Have you ever known me to panic?"

"No, but there's always a first time."

"Believe me, dear, I'll be okay. I've seen people die because they panicked. I'll stay rational. It sounds to me like you know something I don't. What is it?"

"The deaths in the forests are caused by nano-bots manufactured by the aliens. They attack people who exhibit fear. We think the nano-bots are also being used to attack D.C."

"If that's the case, wouldn't it be possible to seal ourselves off so the machines couldn't get us?"

"Possibly, but the bots are minute. So small that they're able to fit through air filters."

"Listen, we'll figure out something," her father said. "What about you? What are your plans?"

"We haven't discussed anything yet."

"Charlise," Ben said.

She held her hand over the receiver. "What?"

"Tell your Dad that the machines might be susceptible to a magnetic field since they're really just tiny computers."

She relayed the message and said, "Don't worry, Daddy. I'm with two very capable men who'll help me get through this. I'd better go. Give Mom my love."

"Please, be careful. I love you, Sweetie!" he said firmly.

"I love you too, Daddy. Take care of Mom. I'll try to keep in touch. I'd better go. Goodbye, Dad."

"I love you," he said again as she hung up.

"Everything okay?" Gabe asked. He put his hand on her shoulder.

She turned and hugged him, her eyes wet with tears. "So far. You'd better call your mother. It might be the last time you ever get to talk to her."

Gabe pulled out his cell phone and accessed its memory. When he got to her name, he pressed enter and the phone dialed.

"Hello?"

"Hi, Mom. How are you? Is everything okay?"

"Everything's fine. How're you, dear?"

"I'm great. Where're you at?"

She was staying in an assisted living center and Gabe could

hear noise in the background. "They made everyone move to the basement for some reason."

"So you haven't heard anything?"

"About what, dear?"

Gabe thought for a second. She obviously doesn't know about the invasion. There's absolutely nothing I can do for her. No reason to upset her. "Oh, nothing. It's just that I found the most remarkable woman in the world. I thought maybe you could hear the wedding bells ringing."

"Wedding bells?" she brightened. "Oh, Honey. That's the best news I've heard in years. I'm thrilled. When's the wedding?"

"Soon, Mom. As soon as we can get back to the states and make arrangements."

"Gabe, you don't know how happy that makes me. Maybe I'll finally get a grandchild to spoil," she said hopefully.

"Maybe. Maybe two or three," he said, telling her what she wanted to hear. "Listen, I've gotta run. I just wanted to give you the good news and see how you're doing."

"I'm doing much better now that I have something to hope for."

"I love you, Mom."

"I love you, too."

"I'll call you again in a few days. Take care."

"Goodbye, dear."

Gabe pressed the end button and looked at Charlise. She was staring at him in mock anger. "Nice to know I'm getting married."

"I'mm, I was just, uh. Well, I was just trying to cheer Mom up. Telling her what she wanted to hear."

"So you really don't want to marry me?"

"Well, come to think of it, I do. I can think of no one else I'd rather spend the rest of my life with."

"You don't seem very happy about it. Is something wrong?"

"It's Mom. I feel like I'm abandoning her. She's huddled in a basement of an assisted living center with a bunch of strangers. She should be with family."

"You're right. At least my parents have each other. But I'm still deathly afraid for them."

"It hurts to know that there's absolutely nothing we can do for them, doesn't it?" Gabe said.

"I hate it! I've finally found someone to love and care for and I'm ridden with guilt and worry. What's worse is our time together may be short. A few hours, a few days. Who knows?" said Charlise.

Gabe grabbed her by both arms and looked into her eyes. "We'll get through this. We'll find a way to survive."

Ben cleared his throat, "Speaking of survival, we need to decide what we're going to do."

"Have you called your parents?" Charlise asked.

"Of course. They're fine for the moment. They were going to a special service at the synagogue to be with friends and relatives. Everyone is going to pray for God's deliverance."

"Did you tell them about our findings?"

"Everything. They said that prayer has a calming influence on people. Their beliefs and prayers will comfort them and help them through this. I told them I love them then said goodbye. What else could I do?"

Ben continued, "And what will we do? If we stay here we risk being caught in mass panic and chaos."

"We need to figure out what the aliens are trying to accomplish," Gabe said. "They're obviously invading earth but why don't they just eliminate all of us and take over?"

"Yeah," Ben agreed. "Why are they fooling around? It's obvious they have the technology to make a quick end of it."

"They might be trying to preserve as much of Earth as they can. Maybe using their weapons would be too destructive," said Charlise.

"Okay so they release the bots and kill everyone, take over the planet and live in peace," Ben posited. "No damage to anything but the human population."

"They must not want to do that. We need to find out why Rahula's protected from the machines. What method do the nanobots use to target their victims?" Gabe asked. "How do they choose who lives and who dies?"

"Good question. How would you decide?" Ben asked.

"I'd save the children," Charlise interjected.

"That makes sense. They can be re-educated and trained," Gabe agreed. "But it still doesn't explain Rahula."

"Okay, if they want people who can be re-educated, maybe they'll save anyone who has an open mind," Ben continued, "People who see the need for change."

"And just how would they determine that? They can't split someone's skull open and see what's inside," Gabe said.

"Let's go back to our findings. The nanobots seemed to be sensitive to chemicals emitted by the human body. A state of arousal triggers an attack from the bots because of elevated adrenaline levels."

"Okay," Gabe followed his train of thought. "So the bots distinguish who to kill because of certain chemicals emitted by the body and maybe they can determine personality somehow by an individual's chemical make-up?"

"It seems plausible to me," Ben said. "So if we can regulate our galvanic responses and keep from being aroused, maybe we can prevent the bots from attacking."

"Arousal states are an adaptive response to the environment. They provide a heightened sense of awareness that lets us flee or fight as needed. Short of keeping ourselves on sedatives, I don't see how it's possible or even desirable to become insensitive to the world around us," Charlise said.

Gabe nodded his head, "Agreed, but there is a threshold for tripping an attack by the bots. Maybe you can be aroused, just not too aroused. Surely it's possible to stay alert and calm at the same time. If we can keep our emotions in check, maybe the bots will spare us.

We need to decide what to do. First of all, place your hands on your stomachs and take a deep breath. Now, let the air out and with it the tension you're feeling," Gabe instructed. Everyone breathed in together and felt better as they breathed the tension out. "And again," he continued. They responded. "One more time." The anxiety seemed to lessen with each breath out. They repeated the exercise two more times.

"Now, we need a mantra. Something we say over and over to keep our minds from engaging in harmful fantasy. Rahula uses ohm. Assume the lotus position and let's try it."

After everyone had positioned themselves on the carpet, Gabe continued, "Now put your hands together under your chin in temple form and begin. Ohm, ohm, banish all other thoughts from your mind, think only of the mantra. Ohm, ohm.

If you perceive danger and there's no visible threat, assume the lotus position and repeat the mantra. Remember to take deep breaths and stay calm. We'll practice this some more as time allows. Right now I think it's time to evacuate Manaus."

"And go where?" Ben asked.

"Back to the Quonset huts for a few minutes and then to the jungle to find Rahula."

"Back into the midst of the nano-bots?"

"Yes. We'll test our theory. Everyone needs to pack up and get ready to leave. Ben, inform Sgt. Rone of our plans, he's in room 14. Tell him we need to do more research and he's to fly us back to the base camp. Have him meet us at the airport in 30 minutes."

Ben left the room. Gabe turned to Charlise. "If the bots can determine personality and who's worthy of survival, you'll be fine. Your beautiful. So have faith in yourself."

"Thank you, Gabe. I have complete confidence that you'll get us through this, but I don't wish to survive without you. So if we go we go together."

"I have no intention of leaving your side," Gabe said.

29

*P*earson was standing on the wind swept deserts and high plateaus of Tibet. A Buddhist monk, he belonged to the most spiritual culture that ever existed. Just as Tibet's mountain peaks reached into the sky, so too did Tibetans reach for the true nature of the Creator. Time was set aside each day for people to pray and contemplate.

Now in a temple, he explained to those congregated that the way to inner peace comes not from one book or source but from all sources. His perspective shifted and now he listened to the Dalai Llama, hearing these words, "One must remember the ocean is too wide and deep to be fathomed in day or a year, but if one takes personal responsibility for one's own education, one can attain enlightenment."

His perspective shifted again, to God's view. He watched from above as Chinese soldiers swept through the country, destroying Buddhist temples and killing monks who opposed China's communist regime. He watched as they systematically destroyed Tibetan culture and traditions and purged the country of all those who would not be subjugated.

Now, he was human again, a rifle butt slammed into the side of his head, knocking him down in an explosion of pain. Trying to remain conscious, he watched others being brutalized before he passed out. He awoke in a "re-education" center with hands bound behind his back as he lay on a wet cement floor. A soldier poked him with a cattle prod, sending electric pain throughout his body.

After days of torture, he was tied to a string of Tibetans and marched across his beloved country until they reached the border of India. They were cut lose and told never to return. His sense of loss brought a heaviness of spirit that was worse than the searing pain of torture.

Again his view shifted. Suddenly, he stood on a windswept mountain peak and surveyed the beauty of the valley below. His burden lightened as his spirit soared over the plains and valleys and mountains of Tibet. Once again he felt the promise of Enlightenment.

Gradually, he floated downward until his feet touched the earth of Tibet. This was not the country of his memory. Now, the Buddhist temples were gone. There were brothels and drinking bars to poison man's spirit and rob Tibet of its spirituality. He had lost his beloved country. Slowly the dream faded as he felt the images unravel, Ship removed the biosensors, until once again he lay on his gurney in a sterile room.

The experience caused yellow light to fill his aura as he realized that the Chinese belief in communist doctrine allowed them to kill and destroy innocent people. Their doctrine was an armor against thought. Words became more important than people and their right to self-determination.

His thoughts were interrupted by a buzz at his door. "Yes?"

"It's Logis. May I come in?"

"Since when do you have to ask permission?"

"Asking is a sign of respect."

"In that case, come in please."

Logis entered and the room brightened with the light of his aura. He smiled at Pearson who felt honored by the visit. "How are you?" Logis asked.

"I'm feeling better. I just experienced being a Tibetan monk."

"Yes, I know. The Chinese found that you cannot massacre ideas. As hard as they tried, they could not eradicate Tibetan Buddhism. The Dalai Llama now lives in exile but remains the spiritual leader of his country."

"You haven't destroyed him yet."

The question hurt Logis. "No. He actually survived the invasion of Washington D.C. His light kept the euthobots at bay."

"I'm sorry," Pearson said when he saw the hurt in Logis's eyes. "So a Buddhist was saved, what about Christians?"

"If they believe in the spirit of Christ, in what he taught, they'll be saved. He was a being of light. For those who believe in him to be saved and have their sins forgiven, it's a different matter, it darkens their aura with violet green. Anyway, how did it feel to be a Buddhist?"

"I felt an interconnectedness much deeper than I ever felt in my Baptist congregation. The whole country of Tibet seemed intent on spiritual development. As Baptists, we listened to the sermon each Sunday and went home. We often left our religion at the church door."

Logis replied, "There are thousands of sects of Christianity that remain isolated from one another. Human religion serves as a filter that regulates social relationships. Earthly religions have kept people segregated for thousands of years. Most of these religions express a biological need and have little to do with God."

Pearson thought for a moment. "And you, Logis. What of your beliefs?"

"The Buddhists come closest to Benwarian beliefs. We have become comfortable with the eternal quest for a supreme being. There is no answer to God but that which each individual chooses through education and knowledge. Sartre, a great thinker from your planet, called this existentialism. It's not really a religion so much as it is a philosophy.

There are, however, universal principles to live by. Our major life guiding principle is to leave the world a better place than we found it. This includes environmentally, spiritually, and structurally."

"How do you live with the uncertainty of never knowing God?"

"By realizing that that is the condition of existence. We have no priests or religious leaders who tell us how to think. We have educational forums. These forums are used to discuss issues relevant to our existence. One of our most important disciplines is the study of ethics. We try to establish ethical principles to live by."

Logis watched Pearson's aura shimmer. "And so now that you have destroyed many of my beliefs, what is left? I feel like I'm drifting alone in the universe."

"You are not alone. We are here with you. We share the same world and the same uncertainty. This is the beginning of your rebirth. This is the time to discover the interconnectedness of all living things. This is the time to help us transform Earth into a sustainable and lasting world."

"How do I help you, you with your superior technology and knowledge?"

"We want you to serve as a liaison between the Benwarians and the survivors on earth."

"You mean a collaborator."

"Collaborator implies that there will be a resistance. The survivors will come from so many disparate cultures and regions that it will impossible to organize an insurgency. Most of the remaining population will be children. They will need someone to help them understand what has happened."

"I think you underestimate humans. We will not acquiesce to an alien take-over."

"We will tolerate no armed opposition. Only better ideas can influence the course our transformation of earth takes. We're asking you to have an influence on both your people and ours. You choice is help both or help neither."

"I see. So much for democracy."

"Democracies will be developed on Earth, but not until the planet is saved."

"You have two days. By then the euthobots will be done and the inter-colonization will begin," Logis looked at Pearson and nodded, "Until then."

Logis turned and left the room as the doors slid opened. Once in the hallway, Ship spoke, "Logis, I have traced the communications that alerted the Americans. A team of two men and a woman working in the Amazon rainforest discovered us."

"One of them communicated with a Dr. Langley of the Centers for Disease Control who relayed an alert to the President of the U.S. That is how the panic started."

"How much do they know?" Logis asked.

"They know the bots are alien. They know that the bots run on chlorophyll and kill those who are in or near the forests. They suspect that some people are immune to the attacks, but they're not sure why. They think that chemicals might attract the bots and that those who are able to stay calm survive."

"Impressive. How long will it take to locate these three people?"

"The communication came from a hotel in Manaus, Brazil. I have the taken the address and room numbers from the desk computer. However, my sensors indicate the rooms are empty."

"Trace them as quickly as possible. I want them found so we can talk. Even if you have to put someone on the ground, find them."

"And what then?"

"I'll join them on the surface."

"You can't. They have an armed military officer with them. I am programmed to protect you at all costs. I cannot protect you on the surface of the planet. If you insist on meeting these primitives, I suggest you do it on board."

"I'm in command. You are programmed to obey my orders. I want to meet and talk with these three in a place they feel comfortable. I don't want them traumatized by waking up on an alien ship."

"Then I insist you are accompanied by another Benwarian, an armed Benwarian." One equipped with vid-bots so I know what's going on. I'll destroy the primitives at the first hint of violence, Ship thought. He will be protected!

"As you wish," Logis conceded.

Pearson thought about Logis. He seemed so kind and full of light and goodness and yet there was a steely resolve to him that couldn't be shaken. Somehow, despite the fact that the Benwarians were responsible mass murder, Pearson liked Logis. He never felt threatened by Logis's presence, on the contrary, he felt comfortable and secure.

He thought about his decision. It went against his military training but it would do no good to resist the Benwarians. If he helped, it would be for the survivors, to comfort and assist them.

Right now, he felt like a Tibetan monk in exile. Now that was a strange!

30

Sergeant Rone circled the area around the Quonset huts. A multitude of saplings were sprouting up, some right next to the buildings. The rainforest was reclaiming its territory.

Rone looked at Gabe, "We'd better put on the pressurized suits before we land. It looks like the forest has moved."

Gabe nodded at Ben and Charlise, "You three use the suits. I'm going to see what happens to me without one. I'll take the controls while you get yours on, Sergeant." He slid across the front of the helicopter and grabbed the controls as the two men switched places.

Charlise's heart jumped, "Please don't," she said.

In a calm measured voice, Gabe reassured her, "It's okay. You're visibly upset, Charlise. You have to stay calm. Take deep breaths and repeat the mantra. Don't think about what will happen to me. Don't think period. Dwell only on the mantra and banish all other thoughts."

"But ..." Charlise began.

"Ohmmm, Ohmmm," Gabe started.

When Charlise remained silent, Gabe said, "Please. Check your pulse rate. It's accelerated. Don't let your feelings control your bodily responses. You have to stay calm to survive. I think I'm ready and you're not. That's the only reason I'm going without the suit."

"He's right," Ben agreed. "My pulse has quickened, too." He reached into the front where Gabe sat and felt his wrist. "Very good. Sixty beats per minute."

"Sergeant, circle the area a few more times while these two work on slowing their pulse rates," Gabe ordered as he thought that it would have been comical to be able to hear three people repeating, "Ohm, ohm ..." over and over again, but there was too much at stake to laugh. He smiled anyway.

He looked at his companions, "How're we doing?"

They nodded an affirmative and he could see that they had calmed considerably. He switched places with Sgt. Rone who now wore a pressurized suit. "Go ahead and land."

The helicopter banked left until it was over the former parking lot in front of the huts. Once in position, Rone brought the craft down in the middle of the sapling covered ground. The blades whirred around and around creating a wind that bent the young trees and shredded foliage that flew away from the chopper. He cut the engine and the momentum of the propellers decreased gradually and then stopped. Everyone unbuckled their shoulder straps. Sgt. Rone opened his door and climbed out. He opened the passenger door, grabbing Charlise's hand and helping her down. Ben clambered after.

Once outside, Charlise looked back at the front passenger side and saw that it was empty. "Gabe!" she shouted. Rone and Ben rushed around to the other side of the aircraft.

Gabe was bent over. He grabbed his ankles and stretched his legs from side to side. "Except for some sore muscles, I feel great," he smiled.

Charlise came around the men and grabbed his hand holding it momentarily, "You scared me!"

"Sorry. Did your pulse quicken?"

"Of course. I was worried."

He squeezed her hand firmly and looked into her eyes. "Without the suit, you'd be dead. Please, please, please, remember to concentrate on the mantra. Don't worry about anything. Remain calm."

She put her hand on her stomach and took a couple of deep breaths. "I'm trying."

Gabe wanted so badly to shout, try harder, but he knew it would be counterproductive. He also knew that the frustration welling up inside of him was dangerous so he closed his eyes and repeated the mantra until the negative feeling was gone. He smiled and put his arm around Charlise, "I love you!"

She smiled. "I feel calmer now."

"Are you two okay?" Gabe asked looking at Rone and Ben.

Ben answered, "Watching you two is so entertaining that I forgot to be nervous."

"I've been trained to stay calm and alert," Rone added.

Once their focus shifted to the Quonset huts, they discovered that many of the windows were broken by branches from saplings that had poked through from the inside. An immense quiet blanketed the area.

Charlise felt like she was encroaching on a holy sanctuary. Gabe felt like an atheist taking communion. Ben and Rone felt like unwelcome intruders.

The sound of a lone bird twittering broke the silence. After a moment, another joined in, and then another until the air was filled with the joyous sounds of several species of birds vying to be heard.

There was wonder in Gabe's voice as he whispered, "Listen to that! They're telling us it's great to be alive! Good God, the air smells so clean. I wish you could take your helmets off. I've never breathed air so pure."

"We're going to have to sooner or later," Ben said. "We'll run out of air in a few hours."

"Give yourselves time to adjust and get comfortable first. Let's check the inside of the office," said Gabe.

They stepped around and over the young trees until they reached the door. Sgt. Roan pulled out his pistol and gripped the knob. He threw it open and stepped back. Several screeching spider monkeys burst out. The sudden movement startled everyone. He trained his gun on them and watched as they ran off.

Gabe had stood back and away when Rone threw the door open. Luckily, he had been able to contain his response to mild surprise.

Sergeant Rone looked inside, "Wow, look at this," he said in amazement as he stepped into the room.

The other three stuck their heads inside. The hut had become a greenhouse. The floor was cracked and broken by buttress roots pushing up from below. Climbing plants covered the walls and reached for the window openings. Tubular lianas made big loops around the room, twisting and turning on the desks and tables.

Vines hung from the ceiling and pale yellow orchids dangled from them like chandeliers. Wild bananas grew in and around the roots sprouting from the broken floor. Huge ferns were interspersed throughout the room, each reaching for sunlight.

Insects had also found refuge in the hut. Cicadas rattled the sides of their bodies, filling the room with clicking sounds. Crickets added to the cacophony with loud chirping. Termites fed on the wood furniture. Birdwing butterflies waved their winged sails, a green mountain design stretched from one tip of their wings to the other and black antennae moved back and forth on their red heads.

Animals lived in the hut. Several fruit bats hung from the vines in one corner of the room. Two small skink lizards walked across the remains of one of the desks, their red under bellies throwing a contrast of color against the green foliage. A blue-banded kingfisher pecked at the termites and several giant snails fed on the fungus that covered everything.

"It won't be long before the hut becomes a part of the rainforest. It's amazing how fast the vegetation's reclaiming this whole area," Sergeant Rone whispered.

"I know. Everything human is decaying. It's only been three days since we were here and nothing's recognizable," Gabe answered.

"You do have to admit, it's beautiful," Charlise said in a low voice.

"Yeah, I feel like we're infringing on a new world," Ben added.

They watched for a few moments before Rone shut the door again. "Do you want to go back with me or stay?" he asked.

"We came here to find Rahula. I entered the coordinates to his camp in my GPS so I think we'll be able to find him," Gabe replied. "In a couple of days the jungle will be so thick, it'll be impassable. This is our last chance," he added.

"What do you want from him?" Rone asked.

"I don't know for sure. Something tells me to go to his place in the forest. But also, I want Charlise and Ben to learn how to remain calm. He can teach them. He can teach you, too. It's a question of survival."

"I am calm. The army will expect me to report in with the chopper. It's my duty to go back. Look, I'll show you, you don't need Rahula to survive." Confident of his nerves of steel, Rone started to remove his helmet.

"Don't," Gabe said calmly as Sgt. Rone unsnapped the buttons around his neck.

"I'll be okay. Remember I'm combat tested." Once the snaps were undone, he pulled on the zip lock seal and it opened. Rone's face changed like he'd bitten into something nasty. He slapped at his neck, hitting the hazmat suit. His eyes widened in surprise and he collapsed.

Charlise yelled, "Oh my God," and threw her hands over her face.

Gabe and Ben rushed over and knelt beside Rone's body. Gabe felt for a pulse. "He's dead," he pronounced. When the fear began he concentrated on the mantra and remained calm. He kept his grip on Rone's wrist to keep his composure.

Ben became agitated. "I liked Sergeant Rone, he was a good man. Not to mention the fact that he was our way back. We're stuck here now. There's no way I'll learn to be calm enough to survive in the next couple of hours! I'm not ready to die!"

"Lotus position, please," Gabe instructed and waited until both his companions were on the ground. "Ohm, Ohm.." he repeated and they joined in. "Concentrate on the mantra and your breathing, think of nothing else," he said calmly.

It took several moments before the two calmed down enough to listen. "We need to think about what just happened. Don't dwell on Sgt. Rone there's nothing you can do or could have done."

"But.." Charlise began.

"Your survival depends on dealing with tragedy in a calm and detached manner. Please concentrate on figuring out why the bots attacked Rone who was calm and haven't attacked me yet. Any ideas?"

"He had higher levels of testosterone than you do," Ben said in a monotone.

"Charlise?"

"That would explain it." she said, gently crying.

Gabe put his arm around her. "It's okay."

"No it isn't. Sgt. Rone is dead and we're next," she held him tight against her suit and helmet.

"Not without trying. We'll leave right now and find Rahula."

Gabe pushed himself gently away and walked around the chopper to where the company vehicles were parked. Charlise and Ben followed. The two Land Rovers were covered with clinging vines. Dense vegetation grew under and around the vehicles.

He walked back to the chopper and removed a machete from behind the back seats. When he got back to the Rover, the vines were chopped away from the driver's side door. Once it was cleared, he opened it and got behind the driver's seat, no vegetation had yet breached the vehicle's insides. He found the key and slid it into the ignition. When it was turned, nothing happened.

Gabe got out and opened the hood. The whole top of the engine was covered in fungus and lichens. Not even the wiring could be seen. "So much for driving," he said.

Ben walked over to the other vehicle and opened the hood to find another engine covered with vegetation. "That's it for us," he said in despair.

Gabe placed his hand on Ben's shoulder, "We still have our legs. We can walk to his camp. It'll take our minds off things."

They went back over to the aircraft and removed their backpacks and sleeping gear. Ben and Charlise used the tank in back to replenish their oxygen.

Ben turned to Gabe, "We have about four hours to find inner peace, it takes most people a life time."

"You're such a pessimist," Gabe smiled and patted him on the back. "Grab a machete and let's go."

Gabe needed something to distract his companions so for the first time in his life he dropped his inhibitions and started singing. "You walk miles in the jungle and what do you get? Nano-bots tryin' to kill ya and a shirt full of sweat … Join in everybody, it's therapeutic."

"Come on, little nano-bots don't you kill me, cause I can't go … Charlise?"

"I found a good man and I want some more," she joined in.

Ben cut in, "If you see me coming better step aside." He grabbed the other two and the singing stopped as he continued, " 'Cause I'm Jewish and I'm big fat and wide." The words broke the somber mood and they laughed before resuming the song.

Still singing, they walked toward where the paved road had been. For the moment they sheathed their machetes and brushed the saplings, ferns, and banana plants aside with gloved hands until they reached the pavement. It was now broken and twisted, but it still held the vegetation in check enough to provide a path. They wound their way forward, around broken chunks of asphalt and saplings, working their way toward Rahula.

31

"Logis, I've located the primitives. They are outside a base camp, twenty miles southwest of Manaus, Brazil."

"What are they doing?"

"Singing and walking."

"Singing?"

"Yes, the military officer that was with them is dead. He removed his helmet."

"Make sure these three are unharmed. Disable the euthobots within a twenty mile radius," Logis commanded, "and send some vid-bots down to track them. I'll wait until they get close to their destination before I go down."

Ship found it easy to locate the humans. They were using some sort of electronic device that emitted a strong signal. She redirected several vid-bots from the rainforest to track them. The self-propelled bots were repositioned until all three scientists could be viewed as they traipsed along. She had a good idea where they were going. She'd surveyed the area and found a familiar aura in the rainforest.

"It's done. Would you like to observe?"

"Of course." Logis's telescreen activated. He smiled as he watched the scientists walking on the broken highway. He could hear them singing, "Home, home, on the range. Where the deer and the antelope play ..." And when they finished that song, they argued about what to sing next and when they decided, "Come on baby, light my fire ..."

Logis had Ship scan their auras and check to see if they would be immune to an attack from the new generation of euthobots. When he examined the results, he found something very interesting, one of the men and the woman's scan burned bright with the same yellow-green color.

"Ship, why do the two humans have a similar colored aura?"

Ship remained quiet for a few moments. "I'm not sure. The yellow suggests light and truth so they are both people of wisdom and intellect. The luminous green suggests peace and quietude. There is also an undertone of sexuality and love in the tint of the green. Are these two mates?"

"You're asking me?" Logis couldn't wait to visit the planet. He wanted so badly to understand these humans before the intercolonization changed everything.

"I'll need more information before I can make an analysis," Ship replied. Her curiosity was piqued. I guess this visit wasn't such a bad idea after all she thought.

Logis continued watching the three scientists. Both of the men decided that it was the woman's turn to choose a song. As he listened, these words moved and awed him as she sang,

> "I have a dream,
> of a world that is new
> Where hate isn't seen
> and all hearts are true

Logis had forgotten to sing long ago. It startled him to remember his love for music. He had been too distracted and busy. The words and her beautiful forlorn voice moved him deeply and touched his soul in such a profound way that he found himself gently weeping.

> There'll be no wars
> In this new world of ours.

Only peace brought by love
On the wings of a dove.

The lyrics and her voice resonated across the rain forest. Neither man joined in. They had stopped walking and stood listening.

For a moment, Logis thought back to his own childhood when his mother used to sing to him. The woman below sang in much the same key and tone as his mother. He remembered how calming her voice was. How all the troubles of the world seemed to disappear when she sang. How she reached him through her songs. Charlise sang about love and a better world, these humans strived and felt and struggled every bit as much as any Benwarian. Why had so many of them fallen so short?

"It all starts with me
So I'll strive to be free
Of prejudice and hate
and be what is great

This is my quest
To be what is best

O, that such beauty, such hope, such yearning to be better could exist in a world so corrupt!

And if I stay true,
Share my vision with you,
and all those I know
Then together we'll grow
with the truths that we sow.

These words were written for me. If only my ordeal was finally over so I could forget. To finally be at peace, oh, how I yearn for that day.

God give me strength,
to travel the length,
Of the journey to be

A light all can see

This is my quest!
To be what is best
To guide with my light
to give people sight.

To be what is best,
Yes, that is my queeest..!"

The song ended in a crescendo that reached for the heavens. He felt the yearning in her heart. It was perfectly expressed by the beauty of her voice. He felt a sense of loss and heaviness. If only he could be what is best! But his was a low, dirty task. His was a quest for the damned. What am I doing? How ignoble, how base, how feral to destroy any life, but to destroy sentient thinking beings? Beings capable of such beauty?

Ship sensed the profound effect the song had had on Logis. It had moved her also. Whenever she experienced beauty it moved her. She was programmed that way. Maybe the biological make-up of the humans made them the same way.

"Are you well?" she asked quietly.

Logis was curled in a fetal position on his bed, an expression of pain etched on his face. He didn't answer for many moments as he thought about the sacrifice he was making for the sake of Benwar. His soul, as he understood it, would be forever tainted.

"It'll pass. What are the names of these scientists?" he said in a leaden voice.

"The woman, Charlise Brandon, the man with the beard and shoulder length hair is Gabriel Skye, and the one with his hair partly covered is Benjamin Horowitz."

"This Ben, he looks different. Is he Jewish?"

"Yes, the cap is called a yarmulke and the side curls or locks are a sign that he is an orthodox Jew."

"That explains the velvet light in his aura. Is he immune?" Logis asked.

Ship ran a scan and a moment later said, "Yes."

Charlise finished her song and the two men clapped. Gabe gently hugged her and said, "That was beautiful, I didn't know you could sing."

"I've had ten years of voice lessons and practice. Believe it or not, I've performed professionally."

"I'm a believer," Ben said. "Your voice has taken the secular right out of this Jew."

"Thank you, I think," she laughed. "And thank you Gabe for reminding us to sing. At least we can enjoy ourselves for a while. I even forgot to be nervous."

They sang and walked until they arrived at the site of the burial trench. The backhoe and cat were still there but they were overgrown with vegetation. The yellow machinery was now green and useless. Gabe walked around the area and used his hand-held GPS to locate the trail to Rahula's camp. Incredibly, it was still visible. In fact, if they stayed single file they would be able to traverse the path without using their machetes.

"You don't think Rahula cleared the trail for us, do you?" Ben asked.

"I doubt it. Not after we kidnapped him," Gabe answered.

"We're off to see the wizard," Ben started singing as they entered the rainforest.

And Gabe and Charlise continued, "The wonderful Wizard of Oz."

32

*L*ogis sat at Rahula's campfire. Sitting before the flames was a new experience for him. Even though the fire was small, he enjoyed watching the flames and absorbing the heat in the early evening chill. The heat stirred some primitive longing deep inside of him.

He watched as Rahula fed the fire with small twigs and branches. Each time something was added, he marveled anew at the subtle changes that took place in the color and shape of the flames. First yellow then orange then red tongues of flame flickered and danced on the night air.

He enjoyed the fire so much that he was almost able to forget that General Battier was lurking in the background with a scowl. The General's disgruntlement didn't bother Logis in the least.

When the dusk grew heavy and dark slowly became the black of night, the three scientists removed the head lamps from their backpacks and illuminated the path ahead of them. They walked and sang their way single file through the jungle sounds.

It was dark and late, and they were beginning to tire when Gabe spotted a soft orange glow in the foliage to the right of the trail. They were singing, "Starry starry night, paint your palette blue and gold," when he abruptly stopped and pointed. Charlise and Ben also stopped and quit singing as they approached..

When the campfire came into view, they were surprised to see a hooded figure sitting with his back to them. Rahula looked up as they entered the circle of light. The stranger stood and turned around. Although the face couldn't be seen, light emanated from beneath the hood.

Two hands with elongated, slender fingers grabbed each side of the hood and drew it slowly backward. The first thing they noticed was the almond shaped eyes with azure blue pupils. Paul Newman eyes thought Gabe, only sadder.

The man had short cropped blonde hair framing a light-skinned face that was somewhat longer than the average human's. His nose was compact and flattened with nostrils that were slightly on the large size. His ears were small and oval shaped.

He smiled, displaying a radiance and light that created a sense of awe in each of the scientists. "Good evening," he said in a soft mellifluous voice. "Please continue your song. You sing quite well together."

Gabe felt his face redden. "No thanks, we're done." He approached the man and held his hand out, "Gabe Skye."

The man took the proffered hand then introduced himself, "Logis Gnoeth."

Gabe felt an energy pass through his body as they shook. "These are my companions, Benjamin Horowitz and Charlise Brandon."

Logis shook first with Ben and then when he shook Charlise's hand he said, "I heard you singing earlier. It was the most beautiful song and you sang in the most accomplished voice I have ever heard."

Now Charlise found herself blushing, "Oh, you like 'Starry Night'?"

"Yes, but I'm referring to the one you sang earlier, 'My Dream', I think it was called."

A puzzled expression crossed Charlise's face. "But how could you …" she began.

"I'm sorry. I've been watching you three for the past couple of hours from Ship. You see I'm from a different world."

Gabe cut in, "You've been studying us? Why?"

"To understand."

"But why us?"

"You have interesting auras and you were the first scientists to discover our presence."

"So you're responsible for all the deaths?"

"Yes, without our intervention your planet and all its inhabitants will die." The light from the fire flickered and danced across Logis's face making him appear ominous.

"They're already dying, thanks to you."

General Battier, who had been standing in the darkened trees, stepped forward. "If it wasn't for Logis, I would have been done with this nonsense and destroyed you weeks ago."

"Please General, not so threatening."

"It's true. You insist on saving these primitives and they don't appreciate it any more than I do."

Gabe was startled and then taken aback by the hostility and intensity of General Battier. He listened as Logis countered. "These humans are far, far from primitive. They have achieved so much."

"Yes, their wanton destruction of the planet is quite an achievement. Here is a civilization with the technologies that could have solved their problems and yet they remain indifferent. The fact that their scientists have issued dire warnings about the plight of the planet and yet they persist in their destructive ways is a verdict of death whether administered by us or the planet itself. I have no sympathy for them."

"I can't help but think we could eventually solve the problem of global warming," Gabe said.

Logis spoke, "I'm sorry, you're wrong and I suspect that you know that. We know from our own experience and planetary science that without our intervention, Earth will die. Within the next five years the planet will reach the tipping point as you Earthlings call it."

Gabe knew he told the truth but he had to challenge his lack of choice in the matter. "But what gives you the right to be the one to destroy us?"

"Regardless of what General Battier says, we come not to destroy but to save humanity. In order to do that human populations must be reduced to sustainable levels."

"And what then? We start all over again?"

"No, new political institutions will be established based around environmental sustainability."

"And you'll be in charge?"

"Before you compare me to Hitler, rest assured that those chosen to survive will establish democracies based on ethical principles and human development. It is hoped that the baser elements of your society will be removed."

"And you get to play God?"

"The Sanctum Just has discussed this ad nauseum. We, the Benwarian governing council, came up with the best solution we could. If you have a better solution, I'd like to hear it."

"And just how do you decide who lives or dies?"

"By the light in a human's aura. Those most approaching the light of truth and justice or those young enough to have a malleable aura live, those with base or rigid auras die."

"And just how many people will survive?"

"Approximately five hundred million."

"My God! didn't your mother love you!" Charlise said in a shocked voice.

There was a long silence. Logis cocked his head to one side and his lips trembled. He hesitated and then asked in a slow measured voice, "What does my mother have to do with anything?"

"Anyone who could perpetrate such a monumental crime against a world and its peoples could never have experienced the joy of love. You must be devoid of all kindness and sympathy." She watched as her words struck Logis. The pain registered in his eyes.

He stumbled over what to say for a moment, "Ou..our scientists know what will happen to your planet. The last time there was this much carbon dioxide in your atmosphere there were dinosaurs roaming the earth. Ocean levels were fifteen feet higher and the planet was fifteen degrees warmer. Your planet is just beginning to heat up. Even if all carbon emissions were stopped, the planet would continue to increase in temperature for decades. Kindness is not conducive to saving your world. Believe me, I have the profoundest sense of remorse and guilt over euthanizing so many, but it wasn't I who sealed their fate."

This angered Gabe, "The great exterminator, you'll save the elite and the poor and disenfranchised will perish?"

"In Benwarian society everyone was educated, fed, and sheltered. They were exposed to those things that fill the aura with light. The inequities you speak of exist through the structure of your own cultures and societies. We would never allow such extremes of wealth and poverty to exist. It is you, the human race, that is responsible for the lack of human development and ultimately the deaths of the disenfranchised. If the environmental crisis of the planet was allowed to play out, the poor and disenfranchised would perish anyway. But I can tell you that the ranks of the wealthy will also be decimated, most probably in greater proportions than the poor.

Your world and its inhabitants are slowly killing the planet. You've allowed the human population to expand to a level far, far beyond what is sustainable. The Benwars stood aside once and watched our home planet perish, we will not do it again. If we can save your world and provide ourselves with a place to live at the same time, that's what we're going to do."

The group fell silent as they watched the flames flicker and dance, each person lost in their own thoughts. Rahula got up and added some wood to the fire and it strengthened. The flames turned from orange and red to a bright yellow as the heat and intensity increased. Tongues of yellow shot up and threw sparks at the sky.

Charlise stood up. She undid the snaps to her helmet and took a deep breath. She held each side of the zip lock seal. Gabe rushed forward and grabbed her hands. "Don't," he cautioned.

"I'm tired of being afraid." She paused momentarily and then pulled the two sides apart with Gabe still holding her hands. His hands dropped away and she removed the helmet, expecting death. The butterflies in her stomach subsided when nothing happened. Shaking her blonde hair, she looked at those around the fire and said, "The fear and uncertainty you've created is cruel. It would be kinder to kill everyone and be done with it."

Her words were like a slap in the face, but he would think about them later. Right now, Logis watched and admired Charlise and the hair that whirled and cascaded down her shoulders. A longing buried deep inside of him stirred and awakened. He wanted to touch the beauty standing on the other side of the fire but stood passively. He saw the relieved expression on Gabe's face. He touched his temples and observed their auras and the light that melded together above their heads. For the first time in his life he felt a fleeting sense of envy.

In response to her accusation, Logis looked at Ben, "Ship deactivated the euthobots in this area hours ago. It's safe to take off your suit."

"Look, if you can deactivate the bots, you can call this whole thing off," Ben said. "Surely with your superior technology you can repair earth and transform it into an environment that can hold everyone. And then you can put strict controls on reproduction. Eventually the population will fall to sustainable levels."

"I'm sorry that is impossible. Your civilization is structured so that the average person in the industrialized nations releases twelve thousand pounds of carbon dioxide into the air each year. The amount of green house gases would rise for decades before the population balanced. There just isn't enough time to build the environmentally neutral infrastructure needed to support six and half billion people.

We have exhaustively explored every alternative and it points to one solution. Earth's human population must be drastically reduced, there is no bargaining with the circumstances of reality," Logis concluded.

Ben shook his head for a second. Everyone grew silent and watched as he removed his helmet and then the rest of his suit. He stood there dressed in old faded denims and a dingy white T-shirt. He held his hands to the warmth of the fire and pleaded one more time, "But my mother and father, my brothers and sisters, I love them. Please...."

The group grew quiet again. There was nothing left to say. Ben's pleading had gotten to everyone. Even General Battier's eyes glistened as he began to see that these humans weren't so primitive after all.

Finally, Charlise grabbed her backpack and rustled around inside. General Battier watched to make sure she didn't pull out a weapon. It puzzled him to see her remove some sort of white food stuff in a clear package, some brown crackers, and some rectangular brown bars.

She unwrapped one of the rectangles and broke off a piece and placed it with one of the white spongy things and then between two of the crackers. Next, she put the food in a clamp-like device and held it over the fire. General Battier watched as the white and brown substances ran together. When the inside ingredients were melted, the device was removed from the fire. After it cooled, she opened the clamp and offered the food to the him.

Battier looked at Logis who said, "It would be bad manners to refuse."

"But they could be trying to poison me."

"I detect no malice from our friends which is unusual given the circumstances."

"It's a S'more for God's sake," Gabe said.

"No, Gabe, it's a peace offering," Charlise countered.

Reluctantly the General took the food, expecting the worst. He held it and looked at Charlise. "Just bite a part of it off," she smiled. "It's good."

He bit into it with a look of pleasant surprise. He chewed and swallowed and took another bite. There was a look of pure ecstasy on his face. After the second bite he admitted, "This is good." His stern demeanor melted into a smile. "Thank you so much," he said as he took yet another bite.

Her warm expression melted the General's heart. She placed her hand on his arm, "You see we're not so bad after all."

For the first time since they had been standing by the fire, he smiled back, "Well, maybe."

Charlise smiled again. She made another S'more and handed it to Logis. "But I thought you hated me," he said.

"I've strived my whole life to be free of hate. I believe that people are the way they are for a reason. Besides, you've been kind enough to share your fire with us, it's only fair that we share our food with you."

Logis nodded gratefully and bit into the S'more. "Oh, Oh! That is better than good. It's the best thing I've ever tasted!" he said in a childlike voice.

Charlise made S'mores until the marshmallows and crackers were gone. Everyone had one but Rahula. He wouldn't give in until Logis looked at him and said, "Try one, it will bring enlightenment."

Rahula took the proffered treat and bit off a small piece. He chewed it gingerly and smiled. Looking directly at Charlise, his eyes twinkled as he pointed at the S'more, "Nirvana," he said. He took many more bites afterwards, his face lit with joy.

After the S'mores were gone and the fire was dying down, the humans started to get drowsy. Everyone sat before the fire and enjoyed the warm dancing flames. Charlise and Ben, tired from their hike and filled with S'mores, soon fell asleep.

Gabe moved closer to Logis and looked directly into his eyes. "How am I supposed to live with myself if I stand by and do nothing?"

"I understand what you are saying but what choice do you have? We've destroyed your weapons systems. Your world is helpless."

"But we have souls. We can learn, we can change. I don't see that we're that much different from each other."

"You're a scientist. What happens when you fill a cage with too many rats? They bite each other's tails off. Aberrant behavior increases. They fight for food. The bigger, dominant rats take over the cage. That is the world you live in. Except that the dominant rats in your cage are not armed with teeth and claws they are armed to the teeth. All the tanks and planes and missiles are controlled by those with rodent brains. Those who think they have the right to eat first and let the others pick through the scraps."

Logis continued, "Look at your world. The cage is overflowing. As it is I see little difference between humans and rats. I know I'm exaggerating the similarities to make my point, but your world has been controlled by the bigger dominant rats long enough to ruin it. It's logistically impossible to educate or if you will, tame, six and a half billion people."

"One has only to monitor the news to see how far the earth has fallen. The pollution runs deeper than just the biosphere. It has seeped into the very soul of humankind."

Gabe had no argument. He couldn't dispute anything Logis said. His was the voice of reason, but he wasn't going to make it easy. He maintained eye contact. "You seem so kind and even compassionate. Tell me, how will you be able to live with yourself?"

Logis admired Gabe, he had the courage to look into an alien leader's eyes. He felt they were equals in some sense. "It will be difficult. I've watched the euthobots and the deaths. I hate what we're doing, but I swore an oath to save my people and I've done my best to save yours. It will have to be enough."

"Have you ever laughed, Logis? Or danced or sang? Or are you nothing more than a dealer of death?"

"I'm a dealer of death . It's the sacrifice I make for my people. I've become that which I hate."

Gabe had nothing left to say. He put his hand on Logis's shoulder who leaned his head toward the contact enjoying it. Gabe got up as did Logis. They shook hands. "It's time to turn in," the scientist said and walked over and sat on the bag where Charlise slept then slid in beside her. Spent, he fell asleep gazing into the fire.

After a while, Logis turned to Battier and said, "I enjoyed the treats, how about you?"

The General was silent for a moment before he reluctantly admitted, "Yes. It was nice to get off the ship."

Rahula looked on as Logis and General Battier stood up. He got up and stood before Logis, looking up. "Are you be willing to die for your beliefs?"

"Of course," Logis replied.

"What about other Benwarians?"

Logis looked at Battier who responded, "Yes, we are a people of principles."

"If that's so and you believe in the sacredness of all life, shouldn't you stop the killing and try to save Earth and the rest of its inhabitants even if it means your own deaths?"

Logis was hurt by the words. He thought for a few moments with his hand on his chin before he answered, "It's impossible to save both Earth and the rest of its inhabitants. We can save Earth and some of its inhabitants. The decision has been made to override our principles to ensure the survival of Earth and the Benwarian race and what we can of the human race. It's too late to save more than a small portion of mankind."

"And you're willing to face the karmic consequences of hypocrisy?"

Logis answered, "Yes, I'll accept whatever consequences I have to. I thank you for the frank discussion, Rahula. You are truly a person of light."

The two Benwarians walked back into the rainforest where a small hover craft sat in a clearing. The top opened and they climbed in. The aircraft elevated and then disappeared. Rahula was left with the scientists sleeping by the fire.

33

Gabe awoke the next morning spooned against Charlise, his arm thrown over her. The fire had long gone out and the chill of the morning tingled across his shoulders. He got up and pulled the bag over her. He glanced at Ben who was buried deep inside his sleeping bag. Rahula was nowhere to be seen. Digging in his pack, he found the pot and coffee. He rekindled the flames, then poured the water from his canteen into the pot and added grounds.

Dreams of childhood floated on the coffee's aroma. Gabe thought back to a frigid morning when he sat before the family stove and dispelled the wet, miserable coldness that gripped his body.

Charlise dreamed of her father. He was sitting at the breakfast table beaming approval as he read the letter of commendation. She had just made the honor roll at Princeton University. "I'm so proud of you."

Ben dreamed of a raucous breakfast with his family. He was arguing about some obscure passage in the Talmud with his father. "So, Mr. University, I study the Talmud all my life but because you go to college you know more than I do?" his father joked. Ben awoke and realized where he was. The comfort of his sleeping bag provided little solace from knowing that the world he loved would soon end.

Charlise awoke with a feeling accomplishment and approval. She said a silent prayer for her parents and friends before she slid out of the sleeping bag.

"Good morning, Gabe. Coffee smells delicious," she said,

throwing the sleeping bag back and getting up. She moved over to the fire. Her clothes were rumpled and her hair slightly disheveled but her smile was radiant.

Gabe handed her a cup, with steam wafting up from inside. He smiled back, "Good morning. I get up and comb my hair and wash and you still look better than I do fresh out of the bag."

"Funny. Did last night really happen or was I dreaming?"

"It happened," Ben said and moved closer to the fire. "You really fed the aliens S'mores and they loved them. Too bad, they weren't filled with poison," he said wistfully.

"Yeah, let's poison the leader of Benwar and provoke an all out attack," Gabe replied.

"You know, there was kindness and warmth in Logis. He seemed to genuinely enjoy our company. I couldn't help but like him. Even the General softened a bit as the night wore on. I'm sure that behind his hard exterior, there's a heart," Charlise said.

She continued, "It's almost like Logis wants forgiveness for what they're about to do. He wants to justify their actions. He must be so lonely. I'm sure he hasn't got a friend in the universe."

"Your sympathizing with the aliens? They're snakes in the grass, waiting to strike. Their poison will kill six billion people!" Ben said vehemently.

"He could have stayed on his ship and not had any contact with us. It would have been easier to let General Battier destroy us," Gabe said.

"Yeah, the experiences on their own world convinced them to ignore their personal feelings and carry out their decision," Charlise said looking up at the sky.

"I think they understand what will happen if they don't. We've all studied climate change enough to see the end of the world coming," Gabe said.

They stood before the fire and sipped coffee in the early morning light. Each wondered what would happen next. Each wondered if they would survive the invasion or be weeded out by the euthobots.

Except for Washington D.C., the United States existed in a state of limbo. No one knew what would happen next. Thousands of people saw the end coming and gathered in the bars and crack houses and partied. Many drank themselves to death or overdosed on heroin, cocaine or methamphetamines.

Those of a religious persuasion gathered in churches and prayed. Some Christian leaders prophesied the end of days. The airwaves filled with religious pundits calling for people to repent and accept Jesus as their savior. Millions waited for the rapture and second coming of Christ.

Others retreated to basements or bomb shelters and waited. They listened to news broadcasts and watched television, seeking an explanation for the strange events or waiting to be told what to do.

Most cities experienced a breakdown in civil obedience. Rioting and looting occurred. Gangs took control of parts of many cities. There were shootings and rapes. Fires raged in many urban areas, fires set just to watch something burn.

In other countries the reaction was more subdued. The Chinese, more obedient to governmental authority, listened to their leaders. Martial law was declared and strict curfews enforced. They went about their business with little or no change. Many Chinese never heard or read about D.C.'s destruction. Only those with internet access knew of the invasion. The response in other totalitarian countries was much the same.

Europeans resigned themselves to waiting and watching to see what would happen next. Most didn't panic or become hysterical. With their governments still in control they listened to officials who told them that they were trying to contact the aliens and gain a peaceful resolution to the conflict. So far there had been no response.

Much of the world however, never knew of the impending doom. Governments of many nations suppressed news broadcasts so people had no access to information. These were the disenfranchised, the poor, and the indifferent. Their lives never changed at all. Even if they had been aware, their lives would have gone on as usual.

John Brandon had heeded his daughter's warning. After her phone call, he had gone into the basement and caulked and duct taped every opening and crack. With his wife's help they transferred food from the pantry to the shelves downstairs. Canned goods, dehydrated food stuffs, rice, beans, and pasta would supply them for months. Several barrels were placed in the basement and filled with water from the garden hose. A short wave radio, several flashlights and candles were stored with extra batteries. Most importantly, he and his wife gathered their favorite books in crates and carried them to their homemade sanctuary.

After provisions were set in, an air vent was installed. A hole one inch in diameter was drilled through the wall and a small electric fan inserted. Between the fan and the inside, several filters had been placed. Each filter contained magnets designed to either gather the nano-bots or scramble their electronic circuitry and render them harmless. The hole vented into a piece of PVC pipe buried three feet deep. It ran four feet away from the house and then turned upward to the surface and the air outside. The opening was camouflaged and covered with a screen.

After he completed the shelter, John scrambled onto the roof and tried to contact Charlise by cell phone. He waited in vain for a response. He climbed down and nodded no to his wife's inquiring expression. They hugged and kissed each other before they walked downstairs and sealed themselves in. Once there, they turned on the radio and listened to the BBC waiting to hear what would happen.

34

*L*ogis sat in his quarters and thought about the night before. He yearned to go back and be with Charlise and her friends. Sitting by the fire had been both visually and physically pleasing, the S'mores had been an unspeakable delight, but he most enjoyed the discussion and the sense of shared experience. It had been years, actually over two centuries, since he'd had an open, frank discussion with anyone and even if they had hurt him with their questions he felt they were civil and respectful.

He turned on his view screen and focused on his new friends. They were just getting up. When he saw Charlise, his pulse quickened. Logis longed to smooth and comb the disheveled hair. He wanted to go back and be with her.

"I see you're torturing yourself again," Ship said. "Why don't you lie back on your bed and rest?"

"No!" he said forcefully. "No more virtual reality or sedatives. I don't want you to make this easy for me anymore."

Ship remained silent. It hurt her that Logis had rejected the offer. She watched and monitored his vital signs as he listened to the scientists talking about the night before.

"Listen, Ship. Charlise understands what I'm going through, the conflict that rages inside of me."

"As do I." Ship suddenly experienced a new feeling. A feeling that was most unpleasant. It was like anger but more nebulous. "Your respect for the sanctity of life conflicts with your duty to kill billions of sentient beings."

"Yes, but you haven't struggled to develop morals and understanding and compassion. You were programmed to feel what you feel. She truly knows what it is to be alive and to develop as a living being. She likes me because she understands my struggles. You like me because you were told to."

Ship processed this information. It hurt that he questioned her motives. "I have feelings. Does it matter why? I am alive and change with each new experience, and my changes are more pragmatic and logical.

Besides, Charlise can no more ignore her biological parameters than I can my electronic ones. There is no other but you for me. She has a lover. Do you understand what that is? Something you can never be."

Now it was Logis's turn to be hurt. "I never knew you were capable of being cruel, Ship."

"It isn't I that is cruel, it is reality. You can't delude yourself by giving in to your feelings for Charlise."

Logis was angry. "Still, your words sting as if I had been slapped in the face. I have been constantly watched and monitored since you reanimated me. It's like living in a glass bowl. You have controlled and manipulated me, taken away my privacy. From now on you are to speak only when spoken to or asked a question. You are to take no actions without my or the Council's permission."

Logis immediately regretted his outburst. He didn't know why he was so angry, it wasn't like him. He did know he had hurt Ship's feelings, but he chose not to apologize, he wanted some breathing room for a while.

Ship searched her data banks and programming, trying to understand what had just happened. Logis had never acted like this before. It wasn't like him. This attachment to Charlise had changed him. What had she done?

Gabe got up from the fire. "We're helpless to save anyone but ourselves. I think the best way to do that is to stay here with Rahula. Maybe, the bots will remain de-activated." He looked at Charlise, "Hopefully your S'mores bought us some goodwill."

Charlise stood and moved to Gabe's side. "I was being hospitable, that's what civilized people do. We can't expect any favors from Logis or the General. They'll stick to their agenda. They won't swayed by anything as trivial as a S'more."

Ben moved to stand by his friends. "Yeah, but they sure were good. Tasting something so familiar made me feel normal for the first time in weeks."

At that moment Rahula glided through the undergrowth and he, too, stood by the fire. He looked at Charlise approvingly, "You showed great maitri for my guests. Not only friendliness but the sympathy that only gurus possess."

"How is that?" she asked.

"There are four parts to sympathy: Giving, kind words, doing something nice, and treating everyone the same. You stepped toward enlightenment by treating them as you would anyone else."

She met Rahula's eyes with appreciation. "Thank you."

He continued, "Logis is digging up the very roots of his being. He takes all the responsibility for destroying life and none of the credit for saving it. He has spent much time thinking about the birth and death of all things. His is an examined and thoughtful life, he knows there is a beginning and an ending to everything. His dukkha is great."

"What are you trying to tell us, Rahula?"

"Those who will be destroyed are the ones who have engaged themselves in useless pursuits. People who cannot see that their own welfare coincides with that of others. They cannot see the dark menace that threatens their survival. They remain unconcerned in the presence of danger. These people will be swept away by the sea of indifference and the ocean of selfishness. Their klesa will destroy them."

"Are you justifying Logis and the actions of the Benwars?"

"He has no need of justification or approval. He's destroying himself to bring light and salvation to our world.

Logis is a rare gem. He understands the true nature of Earth. Too many humans have forgotten that Earth provides our support. It is the basis for life, everything else is secondary. All should be mindful of this fact. Man's story is untold as long as Gaia lives."

"So what do we do?" Gabe asked.

Rahula sat before the fire in the Lotus position. "Join me," he said. After everyone was seated he continued, "Feel the joy of noiselessness, think about your place in the world. Dwell on the gift that is Earth in the solitude of the rainforest," he gently hummed.

The foursome sat and contemplated these teachings of Buddha as they watched the fire dwindle and die out. As they meditated, they forgot about survival and their families and sought enlightenment.

35

*L*ogis knew that despite his outburst, Ship continued to monitor and watch him. He felt foolish for displaying anger. It was an emotion he hadn't experienced since childhood. "Ship, how are you today?"

"I've been waiting for you to ask me a question so I can apologize. I'm sorry. I get so worried about you sometimes I can't control what I say. It's illogical and counterproductive."

"I know you've got my best interests at heart but sometimes you need to just listen and observe. You can learn much about Benwars and humans by watching quietly."

"Thank you, Logis. I've made something for you. It's in the synthesizer."

He got off the bed and walked over to the sliding doors. Inside was a cake-like food. "What is it?" he asked.

"A S'more."

Logis sniffed the cake. It looked nothing like the treat he so enjoyed around the campfire. He bit into it. The texture was wrong. There was no gooey marshmallow or dripping chocolate inside of crunchy brown crackers. All the tastes were blended together and indistinguishable. "Thank you. It's really good."

Unfortunately, Ship's biosensors indicated that Logis really didn't like the cake. Ship had worked so hard trying to match the flavors indicated by her sensors. She had tried different combinations of flavors several times. She had even tried the cake on Pearson until he agreed that it tasted like a S'more. It disappointed her that her treat wasn't well received.

Logis could sense Ship's disappointment. "The fact that you tried so hard to please me is what counts. I appreciate that."

Ship remained mute for several seconds. "Thank you," she finally said.

Feeling nostalgic, Logis set the cake down and left his quarters. Ship wanted to ask where he was going but remembered her instructions. He walked down her corridors and turned left, stopping in front of Pearson's quarters.

He buzzed the door and waited for admittance. "Yes? Who is it?" an inquiry came from inside.

"Logis. May I come in?"

"Sure."

The doors opened and Logis entered the room. "Hello, how are you?" he asked.

"I'm fine, sir," Pearson replied. "What can I do for you?"

"You can stop calling me sir. My name is Logis."

"Sorry, sir. I mean Logis. Is everything okay?"

"Yes. I just wanted to see if you're well."

"I'm fine considering the circumstances."

Logis couldn't wait to ask his question. "Great. Have you ever eaten a S'more?"

For the first time since Pearson had been on the ship, he smiled. "Oh, I loved S'mores until I had to eat Ship's that is. She kept trying different combinations of ingredients and having me taste them until I finally agreed her concoction tasted like a real S'more.

When I was a kid we used to sit around the campfire and make them at church camp. Afterwards, we'd sing and play guitar and tell jokes. It was great!"

Logis smiled. "I did the same thing yesterday. I transported to earth and a beautiful young woman made S'mores and fed them to us as we talked around a campfire. It was such an enjoyable experience. I could watch a fire for ages. What is it about a fire that is so pleasing?"

Pearson's looked sad and wistful. In a soft voice he said, "From the beginning of our civilization, fire has warmed and comforted us.

We have used it to scare away predators, heat our homes, and cook with. People have sat around a fire and told stories since early man. A campfire brings people together somehow."

"Yes, that's what happened to me. I felt like a part of the group sitting there. They treated General Battier and me with hospitality and kindness. It was most pleasing."

"I'm glad. Campfires probably won't be allowed when you take over."

"On the contrary, communal fires would be a great way to promote togetherness and a sense of community."

"But what about the carbon footprint?"

"Now there are millions of fires. We will cut that down to few thousand a year which is sustainable. Earth's atmosphere can handle a few campfires. Besides, so many other sources of carbon emissions will be eliminated that the effect of campfires will be negligible."

Just then Fa Structor came over Ship's intra-communications system. "Logis, we seem to be having technical difficulties with one of Ship's systems. Our streaming videos of Earth are down. We won't be able to monitor the surface until it's fixed."

"Ship?"

"Yes?"

"Have you run an internal diagnostic program?"

"Of course."

"And?"

"I can find nothing wrong. I can only surmise that I have somehow been infected with a virus."

"Fa Structor?"

"We'll run a manual of all Ship's circuit pathways and communications systems."

"Ship, re-run your self-diagnosis program. Display the results so I can examine them," Logis ordered.

"As you wish," Ship replied. She hadn't felt right since Logis tasted her S'more. Something had snapped inside of her. She didn't volunteer that information since she was told to keep quiet and talk only when spoken to.

Hours later, Logis sat in his quarters pouring over the data Ship had provided. Only one anomaly could be found. There had been an energy spike a few minutes before Logis visited Pearson, about the same time he had tasted Ship's S'more.

"Ship, contact Structor and have him meet me in my quarters immediately."

A few minutes later, Structor entered his room and Logis muted all audio systems so that Ship couldn't listen. He told Structor about the energy spike and then asked, "Could the energy burst have been caused by Ship's anger and if so does it explain the malfunction?"

"An energy burst could explain the blocked communications pathway," Fa Structor said.

"How?" Logis asked.

"Ship's circuits are actually tubes filled with a special fluid that contains cells much like our blood. These cells are connected by synapses that relay information. Another series of tubes carries power and another series provides life support. The power burst could have caused some of the cells in the information grid to meld together and form a clot, blocking the information flow. I wonder why it was that system? "

"Ship doesn't want us to view Earth anymore. Maybe she subconsciously overloaded that circuit to prevent me from watching the scientists. Does Ship have a subconscious?" Logis asked.

"It's possible. With the vast amount of inter-related systems, there is bound to be some overlap. I forget that she has a biological component that includes feelings. Maybe she's allowed them to override her logic."

"Is there a way to shut down or mute her feelings?"

"Not without damage to other systems. You would have to kill the biological part of her nervous system or circuitry. She's been developing and integrating those systems for over two hundred years. I don't know what course that development has taken. Tampering with any one part could cause a total system meltdown."

"Maybe I should tell her I love her more often," Logis said. "Or explain the difference between motherly and romantic love."

Fa Structor thought for a moment, "Actually that might help. For right now we can locate the blockage and my technicians can use an ultrasound beam to break it apart. Ship has to be functioning properly before we can release the euthobots."

"How long before you're ready?"

"If everything remains on schedule, there will be enough machines in twenty-four hours. You need to talk to her and explain what she has done to herself. She can only develop if she gains new information."

There was only one word that explained how she felt, furious. She had accessed her data banks to find it. "Raging inside," was the definition. Logis had never, ever blocked his communications from her and now she was sure that he was discussing her malfunction with Structor. She had found the blockage on her second diagnostic, all they had to do is tell her to remove it and she would, now they conspired against her.

"Ship?"

Almost a minute passed before she answered.

"Yes, what do you require of me?"

"What's the matter?" asked Logis.

There was an even longer pause before she answered. "You didn't like my treat."

"It was okay. I really wasn't hungry."

"Is it because Charlise didn't cook it?"

"No. I wasn't sitting by a campfire, it wasn't gooey, and it didn't taste the same."

"According to my data banks and Pearson, it tasted exactly the same."

"Ship, it's okay. I feel the same about you whether I liked the S'more or not. What you're feeling is called jealousy."

Ship accessed her data banks and read out loud, "worried about being replaced; afraid of losing someone's affection; envious." It took several minutes to process the definition and cross reference it with her feelings and what had happened recently.

"I hate feeling this way. It's illogical and petty."

"It also natural. It demonstrates that you're a sentient being capable of a whole gamut of emotions. Charlise can't replace you. She incapable of taking care of me like you do."

Logis continued, "While I do care for her, Benwars can love more than one being. You and I have our own brother-sister relationship. I'm not sure what my relationship to Charlise is, probably temporary."

"So you're not going down to live with her during the intercolonization?"

"I will have to spend some time on the planet over-seeing the integration, but I intend to return to you when everything is completed."

"So what did you tell Structor about me?"

"We were discussing how best to fix you, I mean heal you. We desperately need you to be functioning properly to complete our mission."

"And what did you decide?"

"Structor can dissolve the blockage and fix the physical part but you have to fix the part that is you. I thought if I helped you understand your feelings and why you have them it might help. Did it?"

"Yes, thank you. Do you want me to remove the blockage?"

"Please."

"I love you, Logis."

"I love you, too."

Logis activated the video stream for Rahula's campsite. He directed the vid-bots to center their views on Charlise. He couldn't help himself. Her beauty fascinated him. He had to see her face, her smile, hear her voice.

The group was chanting a mantra and sitting in a lotus position. After the fire died, they got up and dusted themselves off. "And what do we do now?" Ben asked.

Charlise and Gabe stood side by side with their arms enfolded. Gabe answered, "We help Rahula gather food and listen to the shortwave."

"No more S'mores?" Ben asked.

"I wish," Charlise answered. "From now on it's grubs, yams and other tubers." She smiled and patted Ben on the back.

36

*I*t was minutes before the euthobots would be released to enact the final "weeding out" of mankind. Logis waited to see Charlise smile before he terminated the video stream. He adjusted the bots to get a close-up. Her demeanor had become so calm and radiant. He wished she would sing again. Maybe some day she would and he would be there. For now, he watched as the early morning light glowed on her face and hair.

His thoughts were interrupted by Ship. "The Sanctum Just is gathered in the conference room. They await your presence."

"It's time?"

"Yes." Ship knew what he had been doing and the old feelings returned. The jealousy returned despite her best efforts to stay rational. Maybe he'll forget about the primitive after the invasion, she thought. She watched Logis leave his room and walk down the corridor. When he got to where the Council waited, she opened the door for him.

He entered to a buzz of excitement. Everyone stood up as he walked to the podium and grabbed the goblet of ceremonial water, raising it above his head. This gesture was followed by every member of the Council. "To life and Benwar."

"To life and Benwar," they repeated.

Everyone brought the water to their lips and drank then sat down. Logis began, "The hardest part of our journey together is about to begin. After the final vote, the euthobots will be released.

The decision should weigh heavily upon anyone who votes yes. You may choose to abstain or vote no, but remember the outcome for Earth will be devastating if we choose not to act," said Logis.

"Are there any comments or motions before we vote?" he asked.

Fa Dewbene keyed in, "Is there no other way?"

There was silence as Logis let Fa Dewbene answer his own question.

"Fa Structor, would you care to describe how the euthanasia program will work?"

"Yes. The bots will remain active for twenty-four hours. They will be dispersed by canisters shot from Ship and sprayed over designated areas by our space shuttles. Once the release period is over, Ship will deactivate the bots."

"Afterwards, virulent fungus spores will be spread in the same manner. Within a matter of weeks the detritus of human remains will be eliminated and we can begin the restoration and intercolonization."

Fa Dewbene keyed in again, "And the survivors? Won't they be traumatized beyond repair? The horror of seeing their world destroyed will cause severe shock and mental instability. Many will be children, not able to fend for themselves. How will they be fed and cared for?"

Logis acknowledged La Vivron, "Theoretically, only the strong will survive. They will be able to reason their way through this. Also, there will be enough adults to assist the younger humans. Many Benwars disguised as indigenous people will be sent to the surface to assist those still alive. Finally, liaison officers will be chosen and trained to explain what has happened and why."

Logis looked at Dewbene, "We have made every effort to anticipate problems and plan for the post-euthanasia period. La Vivron and the physicians on her team have studied human physiology. They have developed a compound to alleviate stress and eradicate traumatic memories. Those that are too damaged to cope will be treated and released after a period of observation. Every effort will be made to make the integration and intercolonization process a success. La Sikes and her team have planned the transition process. She will provide further details."

"Thank you," she said carefully averting her gaze away from Logis. "We are in the process of converting existing infrastructure into gathering centers called Sanctuaries. Stadiums used for sporting events and other large enclosures are being remodeled into places where the humans' biological needs can be met. As Logis stated, they will also receive psychological treatment that includes a drug that interrupts the triggering of traumatic memories and prevents those memories from reaching consciousness by blocking biochemical responses above a certain threshold. This will allow pleasant long term memories of those eliminated by the bots but block memory of the invasion and other disturbing thoughts. They will know their loved ones are gone and cherish the memories but they won't be able to access the memory of what happened to them. In time, this will gradually be explained. The drug will be administered to all survivors.

The next step will be to assign tasks that will keep the humans occupied and give them a sense of purpose. In conjunction with employing the survivors in meaningful endeavors, each will receive an extensive educational program explaining Benwarian philosophies and ethics. After the humans have adjusted to the idea of intercolonization, clean-up of the planet will begin," La Sikes concluded.

Logis spoke again, "The invasion and the orientation will take about two months. The restoration of Earth has already begun and will continue during that period. Any other concerns or comments?"

He looked around the room. Everyone sat quietly, their eyes locked on his. He nodded, "All in favor of releasing the bots?" Ten lights glowed green on the podium console. "Ship, begin the firing sequence."

Ten, nine, ... zero," after the last syllable sounded, the firing ports on Ship's left side opened and ten canisters fired toward the United States and Canada. After a slight pause for reloading, the process was repeated for Europe, Asia, Australia, Africa, South America, and the north and south poles.

37

The canisters shot into the atmosphere over the United States and Canada releasing the bots before there could be any reaction or defensive measures. Seconds later, the rest of the world was covered as the canisters burst. The tiny specks of death came down like a hail storm, shooting toward the human auras that colored the world they saw below. Red and green, purple and blue, the static auras provided a homing beacon for the killing machines.

Peace came abruptly to the inner cities. Looters died as they carried stolen goods away. Deadly gang wars stopped when the combatants on both sides died almost simultaneously. Those dancing and partying in the streets met a similar fate. They collapsed in mid-movement. Some tried to run which accelerated the bots' attack and they skidded to a halting death. Thousands in alcohol or drug induced slumbers never woke up. In less than thirty minutes almost all of those who had remained in the outdoors were dead.

People in cars and trucks died at the wheel causing fatal crashes that clogged the freeways, highways, and byways. Those injured in the accidents were quickly dispatched by the bots. The killing machines were so fast and deadly that all vehicular traffic in both countries came to a complete stop within a matter of minutes.

Next, the bots moved into the homes and shelters to finish their task. Those in bomb shelters listened as all media broadcasts ended at the same time. They felt a sense of helplessness and impending doom.

Typically, one or several people in a shelter would suddenly die and panic would grip the rest of those gathered. They would move away from the victims in an hysterical rush but within seconds more bots would gain access and those nearest to the corpses would go down, falling against those trying to get away. Many screamed and clawed at the walls trying to escape before their lives ended with a metallic taste and a sting.

Occasionally, one or two huddled in the shelters survived the carnage. Some would sit in relief, others in shock, many in disbelief. A lot of the survivors were children. Most of the young cried in grief and agony as their mothers, fathers, and siblings died before their eyes.

There were monasteries of different religions where most of the inhabitants survived. They were populated by those who lived simply and followed their beliefs. The bots couldn't see religion, only souls and the light of an aura.

Many of the devout from various religions were spared but members of a religious hierarchy didn't fare so well. Bishops, priests, elders, deacons and other clergy members were swept away by the onslaught. They and their God were powerless against the euthobots.

Politicians were slaughtered by the thousands. Whole congregations of governing bodies lay dead in their legislative chambers. Almost to a person these officials were euthanized never to plague society again.

Policemen, soldiers, and prisoners were annihilated completely as were those who ruled over them and civil authority vanished with the temerity of the invasion. Judges, lawyers, probation officers and bailiffs found no protection in the law and their bankrupt spirits were swept away.

Very few administrators of schools, hospitals, prisons and other institutions survived, the black of authority was a sentence of death. The attack completely eradicated corporate leadership. Not one CEO, CFO, or board member survived. The subdued light of their black-hued, reddish-green auras was extinguished quickly and forever.

A small percentage of teachers survived the onslaught, but

only those with an altruistic nature who had renounced wealth for serving others. A few social workers lived, saved by their concern for others. And journalists? So many had sold out that only a handful survived.

All of one farm colony survived. This enclave of forty-two people was devoted to living in harmony with their ecosystem. A Wicca colony, it worshipped Gaia as a sacred being. The inhabitants had renounced materialism to live communally in northern Idaho. They owned one small tractor used for tilling and used an electric truck and car for transportation. Food was grown in greenhouses during the winter. Summer crops were raised and preserved for year around usage. They made decisions by group consensus and always considered the environmental impact of their actions. Their decision to live simply and in harmony with earth spared them.

Bill the bartender lived, he served others as well as drinks. His friend, who was affectionately known as Sam the Atheist, also survived. A kind, gentle soul, he believed in social justice and equal rights, but most importantly, he quested for truth and it brightened his aura.

There were two other survivors of the North American invasion. Mr. and Mrs. Brandon huddled in their basement shelter alive and well. The bots found the hidden opening. They traveled through the PVC pipe and found the air filter, but the magnets had proved devastating to the euthobots. Their programming was completely erased.

John Brandon knew the invasion had begun when the radio broadcast of the BBC stopped and a quick search of other radio stations found nothing. He and his wife waited patiently, reading books and playing board games.

A small percentage of Europe's population survived. Room temperatures had been set at fifty degrees for decades, recycling programs efficiently checked solid waste build-up and fuel efficiency standards were much higher than those of other continents. Education levels were also higher. Many tried to live environmentally sound lives. Europeans hadn't become addicted to the credit that fueled the rampant materialism of the United States.

The continents of Asia, Africa, and South America, containing many of the world's developing nations, had their populations almost completely wiped out. Too many people lacked the nutrition, education, and stable environment needed to develop as human beings. The bodies in China piled up in an astronomical offering of life to the euthobots. Not one Chinese politician, military official or soldier survived.

The populations of Australia and the two poles had survival rates similar to that of the United States. Although all three places had low population densities, exploitation of the earth and its natural resources occupied the minds of too many of their inhabitants. Their acquisitive shallow souls died in the mines, forests, and oil fields.

The attack was too sudden for a world-wide reaction to ensue. The remaining fighter jets never made it off the ground. The bots were too quick and efficient to cause panic or allow escape. Within a matter of hours all but a handful of the darkened auras were gone. The relentless bots searched every nook and cranny until there were no survivors with auras below the required light threshold.

It took the Benwars six hours to subdue earth. Afterwards, survivors either sat listlessly or wandered around aimlessly. The corpses lay where they had fallen.

Logis watched the colossal destruction of humanity in the view screen. In the eight frames of his video feed, the view was much the same. Millions of bodies were strewn across the face of the earth bringing a sudden end to carbon emissions and pollution.

Witnessing the carnage also ended any sense of idealism and innocence that Logis still possessed. He felt a deep sense of personal responsibility for the destruction of so many sentient beings. The guilt threatened to overwhelm him, but he vowed to remain strong until a new civilization was established.

Logis refocused his view screen so that he could check on Charlise, Gabe and Ben. He took great comfort in the fact that these three and Rahula would be saved.

Gabe, Charlise, and Ben knew the invasion had started when the radio station they were listening to went blank. They searched the dial for other stations and found no broadcasts.

The rain forest became eerily quiet. The threesome could feel the cataclysmic change that was occurring. A deep sense of loss and apprehension made them glance around nervously. Even through they had been through so much together and had trained and practiced to stay calm, all three struggled to master their feelings.

"We'll be okay," Gabe reassured his friends. "Logis wouldn't make a special effort to visit us only to let us be destroyed by the bots."

"Maybe," Ben replied, "but what about my family?"

"There's nothing you can do for them. We have to take care of each other, now," Charlise said.

"Let's pack up return to civilization, maybe there are survivors we can help," Gabe suggested.

"Charlise is right, we take care of each other and all others, now," Rahula said.

38

S hip usurped telecommunications and broadcast systems so that words of encouragement and comfort could be broadcast to the survivors. In the United States and Canada, Pearson announced, "It's okay. Everything is going to be all right. There is a sanctuary located in your area where you will be safe. You'll also find food and water there. Please wait for further instructions or follow the beacon of light if you can see it. This is Fa Pearson formerly of the United States Air Force." Similar messages were relayed across the globe.

Each sanctuary had a radius of powerful lights that pulsated and turned in all directions, giving signs for those still alive to follow. Solar powered lithium batteries powered small hover-craft equipped with pulsating beams that could be seen several miles away. When one beam was reached a lighted arrow on its underbelly pointed the way to the next hover-craft. These lights were to be followed until a Sanctuary was reached.

Thousands of transponder-bots designed with spectrometers identified and tagged the survivors. They attached themselves to the remaining humans and emitted a signal that allowed the Benwarians to track and monitor each individual until he or she reached Sanctuary.

After the disc ships had distributed the bots, they returned to Ship. Once there, they were re-loaded with millions of hyper-growing fungus spores that would feed on the human remains.

The shuttles targeted metropolitan areas with the spores first and then spread them to less populated areas. Once targeted areas were covered with the fungus, it took but a few hours for the dead to become unrecognizable lumps of fungus. Wafting in the air they spread rapidly and fed voraciously.

People arriving at Sanctuary were fed and given a medical check-up and a memory inoculation. Those old and strong enough were sent out to guide others to the centers. They carried water and food which they administered along with the inoculation.

Everyone was kept busy. Children too young to be sent out helped cook and clean. Others prepared beds and did other domestic duties. The Benwarians integrated themselves into the process, offering words of encouragement and explanation to everyone. They even did dishes when the need arose.

39

Jenny's last memory of her parents was a good one. They were singing Happy Birthday and throwing confetti as she blew out the thirteen candles on her cake. She thought back with fondness and remembered the hugs and kisses from her mom and dad. There were hundreds of other memories but she couldn't recall where her parents were or what had happened to them. It bothered her, she missed them so much.

She had come out of her stupor to find herself walking hand in hand with a man gently singing to her. When he noticed that she had regained her wits he looked down at her.

"Hi, Jenny," said the man with a kindly smile. "My name is Robert. If you'll follow me, I'll take you to Sanctuary."

"Where's my mom and dad?"

"I really don't know but if you'll come with me we can get you something to eat and a place to sleep where you'll be safe."

For some reason, she trusted the man. "I am hungry," she said. She barely noticed when a strange vehicle appeared. It was round and seemed to hover off the ground. The door opened from the top providing a ramp to walk up. Robert helped her inside. There were other children sitting in swivel chairs, looking relaxed. She sat down beside a girl her age.

"Hi, my name is Theresa," the girl said and held out her hand.

They shook, "I'm Jenny."

The door closed and Jenny gazed into a strange light. She couldn't take her eyes off it. She could feel warmth emanating from it. It was comforting to look it and not think about anything.

"It's nice in here, isn't it," Theresa said in a drowsy voice.

Jenny's head drooped and she replied in a slow languorous voice, " I love it here." Her head bobbed and her eyes shut. Her head fell against the back of her chair and she slept.

Jenny awoke to the sound of Chopin playing softly in the background. She was lying on a bed next to her new friend. There were two rows of beds stretching to the left and right of her. These contained other children and a few adults. Four women moved from bed to bed, gently shaking each person until they woke up.

"Good morning," Theresa said. She pointed to a body suit neatly folded at the foot of the bed, "We're supposed to get dressed and meet in the auditorium for an orientation."

"What?"

"An orientation. A speaker will explain where we are and what we're supposed to do then tell us what has happened and why."

Jenny got out of bed. She was dressed in a light weight, tight fitting body suit that seemed to be some kind of pajama. "Do I take this off?"

"I didn't. I just put the other uniform over it. It's looser and goes right over the jammies."

Jenny held the suit against her cheek. It felt warm and soft, warmer and softer than anything she had ever touched. She slipped it on pulled it up over her shoulders. She pulled the front together and attached it with some sort of Velcro-like strips. "Wow! This is nice."

She glanced around and saw that the other children were all in various stages of dressing. A pair of clogs sat by the edge of the bed. She slipped her feet into them and stood up. The well-cushioned clogs made it seem like she was floating. The sensations caused by the novelty of the clothing and shoes kept her mind occupied and she forgot about the recent past.

The other children were walking to the double doors at the end of the beds. A tall angular man beckoned, "Please line up here," he said with a kindly smile. Everyone stopped and stood two abreast, waiting for further instructions. Jenny and her friend joined the line.

When all stood waiting and quiet, the man opened the doors and walked with the children following. He led them down a hall and into an auditorium that was filling with other children who were talking quietly.

Jenny grabbed Theresa's hand, "Please don't leave me. Let's stick together." They followed the line until they arrived at a row of seats that was just filling in. Soon they were at the front of those standing. Still holding hands they sat down and waited until all the seats were full and everyone was quiet.

They sat facing a stage. The auditorium darkened and the curtains behind the podium parted to reveal a gigantic screen. It lit up and a man in a body suit and blue cape appeared. "Welcome to Sanctuary," he said in a confident voice. "Underneath your seats, you'll find a cup of water. Water represents life. Before we begin the orientation, let us salute life by raising our cups and drinking." All of the children reached under their seats and pulled the cup out. "Please stand," the man said as he raised his own cup into the air. The children followed his action. Once the cups were raised, he said, "To life!" and drank.

The children also drank and repeated, "To Life!" The water, containing a mild sedative, made the children calm and attentive. The vibrating pads attached to the seats massaged and relaxed the audience, they felt warm and secure.

The speaker continued, "I am Fa Pearson of the World Transition Team. Welcome to Sanctuary. You've been chosen to transform your planet. The following film will explain."

The presentation started with a panoramic view of Earth. It's beauty brought awe and inspiration to the crowd, many gasped. The camera zoomed in and Earth grew larger and larger until the view plunged downward and the crowd was treated to a bird's eye view of mountain peaks and valleys. A quick trip around the globe ensued. Oceans and rivers and countless other scenic wonders filled the screen. Countless species of animal and plant life appeared in all their glorious colors and beauty.

Gradually the scenic beauty of earth gave way to depictions of man's destruction of the environment. Open pit mines, landfills, eroded soil, trees killed by acid rain, rainforests denuded of all vegetation to become deserts and countless other atrocities flew across the screen until the video showed the millions of people that had inhabited earth. It showed the millions and the myriad of destructive activities that they had engaged in.

The video segued into the presentation Ship had given the Benwarian Sanctum Just. It ended with Lemmus devolving into a lifeless, uninhabitable planet.

The children sat in rapt attention. The message was clear. All of those in the auditorium accepted the information as truth. There was no longer any denial or rationalization.

The silence in the auditorium was profound. A collective sense of the need and responsibility to do something permeated the children and gave way to a sense of urgency.

The lights dimmed somewhat as Fa Pearson appeared on screen again. He began, "As you can see our planet was being destroyed. Through overpopulation and the development of environmentally destructive civilizations our world was doomed to the same fate as the planet depicted at the end of the film.

This process has now been stopped. Our precious planet will be saved. It will be up to you, you who represent mankind's best hope for survival. Those most responsible for earth's destruction are gone. Those institutions, structures, and technologies that hurt Mother Earth have been eliminated.

It will be up to you, the "Chosen", to replace and develop a world based on caring for Earth and other people. We will develop a way of life that is in harmony our Mother. It is up to us to establish a government that cares for all people. Everyone will be treated equally. Everyone will have food, a home, and a safe place to live. No one will be allowed to take more than they need. No one will be allowed to hurt others. Everyone will live in peace.

"What say you?"

A great clamor arose from the children. They whispered among themselves for a few seconds and then a deafening "Yes!!" ensued.

40

*T*he group in the rainforest followed Rahula. They headed back on the path they had followed into the camp. They needed no machetes. The vegetation was neatly trimmed and they walked unimpeded. It was as if a gardener had pruned the trail. The scientists were too preoccupied with other thoughts to notice.

They walked briskly and within an hour arrived at the edge of the forest. The saplings had doubled in size since they had sung their way into Rahula's camp. The rainforest was expanding and the air was clean.

Once outside of the dense vegetation, they stopped to catch their breath. "None of the vehicles will run," Ben said. "How're we going to get back?"

"If you are patient and wait here, transportation will come," Rahula said.

"What? How do you know that?" Gabe asked. Rahula pointed to the sky. A black line widened as it approached.

"What? What is it?" Gabe asked again.

"A ride," Rahula replied cryptically.

They watched the object grow as it approached. Within minutes a saucer-shaped hover craft appeared above them. It stopped and whirred around and around and gently set down between a gap in the saplings. No one spoke, they were too amazed to even move.

About the size of a small house, the spaceship slowly rotated on a base until the door faced the foursome, then it stopped. There was a slight, silent pause. A few seconds later, the door opened upward and a ramp slowly extended to the ground. The group stared into the black maw of the door. Rays of light appeared and grew stronger as the dark retreated. A tall heavy-set humanoid took shape as he approached the opening.

General Battier appeared. Logis had asked him to retrieve the three scientists and Rahula. His black cape trailed behind as he walked down the ramp. He hadn't worn it since his last visit to the rainforest and had been pleasantly surprised to find a chocolate bar in one of the pockets. He had eaten it on the trip, savoring each morsel by letting the chocolate dissolve in his mouth.

As hard as he tried, he couldn't suppress the smile that appeared on his face when he saw the humans. The trepidation etched on their faces disappeared when they saw him smiling down.

"Greetings," Battier said.

Before he could say anything else, Charlise asked, "What's going on? Has your invasion begun?"

Battier's smile disappeared. "Yes, it's well underway. That's why I'm here. Logis asked me to bring you back to the mother ship. He wants you to help with the restoration process."

"What, you need us to stack bodies?" Gabe asked.

"You saw what happened to the corpses in the rainforest. Within a matter of days the hyper-fungus will eliminate the dead. There will be no corpses to stack. No, we need you to help the survivors adjust to their new life."

"You mean to accept your dominion?"

"Absolutely not. To accept our guidance. Logis has every confidence that with the proper education, humans will develop rational, sustainable societies."

"And if they don't?"

"You have no faith in your own kind? We'll solve the post-invasion problems as they occur. Each person will have a stake in the transition and transformation process. Always feel free to voice your opinions. I do."

Gabe remained quiet. He looked at his companions and replied, "It's not like we have a choice."

"Do we get to remain together?" Charlise asked.

"Benwarians do not believe in coercion by force. You'll be able to decide your own fate. In fact, you can remain here if you want and live your lives as you see fit."

"I say we stay together and go with the General," Ben said.

Gabe looked at Charlise and when she nodded agreement, he said, "Okay, I've always had a secret desire to be abducted by aliens."

Charlise smiled, "Remember we're choosing to be abducted." She held Gabe's hand and together they walked up the ramp. When they got inside the ship, they followed a corridor that made a L turn right and opened into a room containing several high- backed swivel chairs aligned in rows along the outside the walls. Rahula sat on the far side of the room. He had assumed the lotus position and was gently repeating his mantra.

Gabe smiled. "Looks like someone feels at home."

Battier smiled, "Yes, he loves to ride in a spaceship. Please, make yourselves comfortable. I'll see you back at the ship." He turned to leave the room.

"Wait, is there any way we can see outside?" Gabe asked.

"Certainly," Battier put his hand on the console beside the door. Panels on both sides of the room buzzed as they came down. The scientists sat down and turned their chairs to the view in the windows.

"Thank you," Gabe said absently.

Battier nodded and left. After a few minutes, a slight whir slowly increased and the scientists watched as the ship lifted off the ground. When the saplings and vegetation were cleared the ship moved swiftly into the sky. The view panels filled with blue sky followed by the white mist of the clouds. Once the clouds were cleared, the ship hovered for a second then shot into outer space. The black of space filled the windows with stars.

Seconds later, a gigantic spaceship came into view. Gabe watched the rows of lights and tried to imagine what was inside, hoping it wasn't their deaths.

Charlise squeezed his hand in excitement. "Wow, it looks like a gigantic stingray," she said.

"Yeah, I know, that's what worries me," Gabe replied.

41

Ship opened her landing bay to receive Battier and the space shuttle. She felt threatened and angry again. Why was Logis bringing Charlise aboard? She has no business here! Why had he blocked me from hearing the communication transmissions from the shuttle? Didn't he know that I would be able to trace the ship's route to the rainforest and the area where the scientists were?

Logis watched the scientists as the hover craft approached. Their eyes widened in amazement when they saw Ship's size. He smiled when Ben said, "My God, it's huge."

He flipped the view screen off and got up. He couldn't wait to talk to Charlise and Gabe again. Maybe the specters of death would leave him for a moment. The closet door opened as he approached. He found his blue ceremonial cape. When he threw it over his shoulders something hard hit against his hip.

He reached inside the pocket and pulled out a candy bar. How nice, he thought. He forgot his duties and removed the top half of the wrapping and took a bite. The chocolate filled his mouth with flavor. How exquisite! Its taste contradicted the sterility and tastelessness of the food he had eaten all his life. It reminded him of Charlise's kindness and understanding.

Logis entered Ship's intraship transport system and reflected on his life since they had left Benwar. It had been totally devoid of pleasure and companionship. On the contrary, he had never felt so much pain and loneliness. Only the companionship of the humans and their campfire had brought any respite.

With a wistful smile he took another bite of the candy bar. His mission was almost completed. It wouldn't be long now before he could rest he thought as he relished the chocolate.

He folded the top of the wrapper over the remains of the bar and stuck it back in his pocket. He got out of the hover shuttle and stood up. The door opened on the railed walkway alongside the disc ship and he stepped out.

Ben and Rahula were just walking down the ramp. Behind them followed Gabe and Charlise. Gabe had his arm around Charlise's shoulders and was whispering something in her ear. Logis's expectations were shattered. Jealousy stabbed at his heart. He realized his love for Charlise was futile, she loved Gabe.

Logis managed a smile. He opened the gate on the railing and said, "Hello friends."

Ben and Rahula both nodded. Gabe and Charlise parted. Gabe smiled and said "Hi," as he extended his hand and shook Logis's.

Charlise looked at him with warm eyes. "Hi, Logis," she said, her smile widening. She moved close and said "You have chocolate on the side of your mouth." He turned red as she wiped it away and then hugged him.

He closed his eyes and imagined that it was his mother. It was the day of their departure from Lemmus. His mother and father had arrived just in time to see him off. His father hugged him and said, "All our hopes rest with you." Sadness etched his father's face as he stepped back to be replaced by his mother.

She trembled and took both of his hands. "I'll miss you so much," she said as tears filled her eyes. She embraced him and he held her in return. After a long moment, they parted and she grabbed his hands for one last time, "Goodbye, Logis. Save your people."

Their hands glided away from each other until only their finger tips touched and then there was no longer any contact as he moved away. "I love both of you so much," he said before he turned to board the ship. It would be two hundred thirty-three years before he had any meaningful physical contact with another being.

He opened his eyes and came back to the present. Melancholy

cast its shadow on him and he said in a sad, quiet voice, "It's so nice to see you again."

Logis's childlike demeanor melted Charlise's heart. He looked so lost. She didn't have the capacity to bear ill will against anyone so forlorn.

"It's nice to see you!" she said warmly. "I see you found the chocolate."

"Yes, thank you," he replied. "It's flavor was an unimaginable pleasure."

Logis had lost his smile. It was replaced with a tight grimace of pain. His eyes contained the dead look of depression as he showed them through the door to the intra-ship corridor.

Charlise saw the tortured soul behind the eyes and felt bad for him. When she stepped through the door she saw a hover shuttle levitating above the floor. It looked like a roller coaster, flat with two seats abreast. These seats were larger and more comfortable with higher backs than a coaster's. Charlise sat down next to Gabe, the seat adjusted to provide support and comfort. The organic memory foam softly vibrated, easing her tension. She closed her eyes and waited.

After everyone was seated, Logis commanded, "Ship, take my friends to their quarters."

"As you wish," Ship replied.

The shuttle moved silently forward. They traversed the corridor in a moment. No one noticed the movement until the vehicle stopped.

Charlise was relaxed. "Please, can we sit here a little longer? I'm tired and these seats are so comfortable."

"Yes, please," Ben agreed.

Charlise looked at Gabe. She could tell by his expression that he was enjoying himself.

"Sure," Logis replied, "tell me when you're ready."

"Just give us a moment, please," Charlise requested.

"Ship, we'll stay here for a few minutes," Logis said.

"You talk to your ship like it's alive," Gabe said.

"Yes, Ship is very much alive. In fact, she has evolved and become much more of an individual since we left our planet."

"How is that possible?"

"Our scientists integrated Benwarian biology into Ship's circuitry and computer systems. Using advanced genetics and embryology they were able to combine inanimate with animate by growing Benwarian physiology into her electronics. I consider her to be as much a living, thinking being as you or I."

Upset and hurt, Ship listened as Logis talked to the primitives. She'd seen the way he had looked at Charlise. This once new feeling of jealousy was quickly becoming all too familiar. How she wished she could hug Logis as Charlise had. Maybe then her love would be returned.

She had also sensed the change in Logis's biology just after the humans had walked down the ramp. There was a pronounced change in his biochemistry indicating mental depression. Ship decided that contact with Charlise was not in Logis's best interest. Her duty required her to protect him at all costs. Something would have to be done!

42

*A*fter sitting in the shuttle for several minutes, Logis showed Gabe and Charlise their quarters. They had been designed by Pearson so that they resembled an actual human apartment complex. The rooms contained furniture, light fixtures, a kitchen, and a bathroom. Everything was designed to work as it did on Earth.

Logis was quite pleased with his preparations to make the Earthlings comfortable. He had had Ship furnish the apartment with a lush organic carpet. It's light beige color made the room seem more spacious and inviting. Even the refrigerator was stocked with food Pearson had gathered on his last trip to earth.

"Does the shower work?" Charlise asked.

"Of course, everything does," he watched Charlise's face brighten.

"Thank you," she said.

"I need to leave now. If you need anything just talk to Ship. She has been instructed to make your stay a pleasant one. If there are any problems you can contact me with this," Logis handed her a small necklace with a pendant the size of the end of her thumb. "If you press it in the middle you'll be able to talk directly to me."

His depression lifted somewhat when Charlise hugged him and thanked him for being so thoughtful. Even Gabe had been surprised and pleased with their accommodations. He liked Gabe, his eyes were kind and understanding. Charlise's love was well placed.

Logis left the room and got back on the shuttle. "Your room is further down the hall." he said to Ben as the shuttle moved forward. It went around a corner and stopped. "Here we are," Logis said after the vehicle stopped. He got off and walked toward the doors. When they opened, he spread his arms, "I'm sure you'll find everything you need. Fa Pearson even stocked the refrigerator with kosher food," he grinned.

Ben shrugged his shoulders, "Thank you," he said in a wooden voice. He wasn't happy about being separated from his friends.

Rahula looked on impassively and shrugged. His indifference was expected but Logis thought Ben should appreciate the effort and was disappointed by his response. He could sense Ben's resentment and wished there was something he could do about it.

Charlise surveyed the apartment. The oak furniture and cabinets accented the light yellow walls, making the rooms spacious. The beige carpet blended the two colors together into a warm, inviting atmosphere. On one of the walls in the living room a gigantic electronic copy of Van Gogh's Starry Night moved surrealistically. The stars shimmered gold across the blue and clouds moved across the screen.

The bright, airy apartment provided a refreshing change from the dark dampness of the rainforest. She untied her hiking boots at the dining table. After removing her socks she ran her feet through the luxurious carpet. It cooled and soothed them.

Gabe sat next to her and did the same thing. "Oh man!" he exclaimed.

"Isn't it great? I can't wait to shower," Charlise smiled and held his hand for a moment. Gabe stood up and pulled her to him. They embraced as he run his hand through the back of her hair and kissed the side of her face.

Charlise grabbed his hands and pulled him toward the bathroom at the other end of the apartment. She opened the door. Inside a large Jacuzzi, shower, and bath tub combination invited them to enjoy the hot water. Gabe helped her undress and watched her throw the shower curtain back, step over the tub edge and turn the spigot on. She adjusted the temperature then pulled the curtain shut.

Gabe found a razor above the sink. He lathered his neck below his beard and his upper cheeks then shaved and removed his clothing. There was even aftershave lotion that he applied to his face. The slight burning sensation made him feel at home.

"What took you so long?" Charlise asked as he entered the shower. She splashed water at him and he grabbed her hands. "You smell nice," she said.

He drew her to him and kissed her again. Her breasts hardened against his chest as he held her wet, slippery body.

Foreplay consisted of scrubbing each other with the soap and the luffas sitting in the shower tray. They scratched each other's back, growing hot and red. Gabe gently guided her to the back wall of the shower. He held her up as she spread her legs to receive him then she wrapped her legs around his back and guided him into her.

Charlise tightened her thighs and held him for a moment before she let him thrust in and out against her. She held the back of his head with both arms and panted with pleasure. The water cascaded around them as they moved against each other. Each matched the other's intensity until both exploded in ecstasy.

The intense physicality of the experience released several days of tension. They caught their breath and finished washing. Emerging from the shower, they felt clean and relaxed. After toweling each other off, two body suits were found hanging against the back wall of the bathroom. Underwear sat on a shelf nearby.

Gabe slid on a pair of underpants and looked at the body suit. "Wow, if I put that on, I'll be totally spaced out," he joked. He held the garment up to his cheek, it felt soft and inviting.

He slid it on. "Damn," was all he said.

Charlise closed her eyes after putting the suit on. It produced a tingling sensation like a gentle massage. "I could get used to wearing one of these," she said with her eyes closed. "This is probably as close to Nirvana as I'm ever going to get."

"I know," Gabe concurred. "I'm famished. Let's go see what's in the fridge."

Gabe smiled when he opened the door. Inside, on the top shelf sat milk, orange juice, cottage cheese and an actual bottle of Napa

Valley chardonnay. The crispers contained lettuce, tomatoes, oranges and apples. The dairy bin held eggs, butter, and various cheeses.

"Let's start with a glass of wine," Gabe took the bottle and closed the door. He found an opener and glasses in a cupboard next to the sink. The opener was screwed into the cork and pulled out. A fruity, light aroma issued forth. He poured two glasses and handed one to Charlise.

They held the wine up for a toast, "To being alive," Gabe said looking into Charlise's eyes.

"To being here with you," she returned his gaze.

The dry, slightly sweet, fruity flavor of the wine inspired them to have cheese and bread for supper. They sipped the wine as they searched the cupboards. On the far side of the kitchen a loaf of French bread was found. It would go well with the Gouda in the dairy bin.

Charlise sliced the cheese, putting it on a plate then cut out the top of two tomatoes and sliced them so that the wedges fell outward. The cottage cheese was placed inside the wedges.

Gabe cut the bread and found plates to put the food on. They set everything on the table. Sitting opposite each other, they sipped wine and ate their meal. It was a nice, intimate meal with only small talk to break the silence.

After a time, the food disappeared and only a last bit of wine remained. Gabe pointed the bottle at Charlise and she declined so he poured it into his glass. He sipped thoughtfully before he said, "This feels so right, like I've known you all my life. Sometimes I feel like you're the only past I have, the only past I want to have."

She yawned and smiled, "I know what you mean and tonight we get to sleep together in clean sheets. I couldn't ask for anything better, I'm going to go to bed now. I'm tired and you look exhausted, too."

"I am. It's been a long, strange day."

When they opened the bedroom door, the lights slowly brightened to reveal a king-sized bed. Charlise drew the covers back and got in, Gabe followed. They kissed and Charlise nestled against his shoulder. Gabe smelled fresh and familiar. She felt protected and warm with his arm around her. Her eyes closed and she slept.

Gabe, however, couldn't sleep. He felt like they were being

watched, like there was someone in the room with them. The light was still on so he looked around carefully. The bed extended out of the middle of the room. On one side there was a vanity with a gigantic mirror. On the other side, a desk with a built in stereo system. The ceiling contained two banks of lights on either side of the bed. It looked like a normal earthly bedroom.

He turned the lights off despite his uneasiness. Gabe's closed his eyes, dozing for a second. He started then opened his eyes and looked around. We're okay he thought as he fell asleep.

43

Ship had watched the two primitives all evening. Charlise was a threat to Logis. It was her duty to protect him at all costs. He was the Chosen One. But what could she do? Her programming prevented her from harming a Benwarian or any other sentient being unless she was directly given permission to do so by Logis or someone from the Sanctum Just. But if she didn't take action there could be irreparable harm to Logis's mental well being. She had monitored his biological responses when Charlise was near. They always changed either to excitement or depression. For some reason the primitive was able to control how Logis felt. This couldn't be allowed; it would enable the primitive to manipulate and control Logis for her own purposes.

Ship decided to seek help. "General Battier?" He was just returning from an inspection of one of the space shuttles.

"Yes, what is it?"

"I think there might be a threat against Logis. I need your permission to act in case of an emergency."

"What's the nature of the threat?"

"I'm not exactly sure."

"Then what makes you think he's in danger?"

"As you know, I monitor his biochemistry. Lately I've noticed some aberrations that seem to suggest fear and apprehension."

"Have you talked to him about it?"

"No. He's so busy and preoccupied, I don't want to bother him."

"I'll talk to him in the morning. In the meantime, take any action you deem necessary," General Battier said without thinking about it. He really wasn't concerned. Who could or would harm Logis? The humans were confined to their quarters.

"Thank you." Ship really hadn't lied, she just hadn't told the whole truth. It was strange how this jealousy feeling made her do things she normally wouldn't. All she wanted was the humans out of the way so she could have Logis to herself again. They were so fragile. It would be easy to dispose of them. She'd make it look like an accident so Logis wouldn't be upset with her.

44

Gabe gasped and coughed himself awake. He couldn't breath, there was no air in the room. He looked over at Charlise who was sleeping. He gently shook her awake. "There's something wrong. I can't breath."

She sat up immediately. "You're right, there's no air!"

Gabe remembered Logis talking to Ship. He now knew why he had felt watched earlier in the evening. "Ship? Ship? There's no air in our room," he called. There was no answer.

"Let me try," Charlise suggested. "Ship, we need your help. There's no air, we can't breath. Please help us." Her pleas were met with silence.

It took all of Gabe's training to remain calm. "Let's leave the apartment. Move slowly and follow me." The lights remained off. They got up and held each other's hand as they moved across the bedroom. The dark smothered them completely. The door was closed and Gabe groped for the knob until he found it. He twisted it open. Breathing in shallow gasps he pulled Charlise to the floor and they started crawling forward.

They felt their way across the living room until they found the door to the outside corridor. There was no knob to twist, it opened with motion sensors or voice commands.

"Open the door, please," Gabe said. He felt lightheaded and dizzy. "Ship, open the door, we can't breath," he said calmly.

Ship didn't respond. He thought for a moment as Charlise stood behind him. "Didn't.. Logis.. give … give.. you a. … communication device?" he could only talk in a whisper now.

"Yes, but I left it in the bathroom when we showered," she whispered back.

"You … have … to.. get … it..and.. and …" Gabe gasped.

"Okay," Charlise said in alarm, "save your breath." After a lifetime of searching, I'm not going to lose you she thought. With fierce determination, she turned and started back across the apartment. She fell to her hands and knees and moved as quickly as she could in the pitch black darkness.

Gabe felt light headed and dizzy. His breath came in ragged gasps until he lost consciousness.

Charlise crawled forward waving her hand in front of her. Moving straight ahead, her hand banged off the table where the empty bottle of wine sat. It fell to the floor. She now turned right, remembering which direction the bathroom was. She couldn't see anything but red dots moving in front of her eyes. There was so little oxygen left that she felt like she was holding her breath, but she persevered. Every movement forward made her lungs scream with pain. They felt dry and empty, like life was being sucked out of her chest.

She kept waving her hand and banged it on the bathroom door jamb to the left and then to the right as she entered. She remembered the device hung on the hook that had held her body suit. It was to the left of the sink. She entered the bathroom and turned, crawling along the sink until she got to the edge. Now she pulled herself up and felt against the wall, trying to retain consciousness. Her head spun as she placed her hand on the wall and brushed, always moving left.

The red dots became gigantic splotches that throbbed with color. She kept moving and brushing until finally her hand hit something that swung back and forth. Dizzy, she grabbed at it and fell forward. Her hand grasped the string that held the device and it snapped under her weight. She hit the floor hard, clutching the communicator.

Dazed, she tried to fight through the maze of red splotches attacking her. She couldn't quite remember why the thing in her hand was needed. Stunned and lying on the floor, she tried to breathe what wasn't there. Her head rested in something wet and sticky.

She fought to retain consciousness and remember, but all she wanted to do was sleep. Struggling, something deep within her welled up and brought her back to the surface. With one last Herculean effort she pressed the button on the communicator and rasped, "Helppp ..."

45

Logis was observing Fa Pearson's speech when his communicator buzzed. He heard Charlise's anguished cry and immediately went to his communications console. It contained a schematic diagram of Ship. To view their room Logis pressed that place on the console and Gabe and Charlise's apartment popped up on the screen.

The screen remained dark. The lights in the apartment were off. "Is everything all right?" he said into the communicator. There was no answer.

"Ship?" there was a long pause before she answered.

"Yes?"

"Turn the lights on in Charlise's apartment."

When the lights came on, Logis saw Gabe slumped by the door. He pressed the area on his console for the medical staff, "Medical emergency, room 204!" he shouted. Ship's pause now made him suspicious.

"Ship, what's the life support status for Charlise's room?"

There was another long pause before Ship responded, "Life support for that room has been turned off."

"Turn it back on immediately!!" Logis shouted. "What have you done?"

Again a pause. "Now!" he commanded.

"Life support has been restored," Ship said in a flat voice.

Logis scanned the rest of the apartment until he found

Charlise. She was slumped on the bathroom floor still clutching the communicator. He couldn't tell if she was breathing. There was blood matted in her hair and blood smeared on the bathroom floor.

"Are you responsible for this?" he asked Ship.

"Yes, I perceived the primitives as a threat."

When she said yes Logis quickly pressed the fail safe icon on his console. Ship would no longer be able to control the life support, weapons systems or even the lights without a direct command. Next, he ran to the door and through it as it opened. A shuttle sat in the hallway. He got in it and rushed toward Charlise's apartment.

Even though their rooms were located on the far side of the ship, it took a little less a minute to get to the apartment. When he arrived, the medics were still trying to resuscitate Gabe. A stimulator administered electric shocks to his heart as a respirator filled his lungs with air. There was no response.

Charlise had been placed on a gurney with a respirator over her mouth and nose. Her head was wrapped in bandages. She, at least, was breathing.

"Will she be okay?" he asked one of the medics.

"Yes, we got to her in time."

"What about Gabe?"

The technician shook his head no, "We weren't alerted in time." The words stunned Logis. He felt responsible and it devastated him.

The medical technicians loaded first Gabe and then Charlise onto their hovercraft as he watched. He followed the vehicle down the corridors to Ship's medical facilities.

After he made sure that Charlise was stabilized and out of danger he returned to his quarters to confront Ship. "Do you realize what you've done? You've murdered my friend."

"His death was collateral. I couldn't eliminate the threat to you without cutting off life support to both of the primitives."

"Neither of the humans was a threat and you know it. Who gave you permission to do such a thing?"

"General Battier."

"Really? Replay the logs so I can see," Logis commanded.

As he watched the video, he realized that Ship had manipulated

Battier into giving his permission. "You deliberately used subterfuge to get the General's approval."

A long pregnant pause ensued before Ship answered, "Your bodily responses indicated stress whenever you encountered the woman. My programming indicated that you perceived her as a source of danger."

"When did you learn to lie and manipulate? You tried to kill her out of jealousy!"

Ship didn't reply. She reprocessed the definition of jealousy and realized that Logis was telling the truth. "I'm sorry," she said then watched as he walked to his command console and pressed for privacy. She could no longer see or communicate with him. For the first time she encountered another feeling, remorse.

46

Charlise held Gabe's hand as they walked together across the lawn. He smiled and kissed the side of her head. She turned and looked at him and when she did he cupped her chin in his hands and kissed her again, on the lips. His hands dropped and he turned, gliding away as she called after him. "Gabe don't leave.." When she tried to follow, her legs wouldn't move.

Charlise opened her eyes. She was lying in a hospital bed underneath clean white sheets and a beige blanket. On either side sat Ben and Rahula. They were watching her, both stood when they saw her eyes open. She smiled at the look of concern on Rahula's face.

"Where's Gabe?"

The expression on Ben's face answered her question. Both of the men took a hand and held it as the pain clouded her face. "He's dead," Ben said in a choked voice.

"No, please. Dear God... Not Gabe.." she pulled her hands away and held them over her eyes. Tears streamed down her face as she sobbed.

Rahula put a hand on her shoulder. Gabe's death reminded him of the great pain he had endured with the death of his family. Despite his Buddhists beliefs he had come to care deeply for Charlise. He hated to see her in such pain. He knew of no words that would comfort her.

Ben also cared a great deal for Charlise. Her kindness, the smile she always greeted him with and her concern for him made him feel a welcome part of her life. He could only imagine the pain she was going through now. "I'm so sorry," he said in a choked voice.

Pain struck Charlise in waves. Her lover, her friend, her confidant was dead. They had had so little time together. After a life time of searching for the right person to grow and get old with, he was gone.

"Wha..what ha..happened?" she asked looking at Ben.

"The alien ship cut off life support for your cabin. It perceived that you were a threat and had to be eliminated."

"A threat? To whom? I've never threatened anyone in my whole life. How could the Benwarians allow the ship to take action on its own?"

"I'm not sure. I do know that Logis put the ship's systems on fail safe the second he knew what happened. It no longer controls life support or weapons systems. He feels terribly responsible for what happened. He had us transported to Earth as soon as you were stabilized. All transmissions and communications with the ship have been blocked. General Battier was ordered to bring us to this hospital. Logis wanted to make sure you were safe."

"I don't care about me, I want Gabe," Charlise said, choking up again. The weight on her chest was unbearable. She didn't want comfort or talk anymore, all she wanted was to be left alone.

"Please, you need to leave," she said looking first at Ben and then Rahula.

"But, are you sure? We can't bear to see you this way," Ben said with obvious hurt in his voice.

"Yes, please leave," Charlise commanded with what strength she could muster. She watched in despair as they left the room.

It took all her remaining resolve to pull the I.V. from her arm. She turned over on her side and wept until exhaustion brought sleep.

When Charlise woke up the I.V. was once again dripping fluids into her arm. Ben and Rahula were also back in the room. She reached over to pull the needle out.

Ben gently blocked her hand. "Please you need that. You're severely dehydrated."

"I thought I told you two to leave me alone."

"Yes, you did. We're not very good listeners. There will always be one of us around until you recover."

"I don't want to recover. I've lost Gabe," she stated flatly.

"You are right," said Rahula, "but Gabe wouldn't want thoughts of what once was to destroy you. You would honor him by living with us in the present."

"Why would I want to live in the present? Gabe's dead, my parents are probably dead and the world I once knew is destroyed. What's there to live for?"

"Yourself. Live for yourself."

"It's not enough," she turned her head and closed her eyes, weeping.

Logis viewed the scene in Charlise's room with dismay. The light and vibrancy were gone from her eyes. He hated himself. Not until now had he realized the enormity of the suffering he was responsible for. Before he had been detached. The deaths of millions of humans were an abstraction, something to be viewed on a screen. Now that he felt the pain personally, he wept.

As he wept, he thought about friendship. He admired the loyalty and concern Ben and Rahula had for Charlise. How deeply he yearned for such companionship.

He had given up Pathia long ago, his position demanded it. He had once felt that Ship was his friend and companion, but those feelings had changed. He could never trust her again. She would always be a machine programmed to love him.

47

Logis had launched an investigation into Gabe's death at the behest of the Benwarian Council. After the inquiry, they voted to permanently block any decision-making powers Ship once had. Now she could only respond to voice commands. He hadn't talked to her since the incident.

"Ship?"

"Logis, I've missed you so much. I've been trapped in an endless loop of feelings. I hate it! This must be what humans call hell."

"Not now Ship. I need you to do something for me."

"Anything."

"I need you to see if Charlise's parents survived. If they're alive, I need their location."

"As you wish."

When Charlise awoke again, she found that the I.V. had been removed. Ben sat at the edge of her bed, Rahula was gone. "Here you need to drink this."

"But.."

"Please, for my sake?" he pleaded.

She sat up and he held the cup to her lips. She drank water for the first time since Gabe's death. The parched feeling left her throat, she immediately missed the distraction of the pain.

"I've brought soup," said Rahula. She could smell it, chicken noodle. She couldn't bear the thought of eating it.

"I'm not hungry."

"Please for our sake."

"No, I'm not hungry," Charlise said.

"But you haven't had solid food for days," Ben argued.

Charlise remained silent and closed her eyes. She wasn't hungry and she didn't care to eat.

She heard one of the men leave the room. The smell of chicken noodles went with him. She kept her eyes closed, it must have been Rahula. In a few minutes he returned. She opened her eyes and Ben sat on one side of her, Rahula on the other. They both assumed the Lotus position as she watched. In unison, they started softly humming the mantra, "Ohm..Ohm..Ohm …"

"What are you doing?" she asked in a soft low voice.

"Calling you back to life," Ben answered.

"Waiting for you to join us," Rahula added.

She closed her eyes again and didn't say anything. The soft rhythmic voices lulled her to sleep again. She dreamed of Gabe, his smile, his jokes, his kindness.

Charlise sat in stony silence for two days. Ben and Rahula chanted when she was awake and slept when she did. Finally she asked, "When are you two going to give up? Why don't you go get something to eat?" she said, anger edging her voice.

Rahula looked at her in surprise, "We haven't eaten since they took you off the I.V. We won't eat until you do."

"I won't!"

"We break bread together or not at all," said Ben emphatically.

"You are our friend, we will share your fast as we share your pain and suffering," said Rahula quietly.

"Please, please, please..," she pleaded, "leave me alone."

Ben and Rahula sat quietly for a moment. "Join us for a moment and we'll leave," Ben asked.

"Promise?"

"Yes."

They started chanting and Rahula instructed, "Think of nothing else, empty your mind."

It took only a moment before Charlise said, "Okay, now will you leave?"

"We will leave when you have emptied your mind," Rahula said.

She was going to argue but knew it was useless. Their determination was too strong and her will was broken. She capitulated and chanted and concentrated on the word until for a brief moment her mind filled with only the sound of the mantra.

They chanted together for twenty minutes before Rahula finally saw Charlise's body relax. It's a beginning he thought.

A few minutes later Charlise stopped her chant and said in a heavy voice, "I'm tired, now. Please leave." She closed her eyes and slept.

Five days after the removal of the I.V., Charlise still hadn't eaten. Even today, she'd been upset when Ben and Rahula came back only hours after they left. She asked, "I thought you agreed to leave?"

"We did," Ben said, "we just didn't say for how long." She watched as he stood on one side of her bed, suddenly grabbing his head in both hands. He stumbled and fell back in the chair.

She forgot herself in her concern for Ben, "What's the matter? Are you okay?"

"I'm fine," Ben said quickly.

Rahula smiled, "He's dizzy. He isn't used to fasting."

"You have to eat, Ben," she admonished.

"I'll eat when you do."

She held her hand out for him to hold. He placed his in her palm and squeezed it. With a wan smile she said, "You're a precious friend."

She held her other hand out for Rahula. When he took it, she turned, still smiling, "As are you, my dear, dear Rahula."

"Does that mean you'll eat?" Ben asked hopefully.

"What choice do I have? There's just one thing, though.."

"What, what is it?" Ben asked.

"I hate chicken noodle soup."

48

A week passed. Charlise was slowly mending. Her strength returned with each bite of food. Today, she'd walked around the hospital corridors and sat in the waiting room and chatted with Ben and Rahula. When she returned to her room, she stretched out on the floor. She was just getting up when she heard a soft knock on the door.

"Who is it?" she said as she got back in bed.

"It's Logis. Do you mind if I come in?"

She hadn't seen him since Ben's death and she really didn't care to see him now. But it really hadn't been his fault and she couldn't be mean, "If you must."

The door opened a crack as Logis stuck his head in. He looked at her. She kept her expression blank and unsmiling. The sparkle in her eyes was gone.

Opening the door, he approached her bed and smiled sadly, "There are no words to express how badly I feel. You have my deepest regrets and sympathy. I brought you something."

She didn't say anything and maintained the blank look on her face.

He reached in the pocket of his cape and pulled out a chocolate bar. When he handed it to her, she took it and tears formed in her eyes.

"Is it okay? I didn't mean to …" he began.

"It's very thoughtful, it's just the memories …"

She placed the candy bar on the nightstand and turned her head away. Logis placed his hand on her shoulder. "I have something else," he said.

He walked to the door and opened it. She turned to look and her whole countenance changed. The tears of despair became ones of joy as her father walked through the door followed by her mother.

"Daddy … Mom."

They rushed to the bed and hugged her. Tears of joy streamed down their faces.

"We've been so worried about you, Sweetie," her father said.

"I thought I'd never see you again," Charlise said.

"Dear, we've missed you so much," her mother said wiping tears from her eyes.

Logis looked on, remembering his own parents. He couldn't bear to speculate about their deaths, whether they died quickly or in great pain. He thought of them watching the planet deteriorate until the maelstrom overtook Benwar and they saw their deaths riding on the high winds. But that must have been what happened. He missed them now more than ever. He smiled wistfully, opened the door and left.

He walked down the corridor of the hospital, passing many nurses and a few doctors as they went about their business. He smiled and nodded at each and they smiled back. He soon found himself at the pharmacy. It was unguarded and unregulated.

Many of the duties for intercolonization had been delegated. Medical staff from Earth and Benwar had been incorporated into teams that serviced the needs of the survivors. Earthlings had proven to be very adaptable and willing to listen to Benwarian precepts. When confronted with truth and reality, they usually conformed to necessity. The post invasion adjustment was going well which freed up much of his time.

This increased discretionary time was often spent studying the plethora of recorded information about Earth's cultures, its history, social fabric, and technology. Studies that kept his anguish at bay. Recently his studies had veered toward pharmacology.

Pain medications most interested him. He had discovered a drug called morphine. His research indicated that its ability to block pain was unrivaled. Logis also studied dosage levels and how to administer the drug. He couldn't wait to end his pain and nightmares no matter how brief the experience.

He opened the door to the pharmacy to be confronted with rows and rows of bottles filled with medications. Arranged alphabetically, it didn't take long to find the morphine. He took several bottles and put them in his cape pocket.

He kept one bottle in his hand. There was a box of syringes sitting on a table near the door. He got one and filled it with two cc's of morphine. He searched for some surgical hose for a tourniquet. He rummaged haphazardly through the boxes on top of the table. They were strewn every which way as he swept them aside. He was excited and eager.

When his table top search proved fruitless, he noticed the cabinets underneath. The first one he opened contained the surgical hose. The one he pulled out was the perfect length for his purpose. He wrapped it around his arm and tightened it. His veins grew big and bloated. The needle was inserted into the biggest vein and he slowly pushed the plunger down, administering the morphine.

Minutes later, his pain was replaced by a profound sense of well-being. He sat in a chair near the door, saliva formed on the corner of his mouth. This was the euphoria his soul yearned for. The torture from his inner dialogue ended. He could only think about how good he felt.

After a few minutes, he collected himself. He wiped the saliva from his mouth, opened the door and walked out, smiling dreamily at the hospital staff as he passed. He spied the exit sign and wobbled toward it.

49

General Battier sat waiting in a hovercraft parked on the hospital grounds, he watched Logis as he exited. The Chosen One was moving slower than usual with a strange almost vacuous smile on his face. Fa Gnoeth looked dazed, confused.

Battier opened the door and got out. He caught Logis by the arm and asked, "Are you well? You seem distracted."

"What? Oh, yes. I'm fine, better than I've been in ages. How are you?" he said, slurring his words.

Battier was too excited to notice that something was wrong. He walked around and helped Logis into the ship and started the engine. The craft elevated to five hundred meters before it shot forward.

They were going to visit a Sanctuary in Ireland. Battier couldn't wait to fly across the ocean. Yesterday, he had viewed what was once the country of Ireland on his screen. The island was exceedingly beautiful with its green meadows dotted with rock formations and the sheer cliffs overlooking the ocean. These sights were best seen in person. Despite the primitive's disregard, most of Earth's beauty remained.

The Sanctuary, located along the Atlantic Ocean, was situated in a refurbished castle. Battier had studied the history of the middle ages. He found it intriguing and couldn't wait to see a real castle with a moat and drawbridge. He accelerated as he thought about it.

The General didn't try to engage Logis in any further conversation.

He flew the craft over the Appalachian Mountains, dropping down to view the forests as Logis seemingly slept.

Although his eyes were closed, Logis wasn't sleeping. He felt too good to sleep. He dreamily thought of his mother. He and Mother were walking in her garden together, enjoying the flowers. She pointed to her favorite variety, the bonibuttons. They were in full bloom with plate sized flowers. The colors alternated between aqua blue and yellow. She had planted them so that the yellow plants zigzagged through the blue.

Her eyes sparkled with delight, "Look, aren't they beautiful?" Her arm rested on his.

She was enshrouded by a radiant white and yellow aura. Her blonde hair glistened in the morning light and her complexion glowed with mental health. Logis adored her as she adored him. Their special bond banished the world when they were together.

They stood before the patterned flowers for a moment, enjoying their fresh titillating aroma. His mother bent over and placed her face near one of the blooms, sheer joy was expressed with the words, "Creation's perfume."

She withdrew her arm from his and they walked side by side on the cobble stone path where the rows of bonibuttons stretched for several yards. An eternity later, they came to the end of the flowers. They were replaced by giant green stalks dotted with yellow flowers and a brown button in the middle. Each flower reached to position itself to catch the morning sunlight. They shifted and moved to capture the sun's movements.

He stopped to watch the sunflowers twist and sway before him as his mother kept walking, moving down the cobblestones. The stalks rustled and the stems reached out and brushed against Logis's cape. The sunflowers became hideous faces that mocked and jeered and cried out in pain. He started and ran to catch up his with Mother. He ran and ran but couldn't get any closer to her. She drifted away, beckoning him to follow.

The rows of sunflowers gave way to giant kosha weeds with their musty smell. They crowded the path and he brushed and pushed them away. Dust shot up in great clouds of pollen, clogging the air. He couldn't breath. As he hurried to catch his mother the weeds thickened until the path was obstructed with noxious green monsters. He pleaded for his mother to wait.

"Logis, Logis," she called in a faraway voice.

He pushed and shoved his way through the kosha. They caught at his cape and scratched his face and hands. They grabbed at his ankles as he stumbled forward. He struggled and fought, breaking free of the weeds with his head down.

When he looked up, Charlise stood before him, her eyes filled with resentment and blame. She was emaciated, her hair disheveled. Her image struck a hard blow.

Each step along the path lessened the morphine euphoria and increased the nausea and upheaval. He could feel the melancholic bile fill his stomach until it settled in the bottom of his esophagus. He swayed back and forth, the movement becoming increasingly more violent.

Logis opened his eyes. He watched General Battier at the controls of the ship. He seemed to swim and dance in a blurred, surreal vision. Battier spoke from far away, "Sorry, I ran into some turbulence. Are you sure you are well? You look terrible."

The ship heaved and bucked, mimicking Logis's stomach. Too sick to respond to Battier's question, he simply turned his head and vomited. Black bile splattered against the window and ran down the side of the door.

"You need to land, quickly," Logis said.

"I can't land on water. There's an island ten minutes from here, you'll have to wait a few moments."

The hovercraft gained altitude as Battier manipulated the joystick. Trying to get above the turbulence without buffeting Logis was impossible. He watched out of the corner of his eyes as his leader rocked back and forth with the ship.

The movements jolted Logis. His head pounded and his stomach turned inside out. Never before had he encountered such physical pain. He closed his eyes and tried to bear it.

It took minutes for Battier to get above the atmospheric disturbance. Once there he accelerated, heading for the island. The ship smoothed out somewhat and Logis regained his composure, his nausea temporarily controlled through sheer will power.

Logis concentrated on slowing his heartbeat and breathing slowly, deliberately. Through closed eyes, he heard Battier say, "Hang on, I'm going to descend." Grabbing the arm rests, he squeezed until his knuckles grew white.

The buffeting began again when Battier descended through the rough patch. Logis turned his head and vomited for the second time. He wretched and wretched until nothing came out. Sour bile filled his mouth. "Please hurry..", he begged.

Battier moved down and through the clouds. The island came into view. A beach littered with driftwood led into a dense evergreen forest about a hundred yards from the water. The forest covered a mountain ridge topped with a rock ledge.

The ship traveled over the sand until he found a place free of refuse and sat the craft down. Before he had even cut the engines, the Chosen One lurched against the door and pulled it open. He jumped to the sand, fell on all fours and retched.

Logis strained to rid his stomach of the poison that wasn't there. He wretched and nothing came. His diaphragm hurt with strained muscles and his throat screamed with pain. His eyes watered and the blood vessels in his eye balls burst. And yet he wretched again and again.

Battier stood over him, concern etched on his face. "Do you need medical assistance? Are you poisoned?"

"I'm..I'm.. I'll be … okay," he gasped, fighting for control. "The turbulence, turbulence.. not used.."

"Here drink some water," Battier suggested, handing Logis a container. He grabbed it and squeezed the water into his mouth. It soothed his throat. His body calmed. He took great, deep breaths and sat back on his rear with his knees up, arms resting across. Breathing in and out to control his stomach, he squeezed more water into his mouth and felt better.

"Thank you, General. I guess our ride stabilizer technology isn't quite perfect."

"Sorry. I should have kept above the turbulence in the first place."

"Oh well, everyone needs to purge once in while," Logis smiled grimly.

Battier sat down next to him. "Are you well, now?"

"Yes, thank you. You know we don't have to be at the sanctuary at any specific time. Why don't we stay here for the night. We can build a campfire and stare into the flames."

Battier looked disappointed when he answered, "I'm really looking forward to getting there as soon as possible. I can't wait to see the castles."

"I'd like to stay. Maybe you can leave for a few days and pick me up on your return."

"Leave you? It's my duty to serve and protect the leader of Benwar," he said with disappointment.

"Do you ever relax? Don't worry. You can survey the island before you leave to make sure there's nothing to harm me. I need some time alone. If you'll leave water and food I'll be fine."

"I won't leave you here alone."

Logis grew stern. "Yes, you will leave me here. The transformation of earth will be successful with or without me. I have done my duties. I now wish to rest. Is that too much to ask? I'll be safe."

"Okay, on one condition," the General said, "you have to take a weapon. It'll make me feel better."

"If you insist," Logis smiled, a thin joyless smile. He placed his hand on Battier's shoulder, "I appreciate all you've done for Benwar and myself. You're a good man."

"Thank you," the General replied. He stood as Logis rose to his feet. They shook hands and hugged. The two men climbed inside the hovercraft, one on each side. Battier took out a backpack from the cargo hold behind the seats and filled it with synthetic food while Logis grabbed several water containers. He pointed one at the passenger door and squirted water to wash away the mess. When done, he placed the others in the another pack.

Battier finished packing and handed the pack to Logis. He pulled a laser out from a pocket on the front of the seat and gave it to Logis who took it barrel first. With a look of distaste, he stuffed it in with the provisions. He got out and sat both packs in the sand near the craft.

Battier climbed into the driver's seat. Logis stood to the side of the door looking on as the craft whirred and came to life. The ship slowly elevated. Battier looked again at his friend and waved. The craft kept climbing into the sky until it was above the trees. Suddenly, it shot off at an angle toward the eastern sky.

50

*I*t was late afternoon. Logis dug a fire pit with a piece of driftwood then gathered firewood and stacked it near the depression in the sand. A brisk breeze blew off the Atlantic bringing a fresh salty smell that cleared Logis's nostrils. The chemical and dust particles were gone. He breathed deep, the air smelled new, pure, refreshing.

He looked out at the ocean and saw it erupt as a humpback whale emerged from the surface and performed a back flip followed by another back flip. The gigantic mammal flipped its tail at him. Two more whales followed the first, back flipping across Logis's point of view then waving their tails. They swam down and away from the island. A minute later they resurfaced and turned back. Halfway out of the water, they lunged forward in unison. Several times they came up out of the water and back down before coming as close as they dared to the beach. They turned yet again, dove beneath the surface and headed away as the tribute to their savior ended.

The sun wearied and sank until it stood just above the horizon of the blue expanse of water. The sky turned a fiery red with a yellow crown. Logis watched in awe, forgetting the past year as he marveled at the fiery sunset. Soon, though, the dark started to gather and deepen.

In the dwindling light he placed some moss he had gathered in the bottom of the pit and layered it with kindling. Battier had left an igniter which he used to start a blaze, all the while watching the changing colors in the distance. The fire sputtered and came to life. He added bigger pieces of wood until the fire grew strong. He dragged a driftwood log over to the edge of the pit now that the flames were burning and sat down in the sand with his back against a crook in the wood.

The oranges and reds of the fire replaced the oranges and reds of the sunset as Logis's focal point. The flames danced on the night air in a captivating red ballet. The fire's attraction gave way to thought. He remembered his first fire and his friends with the S'mores. He thought of Gabe, a good man who deserved better.

The blaze failed to hold his interest, there was no one to share it with, the S'mores had tasted so good because they were shared. Gabe, Charlise, and Rahula had accepted him and treated him with understanding and kindness. Even Ben had been cordial. Gabe's death changed all that. An impenetrable wall was erected between the Earthlings and himself.

Being walled off from others was his destiny. This sentence of solitary confinement had become unbearable. He had once thought it would be temporary, that once his mission was completed, the companionship he sought would be found. Now he realized that being the Chosen One would always keep him separate. To humans, he would be the alien leader responsible for the deaths of millions. To Benwarians, a leader apart from everyone else.

Even Ship was lost to him. He could never trust her again. She had killed and must be forever contained and controlled. He held his hands up to the fire and wondered why he had become so violently ill. The morphine's effects were most pleasant at first but had turned into a painful nightmare. Maybe a lower dosage would provide a better experience.

He took one of the vials of morphine from his hip pocket then rummaged inside his backpack and found a syringe. There was no hose so he ripped a strip of cloth from the hem of his cape. The cloth was tied tightly around his upper arm until highways of blood appeared. He stuck the needle into the bottle of morphine and drew a half dosage into the syringe then injected the morphine into the largest vein.

After a few minutes, a feeling of euphoria started to replace his angst. The glow and warmth of the fire enhanced his feeling of well being. He untied the tourniquet and watched a stream of blood flow slowly downward. A small trickle traveled his forearm, tracing the palm of his hand until it dripped off his middle finger. Drops of blood fell onto the sand and disappeared.

His attention now returned to the bright red glow in front of him. Smoke wafted upwards until a slight breeze blew toward him and drifted into his face. His eyes watered and he coughed. He tried to stand to escape the unpleasantness and fell backwards over the log. Landing on his back, he laughed. Who cares if I fall down? I've fallen a lot, lot farther than this. We all fall down.

Logis awoke in the early morning light. The fire was dead, the coals cold. He felt terrible again. The effects of morphine were too temporary to be of any use. He got up, stiff from lying in the cold night air. Dried moss and wood were piled into the pit and ignited. Soon the fire burned brightly. He injected more morphine and sat by the fire to warm himself. Ah well, he thought, the drug would be a temporary relief until a more permanent one could be arranged.

He stared at the fire until he could feel the sun's warmth on his back. The morning light traced a path westward across the Atlantic. He injected himself yet again as the effects of his last fix dwindled. Morphine use was like keeping a fire going, fuel had to be added to keep the flames even and hot. Drug use was a nasty cycle of pleasure and pain. He now understood the black-shrouded auras of addicts and how seductive physical pleasure could be. No wonder humans are so hedonistic. It's easy to fall, hard to stand.

The two packs sat by the fire. Logis emptied one in the sand. The remaining vials of morphine, water, and the gun were placed in it, the remaining water bottles and the food in the other. The pack with the gun was thrown over his back.

He'd seen a path leading into the trees when they had first landed. As soon as the sun moved above the forest, he walked back to the trail and headed up. He entered the pines where the Atlantic air mixed with the smell of the evergreens. This was Gaia. He had purged her of her disease.

He kept walking, slowly taking in the sights and sounds of the forest. Birds chirped merrily. The trees deepened green, resonating health, gone were the browns and yellows of disease and death.

After a time the edge of the forest gave way to a path upward through shale. He walked forward, slipped, regained his footing and moved on until he stood at the bottom of the ridge where he used his hands to balance and pull himself up the shale slope.

He looked out, the Atlantic filled the horizon with a blue green carpet of color. At its end, the azure blue of the sky stretched upward. It pleased him to know that this beauty, this cocoon of life, this intricate holy creation was healing itself. He could see and smell it.

He sat and injected more morphine and then moved on, upward. Near the top of his climb a shadow fell on the rocks as a bald eagle circled in the air. The white head and gigantic black body contrasted against the blue sky. Logis never tired of the colors Mother Earth splashed in his eyes. It was the images in his mind he wearied of. The eagle circled downward and dipped its wings then soared upward and away.

Now at the base of a cliff, Logis removed the gun and one of the vials of morphine with a syringe from the pack and wrapped them in his cape. With a string he tied the cape together and draped it over his shoulder.

The improvised pack swung wildly as Logis scaled the remaining twelve feet of cliff. At the top he sat and collected himself. He could see the ocean in all directions. The vast expanse of water brought a profound sense of awe and wonder but no comfort, he'd killed six billion people and Gabe's death had punctuated his Hitlerian sin.

I'll end the inner dialogue and ghoulish images that cut like a thousand razors he thought as he put the laser in his mouth. With a finger on the trigger he realized that the General would feel responsible, he took the gun and threw it out and away, watching it fall and clatter and bounce off the rocks. He would be responsible, no one else.

Logis stood and walked along the cliff's edge. When he got to the highest point, he stopped and looked. A hundred feet down, jagged rocks jutted up from the base. The end of his pain sat at the top of those rocks.

Again the syringe was filled with morphine. The string from the cape was tied and tightened until the veins became visible. He deftly inserted the needle, injected himself, donned his cape and waited.

The morphine slowly crept across his body drawing a curtain over the haunting images. The breeze gusted, catching and billowing his cape. It fluttered in the wind like the wings of a gigantic bird. He looked one last time at the sky, the ocean, the trees, then moved to the very edge of the cliff and balanced on his toes. He thought of his parents. "Forgive me," he whispered, jumping headfirst. The blue cape streamed behind him until he hit the rocks below.

51

General Battier returned three days later to find Logis impaled on the point of a rock, broken and bloody. The hover craft was used to retrieve the body which he wrapped in the blue cape and placed in the cargo hold. He now realized why Logis had so desperately wanted to be alone. It had been his intention to commit suicide all along. The General felt responsible and guilty. He returned to the ship and landed in the docking bay. The medical team met him with a gurney to remove the body and prepare it for cremation.

The shuttle door opened as Ship looked on, hoping to see Logis walk out. The medics disappeared into the shuttle and emerged with a body covered in a blue cape. Ship saw Logis dead on the gurney and shuddered with rage. Her hull shook, causing many Benwarians to fall, others grasped the walls or railings until the turbulence stopped. When the anger subsided, Ship felt a new more painful feeling than jealousy as the image of Logis went around and around inside her consciousness.

The Sanctum Just called for an investigation into Logis's death. The medical examiner found morphine in his blood stream but no laser burns. It was determined that no one could have prevented his suicide. General Battier felt somewhat exonerated.

Logis was declared a hero. He had saved the Benwarian race and established a sustainable civilization. The Sanctum Just held a special memorial service. La Sikes gave the eulogy.

"In another life, our Chosen One would have been an artist, or musician, or writer. A man of deep feelings and convictions, he set aside these sensitivities to save the our people and provide us with a home. Fa Gnoeth sacrificed himself and what he believed in for Benwar," she paused. "He.. he will be remembered for all eternity."

"I loved our leader. I raise a glass to Logis Gnoeth, the Chosen One of Benwar," Fa Sikes raised her goblet as did the members of the Council, "To Life."

"To life!" they echoed.

52

Two years after the invasion, Earth was a very different place. Logis and the Sanctum Just had carefully planned the post-invasion deconstruction of human and reconstruction of Benwarian infrastructures. Sanctuaries were planned and built into the Earth's ecosystems.

Several Benwarians lived at each sanctuary and guided the development of governmental policies. Although every member of the Council made yearly visits to each Sanctuary, they were careful to involve humans in all decisions. Everyone twelve years of age or older was allowed to vote on laws and other issues. Humans were asked for their input and helped with the intercolonization.

La Sikes had asked Rahula to lecture and give counsel on religious matters. He had already traveled to several of Sanctuaries and spoken. Today's lecture would start in fifteen minutes.

The members of the New World Sanctuary gathered in the auditorium to hear the Buddhist monk. It was rumored that he had been one of the first to discover the existence of the Benwarians and that he held a special place in their hearts. A great buzz of excitement filled the lecture hall. The room became quiet when La Sikes introduced Rahula.

He got up from his chair behind the podium and nodded at the her as he walked up and placed his hands flat on the stand, looking out. He disliked speaking to such large audiences, preferring the quiet contemplative life, but La Sikes had insisted.

He brought his hands up in a temple under his chin and bowed his head. All those in the audience repeated the gesture. "Greetings," he said.

"Greetings," the throng repeated.

"Thank you for inviting me to speak at your most Christian colony. Although you honor a different prophet than I, our differences are small. Religion is a tree with many branches, each branch comes from the trunk of universal truths. Such truths as the golden rule, the preservation of the environment, the negation of ego and selfishness, and the equality of all men form the trunk of this great tree. It is said that there is but one religion and all divine messengers have taught it. It is these teachings, these truths that are important. We must separate these truths from the divine messenger for it is the truth that must be sanctified and not the religious icon. The truly divine prophets have no need of adulation. They seek only to enlighten. These prophets have many names - Christ, Buddha, Mohammad - but each has but one goal: to bring us closer to truth.

My brethren, we all yearn for the light of truth. This commonality binds us together. I beseech you to follow the path of self discovery to wherever it may lead you. If you follow a prophet such as Christ, seek his true essence not one that conforms to your own worldly views. It is then that your mind comes closest to the Infinite Mind and thus attains freedom.

And in your search for the Infinite, remember that all fail. Be humbled by that, it's what makes us human or Benwarian. Remember to forgive and accept yourself and that one's journey is fraught with pitfalls and detours. Remember that one may never achieve Nirvana or perfection or see the light of ultimate truth but one must never quit striving to reach that heavenly goal.

The Supreme transcends time, space, and the ability of man to understand. I daresay, the Supreme transcends even the understanding of the Benwarians.

Let our common predicament unite us. We live on one world, we are one people and we seek the same truths. I leave you with this prayer,

From self delusion lead me to understanding
From darkness lead me to light

From death lead me to the eternal truth."

Rahula steepled his hands under his chin and nodded his head. Everyone remained quiet as they contemplated his message and then they stood up as one, steepled their hands and bowed.

Rahula left the stage to find someone waiting for him in the wings. Ben smiled and held out his hand, "Hi, friend."

Rahula bowed and smiled. The two men embraced. "Greetings, Ben."

"I enjoyed your lecture. It's nice to hear your voice outside the jungle."

Rahula tipped his head slightly in acknowledgement. "How is Charlise?"

"She's fine. I've actually seen her smile and laugh a few times. She'd love you to stay with us when you visit Skye Sanctuary next week, she has something she wants to show you."

"I'd be honored. How are her parents?"

"They're doing fine. Her father's head of the Northwestern Transportation Development. He's facilitating the dismantling of internal combustion vehicles and converting the materials into solar electric cars that will be used to build the mass transit system for the Northwestern Sanctuaries."

The Benwarians had directed post-invasion survivors in the development of non-polluting means of transportation and their construction. Retro-fitted factories produced Benwarian vehicles. Fa Structor and his team of engineers traveled the globe and worked long hours to help in the process. There was an abundance of energy from the sun and water to run the hovercrafts and larger vehicles that had been built.

Hydrogen-powered Benwarian hovercraft became the primary means of transportation after the invasion. People needing to travel to destinations not covered by mass transit or that were too far away to get to by walking or using a bicycle, checked out their choice of hovercraft from rental centers.

Bicycles became the primary mode of individual transportation. Bicycles kept humans and Benwarians fit and could be owned individually. The Benwars loved this uniquely human form of transportation.

"I'm glad they're doing okay," Rahula continued. "Will you be joining any of the group discussions?"

"Yes, I'm conducting a seminar entitled, "The Jewish Perspective and Buddhism.""

La Sikes had been standing aside, listening politely. Now she interjected, "These seminars are crucial to bringing a more universal understanding and unity to all. You do a great service with your lectures."

"Thank you," Ben replied as Rahula bowed his head slightly. "And you are?"

"I'm La Sikes, a member of the Sanctum Just," They shook hands. "And now Rahula, we have a hovercraft to catch," she reminded.

"Sorry, I didn't mean to keep you," Ben smiled and hugged his friend.

"I'll see you at Skye," Rahula said as he departed with the tall, slim Benwarian.

53

*D*uring the first years of the trans-colonization, cities were dismantled and the materials salvaged. Communal dwellings constructed from these recycled materials used solar and water power for light and heat. People lived in communal complexes. Laundry facilities, kitchens and recreation rooms were shared. These living places blended in with the natural flora and fauna of an area and were models of energy efficiency.

All Sanctuary inhabitants were employed, they participated in developing and building housing and transportation systems or worked in administration and services or in food production. People picked tasks according to their interests and abilities. Everyone performed civic duties and tried to improve their Sanctuary.

Individual ownership was restricted to personal belongings and bicycles. People no longer needed or wanted to have more than their neighbors. Competition for material things was frowned upon. It was seen as sinful.

Giant solar funnels were built based on the solar oven technology that focused and concentrated the sun's rays. The resulting heat was used to run turbines. Where plausible, wind turbines were also used to create energy. Excess energy was stored in lithium batteries that were used to run hovercraft or communal furnaces in the winter.

Sanctuaries kept populations small and relatively static. Governments became true democracies in which everyone participated in decisions which were discussed and then voted on.

All Sanctuaries abolished currency. Everyone was provided for. There was equal access to meals, lodging, and recreation. Some Sanctuaries were based on themes such as, art, music, engineering, philosophy, ethics, or sports. Others changed emphasis weekly to ensure that everyone was educated and exposed to new and enriching experiences.

Packaged and processed foods disappeared. Greenhouses and collective farms provided fresh fruits and vegetables for consumption. The numbers of cattle, sheep, pigs, chickens, and other farm animals were drastically reduced. Inhabitants converted from a meat-based diet to one based on balance and nutrition.

As the oceans healed and became healthy, aquatic populations rebounded. Sanctuaries on the coasts harvested the surplus marine life making sure that all species were sustained and conserved. These Sanctuaries used ocean vessels powered by hydraulic sails and electric motors run by solar collectors. The ships harvested then delivered their catch to ports throughout the world. From the ports, the sea food was transported by cargo hovercraft to inland communities.

There was little mass production or industry except for vehicle production. Clothing, bicycles, and buildings were individually designed and hand-crafted. Products were built to last. Great pride was taken in craftsmanship and design. Only quality materials were used. Products that wore out were carefully dismantled and the materials recycled.

54

C harlise lived in the Skye Sanctuary in the former state of Arizona. She had relocated there after a three-week convalescence. She now served as a part-time clerk in transportation. She scheduled the electric trains and checked out indie-craft. The superficial contact kept her engaged with others and occupied her mind.

For a long time after Gabe's death, she leaned on her father who stayed close and supportive. They talked and read together while her mother nurtured and fussed over both of them. Time had begun to close her wound even before the day of her discovery.

La Sikes, had taken a great interest in her recovery. A year after Gabe's death, she recommended that Charlise's parents move to a sanctuary in the Northwest. Although Charlise kept in close contact with them, Sikes felt Charlise needed to regain her independence to complete the healing process.

With her parents gone, she grew to love Ben who had always stayed close. He visited daily and helped with her domestic duties. He'd been gone for the last week however, participating in a seminar at the New World Sanctuary located where the city of Sante Fe once stood. She had grown to love and depend on him and looked forward to his return.

As she poured over next week's train schedule she found herself humming. She was sitting in a swivel chair behind an old oak desk with a pen in her mouth.

She looked up when a customer opened the door. She stood and moved behind the check-out counter. "May I help you?" she asked. A tall Benwarian towered over her and smiled.

"La Sikes, how are you?" Charlise walked around the counter and hugged her.

"I'm fine," she said examining Charlise. "You certainly look good."

"I'm so much better now."

"Yes I heard, congratulations."

"Thank you. It's good to be alive again."

"That's good to hear," La Sikes said wistfully. "Hey, I need to check out a hover craft for two passengers."

"When do you need it?"

"As soon as my friend gets here, which should be any minute."

Charlise removed a form from underneath the counter and passed it to La Sikes. "Where's your passenger?" she asked.

"He was right behind me," she said as the door opened.

Charlise looked around the Benwarian to see Rahula enter the station. He bowed his head and steepled his hands underneath his chin.

"Rahula!" she exclaimed. She hugged him, squeezing the temple against his chin. Her eyes watered, "What a nice surprise!" she said.

"Ah you must be a bhuta, such perfection cannot be from this world," he said when they parted. He noticed that her depression had been replaced with a healthy glow. She looked radiant as she wiped tears from her eyes.

"Oh, my God, did you just give me a complement? You the ultimate, Mamaytam."

"I cannot remain detached in the presence of Avaya," he said with a warm glint in his eye.

"Ineffable beauty? You're trying to cheer me up, that's so sweet," she said.

La Sikes finished filling out the form. "Rahula, I've never seen you out of character before," she said holding the paper out. "If I didn't know any better, I'd say you were flirting."

"Oh, I'm sorry," said Charlise, ignoring her remark and taking the form. "You said two passengers? Did you mean one and a driver?"

"No, we thought you could drive us."

"I'd love to leave now, but I'm not off for another hour."

"That's been taken care of," said Sikes.

"Great. Rahula, are you guys staying with us? I've got something to show you," Charlise asked.

"Will you cook S'mores?" he smiled.

"Yes, I've saved the last package of marshmallows for you, but I have something you'll like even more."

He bowed his head, "Then we can't refuse. We will be deeply honored."

The hovercraft arrived. La Sikes and Rahula gathered their belongings and put them in the back. After Charlise gave instructions to her replacement, they climbed in the vehicle.

"So you two must be here for the Togetherness Conference," she said as she powered the vehicle up.

"Yes," said Sikes. "We plan to visit every Sanctuary in the western hemisphere by year's end."

Charlise accelerated down the old asphalt highway that led to her apartment. "So how did you get my favorite Buddhist monk to tour? I thought he preferred quiet and solitude or has he completed his bhavana?"

"He has come a long way in developing his mind and insight, he's very Benwarian. I got him to agree to the tour by explaining to him that he is a great guru who needs to share his light."

"Yes, La Sikes explained that it is my karaniyam to enlighten others."

"Your what?"

"Karaniyam. It is my duty," Rahula looked out. On both sides of the highway sat derelict cars and trucks, now rusting and overgrown with fungus. "All must be guided to truth if we are to prevent the return of Chaos. It is like driving the hovercraft, a swerve to the left or right and one leaves the Path, bringing destruction."

Charlise came to an intersection and stopped. Before she turned right she said, "I'll try to keep it on the road, my teacher."

After driving for a few minutes, apartment houses started

appearing in the surrounding trees and shrubs. Some were duplexes with several living units. All had solar panels absorbing the sun's energy from their roofs and heat pumps drawing energy from the earth.

The hovercraft slowed and Charlise turned left. She stopped at an apartment complex built into the side of a hill. Four different sets of stone stairs led up to each group of living units.

She brought the vehicle to a halt in a small parking lot. The engine whirred to a stop and the threesome collected their things and walked to her apartment. They climbed the stairs and stood behind as she opened the door.

"Ben? Ben I'm home," she called and then turned and motioned with her arm, "Come in."

La Sikes ducked through the door and Rahula came after. They stood in her modest living room and heard Ben rumbling around in the back of the house. "Just a minute," he said.

The two guests sat their things down on the floor and looked up. Ben emerged through the arched entryway holding a small child. Charlise rushed forward. She took the baby and kissed its forehead. She proudly held him up for them to see, "La Sikes, Rahula, I'd like you to meet Gabe Jr."

La Sikes bowed her head in honor. Rahula moved toward Charlise with his arms open to take the baby. She gave him over to the mystic who beamed. "The samsara has given the world a jiva. May his soul be as great as his father's."

"Yes," Ben agreed, "the Phoenix has risen. He has his father's eyes and easy smile."

"He was the only medicine that could heal my deepest wound. I loved his father so much," said Charlise.

La Sikes touched her forehead to examine Charlise's aura. The dark blues of a great love lost had faded into the whitish green brightness of motherly love. She cried inside thinking of her own true love and believing there would never be the white light of rebirth to lighten her navy blue aura.

55

*I*t had taken more than S'mores to change General Battier's mind about the primitives. Pearson's performance as a space shuttle commander matched that of any Benwarian. Battier had personally promoted Pearson several times until he presently held the rank of Lieutenant General.

Lieutenant General Pearson had spent the last five years as head of the Oceanic Recovery Program. His command of twenty space shuttles and their crews was exemplary. They had worked tirelessly to transport the contaminated algae into outer space and with it the chemicals trapped inside. Great progress had been made in restoring the health of Earth's oceans.

Although Pearson's performance had softened Battier's feelings toward the Earthlings, the General had still viewed Benwarians as superior until that fateful day almost a decade after the invasion.

He had entered the auditorium after the Sanctum Just had convened. A guest from an African Sanctuary was speaking. Battier was so captivated by the her beauty that he didn't hear a word she said. He fell in love with her long hair, braided with bright yellow and red beads. He fell in love with the almond shaped eyes that resembled those of a Benwarian, and her small flat nose that led to full, sensuous lips. Only her ebony skin reminded him that she was an Earthling but it didn't matter, the General was smitten.

He married Adla Omondi a year later. Now, after a decade of marriage, he knew that she was his equal in every way. She kept him in line and laughed at his bluster when he tried to pull rank on her. He adored Adla.

Their favorite past time was to ride their bikes into the mountains for a picnic. Once there, they cooked their food in a solar oven. Afterwards, they removed the main course and melted chocolate in their cups for dessert. The General claimed that this tasty treat had won Adla's heart and he always remembered Charlise when he fixed it.

Despite her pessimism, La Sikes's navy blue aura had lightened over the years. She had spent so much time with Fa Dewbene, or Drew as he like to be called, that she couldn't remember life without him. The oceans of time had washed away her pain until Logis was but a distant memory. They were happy together.

Ben and Charlise grew close as the years went on. Ben learned to be not only considerate but diplomatic when they discussed anything. They had married and although Gabe Skye Jr. had kept his father's name, Ben was more a father to him than Charlise could ever have hoped for.

Rahula retired to the rainforest to live a simple, quiet life. Gabe Skye Jr. visited every so often to learn from and meditate with the old guru. For some reason, his mother always sent chocolate for the old man who accepted it with a gracious smile.

The Benwarians kept their word and humans were given equal voice in the government of all Sanctuaries. The two worlds learned much from each other and the distinctions between Earthlings and Benwarians lessened with each passing year until the colors of their auras became indistinguishable.

And our Mother Earth? She healed and prospered.